This book should be returned to any branch of the
Lancashire County Library on or before the date

SCH
GRAY 15 MAY 2009

2 4 SEP 2016

3 1 OCT 2016

2 0 JUN 2019

1 2 JUN 2009 1 OCT 2016

1 2 AUG 2019

2 9 DEC 2016

1 3 NOV 2019

2 0 JUL 2009

2 5 MAY 2018

—

2 0 JUL 2009

2 8 JUN 2018

05 . 07 . 13

1 8 JUN 2015

— 5 AUG 2015

— 7 OCT 2015

1 3 JAN 2016

Lancashire County Library
Bowran Street
Preston PR1 2UX

Lancashire
County Council

www.lancashire.gov.uk/libraries

LANCASHIRE COUNTY LIBRARY

3011811500035 5

D0529135

A PERFECTLY GOOD FAMILY

Lionel Shriver is the author of eight novels, as well as a journalist for the *Guardian*, the *New York Times*, and the *Daily Telegraph*, among many other publications. An international bestseller, *We Need to Talk About Kevin* won the Orange Prize for Fiction in 2005, and has been translated into more than twenty languages. A *New York Times* bestseller, *Time* magazine top-ten pick of 2007, *Entertainment Weekly's* Book of the Year and rising to number two on the Canadian bestseller list, *The Post-Birthday World* has already secured eleven foreign translation deals.

Lionel Shriver lives in London and New York City.

Acclaim for *The Post-Birthday World*:

'*We Need to Talk About Kevin* was a modern masterpiece but this is even more exciting and exhilarating.' *Sunday Express*

'Before it was co-opted and trivialized by chick lit, romantic love was a subject that writers from Flaubert to Tolstoy deemed worthy of artistic and moral scrutiny. This is the tradition into which Shriver's novel fits. In 50 years, we'll still be wild about Harry. And a lucky handful of readers may stumble across *The Post-Birthday World* and wonder why they've never heard of it.' Voted Number One Best Fiction Book of 2007, *Entertainment Weekly*

'A wise and moving novel, touching us most deeply when it shows us how finite our lives are, and how infinite we want them to be.' *Daily Telegraph*

'A playful, psychologically acute, and luxuriously textured meditation on the nature of love.' *The New Yorker*

'Shriver chalks her narrative cue with relish and, once the story gets underway, it's hard to take your eyes off the green baize.' *Tatler*

'Brutally wise, viciously funny and at times unflinchingly cruel.' *Sunday Telegraph*

'Complex and nervy, Shriver's clever meditation will intrigue anyone who has ever wondered how things might have turned out had they followed, or ignored, a life changing impulse.' *People*

'The writing is continually engaging, the 1990s period detail rich, and the novel itself is a compelling take on the desire to have more than one opinion, or passion, at a time.' *New Statesman*

'Hugely entertaining . . . tackles the duelling human needs for passion and security with fierce, witty honesty.' *Vogue*

'Irina is a thoroughly compelling character, an idiosyncratic yet recognisable heroine about whom it's impossible not to care.' *New York Times*

'This almost chicklit plot is transmuted to literary gold by the sheer quality of Shriver's writing, the thoughtfulness and accuracy of her observations on life and relationships, and some sublime structuring . . . . For the last five hours I didn't stop reading for a moment; the last author who achieved that was probably Enid Blyton.' *Daily Mail*

'It's extremely clever but the cleverness never overwhelms the emotional power of the whole. As a reader you're both impressed by the form but still completely enthralled by Irina's inner life and passions. . . . . .one of the best novels I've read in ages.' *Daily Express*

'Unflinching . . . . One certainty is that Ms Shriver is not interested in fostering illusions about love . . . .*The Post-Birthday World* is disturbing because it seems real: Irina's wavering and soul-searching are not the comic vacillations of Bridget Jones, and the choices she makes are not the pragmatic decisions of an emblematic woman ambitious to 'have it all' . . . .' *Wall Street Journal*

'A compulsive, clever, wise and witty novel.' *The Times*

'With its gimlet view of the vagaries and varieties of human love and its inventive double story line, Shriver's eighth novel is a piercingly funny follow-up to her tragedy-laden 2005 Orange Prize winner, *We Need to Talk About Kevin.' Elle*

Acclaim for *We Need to Talk About Kevin*:

'This is an important book . . . here is a fierce challenge of a novel that forces the reader to confront assumptions about love and parenting, about how and why we apportion blame, about crime and punishment, forgiveness and redemption.' *Independent*

'One of my favourite novels . . . the best thing I've read in years.' Jeremy Vine

'This superb, many-layered novel intelligently weighs the culpability of parental nurture against the nightmarish possibilities of an innately evil child.' *Daily Telegraph*

'Urgent, unblinking and articulate fiction.' *Sunday Times*

'Shriver keeps up an almost unbearable suspense . . . It's hard to imagine a more striking demolition job on the American myth of the perfect suburban family.' *Sunday Telegraph*

'Shriver has skilfully hit the bulls-eye on two best-selling targets in the American market: the fear of rampage killings by teenagers at school, and the guilt of working mothers . . . ' *TLS*

'An awesomely smart, stylish and pitiless achievement . . . . Franz Kafka wrote that a book should be the ice-pick that breaks open the frozen seas inside us, because the books that make us happy we could have written ourselves. With *We Need to Talk About Kevin*, Shriver has wielded Kafka's axe with devastating force.' *Independent*

'One of the most striking works of fiction to be published this year. It is Desperate Housewives as written by Euripides . . . A powerful, gripping and original meditation on evil.' *New Statesman*

'A great read with horrifying twists and turns.' *Marie Claire*

'It is a book about the dangerous distance that exists between what we feel and what we are actually prepared to admit when it comes to family life. (. . .) It is a book about what we need to talk about, but can't. (. . .) Shriver's satire on child-centered families captained by adult buffoons whose intellectual, not to mention erotic, life is in pieces, could not be more timely.' *Guardian Weekend*

'Harrowing, tense and thought-provoking, this is a vocal challenge to every accepted parenting manual you've ever read.' *Daily Mail*

'An elegant psychological and philosophical investigation of culpability with a brilliant denouement . . . although (Eva's) reliability as a narrator becomes increasingly questionable as she oscillates between anger, self-pity and regret, her search for answers becomes just as compulsive for the reader.' *Observer*

Acclaim for *Game Control*:

'Every now and then a modern novel about Africa comes along that neither trades on the continent as "exotica" nor piously makes literary capital out of human misery—that doesn't go woozy at the sight of a wildebeest, that might be more cruel than caring, but in fact isn't. John Updike's *The Coup* was one such, as was Paul Theroux's *Jungle Lovers*; Lionel Shriver, an American woman already praised for *Ordinary Decent Criminals*, has produced another. . . . The darkness is dissolved, but an unpleasant taste is left in the mouth along with our passing laughter. Playing with genres, Shriver encourages the reader to consider serious matters, without serving up tedious ethical fiction.' *The Times Literary Supplement*

'Rare is the novel driven by science that does not collapse into a techno-thriller or the book about Africa that does not disgorge condescending sentimentality of the "white man's burden" variety. Yet Lionel Shriver has produced a book that qualifies on both counts. . . . Shriver has no rigorous prescription for this hefty problem of humankind. Nobody does. It is more than enough that she has illuminated the quandary of human need with such subtlety, perspicacity, and—tempered with a sensible measure of skepticism—such a durable and salient affection for all people.' *The Scotsman*

'Her work is all the more valuable for its flagrant defiance of political correctness.' *Times*

'Shriver makes sharp, interesting points on both the futility of white guilt and the necessary narrowness of Western aid organisations. Shriver is an intelligent writer and is astute on the arbitrariness and arrogance underlying white efforts at population control in Africa.' *The Guardian*

'Lionel Shriver's debut [sic] novel, *Ordinary Decent Criminals*, outclassed nearly all the macho but humdrum fiction spawned by the Irish Troubles. *Game Control* mixes dark comedy, intellectual sparring, doomsday thrills and psychological scrutiny into a bold and bracing cocktail. . . . Shriver skirts the edge of tragedy with superb aplomb. Her speculations chill the blood; her language glistens with a diamond-hard wit. . . . [*Game Control*] depicts not only Africa—though Shriver conjures up a vivid Nairobi—but western attitudes to the third world; the messianic, the masochistic, and the plain murderous.' *New Statesman & Society*

Also by Lionel Shriver

The Female of the Species
Checker and the Derailleurs
Ordinary Decent Criminals
Game Control
Double Fault
We Need to Talk About Kevin
The Post-Birthday World

LIONEL SHRIVER

a perfectly good family

HARPER

This novel is entirely a work of fiction.
The names, characters and incidents portrayed in it are
the work of the author's imagination. Any resemblance to
actual persons, living or dead, events or localities is
entirely coincidental.

Harper
An imprint of HarperCollins*Publishers*
77–85 Fulham Palace Road,
Hammersmith, London W6 8JB

www.harpercollins.co.uk

This paperback edition 2009
1

First published in Great Britain by
Faber and Faber 1996

Copyright © Lionel Shriver 2009

Lionel Shriver asserts the moral right to
be identified as the author of this work

A catalogue record for this book is
available from the British Library

ISBN: 978 000 727111 5

Set in Minion by Palimpsest Book Production Limited,
Grangemouth, Stirlingshire

Printed and bound in Great Britain by
Clays Ltd. St Ives plc.

All rights reserved. No part of this publication may be
reproduced, stored in a retrieval system, or transmitted,
in any form or by any means, electronic, mechanical,
photocopying, recording or otherwise, without the prior
permission of the publishers.

This book is sold subject to the condition that it shall not,
by way of trade or otherwise, be lent, re-sold, hired out or
otherwise circulated without the publisher's prior consent
in any form of binding or cover other than that in which it
is published and without a similar condition including this
condition being imposed on the subsequent purchaser.

Mixed Sources
Product group from well-managed
forests and other controlled sources
www.fsc.org   Cert no. SW-COC-1806
© 1996 Forest Stewardship Council

FSC is a non-profit international organisation established
to promote the responsible management of the world's forests.
Products carrying the FSC label are independently certified
to assure consumers that they come from forests that are managed
to meet the social, economic and ecological needs
of present and future generations.

Find out more about HarperCollins and the environment at
www.harpercollins.co.uk/green

SOUTH LANCASHIRE LIBRARIES

| S CH 4/09 | S | S | S | S |

To DON AND PEGGY SHRIVER
*from whom, on balance, I have inherited more strengths
than foibles—the most parents could hope for any child*

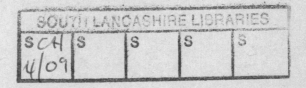

LANCASHIRE COUNTY LIBRARY	
3011811500835 5	
HJ	15-Apr-2009
AF	£7.99

A son could bear complacently the death of his father, while the loss of his inheritance might drive him to despair.

Machiavelli, *The Prince*

'Don't tell me,' said the taxi driver, rubber-necking at the formidable Victorian manor. 'Your mother's Norman Bates.'

'My mother's dead,' I said. Harsh, but the information was so fresh for me, only two weeks old, that I was still repeating it to myself.

'Don't you strain yourself, Missy.' He lunged from the front seat to take the luggage from me: two leather monsters and a bulging carry-on. I'd been overweight at Heathrow, and lucky that in November the plane was not too full.

'You want, I'll haul these to the porch –'

'Not at all,' I said. 'My brother likes to give me a hand. He always has.'

I pulled out a wad of dollars crumpled with fivers, unsure of the form for tipping taxis in North Carolina. An ostensible native, I clung to any ignorance about Raleigh as proof that I no longer belonged here. Skint most of my adult life, I reminded myself I would have more money soon and forced myself to hand over twenty per cent. The generosity didn't come naturally. McCreas are Scots-Presbyterian stock; I have stingy genes.

'But you're spot on about the house,' I nodded upwards. 'It does look like *Psycho*, all right. The neighbourhood children all think it's haunted.'

And wasn't it? Handing over the bills, I thumbed Alexander Hamilton; after five years of starchy London tenners, a dollar felt like pyjamas.

'Or *The Addams Family*, mehbe. Take care now, ma'am. Hope your brother's a muscly guy. Those cases is killers.'

'He's pretty powerful.' I frowned. Since I still envisaged Truman as a delicate, timid tag-along about two feet high, that he was a beefy man of thirty-one who lifted weights in his attic living room was disconcerting.

The cab ploughed down Blount Street, leaving me by chattel that would have been, until a fortnight before, all I owned. I turned to face what else I owned: a great, gaunt mansion built just after the Civil War.

There was no denying its magnificence. I had shown friends in London pictures of my family: my dark, glamorously beautiful mother in the days when she was genuinely happy instead of pretending to be; my father sporting his lopsided, hangdog grin as he accepted another award from the NAACP; my little brother Truman when he was photographed by the *Raleigh Times* throwing himself in front of a bulldozer; though I had no pictures, I discovered, of my older brother. None of these snaps made the slightest impression. Yet when I showed them a picture of my house, faces lit, hands clapped, eyebrows lifted. For the English, Heck-Andrews was everything a Southern residence was meant to be: remote, anachronistic, both inviting and forbidding at the same time. It fulfilled their tritest expectations, though I received complaints that there was no Spanish moss. That's in South Carolina, I'd explain. And then we would get on to why I didn't seem to have a Southern accent, and I'd be reassured that tell-tale traces had been eradicated.

Even in the last light of the day I could see the clapboard was flaking; so the failing manila paint was now my problem. It was apparent from the pavement that the ceilings of the first two floors were vaulting, all very exhilarating except they were murderously dear to heat, and the price of oil was now, I supposed, my problem as well. Yet paint and heat were only a third my responsibility – and this in itself would shortly become my biggest problem.

It was the Sunday of Thanksgiving weekend, a holiday which I only ever remembered in Raleigh-Durham, where gift shops were flogging pop-up pilgrim books; letting this exclusively American holiday nearly slip by unnoticed gave me a sense of accomplishment. I zipped up my jacket. No doubt the English didn't picture the South in winter, but North Carolina has one, albeit mild. In fact, I remembered dressing for school huddled by the floor vent, stuffing my bunched knee-highs by its breath to pre-warm my socks. My parents were McCreas, too, and their remedy to the heating problem was all too simple.

I left the bags on the pavement and strode towards the broad, intricately ornamented front porch that skirted the mansion. This opulent, gregarious-looking expanse with a swing on one end was designed for mint juleps; but my parents had been teetotallers and, rather than recall long languid summer nights with fireflies and low laughter, I pictured squeaking morosely with Truman on the swing, frantic for my parents to go to bed. We hadn't been very nice to them. Ordinarily on one of my visits home as I approached this same front door I'd be bracing myself for my mother's protracted, claim-laying embrace – when the more I stiffened, the harder she would squeeze. Once my father died, her hugs had become only longer and tighter and were laced with hysteria. Now I was spared. A dubious reprieve.

We rarely entered through the front door, more comfortable with the side entrance into the kitchen. Ringing the bell, I touched the cold curlicued polygonal panes in the door, one of which had been replaced with plain window glass. The asymmetry never failed to vex Truman. But because the original had been shattered when my older brother put his arm through it – my father had been chasing him through the house to force him to turn down the volume of Three Dog Night – I treasured the flaw. There weren't many signs of Mordecai left here.

'Corlis!'

In the open door my brother hugged me. He knew how: his hands were firm on my back and he waited a single beat during which he was plausibly thinking about being glad to see me and then he let go. I didn't take these capacities for granted.

'You should have let us pick you up.'

'Not during rush hour.' The consideration was unlike me. When I gestured to my luggage on the pavement, I thought I was doing Truman a favour by allowing him to heave it in.

'What have you got in these things, a dead body?'

'You might say that.'

'I thought you were only here for a few days.' He muttered, 'Girls!' with a smile.

I watched my little brother. He was broad, though to say stocky would suggest fat, which he was not. He liked carrying suitcases because he was a practical person and enjoyed putting his muscles to more beneficial use than for sandbagged press-ups. His face, too, was wide, though in my mind's eye it remained insubstantial. Likewise, his hair had coarsened and curled; though we were both born blondes, our driving licences now would read, 'Hair: brown.' Yet I refused to relinquish the notion that my brother's mop was bright gold, a cowlick sprouting from his parting with the spontaneous whimsy of Truman's childhood, of which there was, in fact, little remnant.

My vision was so corrupted that if I blinked, he no longer sported a close-cropped beard. They don't make corrective lenses for people unable to focus on the present tense, so that this myopia of mine would soon have me banging into things all over our house which were there now and not in the past – like my brother's hair-trigger temper. While Truman McCrea as an adult was depressive and given to bilious explosions, I would continue to treat him carelessly, as if he remained the ingenuous, piping, cooperative boy who would do whatever I told him with unfailing trustfulness. He was still, God help him, trusting.

I nudged the cases past the transom and clumped the door shut, rubbing my hands. With Truman controlling the thermostat it was warm in the foyer. Inside Heck-Andrews, with its seasoned oak floor and mahogany panelling absorbing the late sun, evening had arrived. The lamps were lit and for a moment I was taken in: that this was the enclosed, safe, self-contained haven that other people called home. Leering back at me from the facing staircase were the gargoyles on whose pointed ears I'd impaled my crotch as a girl when sliding down the black walnut banisters. It was amazing I could still have children – though not for many years longer.

'Hey, there,' said Averil shyly, hanging back.

I kissed my sister-in-law diffidently, on both cheeks, and stood back to appraise her. There was no reason why Averil should not have been pretty. Her hair was brown as well, but lustrous, while our own was embittered by the memory of its former golden glory and ate the light. She cut hers shoulder length and the locks coiled, turning to her ears as if also shy. She was medium height, though maybe that was the trouble: too much of her was simply medium. Nourished by my brother's obsessively perfect diet, her figure was trim, though her sway-backed posture was pre-pubescent. Her nose was upturned, expectant, and her eyes were enormous with bashful long lashes, and when they turned to my brother they widened still further, colouring with big brown awe. She adored him. Averil, too, was far older than I pictured her – twenty-eight. I thought: she is nicely proportioned and really ought to be lovely, though I did not think: maybe she is lovely.

I nodded at the stand in the hall. 'It's still there.'

'Yep,' said Truman, pressing his lips like my mother.

Mother's pocketbook always rested on this doorside table, where it continued to rest, clasped, reposed like a body in a casket. I knew what was inside: a tin of Sucrets gone sticky, the medicine she didn't take for her heart, and a vast crumple of multiply re-used Kleenex pressed with pink lipstick. When we sniffled in church, she would hand us a damp tatter; repelled, we'd snort the mucus down our throats.

'You should cancel the credit cards,' I advised.

I delivered duties to my brother as privileges. For the funeral ten days earlier, I had allowed him to buy the cold cuts and to ring her colleagues at the hospice. This was the kind of graciousness in which I specialized.

We drifted to the formal parlour, though traditionally we'd have preferred the sitting room opposite, a less pompous environment with the TV and torn naugahide sofas that was comfortably messy. Some solemnity had entered these proceedings which I didn't know how to kick. I felt polite.

'My whole life,' said Truman, in his minor key, 'I've been taught not to go into Mother's purse without asking. Pawing through her wallet doesn't come easily.'

Truman fetched us glasses of wine, and I scanned the parlour, no longer milling with Raleigh's community leaders, hands on my shoulder assuring me what a *good* woman my mother had been, how *deeply committed* my father had been to civil rights, and all the while me squirming at their touch, not feeling flattered even on my parents' account and hoping that when I died no one called me 'good' – though considering what I had just left behind me in London, there was little danger of that.

'I don't know what we're going to do with all this junk,' said Averil.

At least she was candid. However laborious the task of cluttering such vast floor space, my parents had undertaken the chore with some success. With no less than twenty-four rooms in this house, it was substantially over-furnished. The parlour, for example, was fat

5

with low-riding Danish modern. If Truman is to be believed, my parents did not understand (I would say, did not even like) their own house, and were always fighting its retrograde nature and trying to haul it wholesale into the twentieth century, where, according to Truman, Heck-Andrews not only did not belong but refused to go. Thus none of their 'improvements' would take – when my father repapered the upstairs hall with purple peonies, the panels curled to the baseboards that same night. When they splurged on shag for the sitting room, none of the carpet tacks would stay in the floor. I claimed their additions didn't adhere because my father was a do-it-yourself incompetent – his glue was too thin and he used the wrong nails. Truman, one of the last great anthropomorphizers, was convinced that the house itself had revolted, moulting loud wallpaper and shuddering tatty shag from her boards.

As for the 'junk' of which Averil despaired, my parents had been avid travellers, favouring countries with anguishing social ailments: South Africa, Burma, Korea, where they would meet with pastors just out of prison, dissidents running underground presses, and Amnesty International task forces. Somewhere in all that hand-wringing over human rights they'd found time to shop, for this room was busy with been-to bric-a-brac: Namibian carvings, Korean celadon, hand-painted Russian dolls, while the walls were smattered with a mismatch of Japanese sumi birdlife, Indonesian batiks and Masai ceremonial masks.

'I suppose we can help ourselves,' I said. 'Like a boot sale at the end of the day, and everything's free.'

'I wish they'd taken this stuff with them,' said Truman glumly.

'The house, too?' I proposed. 'Like *Carrie*.'

He glared. 'How was the opening? Of your show?'

I sculpt. I had flown back to Heathrow after my mother's funeral to attend my first big break, a one-woman show at a decent London gallery. My mother had been so pleased for me when she heard about it that I didn't think she'd want me to miss my limelight to moon around this house deciding who got her crockery. Truman had been annoyed by my departure, but no life outside this house was real to him; other cities – Raleigh itself, come to think of it – were names in the air. And I'd done as I promised: I'd come back to haggle over our inheritance.

'It was smashing,' I said.

Coy, but with catastrophes you have to salvage something, if only the odd wisecrack.

My wine had evaporated; I was nervous. I *pinged* for more, to discover there wasn't much difference between drinking around my mother and drinking around my younger brother. They both eyed your glass and kept a running count. I often wondered what it was Mother thought I might do or say when I became so fearfully uninhibited. Once she'd become sufficiently alarmed – after two glasses – my bottle would get whisked off and corked, so to slake my thirst I would have to scrounge for my good cabernet hidden gauchely in the back of the fridge. This was subtle strategy. Once we were adults, she couldn't forbid booze exactly, but she made you go public with how you couldn't make it through an ordinary evening with your family without drink. She was right. I couldn't.

I leaned forward and traced the ceramic basketry of a bulbous celadon vase on the coffee table. I worked with clay myself, and had to admire the craftsmanship of its intricate crosshatching, though the aura of the object was cool. If the serene sea-green vase had any thematic content, it was self-congratulation: wasn't-this-difficult-to-make. It was a gift from a grateful Korean graduate student with wayward political views, whom my father had smuggled into NC State out of Seoul. My parents had been so proud of this thing and it meant nothing to me and now it was mine.

Like my father, Truman couldn't keep his hands still, but sprang them against each other or twisted his wedding band and then kneaded the back of his neck as if trying to give himself a massage.

He nodded at the tomes to my left, each volume five inches thick. 'I don't think we should let Mordecai have the Britannicas.'

Matt black with gold inlay, the Britannicas' aura resembled that of the vase, though where the celadon was smug the encyclopedias were scholarly, old-school, elitist. Written before HIV and even the Second World War, they were pure, withdrawn; they dwelt on antiquity, and it was hard to imagine they chronicled anything sordid. The volumes were redolent of my father, with his imposing memory for dates and the first names of historical figures. As the only girl, I was raised to think of myself as not very bright: the Britannicas were smarter than I was; they shut me out.

7

'A 1921 reference book?' I shrugged. 'Try looking up "microchip".'

'That first edition is valuable.'

'The stereo is valuable,' I said. 'So's that vase.' *So's the house*. It was marvellous, what people in my family left out.

Truman tapped the black spines. 'Every time Mordecai deigned to come back home – to ask for another "loan" – he'd drool over these books and talk about how he could hardly wait to inherit the set. To their faces. While they were alive and not very old and in good health! That call you got from me two weeks ago, you knew you'd get it some day, but I'm sure you were dreading it. Mordecai had been drumming his fingers by the phone. When I called him the day she died, I was sure the first thing that went through his mind was, *goodie*, now I get the Britannicas. For that matter, remember the Living Will?'

'Who could forget?' I groaned.

'Not Mother, that's for sure. Mother remembered it, all right. Often.'

This is not the kindest introduction to my older brother. Seven years earlier, in 1985, we had gathered in this parlour at my parents' request. I'd flown down from New York City where I was living at the time, though summoning Mordecai from only a mile away was the greater achievement. He'd only agreed to come when he heard their family conference had something to do with money.

My parents had arranged themselves on the couch, not wanting to begin without Mordecai, who had learned from my father that important people keep others waiting. Once my older brother galumphed in the door an hour late, with a curious glance around the mansion as if he'd never been here before, we three children faced the couch and fidgeted; all that was on offer was black coffee.

My mother took photocopies out of a file folder and passed them around like a handout in school. She presided. In bold on the top of my copy read: A LIVING WILL. My mother proceeded to explain that as medical advances these days often make it possible for comatose or vegetative patients to live for years on life support, it was increasingly common for adults of sound mind to record in writing what their wishes might be in circumstances where they were no longer competent.

'Father and I –' she never called him Sturges to us, only Father. '– wanted you children to know that we've signed these pledges, verifying that we don't want any heroic measures –'

'You mean, expensive measures,' Mordecai had interrupted.

'Yes,' Mother agreed evenly, 'hospital costs for PVS patients can be quite high –'

'A thousand bucks a day,' Mordecai provided. 'And that's before the twenty-dollar aspirins.'

Mother may have coloured slightly, but she kept her composure.

'These forms are not binding contracts in court,' chimed in my father, the lawyer. 'But they are admissible evidence, and doctors have increasingly used them consultatively when a family needs to make a decision. Euthanasia *per se* is not legal in the United States, but there have been precedents –'

The photocopy was sticking to my fingers. My mother crafted an emotion in front of herself, much the way I worked up a sculpture – patting here, smoothing the rough edges, and only presenting it when fashioned to her satisfaction. My experience of real feelings, however, is that they do not take shape on a turntable in view, but loom from behind, brutal and square and heavily dangerous like a bag of unwedged clay hurtled at the back of your neck. Feelings for me are less like sculpture and more like being mugged. Consequently, with no warning, I burst into tears.

'Corrie Lou, whatever's the matter?'

I snuffled, 'I don't want to think about your dying,' not sounding anywhere near twenty-eight years old.

My father was probably embarrassed, maybe even touched, but his expression was one of irritation.

Mother came over and stroked my hair, as she had when, rough-housing with my brothers, I'd skinned my knee – tender and purring, she was not really worried. She surprised me. Histrionic of the family, my mother should have, I thought, thrown both arms around me and wept as well, hearing those unheralded phone rings in my South Ealing flat years hence. But she was matter-of-fact. That was when I realized that most people do not fear their own deaths, really. Yours is the one death you are guaranteed not to live through; you will never have to suffer the world without you in it. She was in terror, I knew, of anything happening to my father, but as for the prospect of something happening to her beforehand she was positively hopeful.

Mother scuttled to the foyer and retrieved one of those recycled Kleenex. Once I'd blown my nose in the shreds, I swabbed drips from their Living Will, smearing the print with pink lipstick. Meanwhile my father was explaining that your mother and I don't consider life worth living if our minds are gone, and we would hate for your lasting memory of us to be as the parents who couldn't remember your names.

Meanwhile, Truman sat mutely in his chair and folded his Living Will in thirds. That he, too, did not get weepy was no testimony to lack of affection for his parents; if anything, Truman's attachment to his forebears was of the three of us the most profound – too profound, in my view. He merely lacked imagination. Like foreign cities, the future was abstract; Mr Practicality would not mourn an event that hadn't occurred yet.

Mordecai, however, couldn't keep seated. He was buoyant. 'This is a bang-up idea.' He fanned the photocopy, his three pigtails wagging across his leather vest. 'Christ, we wouldn't want what happened to Grandmother to happen to you guys. She just lay there for years, it must have cost a fortune! And insurance doesn't always cover it, you know. Exceed the liability, that's it, you sell the house, liquidate assets, a whole life's savings down the IV tube.'

At the mention of 'sell the house', Truman's eyes had shot black.

'You know,' Mordecai went on, 'sometimes photocopied signatures don't hold up in court. You want to re-sign my copy? I'll keep the form in my deposit box. Wouldn't want it to get misplaced, right?'

Allowing one corner of his mouth a spasm of incredulity, my father scrawled on Mordecai's copy *Sturges Harcourt McCrea*, disdainfully illegible; my mother penned her neat initials, *EHHM*, wincing.

She bent to refill our coffee cups from the thermos and offered me another biscuit; my father scowled over *The Christian Century* – anything to avoid glancing at their eldest son. Before Mordecai lunged ebulliently to the door, one more time he sauntered to the Britannicas and caressed them, intoning, 'The new edition is nowhere near as comprehensive.'

'You got the feeling,' Truman recalled, 'that Mordecai would speed his army truck across town, running lights, in order personally to whip the life support from its socket the moment either of them drifted into a light sleep.'

I conceded reluctantly, 'He didn't want them to waste *his* money on *their* hospital bills.'

'Mordecai is crass,' said Averil.

It was an ugly word. 'He's thoughtless,' I tempered. 'A little avaricious, and he's always broke.'

'He's *crass*.' Quiet and verbally economical, my sister-in-law seemed to have been searching for years for the right adjective, which she would not relinquish, like a prize.

'As for the encyclopedias,' said Truman, 'it's not that I want them, I just don't want Mordecai to get them. They're yours, Corlis, if you like. Though I doubt you'd want to pay to box and ship them all the way to England. Nuts, you know, nobody's unshelved one in my lifetime.'

Now I understood why I was nervous. There was something Truman hadn't twigged yet, hardly his fault: I hadn't told him. On the issue of the twenty black volumes, though, I wasn't fooled. Truman was no anti-materialist. It wasn't that he didn't care about things, but that he cared about only one thing, in comparison to which the Britannicas were a trifle.

2

I had Truman lug my bags to my old room on the second floor, one of seven spacious bedrooms, two with alcoves for handmaids – Heck-Andrews had been built in an era of visitors with hatboxes who came to stay for weeks. In fact, the house so exceeded our needs that my father had threatened to let out extra bedrooms to low income or homeless families. Through our childhoods Truman and I would plot the pratfall of beastly unwashed ruffians who were going to smell up the room next to mine and break all our toys. We should have relaxed. Yes, Sturges McCrea was sheepish about a mansion whose semi-attached carriage house had accommodated not only the original kitchen, but, in a fraction of the area, more servants than the main structure housed masters by half, when he helped found the SCLC. But Father's guilty magnanimity never put him to personal inconvenience. He paid lip service, for example, to the equality of women, but never encouraged my mother beyond her part-time volunteer work to get a job, lest her distraction delay his supper. There had never been real danger of scruffy truants ransacking our cupboards while we were at school; my father didn't like children any more than we did.

Rather than board the less fortunate, two bedrooms were converted to studies (my mother's half the size of her husband's and doubling as the sewing room). At twenty-one, Truman had deserted his old lair next to mine for his renovated eyrie on the third floor. Mordecai's former bedroom at the front (strategically placed opposite my parents') had many years ago been shorn of its Jimi Hendrix posters, the nail holes gloppily plastered with my father's usual ineptitude, the funk of unlaundered jeans and surreptitious fags air-freshened away; by the time he turned fifteen they'd realized he was not coming back. I was disheartened when they cleaned his desk of SDS handouts, because I used to sneak into his vacated hovel and pocket treasures. At twelve, when I scrounged the Peace armband from his closet and blithely displayed it binding my peasant blouse as I waltzed out the back door, my mother had shrieked, her cheeks streaking, that I was becoming 'just like my older brother!' This, I was led to believe, was the worst thing that could happen to anyone.

Three halls formed a peg-legged H around the stairwell and master bathroom, down the longest of which I lingered as Truman fetched my carry-on. The hall was narrow with a window at the end, the floor slick enough to play Slippery Slidey in socks, indoor skiing with a running start that my mother discouraged because we reliably embedded splinters into our feet. I noted that Truman had replaced the rotting boards that had skewered us, a neat job. Truman inherited all the physical meticulousness that had skipped a generation with my father.

I peeked into the last left-hand door, slammed in my face enough times. I switched on the overhead light, to find a bland bedspread and stark surfaces: no international gewgaws here. I walked to Mordecai's desk, where the booze-bottle rings and reefer burns had been lemon-oiled into the past. The drapes were pulled back – replaced, since Mordecai had caught one of his old set on fire – while in his heyday they were always tightly drawn, even on the brightest of summer days. I scanned the blank walls and bare boards, but aside from the painted-over lumps of lousy spackling and the discernible scrapes in the floor from when my brother would shove his desk over to barricade the door, I detected no trace of Mordecai Delano McCrea. In my own room, midis drooped in my wardrobe, plastic horses spilled from its top shelf, my first clumsy attempts at clay sculpture humbled me on my bureau. Yet here was a malicious erasure. Not a single test tube from his chemistry set rolled in a dresser drawer, and all the old Herman Hesse paperbacks had been bagged and sent off to Goodwill. No stranger would imagine this had ever been anything other than a guest room. As I sometimes fudged to a Londoner that I was born in New York, I wondered if my parents had indulged the pleasant fiction with the odd out-of-towner that they had only two children.

My footfalls rang hollow back down the hall. I had this entire floor to myself: a drastic privacy I had craved as an adolescent,

13

yearning for evenings like this one when my parents would disappear. Now that I had got what I wished I didn't want it, which goes to show there is no pleasing some people. When my father was alive Mahler and Ives thrummed through this mansion all the way to the tower deck, but with no symphonic bombast tyrannizing the stairwell, no more 'Tommy' pounding from down the hall, no lilting alto of 'I am a Poor Wayfaring Stranger' wending from the kitchen while my mother made pies, this cavernous structure was deathly quiet, and I was grateful for so much as the thump of my case as it fell from Truman's exhausted hand, and even for the piping of my sister-in-law, whose nasal, peevish voice would ordinarily annoy me.

As Truman lumbered up the next flight to grill chicken thighs, I shouted after him. 'Why are you cooking up there? You've an enormous kitchen downstairs, and your kitchen is a closet.'

'I always cook in the dovecot.' He kept walking.

He *always* cooked in the dovecot, and that was reason enough, as he always had the same breakfast, mowed the lawn the same day of the week, and now that he was in college I figured that Duke's varying his academic schedule must have plunged him into interior disarray for half of every semester. Truman's disciplines were so strict not because they were solid but because they were shaky. In my little brother's personal mythology, should he nibble a single biscuit between meals, lift weights on Friday instead of Thursday, or allow himself an extra half-shot of bourbon before bed, he would degenerate into a flabby dissolute overnight. Truman trusted everyone but himself.

As I unpacked, Averil swayed in the doorway, her eyes following each pair of jeans to its drawer. She seemed to be counting them, like Truman and my glasses of wine.

'Whatever happened with your room-mates?' she enquired. 'You said one was cute.'

'I said they were both cute.'

'Which one did you like better? The runty guy with glasses, or the drunken thug?'

I laughed. 'In Britain, you'd say *hooligan*. Which he wasn't, quite. But which did I like better? I guess I never made up my mind.'

'Well, did you ever, you know?' Averil may have found my sexual peripatetics 'disgusting' – her favourite word – just as

14

Truman himself lumped everyone I had ever dated into the categories of 'lunatic' or 'waste product'. Yet like most who married as virgins or nearly so, she displayed a disapproving but keenly prurient curiosity about the love lives of the wayward.

'It's inadvisable,' I said, 'to get romantically involved with flatmates. Even in South Ealing, flats are expensive and hard to come by; you don't want to complicate matters. The three of us were agreed on that.'

'So you left them alone after all?'

'After all,' I said, 'they have left me alone. I will miss them.'

'What's *that*?'

I had unwrapped a piece of ceramic from my leggings, and set it on the dresser by the wobbly elephant from my first firing at ten. 'A souvenir.'

'Can I see it?'

I shrugged.

My sculptures were distinguished by their hands: oversized in relation to the figure and always finely wrought, attenuated fingers extended from a tendonous metacarpus. The severed hand Averil now rested in her palm was reaching for something, or someone, and without the rest of the figure attached no longer appeared youthfully desirous, but merely grasping.

'It's beautifully done,' she admired. 'I can't imagine making something so delicate out of clay. But why is it broken off?'

'Because that's the left hand,' I explained, 'and it didn't know what the right one was doing.'

We trudged up the second flight of stairs where, according to Truman's lore, we were entering another residence altogether. If I were to assert that my younger brother had never left home by thirty-one, he would object. Ten years before, he'd refurbished the top floor into an independent flat; he liked to regard the fact that his address tags still read '309 Blount Street' and his zip code hadn't changed since he was two as mere coincidence.

We had designated the third floor 'the dovecot', since the mansard roof was infested with pigeons, though the scampering overhead could sound ominously like rats. The pigeons had nested on the pediments over the dormer windows, whose overhangs didn't protect the panes from being continually splattered with bird poo. Truman spent a lot of time squeegeeing. Truman lived to squeegee; all the humdrum toil my father deplored as distraction from the Great Questions my little brother regarded as the meat of life.

I did feel a release on rising to the long central room in Truman's hideaway, with its tall, round-headed window at the end, where the spiral staircase curled to his tower. The rooms adjoining this one all had at least one sloping wall, from the slant of the roof; in the cockeyed tilt lurked a sense of humour, which the ponderous lower floors could well afford. Truman's aesthetic may have been backward-looking, but in the runaway eclecticism of downstairs there was no coherent aesthetic at all. He had a prejudice against any furniture made in his lifetime, which suggested a self-dislike. I think if Truman could have wished himself back a hundred years he would. He was always pining about the days when hard work was rewarded and a man was a man and you did what you had to do and life was simple. I personally didn't believe life was ever simple, though I could see fancying the illusion. Truman hated his own time, and expressed his nostalgia in bygone appointments, mostly glommed from the boot sales of other children with dead parents. His offbeat furniture wasn't restricted to a single era – his couch was Victorian, end-tables Edwardian, and there was one upright armchair in his living room, ridiculously carved, that I do not believe belonged to any era at all. But together the hodge-podge formed a family whose members all got along, which was more than you could say for ours.

Here in the middle room he'd laid their hefty darkwood table, solidly built and lovingly refinished. *They don't make things the way they used to* – if you listened to Truman from around a corner you might mistake him for his grandfather, except that my father's father was not the least bit sentimental about the olden days, was grateful for central heating, and had recently installed his own fax.

We dined on grilled skinned chicken thighs, a mound of rice fluffy with a scant tablespoon of butter and steamed broccoli. I had shared this meal before, and variations followed similar nutritional lines. If I asked my little brother what he *believed*, leaving aside his convictions about architecture which were equally fanatical, his leading catechism would underscore that carbohydrates must be relied upon for caloric mainstay; in place of deity he would exalt dietary fibre. Amid the malign influences in Truman's universe, *fat* ranked first. He might not have gone so far as to call obese people evil themselves, but they were at least the devil's playground. While my father had got worked up over a black woman dying because she was not admitted to white Rex hospital, his second son only displayed similar choler when a documentary asserted that some people were born fat and couldn't help it. The worst of determinism, in Truman's mind.

I shouldn't complain; if the food was plain it was impeccably prepared – six and a half minutes per thigh side on the second notch down on the grill, one cup rice to one-and-a-third cups water less one tablespoon. Truman was precise, and, in spite of his highfalutin' and ham-handed father, my brother's world view was essentially mechanical.

'Before we meet with the lawyer tomorrow,' Truman mentioned, and swallowed, 'I thought you and I might talk about –' when he dabbed his mouth casually, his hand trembled '– the house.'

'What about it?'

'Mordecai's going to want his share in cash.'

'Probably.'

'He's a philistine. But what about you?'

We would not hear the details of the will until the following afternoon, but my parents had prepared us for their estate being evenly divided among the three heirs. They must have been sorely tempted to disinherit the eldest altogether, but their idea of themselves as fair liberal parents who did not have preferences among their children won the day.

'Have you a clue how much dosh is left –'

'*Dosh*?' Truman's eyes narrowed.

'Money. On top of the house?'

'Nope. With the *dosh* I saw Father mailing off to every Negro-something charity he could find I bet we're not coming into a windfall. Still, Father's salary from the Supreme Court must have accumulated to something. If my share of the cash is enough, I'd be willing to buy both you and Mordecai out.'

'Uh-huh.' I picked a tendon from my teeth. 'Since Oakwood has gentrified, this place has appreciated by a factor of several times. I doubt you'll have the resources.' I found myself hoping that he would not. 'What's Plan B?'

'Well, you and I could buy Mordecai out together,' said Truman promptly.

'Uh-huh.'

'And then, little by little, after I finish my degree and get a job, I could pay you off and eventually you'd get your money, I promise. We could even draw up a contract, with some moderate interest ...'

'Uh-huh.' I folded my arms. 'In any case, you want to be the one who owns Heck-Andrews. At the end of the day.'

'Well.' He shrugged. 'Yeah.'

'But it's my house, too.'

'In a way.'

'Not *in a way*. Legally, emotionally, historically – I grew up here, they were my parents as well, and it is partly my house.'

'OK!' He backed off, but he still didn't appear to accept that I had, much less Mordecai had, any legitimate claim on what he had already, our mother two weeks dead, assumed as his own property. 'The main thing is, we should try and keep it in the family. The last thing we want is to have to sell. Right?'

I didn't answer.

'Right, Corlis?' He was panicking.

It's chilling how clinical one can be in the midst of grief, but I had given this matter some thought. I did figure Mordecai would want the money, that Truman wouldn't come into enough liquid assets to buy us both out, and I could conceivably force the house on to the market. Just as Truman's impulse with Mordecai and the Britannicas was to deny him the prize, I was tempted to take Heck-Andrews from Truman precisely because it was the one possession he most desired.

'I might go in with you.' I tapped my fork on the table. 'But not with the understanding that you eventually buy my share. If I'm going to have a half-interest in this property, I'm going to stay interested.'

Truman looked mystified, and paused in his hoovering of rice. 'Why? You live in London.'

Averil mumbled, 'Ask her why she brought six pairs of jeans.'

'Don't you?' he pressed.

'And why she packed shorts. And summer dresses. In November.' Averil was talking to her plate.

I tossed my balled napkin at my chicken bones. 'As of today I live in Raleigh.'

I'd fled this town with such desperation that the statement wallowed in my ears with sickening fatalism. The Myth of the

18

Eternal Return: there was no getting away, was there? I felt like one of those paddle balls on an elastic string; the further I bounced away, the harder I would land smack back on my staple.

'Where in Raleigh?'

I rolled my eyes. 'I've been evicted. For now, this is the only place I have to go.'

My brother's jaw jutted forward, like my father's. 'Don't you think you might have asked?'

'Asked? Unless Hugh appoints us otherwise tomorrow, I just inherited a third of this place. Why would I need your permission to live in my own house?'

Averil had started clearing the table, pitching silverware on to stacked plates from inches above, crash-crash; then she made quite a project out of bunching all the napkins into a single, furiously tight wad.

'Because other people live in it,' said Truman.

'If this place is so massive,' I reminded him, 'that Father wanted to donate half of it to the homeless, it's obviously big enough for you and me.'

'But I thought you had this great career going. That you had a gallery and you were going to be famous and you'd made your real life in Britain. All that about applying to British immigration for "settlement" ... How you liked your new *flatmates* ... And a *sidewalk* seems like a *pavement* now.'

'You mean you thought you'd got rid of me.'

'I didn't –'

It happened again, up-side of the head: I was starting to cry. Averil shot me a quick dirty look, as if tears were cheating. As punishment, she cleared my wine glass.

'What did you mean,' Truman prodded, 'you've been "evicted"?'

When I found the spacious flat in South Ealing I was patching together a living from bootlegging films off the BBC for third-world black-market videos, and part-time messengering in town on a gasping second-hand scooter. At thirty-four, I was wearying of odd jobs and empty pockets for the sake of 'my work', and my attitude towards my higher calling had grown sardonic. However, I'd had just enough encouragement from selling the odd piece privately that I hadn't, incredibly, given up. The pretension of being an Artist may have made me cringe, and at low-rent parties I never introduced myself as anything but a bohemian ex-pat scavenger. Still, alone with mud, refining a plane or tapering those delicate fingers, I did not want a drink, a fag, a nap, or a chat; sculpting was the single thing I did that was all I wanted to be doing while I was doing it.

What's more, I savoured that my income was illegal. From girlhood I had been a sneak. For four years I'd limped by on tourist or student visas and wasn't officially allowed to work; I was in my element under the table.

So after I'd made a hash of one more live-in relationship, I may have wished myself beyond the stage of communitarian arrangements with names on milk cartons, but I could not afford a flat on my own, full stop. I posted for flatmates at universities. I knew it was safer – and wouldn't it have been – to advertise for females, but girls bored me and I grew up flanked by boys.

I had several takers, so I must have selected the winning couple with some care. I don't know what system I applied – the two men were not in the least alike.

Andrew Finlay was a grad student in political science at the London School of Economics, a scrawny bookish-looking boy with sharp shoulders and tapered wrists. His body was knobby and perverse, with a prominent Adam's apple and double joints – his elbows bent backwards. Though twenty-four, he looked twelve, an effect he encouraged by wearing outsized overalls bibbing harlequin jumpers, trouser cuffs rolled high to expose rumpled socks and chunky shoes. His facial features were narrow and weaselly, dwarfed by wide National Health horn-rims. Though his grin was sly and he laughed knowingly from the side of his mouth, it didn't take long to ferret out that Andrew had had meagre experience with women.

Peter Larson was a broader man, still well my junior but older than Andrew by six years. He was a Glaswegian, and it took me weeks of deciphering his accent to understand that his ostensible ambitions were in journalism. Such a future was hard to picture, save the bit about boozing up sources at late-licence pubs. Peter was on the hapless side, as he cheerfully admitted. He subbed for the *Daily Mail* and the *Evening Standard* for a month at a time, but often lost the job for mitching his morning slot, hung over. He was frequently late with his rent, but it was hard to get angry with him; that Peter was unreliable was at the heart of his appeal. While Andrew's jokes were contrived around esoteric puns or the latest cabinet scandal, Peter's humour was bawdy, his laughter salacious and inclusive. Besides, he was handsome, a footballer only recently gone to seed, with a square jaw and strong stomach muscles that would bear up under years more abuse. I knew how he'd end up: a potbellied, pasty would-have-been blustering through tall tales to avoid paying his round, but foresight inspired me to make the most of his company before he declined to welcher and nuisance.

Since Peter would vanish for days on end, on benders or fast-burn romances he'd never say, I spent a lot more time with Andrew. The younger man was light enough to share my scooter, on which the two of us would top-heavily weave to Stop 'n' Shop for provisions, to return flapping with plastic bags. His hands resting deftly on my hips sent a warm glow up the back of my neck. Though I might have dismounted grateful to have made it home without capsizing, I'd feel doleful when our mission was accomplished, already chafing to run out of Marmite – his favourite late snack with cold, burnt toast.

An atavistic socialist and paid-up member of Greenpeace, Andrew would wag his slender double-jointed fingers by the hour, lecturing on the betrayals of the Labour Party; I only half-listened. Our more frolicsome times were spent hunched over sticky oilcloth at the kitchen table, where he taught me the conventions of British crossword puzzles. The *Independent*'s clues were oblique in comparison with the *Herald Tribune*'s, a distinction which would tempt Andrew to extemporize on how Americans had no sense of irony. I'd retort that the British were self-regarding and coy. Andrew hailed from Bath; his *l*s converted to *w*s, his *th*s to *f*s and *v*s. I'd mimic his reading of clues – 'Boat of bwuverwy wuv'; he'd caricature my inattentive lapses into a southern accent – 'Keeyun-sheeyup'.

I liked to think it inevitable that, as we haggled over 19 across, his hand would eventually drop the pen for mine.

I liked to think it equally inevitable that, on a later night, Andrew off to bed, Peter would burst into the flat when I was only wearing a kimono, let the cup of coffee I fixed him cool as he poured the last of his White Horse for me, until at 4a.m. the flaps of my kimono would fall open.

Improbably, this went on for months. I counselled each of them in turn that to keep our household amicable it was paramount they neither blurted to the other about any indiscreet flat-mating. Though the two had little in common, they liked each other, and agreed. Andrew said he could see how Peter might feel left out; Peter said, that poor lad's not getting any crumpet, no reason to shove our sheets under his nose. I doubt two women would have been capable of it, but judging from the ease and hilarity of that period those chaps must have kept their traps shut.

About that time I feel wistful, though I know I shouldn't – playing double-footsie under the oilcloth; rushing to throw on my jeans when Andrew and I heard a key in the door; pretending wakefulness so that Andrew would lumber off to bed before Peter stumbled jovially in after last call. I knew our trio couldn't last, but somehow neither man encroached emotionally on the other in my head. Peter was rambunctious and liked to wrestle; he spent no time analysing 'our relationship' and he still didn't tell me where he went on holidays from our flat. Peter would slam-bam; Andrew was tender, solicitous and adventurous in bed. While Peter was oblivious to the crudest details of my existence, Andrew made meticulous enquiry into my past and grilled me on whether I wanted to have children.

Although I'd never have expected appreciation, from Peter in particular, they both adored my sculpture. I fashioned and fired my pieces at a ceramics cooperative in Clapham, but bubble-wrapped them back to the flat, where I unveiled them to my fans in our spare room, to gratifying oohs and ahs.

Good news seems always paired with bad. A fortnight after the three of us had polished off four bottles of champagne to celebrate my coup with the Curlew Gallery, the phone rang again. It wasn't the middle of the night, which might have prepared me. Truman was admirably factual. He had found my mother in our parlour at ten in the morning, surrounded by old photos of my father. Undoubtedly, her heart.

Both boys were terribly sweet. Andrew got right on the phone to BA, and I hadn't known there were special rates for emergency bereavements – I got on a flight at half price the next day. He fixed me tea while Peter, predictably, ran for vodka. They both saw me off at Heathrow, while I assured them I'd be back in a few days; I had to put up my show at the Curlew when I returned.

Take care of my darlings in the spare room, I said, and kissed each of them, daringly, on the mouth.

They may not have been gossipy girls, but if you put two people of any sex in a room by themselves for long enough they will tell all.

'I'd been flirting,' I told Truman, 'with both of them. I guess while I was gone they had a few beers with each other, and … well, they must have been mad.'

'So they kicked you out.'

'That's not all they kicked. Or one of them. When I flew back, no one met my plane. I took the tube, and came home to the flat empty. I was restless, and headed for the back room thinking I could start swathing my pieces in bubble-wrap for transport to the Curlew …' I sighed.

'The hand,' twigged Averil.

'Oh, nobody had taken a pickaxe to them. I might have preferred that. No, all the hands were lopped off. Every one.'

'Couldn't you glue them back?'

'Not for a toney London gallery, and the breaks weren't clean. No, the sculptures were ruined all right. Three, four years' work at least. I'm back to Go. Do not collect two hundred dollars.'

'I find it hard to believe,' said Truman, 'that those guys would destroy all that work for *flirting*.'

It's true that I sanitize my stories for Truman, but like his mother he's so gruellingly good.

'You said it was only one of them,' said Averil. 'Which?'

'I was surprised. Peter was given to drunken rampages. Andrew was the sensitive, cerebral one. Then, I don't think Peter would have cared so much. He was savvy, he was wild and casual and had other women. Andrew …'

'Was in love,' said Averil.

'Maybe,' I conceded. 'I hadn't noticed. I probably didn't want to.'

That night, my spindly lover had returned, having given me just enough time to discover his get-out-of-my-life present. Behind the glare of his horn-rims, his eyes were anthracite. For once, he did look knowing.

'Why the hands?' pressed Averil.

'Because my hands,' I said, 'had lied. But they hadn't really. I liked each of those men. I liked each of them, in a different way, a great deal.'

Whenever my father was asked if he wanted pie or ice cream he would smirk and say he wanted pie *with* ice cream, so I was raised with the idea I could have both.

3

In my bedroom, I could make out snippets of conversation overhead.

'How long is she –' Averil pierced.

Truman's voice was more muffled. 'Until … she's depressed.'

'Corlis takes over!' My lullaby, and I slept.

I woke early, on UK time, and stumbled down for coffee. Our long, woody kitchen was added to the house around 1900, built on top of what was once a deep back porch. We'd eaten most of our meals at the rectangular table in the middle, the formal dining room reserved for interminable pot-roast dinners after church. I loved this kitchen. It had never been done over with linoleum and Formica, but retained its tacked-tin countertop by the pockmarked porcelain sink; cabinets were thick ash with crazed china knobs. My mother had read that a dishwasher used more hot water, so had washed up by hand; hence, aside from the Cuisinart, the room was free of garish modern appointments. With a few home-jarred pickles and strings of garlic bulbs garlanding the curtains this kitchen might have been the hospitable Southern hearth my English friends would picture, wafting with the rise of baking cornbread.

Instead the smell was stale, sharp with rancid oil and the faintly medicinal residue from 'perfectly good' heels of bread with the mould pinched off, as if no one would know the difference. Counters were littered with fat green broccoli rubber bands my mother couldn't bear to throw away, or the yellow crimps of sweet roll ties, amid an array of rinsed-out jars with the wrong lids and painstakingly smoothed aluminium foil, dull from re-use. A peek in the pantry proved it predictably lined with watery store-brand ketchup and reduced-price dented tins, recalling 'surprise' suppers when we would open *real* bargains without labels;

at my feet the floor was knee-deep in plastic bags. On the refriger-ator, sheaves of coupons were magneted to the door. Beside them, a last grocery list exorted with shy urgency, 't.p.!' She had never bought double-ply in her life.

I rooted around for a spoon among the ancient airline peanuts packets (Piedmont had long before gone to the wall); from between the gas-war glasses, I retrieved a send-away-for-your-free Nestlé's Quik coffee mug. The prospect of a grown woman who is comfortably well off cutting out three logos from succes-sive purchases, stuffing and stamping an envelope and remem-bering to tuck it in the postbox and raise the flag, all for one mug covered in advertising for chocolate powder, frankly made my jaw drop.

Waiting for coffee to drip (through a cone that had never quite fitted the jug and tipped precariously when filled), I slumped to the table. My mother's kill-joy obsession with minuscule frugali-ties was so unnecessary. Her husband had been a successful civil rights lawyer, later a state Supreme Court judge, and despite the cheques to the United Negro College Fund and his assumption of countless down-and-out discrimination cases *pro bono*, they'd never hurt for cash. I'd had a drink with their estate lawyer when my father died to confirm she was provided for, and he'd been reassuring. So why were we raised on A&P powdered milk?

It's true that thrift was a game to my mother, and she must have enjoyed it. And habits like clawing all the cartilage off the chicken carcass and throwing it into the soup would have been installed in childhood: through the depression, her father was a hard-up typewriter repairman; they'd stinted on sugar through the war. She married in the fifties, when whole magazine spreads were devoted to limp-potato-crisp casseroles. She had never held a job, and her only contribution to the family coffers was to not-spend; so day-old baked goods *empowered* her. But I resisted see-ing Eugenia McCrea as a creature of era; I preferred her as uncommonly cheap. Plenty of her cohorts had gone on to reach for new Ziploc bags rather than washing the old ones relentlessly and sealing a lone half of uneaten spud – perish the thought she should throw it away – into greasy plastic. In the scrimping of this larder you could see it: she must have felt so undeserving.

A sensation to which I had only contributed. She had cooled my forehead with damp cloths when I was feverish, whereas my father, when I was carsick, blew his stack. Yet, like my mother herself, to others I promoted my champion-of-the-underprivileged Dad. When I returned home in adulthood, I debated affirmative action with my father in the sitting room while my mother scoured this yellowed sink. Hadn't he told us himself that he'd been 'waiting for his children to grow up' so that we could at last 'engage in adult conversation'? In the meantime we bored him. So he left the raising of his offspring to his wife, and then had the temerity to rage when his eldest didn't turn out as he'd have liked. When I was young he was so rarely in evidence, forever in 'meetings', that my favourite birthday present was to spend an hour with my father alone, and to do so again I would have to wait another year. Gruff, inaccessible, buried in briefs with glasses down his nose, Sturges McCrea had been more icon than parent to me, and in truth I owed him little.

You'd think that the one reward for doing all the puke-wiping and nappy-dunking would be a little credit; instead we dismissed our mother for being so apparently unimportant. So she redeemed herself by mailing off for coffee mugs, and settled for victories of remarkably intact quick-sale vegetables while my father brought home honorary degrees.

'I thought you might want some milk.'

Truman delivered a carton, and sat down with his panda mug.

'You're not spending much time downstairs?'

'It doesn't feel like mine yet.'

Yet. I didn't take issue, for Truman charmed me in the morning. He took hours to wake up, and rubbed his eyes, bear-like, with the backs of his hands. For years he'd collected panda posters from Peking, T-shirts from the National Zoo, and mugs like the one he was slurping from, on which Ling-Ling nibbled bamboo. In fact, he looked like a panda: with dark rings around his eyes and a myopic bumbling amble, especially on rising, like a massive, muscular mammal I knew to be vegetarian and could tease if I liked.

'Ready for the big pow-wow?' Though a question, the sentence fell.

'As I'll ever be. I noticed nobody's cleaned out the fridge.'

'That's right, *nobody* has.'

'There's some furry yellow squash casserole in there that could cure all Tanzania of TB.'

Truman wandered to the sink; he compulsively tidied. 'Nuts.' He stopped. 'The sponge.'

I turned to glimpse, fossilized by the faucet, the horror of Truman's childhood. It had been his job to wipe the kitchen table, and my mother could not have started a fresh sponge more than once a year. The same fastidious boy he'd been then, Truman wet it by knocking it into the sink and running the tap; he squeezed it with a fork. Touching the sponge with only his fingertips, he nudged the foetid greenish square through my sloshed coffee. He scrubbed his hands, sniffed his fingers, and washed them again.

'How much can a new sponge cost?' he despaired. 'Thirty cents?'

As his first act of revolution, Truman pinched the reeking tatter by its very corner and dropped it in the bin.

Not expecting any surprises, I wasn't dreading our conference with the estate lawyer. If anything, I looked forward to seeing Hugh Garrison, who had handled the particulars of my father's death two years before. For a lawyer, he was unprepossessing, big on corduroys and always tugging at his tie; when he resorted to legal jargon, his eyebrows shrugged apologetic inverted commas on either side. He and my father had been colleagues, though I suspect that during our one after-hours beer at Brother's Pizza two years back I got to know him better than my father had over two decades. Had they met socially, my father would have held forth about how Carter was a much better president than reputed to be (he identified with Jimmy Carter, a nuclear engineer maligned as a moron because he had a Southern accent). Sturges McCrea liked issues. Told your wife had just given birth to a paraplegic, he'd start in straight away with the rights of the handicapped; it would never occur to him to ask how you felt.

At Brother's Pizza I'd been braced to move on to what a marvellous spokesman of the downtrodden my father had been, how fair-minded and self-sacrificing, and what a shame ... The usual. Hugh Garrison launched into no such thing.

'I'll never forget,' he began on a second Bud, 'dinner at your parents', oh, fifteen years back. I'd litigated a case, see – some arthritic biddy over in Cary with a fair stack of cash in the mattress had been tended by a black maid for years. Since her kids hadn't been giving her the time of day, the lady'd changed her will and left lock, stock, and barrel to the maid. Seems they'd become good friends, in a funny way. I'd made the amendments myself, but once the old bird kicked it, the kids started to squawk. Challenged their momma's competence. In court, the new will was invalidated, and I lost the case. Felt terrible about it. Sent the maid to your dad for the appeal. No question as to that jury's logic: any dowager of good Southern breeding who left her house to nigger help – pardon my French – was off her rocker. But since the old bat had been hearing the occasional voice, proving racial bias was living hell.

'Point being, Sturges and I had been working long and late and I was plumb tuckered. So we knock off and your mother cracks open a fresh bottle of apple juice –'

I laughed. 'The Hard Stuff.'

'My nose got shoved so far out of joint,' he admitted, 'that I *asked* for a beer. Eugenia looked at me as if I'd farted.'

'My mother thinks beer is low class.'

'So we sipped our apple juice and then came the nubs of cheddar from the bottom of the drawer –'

'With the mould scraped off.'

'Not *all* the mould scraped off. Sturges cranked up the soundtrack to 2001, when I had a yen for Ry Cooder. I thought maybe we'd get around to the Series, but over the trombones your Dad started shouting about third-world debt. Then it hit me: Strauss, stale crackers, hard cheese and guilty politics – this was Sturges McCrea's idea of a *good time*.'

That's when the idea first entered my head that my parents might be tiresome to other people.

Averil pouted at being left behind, but the will-reading was for immediate family only. I paused at my parents' Volvo, while Truman lurched to the driver's seat. I'll drive if you like, I offered, and he said no that's all right and I clued that he *always* drove, never mind that this car now was a third mine. I sensed a burgeoning attitude problem.

'Can we agree to ditch Mordecai after the meeting?' Truman proposed at the wheel.

'We might have dinner. He's your only brother, he lives a mile away from you, and you've seen him twice in two years. For funerals.'

'He's a bore and a know-it-all and he ignores me. He never fails to make some snide crack about my being in school, and then we have to listen for hours about the future of digital recording.'

I would happily describe my brothers' relationship to each other, except that they don't have one.

'A single evening won't kill you.' That was that. With Truman, I am sufficiently accustomed to having my way that I don't even notice when I get it.

We parked on Hillsborough, a leafy and majestic street in summer, T-junctioning into the state capitol, but looking the worse for wear with dogwoods and black walnuts too bare to obscure the failing businesses behind them. Downtown Raleigh was crumbling and dispirited, though like my parents' kitchen I was glad it had not been done up. Several tower blocks broke the skyline, but for the most part Raleigh's architecture had stayed low-lying, and Hillsborough was still lined with pipe shops, diners serving grits and black-eyed gravy, and the flagging Char-coal Grill. The rest of this town had multiplied threefold since I'd lived here, its perimeters bleeding to Durham and Chapel Hill, so it was comforting to find a stretch like this one that hadn't changed much.

There was one more bit of landscape that hadn't changed much.

I had to smile. Two blocks down, in silhouette he might be mistaken for my father, with that distinctive side-to-side swagger and ground-eating galumph. But my father's purposeful headlong look would have aimed at the NC Supreme Court around the corner; Mordecai leaned towards a different sort of bar.

As he drew a few strides closer, the paternal resemblance fell away. For one thing, he's shorter; both my brothers battled the metaphorical notion that they had not risen to their father's stature in any respect. While my father's umber hair had shocked in a Kennedy-style wave and was cropped close at the neck, Mordecai hadn't cut his hair since he was twelve; he bound the waist-long locks into three tight pigtails. His colouring was my mother's: when unbraided, the hair was lush and dark; his brows were rich and low, his lips full. If he weren't always vulturing his forehead and crinkling his mouth into an anal scowl, his face would look pretty.

The sun out, Mordecai was wincing, the cast of his skin a sallower shade than the wan winter light. While my mother's tones were olive, all of Mordecai was yellow, down to his thick rimless glasses whose lenses he special-ordered with a urinous tint. The unhealthy jaundice of his complexion was, I knew, distilled from liquor and heavy food and a vampire's schedule of hibernating all day and working all night. As he cringed down the poppled pavement, I doubted Mordecai's nocturnal flesh had seen more than a few rays of sunshine for twenty-five years. That may have left him safe from skin cancer, though if so that would be the single disease to which he had failed to issue a personalized invitation.

I raised my hand in salute, but not too high, lest Truman see me as eager.

When my big brother grinned back, his teeth matched his skin. At fifteen he'd declared that for his two live-in girlfriends he wanted to 'taste like himself' and refused to brush. The plaque build-up had been sticky and flaxen, and though he now seemed to conform to ordinary standards of hygiene his lopsided smirk remained ochreous.

'How's tricks, Corrie Lou?' Mordecai was the only living person who could employ my childhood's atrocious double-name without my taking his head off.

'Yo, Mortify.'

He kissed me on the forehead; his lips were soft. I caught a tinge of alcohol on his breath. He grazed my temple with his right hand, whose first two fingertips were lutescent with tobacco, the nails saffron and curling. Though Mordecai was only thirty-eight, his hands, creased with wood stain and machine oil, crosshatched with scars from the carelessness of hirelings, were those of a much older man.

'True.' Mordecai granted his brother a perfunctory nod; Truman grunted.

'You lucked out with parking,' I chattered. 'That army truck must take up at least two metres.'

Hee-hee, went Mordecai – his laughter, too, was prematurely aged, geezery and good-old-boy, from slumming with tar-heel construction workers who dropped out of high school. 'Nope. Yellow lines all the way. Remember that Justice Department card Father kept on the dashboard of the Volvo? After his funeral, I swiped it.'

'I wondered what happened to that,' Truman muttered.

31

'I find that hard to credit,' I said. 'The cops believing an army surplus troop transporter belongs to the Supreme Court.'

'Hey, it's worked so far. Not a ticket for two years. Figured True here wouldn't use it. That wouldn't be *right*. That would be *lying*.'

The pavement was too narrow for the three of us to proceed abreast. I didn't feel comfortable coupling clearly with one brother over the other, so trailed a bit behind the elder and a bit before the younger, our trio cutting a diagonal of birth-order down the walk.

'Man, I hope this Garrison character can shuffle paper fast.' Mordecai rubbed his hands. 'I could sure use the cash.'

Truman rolled his eyes.

Hugh Garrison's office was pastel and travel-postery, with a round table and straight-backs next to his desk. I was obscurely disappointed; in my imagination, we'd be seated at a long dark-wood conference table, with portraits on the walls, emerald bankers' lamps and heavy crimson drapes. I'd read too many murder mysteries.

Hugh shook hands and offered condolences about my mother. When he invited us to the table, Mordecai and Truman found themselves next to each other; Truman fussed with his pea coat and managed to insert me between them. 'So what,' I said, 'you read the will aloud to us?'

'Not unless you insist,' said Hugh, spreading over his chair and hiking his pants so the hairs above his socks showed. He was a rangy, casual man with a no-nonsense air. 'I think I can give ya'll the gist without the being-of-sound-mind-and-body nonsense.

'Now,' he began, spreading papers before him. 'I guess your parents told you that their estate would be divided equally between the three kids. So I assume they also apprised you guys of their bequest to the ACLU?'

He must have looked up to find a wave of shock registering across all three faces.

'It's thanks to the ACLU,' Truman grumbled, 'that we never had a clean sponge.'

'Rubbish,' I said, recovering. 'We'd have had a putrid sponge if they hadn't donated a dime. A smelly sponge is a point of view.'

'All I know is that to Father,' said Truman, 'the primary charity of non-profits was to take money off his hands. With the small fortune Father shovelled that ACLU outfit over the years we could have bought enough A&P eight-packs to wipe up the Atlantic Ocean.'

Hugh looked edgy. 'Mean your folks never informed ya'll that the American Civil Liberties Union was willed a quarter of their estate?'

'*What*?' said Truman and Mordecai at once, which may have been the only time in their lives they did something together.

I shot Hugh a droll smile. 'The fourth child.'

'You said "estate" –' The words were strangling in Truman's throat. 'Does that include Heck-Andrews, or not?'

Hugh rubbed his temples. "Fraid so. Last year your momma expressed second thoughts about keeping her house in this bequest, but she never put word-one in writing. Nobody figured her heart condition was so serious, and as usual – that's the way people are with wills – there seemed all the time in the world to change her mind.'

'Could you testify in court –' Mordecai leaned forward '– that she intended to revise the will?'

'No, and besides, she'd been wavering. She wanted to do –'

'*What Sturges would have wanted,*' Truman recited.

'Bingo.'

'Let's talk turkey,' Mordecai demanded, clicking the silver knobs of his bolo tie on the table top. 'In round numbers, what's the lowdown? Cut to the chase, bottom line.'

Hugh's head tilted with a trace of dismay towards my older brother. I myself had never been sure whether to find Mordecai refreshingly down to earth or, as Averil would say, crass.

"Sides the house? I've taken a gander at this portfolio, but couldn't give you an exact figure. There'll be penalties for liquidating long-term investments prematurely, and state taxes –'

'How *much*?' insisted Mordecai.

'Before deductions, ballpark? Round about $300,000. To be divided between the – four of you.' He smiled.

Mordecai fell back. 'That's *all*?'

'I know what it's worth to me,' said Truman, 'but on the market, what do you figure Heck-Andrews is worth?'

'Ya'll'll have to get it assessed. Off the cuff? House that size in Oakwood right now might list for three-eighty, maybe more. Fact, right downtown – Blount Street's commercial zoning – you might get that much for the property alone. Course, they'd level the structure, maybe put up a –'

'NO!'

Truman would have been heard several offices down. Hugh looked mystified.

'Over my dead body,' Troom added. 'But you're telling me that the ACLU owns a quarter of my house. What am I supposed to do, run a bed and breakfast for bleeding-heart lawyers?' His eyebrows neared his hairline; his jaw clenched, its muscles dimpling in and out. In the pugnacious jutting of that chin, I recognized my father in court. 'And what about the furniture? All those doodahs? Is the ACLU going to want my blender?'

"Less your mom was collecting antiques –'

'Only the cheese,' I intruded.

'No art works?' he asked me.

'If that organization wants my fifth-grade clay elephant, they can have it.'

'Most household contents don't assess at more than a few thousand bucks,' Hugh assured us. 'On this point I bet we could convince the ACLU to ease up. It is, after all, a darned gracious bequest. And I bet a lot of your folks' what-all has sentimental value.'

'Oh, absolutely,' said Mordecai.

'But they won't forget the house?' Truman pleaded.

'Not a snowball's chance. Too much do-re-mi. Oh, they'll be nice about it – at first. But those fundraising boys are hungry. That it's for a good cause only makes them more aggressive. They're not ashamed of themselves. Not that shame usually holds anybody back anyways ...'

'Is there no way to contest this?' Truman's nostrils were flaring.

'Contest it!' Mordecai cried. 'Come on, it's got Mother and Father written all over it! Sanctimonious holier-than-thou liberal bullshit!'

'Father wanted to get to heaven,' I mumbled.

'Yeah, well,' said Mordecai, pursing his lips. 'I'm surprised he didn't give his place up there to a black handicapped dyke instead.'

Hugh was leaning back watching the show, and looked weary. Back when we had that beer it had been awkward at first, and I blurted that being an estate lawyer must be awfully dull. I guess that wasn't a nice thing to say about someone's profession, but I'd been thinking about my father's calling, crusading against racism, in comparison. Hugh had said no you'd be surprised. Estate law's sometimes more interesting than you'd like. You see a lot of – He'd cut himself short and said, well, it's hard not to get cynical about people.

Hugh sighed. 'With the ACLU, you got two choices,' he announced when we'd finished bickering. 'You can all chip in and buy out the organization's share as a family –' He scanned us sceptically, as if regarding our trio as a cohesive collective unit were risible – 'or you can sell.'

'We're not selling,' Truman declared.

'That may be something you have to decide with your brother and sister.'

'I live there!'

'For the time being, kid.' Mordecai played with an alligator clip that fixed his braid and worked the jaws up and down.

'Should you retain the property with the non-profit paid off, then you three could decide how or whether to dispense with the real estate at your leisure.'

'The last thing some of us need,' said Mordecai, cutting his eyes towards Truman, 'is more leisure.'

'What if two of us have some feeling for the house we grew up in,' Truman hypothesized, 'but all the other guy cares about is his filthy lucre?'

'If you can raise the funds, two of you buying out the third is one option –'

'Hold on here,' Mordecai railroaded. 'You're saying with the bastions of social justice out of the picture our jolly threesome can blather for months if not years about what happens to Mommy and Daddy's $380,000 ramshackle mansion – ?'

'It's not ramshackle!' said Truman.

'And meanwhile little True here makes up his bed in my house every morning and waters the petunias and grows old. Isn't there any way to push this programme?'

'You're any of you within your rights,' said Hugh, 'to file suit for partition.'

'So that what,' I said hopefully, 'the house is divided up and we each get a floor?'

'Physical partition is recommended once in a blue moon, but unlikely in your case. I dare say the court would regard awarding one floor each to grown siblings as a re-enactment of the Civil War. No, ordinarily the court demands the property be put up for auction. Any of you current part-owners would be free to bid for the house, though in competition with each other or the buying public, either of whom could jack its price out of reach.'

This was getting too complicated for me. 'Mordecai, come over to the house for dinner tonight,' I suggested. 'We'll sort something out.'

'My ass we'll sort something out,' said Mordecai. 'Your kid brother just wants to sit on his hands and keep his little upstairs hideaway intact like a fucking treehouse. And meanwhile my company's scraping along by the seat of its pants –'

'You'll get your damned money!' Truman's face was violet.

'There's one more thing,' Hugh raised reluctantly, 'before we break up and I let you three *amicably confer* on what you want to do about the real estate.' He didn't look envious; I got the impression that if I invited the attorney to our dinner Hugh would suddenly recollect a previous engagement. 'Mordecai ... You borrowed some money from your parents?'

'A pittance,' my brother replied guardedly. 'Why?'

'Say – $14,000?'

Mordecai sniffed. 'I doubt it was that much.'

'If you question the amount, we could verify with back records. 'Cause the loans are to be deducted from your inheritance.'

I did not think it possible for a man of Mordecai's colouring to pale. True, to my parents $14,000 was a stupendous amount of money. They'd never lost touch with the depression dollar, just as I had never quite debunked the exaggerated value of our twenty-five-cent allowance; a quarter still weighed heavy in my hand. But in terms of 1992, the amount was modest. *Forgive your debts*? So my parents were second-rate Christians like most, and that was hard to swallow when they had just piously donated a quarter of their estate to a child who was only an abstraction. They could be charitable as long as the generosity wasn't towards a real, obstreperous issue who used the f-word. Strictly, the deduction was fair, but I suspected my brother had interpreted the word 'loan' loosely.

'See for yourself.' Hugh handed a sheet to Mordecai.

'May 10, 1989,' he muttered, locating the amendment. He turned to me. 'What did I do then?' He handed the paper back the way Truman had held my mother's stinky sponge.

'Now listen. Mind if I leave you three with a bit of advice?' Hugh enquired, perhaps having noticed that we hadn't asked for any. 'I've probated wills like this before; your situation ain't unusual. The simplest solution is almost always the best. I know a house has memories, but memories you can keep for free. With this many tenants, I strongly suggest that you sell.'

Trying to keep him from spontaneously combusting in public, I quickly herded Truman to reception.

4

As we collected back on Hillsborough, Truman loitered a few feet away, a bullish, belligerent aspect disguising the same lost and stricken countenance he displayed when he was four. It would have been like Mordecai to woo us to one of the pricey eateries that had sprung up in Raleigh while I'd been gone, where he could stage the profligate debauch for which he was renowned around town; glaring from a distance, Truman apparently found his brother's enthusiasm for meeting up later at Heck-Andrews suspicious. Truman had grown so fiercely protective of our house that he didn't invite guests of any description, much less his big brother.

But I rather liked Mordecai's effect on my former sidekick; once our trio parted ways and the two of us returned to the Volvo, Truman clapped a hand on my shoulder and said, 'What a mess!' in a tone that suggested that at least it was our mess, together, and then asked if I wanted to drive; for the first time since my arrival I felt he was glad I was there. In the car, too, we had a feast of things to talk about, starting with that charitable bequest.

'Don't that beat all!' said Truman, quoting our childhood favourite, Andy Griffith, who resembled our father.

'Cutting in the ACLU was totally predictable.' I said. 'It's surprising those first amendment flunkies didn't walk off with the lot.'

'Mordecai embarrassed me. Comes into money from parents he never gave howdya-do and then complains it's not enough.'

'Mordecai feels chronically shafted.'

I had promised to lay in provisions for Mordecai's 'secret recipe' spaghetti sauce. Soothed by the shimmy of our cart in Harris Teeter, my little brother cheered up. While many find shopping tedious, Truman looks forward to Harris Teeter all week.

'I know this sounds crazy,' he confided by the paper towels, 'but I love running out of supplies so that I can replace them.'

I'd seen it: the shine in his cheeks when he lathered a soap splinter, from satisfaction it was his last bar; the flourish of his hand when he vanquished the tarragon so he could buy a new jar. When he collapsed a box of Total into the bin he spanked his palms, as if he'd accomplished something. Truman liked to have needs. At least the illogic wasn't lost on him, but I wondered if this delight in dispatching products in order to re-acquire them wasn't a functional definition of the middle class.

Consequently, as our cart mounded my brother's chest expanded and his step sprang – shopping, he was concentrated, efficient, authoritative about brands of tinned tomatoes. In a grocery store, Truman was pig in shite.

We returned having agreed it was time to move operations to the main kitchen. Truman took obvious relish in unpacking. Although I was sometimes frustrated by the close perimeters of his life, within those boundaries he thrived. Maybe to him who celebrates a fresh jar of mayonnaise belongs the kingdom of heaven. Truman shoved the Winn-Dixie ketchup aside for proper Heinz, swept away the broccoli rubber bands, and set about alphabetizing the spice rack. This would be the first time he'd cook here since my mother died, a festive and solemn occasion both. Truman had ambitions to enlarge his world by exactly two floors.

As he burrowed in the pantry, Truman's high spirits precipitously dropped when the back door slammed. He turned to confront, among his nutritionally correct carrots and ten-pound bag of Carolina long grain, a litre bottle of aquavit.

Hee-hee-hee ...

Truman's face folded down like a garage door. Truman claimed to dislike his brother; I thought his dislike was occluded by terror.

I suggested we all have a drink before preparing dinner. Brothers beelined for opposite corners of the parlour, Averil taking the love seat behind her husband's chair so that her view of her brother-in-law was physically blocked. She picked up a copy of *The Christian Century* and looked rapt.

When I solicited Truman with a glass of wine, I found him hunched over a piece of stationery. I recognized the sheet with its black border as the bill for our mother's funeral expenses.

39

(Exorbitant – I suspect that out of sheer frugality she'd have preferred we bury her in the backyard, like a beloved dog.) He scribbled additions and divisions, tortoiseshell reading glasses down his nose.

I brought Mordecai a shot of aquavit, whose single ice cube he fished out and threw in the fireplace. He raised the glass to the lamplight and squinted through his yellow-tinted lenses at the mere finger remaining, knocked it back, and returned the empty glass. I soldiered to the kitchen where the bottle was lodged in the bulging stand-up freezer. I wondered if he really liked caraway schnapps, which smelled like liquor fermented from a ham sandwich, or whether what he liked was the fact it was repulsive.

On a whim I took down my mother's last grocery list, scrawled on old 'Bob Scott for Governor' notepad paper and still magneted to the refrigerator door, and pulled a nubby pencil from a drawer. I had an itch to make my own calculations. The chart I constructed on the back of the list so amazed me that I wondered at having never drawn it up before:

	Mordecai	Truman	Corlis	ACLU
Mother:	1	2	3	4
Father:	4	3	2	1
Total:	5	5	5	5

By way of explication: every child has sooner or later to face down the farcical liberal fiction that his parents love each child equally well, a myth Sturges and Eugenia enshrined in their will, as if to convince themselves. Bullshit. Parents have favourites. Mine did their best to camouflage these preferences, my father by being indiscriminately aloof, my mother by being indiscriminately clingy. But as Sturges McCrea had himself opined, prejudice will out.

Hence my chart. If we counted the ACLU as the fourth child and allowed each parent to rank the McCrea kids on a preference scale from 1 to 4, we all four earned exactly five points. I had to admire the symmetry, contrived by two people neither mathematically minded and only egalitarian in an official sense. My father fought for justice his whole life, so naturally my parents would mete out love along with the real estate in equal portions.

Though Mordecai's glass was beginning to sweat, I paused to

study my handiwork. Unquestionably, the ACLU came first in my father's affections; it did not wet the bed or require a ride to the school play when he planned to take the car. There was equally no question – and I say this in my mother's defence – that however faithfully she parroted his views and encouraged his cheques out the door, for my mother the ACLU straggled in a far fourth. She was incapable of getting exercised over progeny she couldn't treat to a Popsicle, a ward who would never arrive at the back door trying to hide his report card or waving the winning essay on the school cafeteria. She was a real mother.

As for Truman, that of the warm-blooded kids he was the runner-up with both parents explained a doggedness in him, a we-try-harder, like Avis. If he could merely succeed in besting one sibling with each parent he could walk away with first prize. To this effect he had repaired their hot water heater, retacked their stair carpet, and rolled their wheely-bin to the bottom of the drive every Tuesday morning.

Yet my father's choice of Truman over Mordecai betrayed his weaker side. Sturges McCrea vilified his eldest son for being an arrogant, obstinate, pushy, demanding chancer – ergo, for being just like his father. How much easier to manage, that docile, introverted boy who would never dare the f-word in front of his mother; a 'late bloomer' with a queer fancy for architecture that my father found cute; a man (though I doubt my father ever thought of Truman as a man) too practical, or too cowardly, to move out of his parents' house, and married to a wallflower who was inarticulate about politics and therefore failed to impress. Truman didn't give my father competition.

My mother, too, eschewed competition, which is why in her books I came in third. With the wicked timing of the heedless teenager, I began to mature, or 'grow curves', as she would say, right around the time my mother started to sneak a second piece of pie. I always hated that expression, *grow curves*, which implied putting on weight. Instead I was whippet-thin in my teens, and my mother never forgave me.

It would be absurd for me to take her low rating personally; and I still kept an edge on the ACLU. Yet that among his burpy-poopy-screechy children I was my father's favourite was also impersonal. My father adored me and my mother wished I would put a bag over my head from the same neutral ontology: I was the girl.

Perhaps the single surprise on my chart, then, was Mordecai, who would himself have been taken aback that he'd remained, after so many shouting matches, his mother's pet. Maybe all women prefer their first-born sons. She always stuck up for him, though her advocacy often took the form of despair. I was glad for Mordecai that he'd retained a stalwart ally – he needed one.

Still, her partiality had its exasperating aspect. Had Mother's devotion to number-one son been less fierce, she might have dismissed his foul language as puerile defiance best undermined by refusing to take issue. (My mother was one of the last late twentieth-century Americans for whom the f-word still had punch. It truly shocked her, like a physical slap, and left a brilliant red imprint on both cheeks. Since her heart attack, I had reached for an expletive and could not find a word sufficiently crude for my purposes. In the absence of offended audience, there is no obscenity; with my mother dead, it was impossible to be horrid.) But no – she had to dote on Mordecai, and so he could destroy her. She'd coronated the ingrate, which was like crowning the son most likely to chop off your head.

I turned the chart back over, and re-magneted the grocery list to the fridge, savouring that an entire family calculus rested underneath our continuing need for toilet paper.

Having delivered the aquavit, I stood in the parlour doorway, surveying the results of nearly forty years' worth of primary school arithmetic.

'See, no measurement can be perfect,' Mordecai was expostulating. 'But traditional science has always operated on the assumption that niggling influences, small mis-estimations, can be overlooked. Chaos theory trashed that. That one rounding off, the one pesky speck you failed to take into account, can overturn your results completely.'

'Like *The Fly*,' I said, but Truman wasn't listening. Averil wasn't listening. I felt like my mother, who kept up the naïve conviction to the last that all you need do for a 'special time' is put enough blood relations in the same room. And for God's sake, it wasn't as if we had nothing to talk about. Far from wanting for subject matter, we were sitting in it.

'Man,' said Mordecai, as he propped his thick black lace-up boots on my mother's fragile coffee table; its fluted edge began to creak. 'How do you like that pompous horseshit about the

ACLU? That was all Father cared about, causes. Never mind his kids.' On an open Britannica, he arranged a pack of Bambus and tin of Three Castles; shreds of tobacco dribbled across thin pages of cramped paint. 'They felt guilty for living. Mother never splurged on a box of chocolates that she didn't feel bad about.'

'She felt bad,' I added, 'because they made her fat.'

'Hell, by the time you guys came along, they'd got downright profligate,' Mordecai went on. 'Dirt, that was all I had to play with.'

'Dirt,' said Truman, not looking up from his equations, 'and us.'

Mordecai liked to portray his childhood as threadbare, but often omitted that my father hadn't been picking through Belmont's garbage, but going to Harvard Law School. Boasting about your underprivileged background must be one more mark of the middle class. I had a feeling Real Poor People didn't brag about it.

'I'm just floored,' said Mordecai, 'that they didn't salt away more than 300,000 lousy smackers. They saved enough dough on me. Moving out in ninth grade? No college tuition? And then I borrow 14,000 crummy dollars and it gets subtracted. All that we-love-you-we-want-to-help-you and they kept track.'

I knew that when people were hurting they often seemed recriminating and spiteful from the outside, as Andrew had let me know how much he cared for me by smashing years' worth of my best work. Truman, however, would go to no efforts to rationalize his brother's insensitivity, since to whatever degree he enjoyed Mordecai's company at all it was when his brother hanged himself. There was a grim look of satisfaction on Truman's averted face, as if he were already relishing the conversation with me later when he could once again cast his eldest sibling as a grabby, selfish boor.

'Don't worry, Mordecai will make out OK,' Truman muttered, circling a figure in his lap. 'He'll walk away with $156,000, if Hugh's numbers are right.'

'That's if we sell the house,' said Mordecai, who seemed to have already arrived at this figure in his head.

'Or,' said Truman slowly, 'if Corlis and I buy you out.'

'You'd like that, wouldn't you?' Mordecai shut the Britannica on his tobacco threads and tossed it on the floor, where its spine bent at an uncomfortable angle like an accident victim you aren't supposed to move. He leaned forward and tapped ash on the carpet. 'Here's a cheque, buddy, now run along and we'll pretend we never met.'

'Maybe we haven't,' said Truman tersely.

'Buy me out is exactly what Mother and Father did, for years, and got off cheap at that. And now look – even dead, they want it back.'

Finally Truman looked up from the invoice. 'Nobody kicked you out, you left. You never wanted to be a part of our family, and you weren't a part of it, so take your thirty pieces of silver and leave us alone.'

Truman's muscles were straining the shoulders of his green workshirt, whereas Mordecai's shirt only strained at the buttons above his belt. Of the two, Truman was technically much stronger. Yet in the face of the older's impervious relaxation and bemused little smile, Truman may as well have been lofting rubber darts at a tank.

Mordecai reached for the woven celadon vase on the coffee table, turning from his brother as if neglecting an annoying bee that is not worth the trouble of pursuing and swatting at all over the room. 'What's this from?' he asked me, bouncing the ceramic from hand to hand like a basketball.

'Oh, some Korean gratuity …' I stuttered, nervous for it, and feeling apologetic for my parents' trinkets.

'So this is part of my *inheritance*?' he enquired, still hefting the pot back and forth.

'Lucky you,' I said.

Without further ado, he palmed the vase as if for a free throw, and launched it past Truman's nose to the far corner. It smashed into a hundred pieces with a sound as if an entire china cabinet had pitched on its face. Then Mordecai stood to arch his eyebrows at me, holding his empty tumbler upside-down by way of complaint.

'Maybe,' I said unsteadily, 'it's time to make dinner.'

I had learned from my mother to employ food as a proxy in domestic relations, just as Truman had detoured his complex affections for his family into a simpler alliance with our architecture. At least as we four bustled over cutting boards, the chop of cleavers and scrape of spoons filled what would have been, for fifteen minutes, numbed silence.

It may be sissy of me, but I've always been fascinated by how people cook. Take Averil, for instance: I gave her the job of making garlic bread. Easy, right? And quick. But no. First off, she adds a timorous amount of garlic to the butter, and has to be bullied into pressing several more cloves. She mashes the butter for ten minutes, mortified by the prospect of an unbroken clump startling an innocent diner with a burst of zing. When she advances to the baguettes, she saws the bread slowly as wood, and dithers the blade back and forth after every slice before committing to another, intent on identical twins. When in mid-loaf she severs it in half instead of cutting just to the bottom crust, she lets the knife droop dejectedly as if she has just failed a geometry test. Buttering, she dabs and peers and dabs, until I find it too excruciating to watch further. In the time it takes her to make garlic bread, the whole rest of the meal will have been prepared and the table set.

Averil was daunted by food, along with a great deal else. That she was a substitute teacher in the Raleigh public school system suggested that I had either over-estimated the significance of garlic bread or under-estimated the unruliness of North Carolinian teenagers. In the kitchen, she was always looking over her shoulder to make sure she'd done nothing wrong. She wanted to please the food itself, to earn its approval; perhaps someone in her childhood had delivered draconian punishments for piddling mistakes. Of flavour in general she was leary, her primary concern that there should not be too much.

Where Averil is painstaking, Truman is brisk. They share an exactitude – Truman's diced onions are all the same size square. Yet while Averil might take an hour trimming and snapping green beans one by one, my little brother lines them up ten at a time and dispatches two pounds in ten minutes. And where Averil is timid, Truman is judicious. The heat under Truman's sautéing onions is medium. The amount of salt in his pasta water is some.

The confidence with which Truman wielded a cleaver had always meant to me that, beneath his closeted, suspicious-of-strangers, why-go-out-let's-stay-home day-to-day, teemed a brusque, masculine certainty that never got out of the house. About his assembly-line methodicalness I was less enthusiastic. He was capable of experimentation, but if he ever dolloped the beans with pesto and it was tasty, then he would always dollop them with pesto in future. Truman seized on answers and kept them. I think if you presented a meal to Truman and said, *This meal is good; it isn't remarkable or memorable, but it is healthy and competently prepared and it will never make you grow 'love handles'; if you push this button you may have this same dinner for the rest of your life*, he would push the button. On Truman repetition never wore thin. I hadn't ascertained whether he was congenitally incapable of boredom, or whether he was so fantastically bored, all the time, that he was unacquainted with any other state.

Myself? In the kitchen, I am whimsical and I flit. I measure nothing, adding dashes of this and fistfuls of that until I have made either a brilliant dish that can't be repeated or an atrocious one that shouldn't be. This evening I sneak more olive oil into the vinaigrette than Truman would allow. However, I can't choose between adding capers or green peppercorns to the salad and so opt for both, which is foolish. I do this all the time: torn between accents, I'll sacrifice neither, and the flavours conflict. The last thing I am is methodical; I grind a little pepper until my tendons tire, peel one carrot when I will need to peel five, slice a tomato and have a sip of wine. Washing the lettuce I get impatient since I grew up with a younger brother who would do all the drudgery and I am a little spoiled; the salad will later be gritty. Meanwhile, I hover over the others and I pick. I crunch raw green beans, sample the simmering onions, slip off with a surreptitious spoonful of pesto, swipe a heel from Averil's garlic bread. She squeals. By dinnertime I will have ruined my appetite, but I enjoy food I snitch more than whole permitted portions at table. Most of my pleasures are devious.

The real study, however, was Mordecai, extended at the table smoking roll-ups and slurping aquavit. He ran his own audio-engineering company and was used, like me, to drones dispensing with the shit-work. He only roused himself for the foreman's role of spicing the tomato sauce. Mordecai cooked rarely – he and his wife Dix went out nearly every night – but inexperience never stopped my older brother from being an expert at anything.

If Mordecai has a motto in cooking, it reads: *quantitus, extremitus, perversitus*. Compulsively industrial, he promptly opens three times more tinned tomatoes than necessary. He presses two whole bulbs of garlic into the onions (while Averil's eyes pop) and proceeds to dilute the paste with the entire bottle of ten-dollar pinot noir I have opened to breathe for dinner. He shakes the big jar of basil with visible frustration, prises off the perforated top, and dumps in another quarter of a cup. He tastes the sauce, looks dissatisfied, throws in more basil, looks dissatisfied – in point of fact, Mordecai never looks satisfied – throws in some more, and advances to thyme. I peek in the pot to find that the sauce is turning black. But even after he has killed most of the oregano as well he casts about the kitchen as if the insipid slop still tastes like baby pap. He lights on the cone from my coffee that morning, and spoons in about half a cup of grounds. Only with this addition does Mordecai look pleased. His last stroke, a torrent of hot pepper flakes, leaves me praying we are out of cayenne.

When at last we sat down, Truman and Averil each took as small a spoonful of the sauce on their pasta as etiquette allowed. Even with Mordecai, Truman was polite. He did mutter, 'If this recipe is a secret, I think we should keep it,' but under his breath. The spices were chewy, and coffee grounds wedged in my teeth, though all I could taste was red pepper. I commended Averil on her garlic bread, which did a decent job of damping the fire in my mouth.

Mordecai himself made a show of gusto, his serving mountainous, an extra snow of chilli flakes over the top. He kept the schnapps at his elbow by some triple-strength black coffee and alternated slugs of each. At thirty-eight, he still wouldn't eat his vegetables.

'So kid,' said Mordecai, spaghetti worming down his chin, 'how's the *philosophy* degree?'

I intervened, 'He's got a 3.8 grade point average. Don't you?'

Truman looked at me darkly, as if what I had blurted was shameful, which in Mordecai's terms I suppose it was.

Truman's affairs addressed, we moved to mine. 'How about your sculpture, Core?'

Now, Mordecai himself was one of those entrepreneurs whose big break was always around the corner. I couldn't count the times that he had arrived at Heck-Andrews, to stretch back and toss six digits around in the poignantly misguided assumption that money would impress my father. Yet the big round figures floated in on a puff of his chest, and floated out with a shrug of his shoulders; the New York recording studio contract would simply never come up again, and no one would ask. Only because the next time my brother would be back for a 'loan' to see him through a 'cash-flow crisis' would we understand tacitly that one more big break had not come through. In this regard I was truly sorry for my brother: that he was unable to share with his family a single grievous disappointment, of which he must have suffered so many.

However, those who don't share their tragedies don't invite yours. 'I got a gallery interested,' I said, and didn't attempt even an abbreviated version of my disaster.

The rest of our meal was consumed with yet another contract that Mordecai was sure he'd win for Decibelle, Inc. whose syllables he caressed with more sensuousness than he ever used naming his wife. I could only find it ironic that Mordecai was a self-taught audio engineer when the last thing he ever did was listen. We were treated to all the costly components he planned to install in a local nightclub; his rhythmic recitation of brand names and model numbers – the Stanley-Powers-Ebberstein-and-Whosits M2XY 50001-BH – gave his monologue a liturgical lilt, and my head began to list from Sunday morning narcolepsy. I felt an irrational urge to play Hangman on a church bulletin. As with any sermon, you didn't interrupt, you didn't participate, and you didn't take *any* of it on board bar the fact that it was over.

Averil began to clear up, and stared down woefully at the pot where two gallons of Mordecai's 'secret sauce' remained.

'Freeze it,' I advised, and Truman laughed. Mordecai didn't get it.

'Man …' He extended while the table cleared itself, and lit another roll-up. 'This may sound uncool, but Mother dropping out of the game is something of a relief.'

'A relief?' The tendons in Truman's forearms rippled as he carried off a tower of plates.

'Yeah.' When Mordecai tipped the chair back on two legs and slapped his stomach for emphasis, I puzzled how he'd managed to pick up so many of his father's mannerisms, having left home in ninth grade. 'She wasn't ever happy after Father died, right?'

'Sometimes,' Truman objected tightly, scraping his wife's spaghetti into the rubbish. 'Besides, if she didn't have anyone else to live for, whose fault was that?'

'Hers,' insisted Mordecai. 'They lived in a smug self-congratulatory unit of two. Don't kid yourself that we ever meant much to them – or that we could have made the slightest difference when Father was gone.'

Truman ran water in the sink, and kept his back to his brother. 'You didn't make much difference, that's for sure.'

'Didn't you ever imagine what it might be like if she lived to a hundred? Getting heavier and weak in the head, talking about Father all the time? Wetting her bed, no longer able to drive? Hell, yes, I'm relieved. She's better off, and so are we.'

'The important thing, of course,' said Truman, 'is how *we* are.'

As Truman plopped glasses into the soapy water, Mordecai wrapped his hand around his tumbler, and Averil, I noted, did not have the nerve to clear *Mordecai*'s glass.

'I find it a little hard to picture,' Truman went on, his voice almost affable in a way that unnerved me. 'You driving to buy her groceries; you listening to the day they met in the Young Democrats for the eighty millionth time; you rolling up her smelly sheets and tucking in fresh ones. So what all are you relieved of?'

'You're damn right I wouldn't have changed her sheets. You would have, kid. I'm not that much of a sucker.'

Truman gripped the counter on either side of the sink, his head bowed. The veins in his hands were raised, shocks of hair on his crown standing on end like a cat's in a corner.

'She dunked our stinky diapers and mopped up our vomit when we were sick. She cooked supper every night and if it wasn't always gourmet we didn't starve. It seems fair enough to expect something in return.' At last Truman turned his head. 'If I'd have done it and you wouldn't that doesn't make me a sucker but you a cad. If it weren't for Mother, you wouldn't even be here.'

I had the feeling he was blaming her.

'Shit,' said Mordecai, rocking his chair on its back legs with his boot on the table. 'I didn't ask to be born, did I? She wanted to have kids, she had kids. Diapers went with the territory. I'll tell you this, I didn't want their favours. I wiped my own ass as soon as I was able, and at the age I could so much as turn a hamburger I walked. You're the one who chose to stick around home until, what? Twenty-eight?' (Truman was thirty-one.) 'You'd have cooked her strained peas, because she got you – you owed. I didn't. So maybe I'm relieved for you, bro. There aren't a lot of good sides to people kicking it, but she saved you a twenty-year nightmare and I'm just suggesting you admit it.' The front legs of his chair hit the floor.

Truman sudsed glasses furiously, though with his usual system, all the wine glasses at once, lining them on the left; he would rinse them in matching sets.

'What she saved you,' said Truman, 'was money. If she'd lived longer, she'd have used up what you already seem to regard as inadequate compensation for putting up with her company an entire fourteen years of your life.'

'All right,' Mordecai proposed blithely. 'You think I'm so money-grubbing? Let me pose you a hypothetical question. Say, Mother's dead. A fairy appears, and offers you one more evening with your mother. A whole night. There's one catch: you have to *pay* for it, out of your inheritance. Now, how much would that night be worth to you, bro? Would you pay $20,000? $15,000?'

'That's a false dilemma,' Truman croaked. 'It's not fair, it's not real. That's like asking who do you love more, your mother or your father, when you can love both of them.'

'But you do love your mother or your father more, don't you?' pressed Mordecai. 'Besides, my little fairy isn't absurd. You said yourself, the longer she lived the less we got, so every night did cost money, didn't it? You haven't answered me. How much would the hand-squeezing and hot cocoa be worth to you? $1,000? $500? *Ten bucks?*'

'I'd pay anything!' Truman cried.

'Are you so sure? I've looked at Garrison's figures. You and my sister here want to buy me out of my birthright, ain't that so? Bribe me with a bowl of soup?' (Even Mordecai had been forced to go to Sunday school.) 'The way I see it, you two already don't quite have the cash to send both me and the ACLU packing. So what if this one golden evening with Mommy – her arms around your neck, asking how your day went, patting your head and slipping you a big dish of ice cream – cost you just enough money that you had to sell the house? What if keeping your mother around a tiny bit longer meant you lost your beloved fucking house? Would you take the trade? *Really?*'

Truman took one of the unrinsed wine glasses and threw it on the floor. 'Get out!' he shouted.

Yet it was obvious to all present that stressing a point by breaking crockery was derivative. Earlier in the evening, Mordecai had smashed an object of far greater value that made a much more splendid crash.

Mordecai stood and poured himself one more measure of aquavit; its caraway effluvium made me woozy.

'Something of an accomplishment growing up in this lofty loony bin,' he announced, 'I live in a world of balance sheets. I understand that everything costs, and I mean costs money. Even sentimentality you've gotta pay for. So if you're going to go all wobbly over this house here, you're going to have to fork out, OK? And you haven't got all day. No way am I going to wait around for eons while you figure out how to save this dump. I'm going to Garrison next week to file for partition. The clock's ticking, kid. This firetrap is going on the market whether you like it or not. Maybe it'll go for three-eighty, maybe more. Maybe you and Corrie Lou can bid high enough for it, maybe not. Only one way to find out.'

He knocked back the last of his liquor, and capped the bottle to go. 'I've got to get to work. I'll just leave you with the thought, kid: Would you swap your house for your mother? And *be honest*.'

The back door slammed on an ugly question, since in a sense, as Mordecai well knew, Truman had replaced his mother with a house. While she was alive, he had lavished more abundant attention on this structure than he had on her, so that when Truman tenderly retouched baseboards and caulked the bath I suspect she was jealous.

Truman finished the dishes in silence, while I wiped the table with the new sponge we'd bought that afternoon. He swept up the broken wine glass, searching out the least splinter, and left to collect shards of celadon in the parlour.

Meanwhile I tried to jolly him, saying don't worry about Heck-Andrews going up for auction, we'll swing the price tag, whatever, and maybe Mordecai's right, we should get this property settled, but I got no reaction. Truman looked desperate when there was nothing left to wash, and finally sat with Averil and me for a last glass of wine.

'Are you relieved,' Truman asked me, 'that she didn't live a long time?'

'Of course not.'

He slumped. 'I am.'

'Oh?'

'What Mordecai said,' he proceeded morbidly, rubbing his eye with the back of his hand. 'I'd thought about it. I was afraid she'd live forever. You'd be in England … Mordecai's no use … I'd have been stuck. And now I got out of it, didn't I?'

'You're whipping yourself,' I said. 'Give it a rest.'

'You don't know what it was like,' said Averil. 'The last two years. She never left us alone. She was always baking us pies.'

'How terrible,' I said.

'Well, we don't eat pies!' said Averil. 'She was fat. She wanted us to be fat, too. If I even left the crust, she'd slam cupboards.'

Averil was right. When Mother handed my father half her slice, you could see her calculating that if her husband ate three times as much dessert as she did then she had to be dieting. Without him, she'd have plumped someone else to be eating less than. Mother had her truly generous moments, but would not have cannoned lemon meringues at Truman's dovecot – and at his petite young wife – only to be kind. Fudge, pecan, peach crumble – you name it, my mother's pastry shells were impeccably tooled and would have been aimed in a fusillade at her daughter-in-law's gut.

'We told her to stop once,' said Averil quietly.

My wine glass froze at my lips. 'You didn't.'

Truman groaned. 'That was horrible.'

'She left another one,' said Averil, 'apple and walnut, lattice crust, by our door. Truman took it back downstairs. He was hoping to leave a note and sneak away, but she was home.'

'Except for working at the hospice,' Truman lamented, 'she was always home.'

'He said no, thank you,' Averil went on. 'We'd discussed it. We weren't going to accept another pie. We always ate it, and then felt ill. We considered throwing them away, but knowing your mother, she'd find out.'

'What happened? Did she cry?'

Truman raked his fingers though his tight, curly hair. 'It went on for hours! How I didn't like her cooking –'

I got up and banged cabinets, rattled silverware, picked up drying coffee cups and slammed them on the counter with my lips pressed white. 'I *thought* you *liked* my *pie!*' I gasped. (My mother's

52

speech pattern was emphatic, as if were every word not anchored to its sentence with underlines it would wash out to sea.) '*All* these *year*s I suppose you've been *doing* me a *favour*?'

Averil laughed. I stopped, abruptly. The imitation was too perfect.

'Then she got into how I didn't seem to want her around,' said Truman. 'And I didn't, did I? How baking was one way she could be loving and stay out of my hair. So I said I didn't want her affection in pie, damn it –'

'You said damn?'

'I said damn. She turned purple and said there was no need to curse. I said I didn't like to eat a lot of sugar, but then she started on about Father, so ...'

'You ate the pie.'

'Of course I ate the pie! I hugged her and she mopped her nose with those Kleenex used a hundred times and I dragged Averil down and we all sat around the table pretending everything was fine and the pieces she cut were enormous.'

'Don't tell me. With ice cream. And you finished the crust.' I could see the scene clearly. My mother would bustle with napkins and pour root beer they didn't want either and sit down to a 'sliver' herself with her eyes still puffy and bright red. She'd talk about her Aids patients at the hospice with a humble, apologetic lisping that failed to disguise her sense of victory.

'It had raisins,' said Averil blackly.

'After that – did you keep getting pies?'

'Yes.' Truman sighed. 'Only ever since, she acted nervous, maybe we didn't want it and she'd offer to take it back or make an injured little joke, so we had to act exaggeratedly thankful. I think we got slightly fewer pies on average, but from then on we couldn't scoff them upstairs but had to make a show, sharing dessert with Mother in the kitchen and agreeing about how cinnamon with blueberry was a nice touch. We may have had them less often, but the slices were gigantic and the scene was always tense. So tense you really had to wonder why she kept rolling them out.'

'Now, however,' I said, 'no more coconut custard. You can eat cereal and chicken and rice and grapefruit and your diet is impeccable.'

Truman stared at his hands as if they had just wrapped around someone's neck. His chest shuddered, and lay still. 'I raked the yard. I vacuumed. I cleared pine needles from the gutters and installed new pipes in the upstairs bath. I'd do anything but sit down with her for a cup of coffee, and that was all she wanted, wasn't it?'

'Truman –'

He looked up. 'She cried, Corlis. All the time. She'd wrap her arms around me and her fingers clawed into me like – talons. She'd soak my shoulder so that I'd have to change my shirt. Those weird – shotgun – sobs … And I didn't feel any sympathy, Corlis. I wanted to hit her.'

'Who wouldn't?'

'Any normal son with a heart.'

'Truman, I wouldn't even come home for Christmas.'

'I didn't blame you!' He started to pace. 'You know, I trained her – even before we got married – not to come to the dovecot.'

'As I recall, the big accomplishment was to get her to knock.'

'Right. Twenty-one years old, and she'd waltz straight into my room as if I were still in my cot.'

At another time – as I had for so many years that it ceased to make Truman angry and simply bored him – I'd have suggested that if he didn't want his mother walking in unannounced the answer wasn't to 'train her' but to move out.

'So we had that confrontation. After which – theatrically – she'd knock. This turned out to be important, since there were some mornings I had to stuff Averil up the spiral staircase to hide on the tower deck.' He was worked up, but couldn't help smiling.

'In winter it was freezing,' Averil recalled fondly. 'The neighbours must have wondered, a naked woman on the top of your house. And Truman would scurry around hiding my clothes under the sheet and she'd come in and start to make the bed …'

I had heard these favourite stories before.

'Right, well, *sanctified* by marriage,' said Truman, 'we got a little privacy, OK? Dinner upstairs except on Sundays, and we had our own life. After Father died that went to hell. She'd knock, three timid taps, but never waited to be invited, and crept up the stairs calling my name in that kiddie voice, *Twooo-maaannn!* Some days we hid. Some days we both chattered on the tower deck.

'Well, last spring she came up again and it was time for grape-fruit and I wanted to slip the bourbon from under my sandbag and have our nightcap and finish talking about –'

'Mother,' I provided.

'Of course. We stood around the kitchen and gave her yes and no answers to every question and folded our arms and looked at the ceiling and wouldn't even ask her to sit down in the living room – didn't offer her coffee, didn't ask her about the hospice – but does she get the message? NO! So after half an hour, right, after all those hugs and pats on the arm I couldn't control myself. *Gosh, Mother*! I exploded. *You can't be mean enough!*'

Truman sat down with a thud. 'Well, you know how her voice was always fake? Cheery and falsetto? I'll never forget hearing it change. It sank a full octave lower. It wasn't nasal any more. All the muscles in her face dropped. *No, you've done a pretty good job*, she said, and her posture became totally straight with her shoulders squared and she walked calmly down the stairs. That was her real voice. I'd never heard my own mother's real voice before. Amazing. It was almost worth it,' Truman added. 'But not quite.'

'So sometimes,' I noted, 'you did hit her.'

5

'I thought about Mordecai's false dilemma,' Truman admitted as we squealed on the porch swing late the next afternoon. 'I might pay $10,000 for a night with Mother and Father, as long as it were different.'

'Maybe that was his point,' I said, toeing the swing in a figure eight. 'That it couldn't have been different. Therefore, inexorably, if Mother appeared in your dovecot from beyond the grave, in five minutes you'd be fretting for her to leave you alone. That's the way it was, so that's the way it was.' A tautology, but I was groping.

'What do you think was wrong?'

'Mother was miserable.'

'Yes, for the last two years —'

'Long before that.'

'And Father never noticed?'

'Come on. Mother was the one who never noticed.'

I reported a remark she'd made to me when I was twelve, making my mother only forty. Rather out of nowhere, she informed me in the same buoyant, bouncy tone she'd used for reading aloud *The Man with the Yellow Hat*, 'The best of my life is over, of course. I'd be glad to die now, except that would be selfish. I have to think of the family.'

'What she was saying,' I told Truman, 'was she wished she were dead. And this from the happiest woman in the world, according to herself. She thought it a common enough sentiment and went on to propose we have Spanish noodles for dinner.'

'Don't that beat all,' said Truman.

Like my brothers, I, too, had tried all my life to get away from my parents, the underpinning assumption that of course I couldn't get away or I'd not have gone to such extravagant lengths as putting the entire Atlantic Ocean between us. The two deaths, one on the other, had therefore arrived with a dumb surprise. Behold, it was more than possible to flee their company; in the end they fled mine.

Truman and I had talked plenty about my parents and we weren't through. A brother is a gift this way, since no one else would tolerate our interminable dissection for five minutes. Claustrophobically as I might yearn to chat about something else, should we stray to other matters conversation sagged and I was inevitably lured back. Talk of my parents was like candy we couldn't resist but which made us sick.

It was as if we were trying to solve a puzzle, like the *Independent* crossword. Yet Andrew and I had never done anything with our filled-in crosswords but throw them away. Therefore my question was less whether my mother, feeling excluded, tried regularly to divide me from my brothers than to what conceivable use I might put this information.

I suggested we go for a walk (for Truman, that always meant the same walk); he objected that he walked *after* dinner and I kicked him. He grumbled and said all right he'd fetch Averil and I pleaded please don't. 'She'll feel left out!' he objected.

'Sometimes people are left out,' I said, picturing my mother's eyes hood and smoulder while Truman and I conducted whole conversations in a language we had invented. 'So there's nothing wrong with their feeling that way.'

I grabbed a muffler and jittered on the front porch as Truman applied for permission upstairs. At last he emerged, alone but harried. One walk had cost him.

'What's the big deal?' I asked as we tripped down the stoop. 'For Christ's sake, I'm your sister.'

'You're not married,' he said. 'Filling out course registrations can be a big deal. If Averil can get jealous of a pencil, she can certainly manage it with a whole sister.'

I swished through the curling leaves of the black walnut tree.

He side-eyed me. 'You're looking pretty good.'

'Thanks. The last two weeks, I lost some weight.'

'Suits.'

I biffed him lightly on the upper arm, solid as a firm mattress. 'You, too. Not bad.' It was a service we did one another, mutual confirmation that neither of us was falling apart.

As we cornered Blount Street to North, I glanced back at Heck-Andrews; gold light retouched the manila clapboard so it no longer seemed to need painting. Massive for a residence, it was dwarfed by the Bath Building rising behind it, a great white slab for the NC State Laboratory of Public Health. The steady roar of its circulation system Truman claimed to detest, but I'm sure he was used to the noise. It was the hulk of concrete itself he reviled. Erected in 1987, the Bath Building destroyed the view from our back porch, once of an open field used for landing the governor's helicopter. The field was now circumscribed by a mall of polished granite office buildings, and children could no longer play Army there – a game my father had discouraged, and which had therefore been our favourite.

As we strode down Wilmington Street, my eyes swivelled from the Mall on our left to Oakwood on our right. It had taken me years of absence to notice that our neighbourhood was bizarre. Smack in the middle of downtown Raleigh, our Reconstruction enclave might easily be mistaken for a state theme park; add a gruesome dental surgery, a pretty girl pretending to churn butter, and an over-priced beeswax candle factory and I think we'd have got away with charging tourists admission. The houses were all Colonial Revivals and Second Empires, with storm cellars, boarded-up outhouses, and a proliferation of chimneys; happy darkies hauling water from a hand pump would not have looked remotely out of place. The grand, leisurely scale of these dwellings had been made possible by the Civil War, which had ravaged and levelled so many homes around the capitol. Carpetbagging architects had poured down from the north, for land was cheap, pine plentiful, and labour, with freed slaves and veterans equally unemployed, eager to pound clapboard for a meal a day. The yards were grand, their hardwoods grown as lush and steady as their planters intended.

What Oakwood's architects would not have anticipated was the New South on our left: a faceless array of stoic government granite indistinguishable from dozens of other downtowns north and south. This was the land of Internet and sun-dried tomatoes, no longer butt of barefoot bumpkin jokes, but the most rapidly expanding regional economy of the country, whose Research Triangle labs and industrial facilities drew scientists and magnates from all over the States. I cannot explain it, but none of this new-found sophistication stanched my horror when I slipped and said *that's real nahce* or stopped me from lying to Londoners that I was born in New York.

'Do you ever regret not studying architecture?' I asked my brother.

'Oh, not really.' He sighed. 'I'd have been expected to design modern buildings, wouldn't I? I only like the old ones. The last thing I'd want would be to goon up at the Bath Building and realize it's partly my fault.'

'You and Prince Charles,' I said. 'Ever miss the hardware truck?'

'Yes,' he said. 'Often.'

After high school, Truman went through a 'phase' – according to my father. Surely daunted by Sturges McCrea's professional eminence and degree from Harvard Law, Truman decided to be, as he put it, 'regular'. He refused to go to university. I had walked in on several prolix sessions in the parlour – not rows, they were civil – when I visited from Manhattan. Truman would be extolling the simple-honest-man and his simple-honest-job, for wasn't it ordinary hard-working people who built this country …? My father would rub his chin with a smirk until Truman ran out of euphemisms for unskilled labour, then deliver his own monologue about the value of a liberal arts education and what a privilege it was to 'luxuriate in the fields of the mind'.

For years Truman didn't give in, and considering that I think of him as the family toady he deserves some credit for holding out so long. Truman drove deliveries for Ferguson's Hardware for a decade. Averil's father owned the store, and it was there they met; she worked the floor weekends while getting an education degree from NC State. Her father paid my brother execrably even after he became an in-law, though Truman received his fifteen-cent-an-hour raises with the same awed, unquestioning acceptance of divine intervention on his behalf as when his allowance went up to thirty cents from a quarter.

'I understood that job,' he explained. 'I got to know the layout of the city the way you did London on your scooter, right? The truck was cosy. It was my truck. I played tapes and sang along and in the winter the heater kept it snug and in the summer I had air conditioning … And I always packed a swell lunch.'

I wanted to say, come on Truman, wasn't it dull, didn't you

crave something challenging, I mean how can you retain so much affection for a bloody van, for Christ's sake, but I stopped myself. I do not know why this so rarely occurs to me, but I remembered for once that my brother was not me.

'I thought you found philosophy stimulating.'

'It was OK at first. Lately ... Well, you'd think that all those books about is there a God and the implications of mortality and do we have free will would be of some help, right, when your mother dies? If they're not some kind of explanation or resort, what good are they?'

'Not much.'

'These airy-fairy philosophers are no use at all!' He waved his hands. 'I find Mother downstairs one morning, do you think I was going to look up 'Mothers: death' in an index? It's just, Corlis, all these Great Questions, they don't seem to have anything to do with my life. I used to feel ashamed of myself. I was afraid I wasn't smart or serious enough to be edified by all that wordy pondering. But now I wonder if maybe I'm plugged in and it's these cobwebbed old farts who haven't a clue. When Dr Chasson launches into the mind-body problem I sit in the back of the class remembering that tomorrow is Tuesday and it's time to wheel the trash to the curb. But, you know, maybe garbage disposal is actually more important! For that matter, all this, is there a God? Corlis – I don't *care!*'

'Huh,' I considered. 'I guess I don't either.'

'Most people don't! All they care about,' he added grimly, 'is being right.'

Truman had always been given to diatribes, and I found them wonderful.

We had crossed in front of Peace College, passed Krispey Kreme Donuts, and were now ambling down Person Street. Mordecai lived off Person Street, in a basement under the post office to our left, and as if to advertise this fact 'Mordecai Florist' (no relation) blinked in neon on this block. Truman sped up; I lingered. I could feel a pulse here, a thrum up through my feet as if my brother's Rockwell table saw rumbled the whole street; metal shrieked in the distance. Poking off the post office's far wall, DECIBELLE, INC. swung on the plain black sign, and the back end of the army surplus troop transporter loomed up the slanted drive to the curb. I knew better, however, than to suggest we stop by. On the other hand, had Truman not wanted to risk running into his brother at all he could have eliminated Person from a stroll he took every day. An eccentric flirtation.

We reached a parking sign. We about-faced. We turned around here because he always turned here: the usual logic.

'If you're so disaffected,' I said, 'what are you going to do?'

'I'm going to be a professor,' he recited. To me, Truman's assertion had the same colour as his announcement in third grade: I'm-going-to-be-a-fireman.

'That would make Father happy,' I humoured him.

'Father was always happy,' said Truman acidly. 'He didn't care what I did.'

'He spent an awful lot of time convincing you to go to college –'

'He just wanted to win.'

There seethed in both my brothers a resentment I didn't quite share. Oh, I bore a few grudges – my father never fostered my artistic ambitions, for example. Though once exposed to the caprices of Soho I could see his dissuasions as protective, the charge that I was 'no Michelangelo' when I was seventeen still stuck in my craw. He wasn't an aesthetic troglodyte, either – he adored Rembrandt – but regarded art as a ministerial calling for which you must be God-chosen, and he hadn't seen any angel Gabriel descending to my messy room. Wouldn't I consider, he went on to propose, nursing? 'Nurses are much in demand in the Peace Corps,' he commended. For years later I was tortured by visions of being stuck in some African mudhole in a peaked white cap.

After my stint in the Peace Corps I was meant to marry, end of story. Despite his lauding of the institution, in my father's mind once I was boxed off to my wedding he planned to give me no more thought than the Christmas ornaments in his attic: I would be taken out once a year for ceremonial purposes, then restored to my carton. Failing his expectations was the best thing that could have happened to me. Never signed, sealed and delivered to some generic husband, I remained a person, one capable of the 'adult conversation' my father had dreamed of. He delighted that I alone of his children shared his love of travel, and I don't think he ever recovered from his incredulity that the girl of that lot was not, it turned out, a total idiot.

Yet both my brothers fumed, as if denied entry to the garden.

They had tried different routes – Mordecai by beating his own path there, through brambles of his making: he'd no formal education past half of ninth grade, and taught himself to wire a mixing board under a bare bulb with a diagram. Just as furiously as my father had given it away, Mordecai had thrown himself into making pots of money, and spending even more. He would earn my father's respect by doing everything the hard way and anything he wasn't supposed to. But my father was an authoritarian by nature, and would never reward misbehaviour; didn't, to his grave.

But he wouldn't reward good behaviour, either. He never took Truman seriously, even when his youngest capitulated and enrolled in Duke, even when Truman gave up on majoring in architecture because my father chided that while a 'reputable' calling it was not one in which you'd 'make a moral difference'. My father must have known his younger son would adopt properly sublime aspirations eventually because Truman was like that. The youngest had wiped the table and done his homework; he made As and when he wanted to have sex on a regular basis he got married. Surely it was as a very consequence of this obedience that my Father dismissed him, leading me to the disconcerting conclusion that parents don't really want you to do what they say.

My brothers' ire was not even slightly mitigated by the fact that their father was dead. If anything they were angrier still, for in death there is a way in which you get the last word and I think they regarded the accident as underhanded.

As we once again approached Krispey Kreme, I hung back. 'CBC?'

Truman drew himself up. 'It'll ruin your appetite for dinner!'

I looked back at him dully. So this is how it happened: you yearn for years to be old enough to eat doughnuts when you please, at last you grow up, to find yourself reciting platitudes about din-dins. The liberation of adulthood as we'd conceived it from below was a pipe-dream; with oppressors deposed, we became our own tyrants. 'When was the last time you ate a Krispey Kreme?'

'Five years ago. When you made me.' He glared.

'Come on!' I hooked his arm and dragged him through the double doors. Truman could not have looked more glum if he'd been taken hostage in Lebanon.

Krispey Kreme was an institution in Raleigh, and one corner of this town that hadn't updated its decor since I was a kid. Lit with cold neon twenty-four hours a day, the shop had chrome-rimmed stools, counters the colour of surgical gowns, and waitresses in starched nurse-white. With a few crudely drawn posters about breast exams, it would have doubled as a family planning clinic.

'How're ya'll today?' The waitress patted down our napkins, and without asking poured us two cups of coffee the colour of rusty tap water.

'Cheers,' I said. 'We'll have two chocolate bavarian cremes, won't we?'

'We will not,' said Truman hotly.

The waitress looked enquiring, and I shot her the imperious glance of the elder whose baby brother didn't know what was good for him. She recognized authority when she saw it, and retrieved two revolting doughnuts hygienically gripped in wax paper.

'Lovely,' I said.

'You don't sound like you're from around here, missy,' she drawled.

Oh, joy, I thought. 'No, I'm from London.' I straightened my shoulders and set my tiny serviette in my lap, as our waitress started nattering about the Royals, and was it true that Princess Di made herself upchuck.

'Bloody hell,' I muttered when she retreated. 'I thought she'd never stop whittering.'

'Since when,' Truman charged loudly enough for the waitress to hear, 'were you not born in Raleigh, North Carolina?'

I hunched over my pastry and muttered, 'From. I came *from* London, I didn't say I was born there. Now eat your doughnut.'

He wouldn't. He arched back from it stolidly, as I had from cold pot-roast on Sunday afternoons.

My own snack was unexpectedly melancholic. Sure, it was shite – the custard filling hadn't been within miles of an egg, all corn-starch and yellow colouring, but the dough itself was motherly, and the chocolate icing formed a nice crinkly skin over the top. I made a right mess of it, and was enjoying myself until I looked at Truman, arms folded in disgust, doughnut untouched.

'Something wrong with this here creme-fill?'

'Aside from having about six hundred empty calories –'

63

'There is only something wrong,' I interrupted, 'with my kill-joy brother. Can we have that take-away, please?'

'You needn't have been rude,' I whispered out the door.

'And you *needn't* have lied,' said Truman. 'If you've really come back to Raleigh for good, you're going to have to can that *Cheerio*! la-di-da.'

'Just cause Ah come home don't mean Ah have to sayound lahk a moh-ron.'

'Keep practising,' he said as we loped down Bloodworth. He grabbed my waxed paper bag and dropped the bavarian creme summarily in a passing bin. My brother was getting uppity.

'So have you?' asked Truman. 'Come back for good?'

'For a while, I guess. For years I was driven to get away – from this town, from our family. Why do you think I wanted to hit Krispey Kreme? At least it hasn't changed. Because lately, the past is getting away from me.'

I had long regarded my history as a ball and chain, so had spent every spare minute trying to file it off. Raleigh itself had seemed a purgatory of the obscure whose most malevolent power was to suck me back. In two short years I realized that the past was instead terrifyingly evanescent. Increasingly, the town where I grew up did not exist.

'I mean, now Mordecai's going to force our house on the market,' I went on. 'Maybe that's the limit. No house, no parents – I'm not sure I want to be that free.'

We were on the outer edges of Oakwood, where the Colonial Revivals were smaller and closer together, painted in original Reconstruction colours that approached garish – magentas, lavenders, and corals glared on window sashes, which must have suited the onslaught of posh homosexuals that had recently moved in *en masse*. We turned on Polk Street to enter Oakwood Cemetery, where the setting sun lemoned gravestones on hillocks.

We hiked up to the Confederate burial ground, a grid of modest identical slabs a foot high, engraved with nameless dates. After the Civil War, Union troops still occupied Raleigh. They refused to allow Confederate dead to remain in the federal cemetery on Tarboro Road, insisting that the corpses – grey in every sense now – be exhumed to make room for Union graves: one more Southern grudge to bear, and this town thrived on them. In 1867 the Wake County Memorial Association dug up some five hundred bodies and lugged them over here. Later, the same association hauled corpses down from the heathen North, and now there were 3000 Confederate graves on this hill. We used to play here as children, upsetting the caretakers with our shrill irreverence, and swiping plastic stars and bars from headstones to bring home and deliberately appal my father.

The official halfway point in Truman's walk was a small memorial house erected by the United Daughters of the Confederacy, with cold cement benches and flagstone floor. The damp, still air was sweet with unraked leaves. From one of many bronze plaques to fallen rebels inset in granite, Truman read out:

> Furl that banner, softly, slowly!
> Treat it gently it is holy –
> For it droops above the dead.
> Touch it not – unfold it never,
> Let it droop there, furled forever,
> For its people's hopes are dead.

'The American South,' I observed, pretentiously like my father, 'it's the only place I know that revels in defeat. Most countries, after suffering ignominy, try to put it behind them.'

'Did you ever notice,' said Truman, 'that Father's attitude towards the Civil War was a little weird?'

'Weird? It made him mad.'

'But he wouldn't work himself into an abolitionist lather. He was mad at Sherman. Like everyone else.'

True, and I treasured the inconsistency.

We tripped out the south cemetery gate and threaded through the margins of Oakwood, where big black mamas still darned socks on splintered porches. The central part of the neighbourhood had gentrified, and now contained the highest concentration of Ph.Ds in the city limits. It was thanks to the Eighties boom that Heck-Andrews had multiplied into a staggeringly far-sighted investment, for this had not always been an upscale locale.

Oh, it started that way, though these tattier homes we strolled past now had been built for the Negro cooks and housekeepers who toiled in the Big Houses, like ours. Yet little by little the help didn't remember their place and encroached on Oakwood proper, and in their wake many white owners fled.

Besides, by the 1950s it wasn't fashionable for whites to live downtown, and these creaky anachronisms were considered fusty. As remaining whites upgraded to suburban duplexes and bungalows, the real estate market in Oakwood crashed completely. Many houses were boarded, some condemned, all were in wretched disrepair. (Truman can tell this story with far more pathos than I.) By the time my parents were shopping for a house in 1963, this neighbourhood was considered a dangerous jungle-bunny slum.

Which explains why they bought here. My mother couldn't resist a bargain – an entire mansion and outbuildings for $29,000. My father was taken by the concept of inverse integration – in those days, progressive whites would move into areas on the cusp of turning all-black in order to rescue the investments of Negro home-owners. For once architecture was imbued with moral qualities, though my father's high-minded romance with his new house was short-lived.

Because if Truman is to be believed, Heck-Andrews took an immediate dislike to Sturges McCrea. I grant there was something almost deliberate about the way roof slates would slide off right when her owner was leaving the porch. When my father shut a window, putty showered over his new worsted. When my father closed a door, the knob fell off. When my father tightened a spigot, the washer crumbled and cold water spat straight in his eye.

Truman and I took our usual detour past the Moser house, in front of which we remained for a moment in an attitude of prayerful respect. Though not nearly as grand as ours, the Moser house had been designed by the same architect, G. S. H. Appleget, in 1872.

'So is the beltway dead for keeps?' I asked.

'I think so,' Truman said warily. 'But it doesn't hurt to stay vigilant. If they ever shoot *Son of Beltway*, I'll be on hand for the lead.'

In 1972, when Truman was twelve and I sixteen, the city of Raleigh proposed to put a highway right through the middle of Oakwood. The capital was already growing fast, without any major artery to shift workers in and out of downtown. I'll never forget Truman's panic when he collected the *Raleigh Times* from our postbox. He ran to the kitchen and spread the scandalous headline on the table in angry tears. My father read over his shoulder with ill-disguised optimism that maybe the city would tar four lanes through our foyer and spare him those odious DIY weekends.

Though Mordecai and I were politicized early, coming of age in the Sixties, in 1972 Truman's enthusiasms ran to Sting-Ray bikes and Ugly Stickers; Banana Splits Club membership cards were taped to his bedroom door. The beltway changed that. Down came the Banana Splits Club, up went BAN THE BELTWAY bumper stickers and SAVE OUR OAKWOOD posters. The campaign to stop the highway's construction was Truman's first and may have remained his only cause. Though when the city council's plans were made public it became apparent that Heck-Andrews herself was safe, other houses of her ilk were not. Besides, as Truman would readily fume, any major thoroughfare with its attendant Kwik Piks and Sinclair stations would destroy what antebellum ambience Oakwood had left. These were Truman's first halting diatribes, during which he'd turn fuchsia, thrash his hands, and sputter, 'They don't build these houses any more!' I was nasty. *Whoosh!* I'd whisper trucks in his ear. *Bee-beep!* He'd hit me, and he was big enough that the punches were beginning to bruise.

I'd come home from Broughton to lure him to watch *Dark Shadows* with me, to be told he was slogging about the neighbourhood leafleting for a sit-in at the city council. He had a letter to the editor printed in the *Raleigh Times*; he wrote comment pieces for his junior high paper, *The Mustang*, and his social studies projects were obsessive; regardless of the era, he managed to write essays about Oakwood. My little brother was given to instant and enduring if sometimes irrational loyalties from which I had benefited myself.

The battle over the beltway lasted eight years, and Truman's active opposition never flagged. At fourteen he became a founding member of the Society for the Preservation of Historic Oakwood; by fifteen he was volunteering after school for Preservation/NC, a non-profit concern dedicated to rescuing old properties state-wide to which he still donated ten hours of his week. The acme of his martyrdom was in 1976, on the Moser house lawn, where we now stood. At the time, the property was dilapidated and the city had condemned it, though according to Truman their intentions were less than honourable – the Moser house was smack in the path of Raleigh's prospective new road.

The heavy digging equipment assembled, and so did a hodgepodge crowd – hefty black working women, mothers with prams, boys with scooters. Truman, beginning to fill out now, strode from the mêlée and planted himself in front of the bulldozer. Once he encouraged the others to do likewise, the wrecking crew was at a loss, and shrugging, knocked off for the day.

The SPHO got a stay from the courts, and over the winter Truman sawed and hammered through his Saturdays with the owner until they brought the Moser house up to standard. His grand stonewall before the bulldozer had made the front page of our morning paper; I bought five copies. He looked so brave and handsome, his chin thrust in precocious indignation. One of these was framed and yellowing in Truman's dovecot; another travelled with me in my wallet, flannelled from unfolding and smoothing and quietly refolding again.

As for his second son's burgeoning political awareness, my father was underwhelmed. I might describe our father's attitude towards Truman's architectural fervour as *rueful*; Truman would say *derisive*. The civil disobedience and picketing campaign against the beltway may have galvanized blacks and whites together until Oakwood teemed with the 'community spirit' to which my father paid lip-service, but he'd little taste for potluck suppers in real life. He was a man with strict definitions of what qualified as worthwhile. He'd argue that people are more important than houses, don't you think? and Truman would return that people lived in houses. My father accurately divined, however, that it was not the tenants Truman cared about. In Father's defence, he was himself battling lawsuits filed by white parents against the city over bussing, and organizing discussion forums about integrated education that regularly degenerated into punch-ups. He had his hands full, and I can see how in comparison a fight over a freeway might seem small.

Their differences came to a head twice. When Truman was a senior in high school, he suggested Heck-Andrews be listed on the National Register as an historic property. He claimed our house would be a shoo-in; he knew the procedure through Preservation/NC and volunteered to shuffle the paperwork. My father was patently uninterested. On the register you were told what trees to leave standing and what colour to paint your trim and the rigmarole was a waste of time. I agreed with Truman that registry wouldn't have cost the family much bother; I'm afraid that for my father this was largely an opportunity to hammer home just how little he thought of his son's decorative preoccupation. Truman got the message, all right – loud and clear.

So for the final showdown Truman was already haggard. About his son's ambition to study architecture I won't say my father was scathing, but his response was flat. Since Truman's belated enrolment in Duke was primarily designed to earn his father's imprimatur, there seemed little point in a major that left my father cold. After a few desultory discussions, Truman announced he would switch to philosophy, and my mother made pie.

'You know, the city council never did come around for the right reasons,' Truman reflected in front of the house whose life he'd saved. 'Raleigh just grew so much while the beltway was in the courts that the road they planned wouldn't have done the job any more. Those bastards never did concede that tearing down these mansions would have been town-planning pornography. A hollow victory, in the end.'

'But you made a *moral difference*, didn't you? It's still standing. Thanks to you. Good job.' I biffed his arm again, though my congratulations could never proxy for my father's.

Truman was the defender of the helpless, which was sweet except that if you ally yourself with helplessness you can fall prey to it yourself. To Truman, houses were the essence of innocence: they had never done anything to anyone. With this same compulsive empathy for the weak, he was a sucker for kittens and baby rabbits; as a boy he'd nursed doomed robin's eggs in light-bulb-warmed boxes. He still trapped racoons in our garden without poisoning the bait, and drove the scrabbling creatures in their cage ten miles to release them, bounding, in Umstead Park. I had met other youngest children as adults, and they all had incongruous soft spots for small animals.

As we detoured to the capitol to read inscriptions under bronze Confederates with bayonets, I considered that, coming from paternity with such a grand mandate as equality under the law, there was something marvellous about how little Truman wanted: proper diet and a particular house. As he debated out loud how we might best cook a chicken curry without curdling the yoghurt, I thought there might be something to this idea that the

Great Questions were spurious, not pertinent, and the good life was about addressing instead whether you should microwave bagels and why it had become absurdly difficult to buy 100 per cent cotton athletic shorts. My little brother's gumsoles quickened in anticipation as he scattered peanut casings and pigeon feathers because it was getting past seven o'clock, and it was time for rice.

6

That Thursday morning the postbox was stuffed with stiff square envelopes addressed to 'The McCreas', what few of us remained. I ripped open a selection of Christmas cards at the kitchen table, and they disheartened me somehow. The scrawled condolences about my mother commended her 'community service', but never recalled the clear, accurate alto in which she rendered 'Day is Done'. Many cards were from my father's colleagues, whose names rang with the singsong familiarity of state capitals I'd never visited – 'Benson Bonaventure' and 'Leonard Maxwell' had imprinted tunefully on my memory like 'Boise, Idaho' and 'Montpelier, Vermont'. I could no more picture their faces than they could mine, but if these people didn't know me they didn't appear to have known my father, either. Their notes exalted his legal judgement and passion for civil rights, but not one scribble recalled fondly how when he talked in hallways he'd knock his cordovans one against the other, gazing at the floor and obsessively rattling his keys. My father may not have valued his most endearing qualities; goodness, or what passes for it, is not that attractive, and I hearkened back instead to the day my father waggishly stole our peashooter and pelted the dining room while Mother screamed for him to stop. But we often make that mistake about ourselves; I faulted his friends.

Amid the season's greetings, however, I discovered two identical envelopes, one for Truman, one for me. I read mine, and hid Truman's behind the flour canister, where he discovered it while wiping down the counters after one more allotment of chicken thighs that evening. The return address arrested Truman's sponge; rice grains ticked to the floor. 'What – ?' He ripped the envelope none too gently. 'Garrison was right; they sure didn't waste any time.'

He plonked in a chair and spread the expensive stationery on the wet table, where it began to spot. When Truman was very little Mordecai and I would dog him around the house, mirroring his flailing hands as he tried to drive us away and repeating his every word – 'Schtah-ahp it! Cudd id *ou-oud*' – until he cried. Now he read the legalese aloud with the same mincing parodic whine of his childhood tormentors:

November 29, 1992

Hugh Garrison Esq.
Garrison, Jason & Lee
First Union Capitol Center
Raleigh, NC 27605

Re: Estate of Sturges H. McCrea

Dear Mr. Garrison,

We are in receipt of your letter of 26 November 1992, regarding Mr. McCrea's generous bequest to the ACLU. We understand that you are in the process of liquidating assets of the above-captioned estate, the proceeds from which liquidation the ACLU is due 25 per cent.

As you have advised, however, the ACLU is now co-owner, as tenant in common, of the real property located at 309 Blount Street. To determine the precise value of that property, a formal appraisal should proceed forthwith. Should your clients choose to divest, the ACLU is willing to wait for its portion of the proceeds pending the sale of the house, provided the property is immediately put on the market at a price which reflects its market value. If your clients choose instead to retain the property, the ACLU naturally expects its share in cash, not to be unreasonably withheld.

We recognize, of course, the difficulty that can frequently arise in disposing of inherited real estate, and would not presume to press you unduly in this matter. At the same time, as a non-profit organization with an active and growing caseload, we trust you will proceed as expeditiously as possible.

Let me take this opportunity to express to the McCreas, through you, our appreciation for the family's support. On a personal note,

I worked with Sturges McCrea on the Cox vs. Adams case, when he impressed me with his courage, his astute and even wry arguments, and his overweening commitment to civil rights. This state has lost an able lawyer, a judge who never flinched from a dissenting opinion, and a profoundly thoughtful, sincere human being. That this should be reflected even after his death in the form of this bequest impresses but does not surprise me.

Very truly yours,
David Grover
General Counsel

cc: Mordecai D. McCrea
Corlis L. McCrea
Truman A. McCrea

Truman looked up, wafting. 'Makes you want to vomit.'

'It's like all those Christmas cards,' said Averil. 'Your father was such a totally perfect person ...'

'To whom you could never hope to measure up,' said Truman, flapping the page like flypaper stuck to his hand. 'And of course "David Grover" isn't "surprised".'Everyone knew Father was self-righteous.'

'You think Father was a prat,' I submitted, sitting on the opposite end of the table.

'A *prat*?'

'A pillock,' I clarified. 'A wanker.'

The grinding of Truman's molars dimpled his jaw. 'I think he was on his high and mighty horse, and God forbid he should leave what isn't really that much money – and my own house – to his ordinary children who happen to be white and middle class and of course that's something to be ashamed of.'

'Maybe,' I proposed, 'his kids don't need his money.'

'You think the ACLU is more strapped than we are?'

I cocked my head. 'Might there be a difference between self-righteous and plain old righteous?'

'No,' he said staunchly. 'They mean the same thing.'

'So there's no such thing as decency. As a generous man.'

He flung the letter on the table. 'Decency doesn't include having this exalted Jesus opinion of yourself and making other people suffer for it.'

'I don't understand,' I solicited. 'How have we suffered?'

Truman's nostrils flared as he inhaled.

'Look here,' he said, taking a pen from his workshirt and drawing a line down the back of David Grover's smudged request. On the top of the first column, he printed, DAD GIVES MY BIRTHRIGHT TO STRANGERS, above the second, DAD TELLS THE ACLU TO JUMP IN THE LAKE. He must have worked this out more than once; the arithmetic went quickly.

'Take a look.' He shoved the paper down so I could see. 'Say the liquid assets do come to $300,000. Even adding the $14,000 Mordecai forfeits, you and I together come into $164,000, before state taxes, and that's with Hugh probating for free –'

'Hugh's not charging us legal fees?' I interrupted.

'No,' said Truman reluctantly. 'He's doing it as a favour.'

'For us?'

He squirmed. 'For Father.'

'So is Hugh self-righteous, too?'

'Hugh's just a nice guy!'

'Other people can be charitable because they're nice guys, while your own father is a prat.'

'I didn't say *prat*, you did, will you just listen a minute? If this house is appraised at $380,000, that means to buy out both Mordecai and the ACLU, we need $190,000. We don't have it. Know what that means? "Franny's Realtor" poked on our front lawn.

'But look at this.' He scrawled. 'Without the ACLU scoffing up a quarter of everything? We'd each have $100,000 plus Mordecai's $14,000: $214,000, and we'd only have to buy Mordecai out of his third for $126,666. No problem, right? And with $43,667 each left over to cover taxes and stay on our feet. You asked about suffering. Well, yes, I'm suffering. Thanks to Father's *righteousness*, as you call it, I may lose my only home.'

'Do you think maybe Father worked out those equations himself? That he wanted us to sell?'

'Just because he hated this house –'

'He might've thought it time you got out on your own.'

'You had long, confiding talks about it, I suppose.'

'Yes,' I said smoothly. 'We did.'

'I can live without both of your counsel on my welfare, thank you very much – *what*'s so funny?'

I'd started to laugh, like the Good Witch of the North when Dorothy doesn't understand about the shoes yet. 'Oh, Truman,' I said when I caught my breath. 'All your calculations. Bloody hell. This house is paid off. We can take out a mortgage.'

Truman's shoulders dropped two inches in shock.

'Well, yeah,' he said, folding his chart with embarrassment. 'My point stands. Without David Grover the only trouble we'd have keeping Heck-Andrews would be Mordecai, and we'd have a lot more money. A quarter doesn't sound like that much, but it makes a humongous difference.'

'Yes,' I said firmly. 'It makes some difference.'

'So you think –' he tapped the paper – 'Father's donation is swell?'

'I think it's laudable.'

'Why? He didn't give his money away, but ours.'

'That's where we differ. It was his money.' I had held my peace on this matter for as long as I was able, and licked my lips. 'It's still his money.'

Truman snorted. 'Not any more it isn't.'

But I was just getting started. 'And you keep going on about your house. Sometimes you remember and say our house. But it's theirs. We didn't buy this place. It's still theirs.'

'Tell that to David Grover. You're not being very helpful.'

'I simply can't share your outrage. Father earned his money, to do with as he pleased; we don't deserve a penny.'

'I'm supposed to feel guilty?'

I was not about to make myself popular. 'You're supposed to feel lucky. To get so much as a cheese grater, much less a whole house. Just because you come into something doesn't mean it's rightfully yours. That's what's wrong with this country, too, our whole generation – we think the world owes us a living. We think a house and car and credit card come with the territory. When the Good Life doesn't arrive on a plate, we're irate. We think everything should be free. We're spoiled, Troom. You and I are spoiled rotten. And so is the whole frigging United States.'

'You sound just like your father,' said Averil.

'She's right,' said Truman. 'You're imitating him – staking out the moral high ground and surrounding it with an electric fence. I had to put up with it as a kid, but I don't see why I should have to sit still for it from you.'

'What are you saying, we should give the house back?' shrieked Averil. 'They're dead.'

'In which case,' Truman added, 'there's no point in trying to impress Father with your scruples.'

'Notice,' Averil muttered, 'she didn't say any of this stuff when Mordecai was around.'

'It's much harder for our generation than it was for theirs!' Truman cried. 'After the war, the economy was expanding. Now we're in a worldwide recession, and you want me to bust with self-reproach just because I've got a place to live – for now. A fat lot of good that's going to do anybody.'

'I don't know how much harder it is for us,' I countered. 'Our burden is having it too easy. I think –' I was suppressing a smile – 'inheritance is evil.'

'Well, don't that beat all!' Truman exclaimed. 'You wouldn't want to say something mildly intelligent like, "Inheritance perpetuates class divisions". No, no. Inheritance is *evil*.'

'Why don't you give your share away, then?' asked Averil. 'Why don't you donate all your money to the ACLU?'

'Firstly, I wouldn't do that to you and Truman. Without me, you'd never keep the house, never get a mortgage –'

'Spare us your lordly –'

'I'm not finished. Second, I'm as piggy as the next person. I may find Father's compulsion to give his money away magnanimous, but that doesn't mean I could do the same myself. He was better than we are –'

'Leave me out of your –'

'Thirdly,' I overrode, trying to keep my voice level. 'I wouldn't contribute to causes because I don't have any. I have opinions. I don't have beliefs. People like us, all we know is what we don't believe: in God, in country. Mother was right: we are "negative". We take pot shots. We derided Mother and Father for years, but we're hardly improvements. We don't stand for anything, just against it. Honestly, I'm relieved there's not more money coming our way. If the sum were more sizeable, I might feel obliged to donate some, and with a gun to my head I couldn't think of the first organization or university or even person I'd support. We don't have convictions, Truman. Just opinions. Just points of view.'

'I have plenty of convictions!'

76

I shook my head. 'You have allegiances. I don't even have those.' For some reason this rigorous self-castigation was making me feel fresh and tingly, like stepping from a hot bath.

Because meanwhile a memory was tickling the back of my head. I'd been, what, fourteen. I don't remember the pretence for the quarrel, only that this particular evening, parents out, Mordecai living in a trailer park, I had experimented with a new ploy. Truman yelled at me; I laughed. Truman pummelled me; I laughed harder. He backed me into a corner and started to whip his arms at me like a whirlybird, and I wouldn't fight back, or not exactly; all I did was laugh, until the tears streamed down my cheeks, and I slid against the wall to the floor. In truth he was doing plenty of damage; he'd turned beet red, and had utterly lost control. I just rag-dolled on the carpet, wheezing when I could get it out, 'Oh, please. You're too funny. I'm beginning to feel sick.' He might have truly injured me if in the end my guffaws hadn't drained and defeated him, and he blubbered instead.

I hadn't been laughing this evening precisely, but the disarmament strategy was identical. The more cheesed off Truman got, the milder I became. I hadn't reformed.

'You think inheritance is so disgusting –' Averil began, balled in her chair.

'Evil,' I corrected.

'Ee-vil. But wouldn't you want to pass on something to your own children?'

'Yeah,' said Truman. 'What about your own kids?'

'I'd saddle them with as little as possible,' I said. 'Windfall isn't having a great effect on us –'

'Only an inheritance makes it possible for me to stay in school –'

'*And* to stay home.'

'Not that again!'

'And now without Mother to drive you round the twist, you can stay here forever.'

'I've always got you,' he noted sourly. 'And where are you living yourself?'

'Exactly. I shouldn't be here, either. We should give the whole bloody house to David Grover.' I scanned the kitchen. 'I think places have power. I think Heck-Andrews is dangerous.'

'Are you making a serious proposition?' Truman clutched either corner of the table. 'It seems to me you're not suggesting anything but that we take the house and our last measly allowance, just so long as we feel bad. Vintage Sturges McCrea, Corrie Lou. Thanks for your important contribution. We've got to decide what to do about this letter, and you –'

'There's nothing to decide,' I dismissed, taking charge. 'I'll call Hugh and get a recommendation on an appraiser. Legally we're obliged to pay off the ACLU, whether or not you think Father's bequest is post-mortem posturing, whether or not I think his big mistake was ever letting us have more than twenty-five cents a week.'

'What about Mordecai? He said he was going to file for partition! Then we'll be forced to put it on the market and have weirdos poking in our closets and –'

'I'll go talk to Mordecai,' I said. 'And see if he'll accept a settlement out of court. If so, you and I will take out a mortgage and buy them both out.'

'There *is* nothing to decide, then,' said Truman, relieved. 'We take out a mortgage.'

'Tell that to Mordecai.'

'What's the problem, he gets his money –'

I didn't try to explain, but I had an unsettled suspicion about our older brother that we didn't know him as well as we thought. I moved on. 'Furthermore,' I announced, 'Christmas. We have to invite –'

'Oh, no-ooo!' Averil wailed.

'Why do we have to?' Truman objected. 'Our whole family has been run by have-to for years and where did it get us? On stuffy cross-country car trips with cracker crumbs on plastic seat covers, no-touch rules and you throwing up at Welcome to Montana rest stops. We always did stuff together because we had to and now we're grown up and if I don't want to Jingle Bells with my brother who thinks I'm a dork I don't have to.'

'All right,' I said coolly. 'I want to invite him. When Mordecai's around, things happen.'

'You bet they do. Things like earthquakes and plane crashes and houses burning down.'

'Which would solve all our problems.'

'First it's dangerous, now you're burning it up. Leave my house alone!'

'That's enough.' I put my palms flat on the walnut. 'No more

78

my house. And while we're at it: the carriage house. I don't appreciate being told I can't go into any part of *my* house. My house, Truman. You've got the whole top floor. Don't be greedy.'

The first floor of the carriage house was Truman's workshop; the second was a catch-all corner for dead house plants and broken furniture. The day before Truman had instructed me that I was forbidden to enter there. Truman knew me for a snoop; that morning I'd found the upper door freshly padlocked.

Truman stood abruptly, his chair clattering backwards. 'Your house? Thanks to whom does the roof not leak in your house? Why is your garden still full of kale, what mysterious gremlin replastered the ceiling in your upstairs bath? How did you manage to find some poor bastard to hand-router baseboards they don't make any more when your house had dry rot? And who did the cleaning and shopping and cooking in your house when all your mother could do was cry? Who stood down here day after day like some kind of absorbent – fencepost – while Mother sobbed with her arms around his neck, and who ate all that pie he didn't want and put on five pounds? While you were taking the *tyoob* around London and twittering about art in that pretentious English accent and occasionally *ringing up* and talking to Mother for five minutes but then complaining it was too expensive and leaving her in my lap for the rest of the night? Damn straight it's my house, I earned this place slate by slate because you can go on all you want about feeling undeserving since you are. You and Mordecai did nothing but take, and at least I –'

He reached quickly to squeeze the bridge of his nose, to stanch something, as if pressing hard on a vein there he might keep it from spilling over the floor. His chest swelled, and he turned away. Shoulders sagging from what would have been obscure to anyone who didn't know him as well as I, he rasped, 'I'm such a liar.'

If Truman clung to righteousness himself it was the McCrea collective failing, and in Truman's case indignation masked remorse. I had tried to console him that he'd been an attentive son long after both Mordecai and I appeared at Heck-Andrews no more than once a year, and that he'd gone beyond the call of duty in tending the dismal crumple of our mother once her husband died. In truth, not I but Truman had become the family flagellant.

Barring that unconvincing tirade about routering baseboards, Truman overflowed with stories, like the one of Mother's spurned apple pie, that only illustrated his neglect. I knew them all by heart.

The hasp and padlock I'd discovered on the carriage house that morning, for example, was not the first lock Truman installed in Heck-Andrews. At nineteen, he'd decided to move from his old bedroom on the second floor to the third, then a dusty, dilapidated storage area, stacked with cartons of mildewed curtains and old toy trains. He replaced rotten floorboards, installed a half-kitchen and full bath, and papered the walls in hunting scenes. The dovecot took two years of his life, and it was near the end of the project he bought a Medeco for the door to the third floor stairs.

He hadn't mentioned this christening addition to my parents, but mutely went at the frame late one afternoon, chiselling the bolt hole. He wasn't being secretive – as I would have been – but he wasn't asking permission, either.

While he was gouging away, Mother ambushed from behind, an arm over each shoulder, and clasped her hands. She was so much shorter than Truman that her wrists pressed his throat.

'What are you up to, kiddo?' She puled with a pee-wee lisp, since while we were learning to talk my mother was forgetting how.

It would have been obvious what he was up to. He had stared blithely at the perimeters of the hole, in which he planned to conceal so much more than a bar of metal – Averil and Truman were already shacking up. 'Just tinkering, as usual.' His voice was airy – she hadn't let go, and her wrists had tightened against his windpipe.

'Tinkering at what?' She was still palatalizing like a three-year-old, but there'd be a sharpness now, like a razor blade in a stuffed bunny.

Now, if I were installing that lock, I'd have slipped the cylinder in my pocket, kept my back to the job, and decoyed her into fervid concern over Mordecai's drinking.

But no; Truman had this stalwart forthright side that was ruinous with my mother. 'Just a lock.' He chipped on.

'*What* on *earth!*' She'd have dropped the toddler routine for shock-horror; at least she let go of his throat.

He'd been prepared, having rehearsed his excuse upstairs for days, mumbling alternative versions in the hardware truck. But I knew these set pieces always worked better in the mirror.

'I keep some pretty valuable tools up there,' he recited. 'If we're ever broken into, having the top floor sealed off with an extra lock discourages – intruders.' He fitted the female cover plate and screwed it in place.

She waited for my father. By the time she came to fetch her youngest the bright brass cylinder winked at her, its centre jag a miniature lightning bolt of filial defiance. From the dovecot Truman could hear her trying the knob. He was hanging wallpaper, but would have been lining the panels up crooked because his hands were shaking.

'Trooo-maannnn! Could you come down, please? Your father and I would like to talk to you.' Treacly sweet: a sticky trap.

'Just a minute!' He washed his hands, thoroughly.

At the kitchen table, Truman was arraigned, just as he had been when caught peeing in the azaleas aged eight. He was twentyone, but nothing changes; his stomach congealed. *Never* done: he refused the proffered cup of coffee.

'Your mother tells me you've installed a lock to the attic. Don't you think you might have asked us first?'

Truman must have attempted to sound gruff through his burglary patter, but I'm sure his voice squeaked like a PA with feedback.

'Are you planning to give us a key?' I am driven to use the word *rueful* with my father. His tone would have been patient with repressed amusement, as if Truman had done something naughty but adorable.

'Well …' I could see my brother hunched in the doorway, affecting relaxation; with his hands shoved in his pockets, the denim would have scored his wrists. 'I don't see why you need one.'

'You mean no,' said Mother hotly.

'It's my attic! Before I started working on it, the place was all mouldy plaster and boxes of old towels!'

'All right, and we're *proud* of you,' my father emphasized. 'You're doing a very good job of renovation up there. But that doesn't explain why you need a lock, or why we don't get a key to an entire floor of our own house.'

'What if there's a *fire*?'

'I won't start a fire.' Once more, that exhausted minor key.

'How do you know?' pursued my mother. 'You're putting a kitchen up there – as if ours isn't good enough – what if you leave a pot on the stove?'

'I won't leave a pot on the stove.'

'Listen,' said Father, something he never did himself but which a courtroom lawyer comfortably demanded of other people. 'Maybe you've got a point about burglars –'

'What I want to know is what he wants to hide from us up there!'

'Eugenia,' Father had stilled her, then turned to Truman, no longer wry. 'You might have asked, but it's too late for that. Your mother's right, it's not safe. Now give your mother the key.'

However briefly, Truman must have paused to imagine what Mordecai would do in his place: abjectly refuse. Strafe her kitchen cabinets with the f-word like a healthy American lunatic with an AK in a shopping mall. Paralyse my mother with the stun-gun under his zipper and describe in hard-nippled detail just exactly what he would lock her from upstairs. My father would chase him around the house. Mordecai would break a window.

Except that Mordecai would never have been digging boltholes to secure the fiction that he didn't really live at home. He'd leave. He did.

Disdaining my mother's waiting hand, Truman had flipped the spare on to the table, where it skidded to the floor. 'You'd think at twenty-one I could have a little privacy.' He stomped out.

The Medeco scheme backfired entirely. My mother so relished her prize of the key to Truman's lair that she concocted excuses to stick her thorn in his side. Later she took to leaving her spare in the lock all the time, making a farce of his 'break-in' protection, but he left it there. The key had remained in his door since her death, after which she was free to haunt every floor of Heck-Andrews and no Medeco could stop her.

To Truman, the tale was metaphor – this supposedly exemplary son had spent $35 and most of his adulthood trying to lock his mother out of his life. How short-sighted and hateful, when he knew the day would come when he called and got no answer and tapped with trepidation on the parlour door, to spy her curded thighs spread over scattered photographs of my father: behold, she grants his wish, and maybe he regarded her early death as proper reprisal. I'd tried to explain that nothing could have kept him from thrashing to escape when she lassoed his throat, just as nothing could have convinced Eugenia Hadley Hamill McCrea to indulge Truman his dovecot hideaway and let him keep both keys. The workings of families are as fated as they are futile. Truman tortured himself, claiming he had pointlessly, pettily fought with my mother up to the very day before her heart attack. I'd assured him that had we taken him aside and said, 'Truman, tomorrow morning your mother will be dead,' he would still have argued brutally against buying more rickety aluminium lawn furniture on sale off-season. He'd have still called her a *muckworm* and slept that night never having apologized, with every certainty that on waking he would find her mouth open and her panties showing and he would have to decide whether to call first for a doctor or the police. Because that's the real thing, Truman, the real raw stuff of a family and it's *good*.

Yet in his candid moments Truman regarded himself as the cruellest of us three. At least Mordecai and I had had the consideration to be oblivious out of view, and Mother could kid herself we were simply busy. Truman had turned his back to her face. He had replaced the slates because Mother was afraid of heights and the roof was one place he could be free of her. So he had a lot of nerve trying to trump his sister with his beneficent repairs, and that's why my brother was in tears.

I'm afraid that by recoiling from my mother's smothering embraces, in moments of emotion I imitate my father instead: awkward, gruff, abashed, I forced my hand to Truman's shoulder and pressed as if the fingers were operated by remote controls. I have never been sure how to touch my brother as an adult. I kept my hand on his shoulder a stolid beat, looked at it like an object out of place to be tidied, and took it away.

Truman honked into a paper towel. We had a drink. When we arranged our *schedule* for the week, I forced myself to use a hard *ch*, since apparently my Britishisms got up Truman's nose. We stayed up late, the air cleared, discussing approaches to Mordecai, and how much simpler this situation would become when he was no longer 'tenant in common' of our house. Even Truman said it: our house.

I made an appointment with a realty appraiser for Monday, 7

December. As the prospective buyers of our own house, we needed the valuation as low as possible. We didn't hoover.

No, the Sunday before we filthied dishes and chucked them about the kitchen, and carted crusted cereal bowls to guest rooms. We unmade the beds, strewed the spreads, and pulled the fitted bottom sheets to expose mottled mattress covers. As Truman slumped curtain hooks off their rail, I dusted flour on carpets and walked it in; Averil flung socks down the halls. We pulled out dresser drawers to cough jumpers. While Truman sowed cans collected for recycling across our lawn, I unscrewed the bulbs in table lamps so that sickly overheads would defile the interior with a queasy glare. We kicked over our own rubbish bin, and neighbourhood dogs obligingly dragged chicken bones around the back.

Yet there was little chance of returning the house for an afternoon to the astonishing $29,000 price tag my parents had met in cash. Behind wadded newspaper gleamed fine mahogany baseboard; under wet washcloths on doorknobs lurked antique brass; cold grey soapy water couldn't hide the grand claw-footed tub itself. In the dead pall of overheads, delicate dentil cornice nibbled the perimeters of every room. If you drew a finger through the rusty Carolina clay I had painstakingly dribbled across the mantle, there was no mistaking that underneath was solid rose marble.

At lunch before our appointment, Truman saved the crusts from his ham sandwich to mash underfoot. We raced about gaping closets and cabinets open. It was my idea to leave the toilets unflushed, but Truman's horror prevailed.

As the crowning touch we dressed for the occasion ourselves, scrounging nasty dust-balled shirts from under beds. Averil and I teased our hair, while Truman donned an old BASH THE BELTWAY cap backwards. We looked like white trash.

Truman had worked up a vigorous hostility to Tom Wheeler, so when my brother opened the door I saw a superior satisfaction cross his features that the appraiser was fat. The man's dress sense matched ours: thin baggy suit, lavender tie. 'This guy's a hayseed,' Truman whispered to me in the foyer, the assumption being that anyone that overweight couldn't be clued up about architecture.

Truman was arch, his offer of coffee stiff and more graciously declined. Wheeler said he would get right to work, thank you, and we trailed after him as he began touring our mansion with a notebook. In the parlour, he tripped over our splayed Britannicas while ogling the cornice. He ran his finger through my clay to reveal the mantle's marble. 'Looks like the maid hasn't been through here in a while,' he said mildly.

'Mother isn't around to make us clean our rooms any more,' said Truman.

I slouched on the couch, which we'd bunched with army blankets, assuming a slatternly sprawl but failing to distract him from examining the window frames – which were now, thanks to Truman, tightly puttied around nineteenth-century panes.

In the kitchen, Wheeler cooed over the porcelain sink with its perpendicular X-shaped faucets, and the tacked tin countertop, which far from considered inconveniences were now retro-chic. He nudged away Truman's bread crust and examined the oak flooring, reaching for the sponge to dab off the mustard.

As Wheeler caressed our black walnut banisters, Truman despaired up after him. 'It's an awfully old house – falling apart really. No one's maintained it for some time. My parents weren't fixer-upper types.'

'She looks like a solid old girl to me!' When he tickled a gargoyle on the landing, I thought Truman might slap his hand.

Wheeler proceeded to my room, where the stained knickers made less of an impression than the stained glass window. Another note.

'Original fireplaces!' he exclaimed.

'I guess,' Truman grumbled. We'd bunched mine full of my mother's used Kleenex.

'They draw?'

'No, they're totally stuffed up!'

He worked the flu back and forth – oiled – and gawked up the clean brick. 'Looks good to me.'

At the entrance to the dovecot Truman waylaid, 'That's just storage, you know. Junk.' But Mother's key was in the door, and Wheeler proceeded up the refinished stairs, to where Truman's uglification job had been the most half-hearted.

'Separate apartment,' he noted. 'Raises the value considerably.' We peered up as he ascended the spiral staircase to the tower deck, from which he surveyed downtown Raleigh with such a big breath and pat on his chest you'd think he was on the top of the World Trade Center.

I had never seen Truman nearly so jealous over a man's coming on to his wife as he was over the appraiser's swooning at his house. With Truman always a step behind him, eyes following Wheeler's hands, the appraiser assumed a teasing little smile, and delivered a lascivious performance. He ambled back downstairs, stroking and mauling every inset tile and voluted sconce as if feeling up a skirt, and jiggling outside with such a proprietary swagger that I half expected him to ask for a cigar and highball. Circling the outside of Heck-Andrews the man had a field day, wolf-whistling at the buttress-flanked dormer windows, palpating pilasters and engaged balustrades on the bays, retreating out on to the front walk to leer over the attractive alternation of rectangular and imbricated tiles on the mansard roof. He sucked back a burble of drool to commend the ornamentation of the hoodmoulds in the four circular windows piercing Truman's tower; spittle webbed his mouth.

'Pity about the missing corbels,' Wheeler hummed sadly, 'but they could be replaced.'

On the porch the man gorged himself, cupping the bulbous turned balusters like breasts, fingering up the chamfered posts to fondle the faceted panels and decorative studs, patting the door's surround from ramp to backbend to fleur-de-lis.

'One of the old panes is out,' Truman noted, but by this time his intrusions were lacklustre.

'Congratulations,' Wheeler announced when he was through. 'You're sitting on a gold mine.'

Bollocks.

When they shook Truman's hand was limp. 'Sorry to put you to so much trouble,' Wheeler winked. 'Hell of a project, cleaning that up.'

I sensed we were amateurs.

The official appraisal arrived two days later: $410,000, and Wheeler included a note saying he wouldn't be surprised if we could get half a million bucks. The valuation was inconvenient, it would cost us, but at the same time I could tell Truman felt proud. He swept the clay, hoovered the flour and smoothed the bedding, in the affectionate repossession with which a gentleman takes a woman's arm after she has been insulted by the attentions of strangers.

As for my grandstand – about how our father had the right to give his money to charity, how we deserved nothing, how inheritance is 'evil' – I never retracted it. Frankly, I had learned not only these magisterial sentiments from my father, but also how to use them as a cudgel.

It's true that our generation was strong on uncertainties – we didn't believe in God, were embarrassed by our country, and had even flirted with right-wing departures from the Democratic Party. There was a price to pay for sand under our feet, and though I am not sure I would trade for the pavement on which my parents stood – or thought they stood – I could be envious of the illusion. Sturges McCrea had a way of making both his sons feel dilute, and he might have encouraged them instead to feel akin. Our father did have principles. Granted, he also had hypocrisies – he was officially a democrat and personally a demagogue – but you have to have standards in the first place to fail to live up to them.

Though I don't recall his discussing the subject, my father probably would have looked askance at inherited wealth, though he would also, like a normal parent, have wished to leave something to his children – he did. I doubt he ever considered bequeathing the whole of his modest estate to the Fourth Child. It was devious of me to deploy Truman's inheritance to part him from it.

7

I was accustomed to running messages from Heck-Andrews to Mordecai's Basement; for years the only sparse communication between my parents and their eldest was through me. I would be sent with their forlorn invitation to Easter Sunday's leg of lamb, and though I'd know the answer beforehand I'd leap at the pretext. My parents would be nervous on my account, as if sending me into an uncharted and perilous country from which they themselves were banished, and they always looked relieved when I returned seemingly unscathed.

Then, I was a double agent. At sixteen, I would slink into the Basement and report how last week our mother thought a 'hooker' was 'someone who hooked people on drugs,' and we'd hoot. On return home, I'd share my dismay that Mordecai had killed half a bottle of cognac in a sitting. I was everybody's friend.

As a girl I had adored escaping to my older brother's burrow, so when I took on the mission to appeal to him to settle the house partition out of court the eagerness returned. I had never lost my awe of this brother. Historically, I was perfidious – I got away with things, but I lied. Mordecai, however, had flaunted the very indiscretions I concealed. Craning over the banisters, I'd gawked at my brother in the foyer as he shouted at my mother for all the neighbourhood to hear that she 'couldn't tell him what to do with his own cock'. Cock! He said cock! He hadn't disposed of gin bottles in next-door's rubbish, but baldly upended them in our kitchen bin. He didn't slip condoms in a sleeve of his wallet, but tossed them on his desk or, if used, in an unflushed commode. Once the eldest cut and run, Truman and I still had to be in bed by ten o'clock while Mordecai was living with two older women and shagging them both at the same time.

The reason we were given that Mordecai became so unruly was

88

that our older brother was a genius. When at fourteen Mordecai took an intelligence test at NC State, he scored upwards of 160, in the range my parents informed us was 'immeasurable'. My father often bemoaned that his eldest was 'too intelligent for his own good' – the poor guy.

Meanwhile, neither of Mordecai's successors was pegged as an intellectual powerhouse. My nickname was The Scatterbrain, since I often forgot my lunchbox, and no one thought to connect these amnesias with the days my mother packed ketchup and bologna sandwiches. Truman was christened The Tender Flower, as he cried a lot and was easily wilted. Surely recourse to Mordecai's IQ was pure parental conceit – if Mordecai was unmanageable because he was brilliant, their genes were redeemed and their parenthood absolved. I can spot the self-interest as an adult; as kids we took our labels at face value. We believed that Mordecai was brainier than we were, and genius exempted him from the don't-cuss/don't-drink/don't-fuck rules that continued to apply to us mental mortals.

If curse, hooch and nookie seem the lesser seditions of the time, rebelling against my father in the Sixties was problematic. Other Raleigh-ites were blessed with proper flag-waving dads, dedicated Nixonians who wanted the *niggrahs* kept in their place and the Vietnam War to go on forever. These fortunate sons had strengthening family rows over whether they marched on Washington or cut their hair. But my father's attitude towards Mordecai's sprouting pigtails was *rueful*. A delegate for Eugene McCarthy in the Chicago convention of '68, my father encouraged Mordecai to march on Washington, and threatened to come along. In retrospect, it's surprising that my obtuse brother didn't take to burning crosses on our own Oakwood lawn.

Instead, at nineteen Mordecai built a shrine under the Franklin Street post office to a whole aspect of reality my father abhorred: the physical world. While Mordecai stockpiled every drill and sander he could lay hands on, my father despised and abused mechanisms of any kind. Technology expressed its animosity in return: chainsaws sputtered in his hands; two laptops in a row exploded. On winter mornings when the Volvo wouldn't start, Truman took to commanding my father to get out of the car and to step back three feet, at which point, for Truman, the station wagon turned over like a charm.

My father felt superior to objects and refused to stoop to their level. As a result, he was always putting the wrong oil in the lawnmower or savaging the gearbox in the Volvo with a ruthless, careless arrogance he sometimes transferred to his children. He would botch plastering drywall because he regarded himself as above drywall, though the plaster always got the last laugh. My father was an ambitious, wilful man used to getting his own way, and this showed in his strong-arming of the inanimate. People, in fact, were easier to push around; the objects fought back. I'm sure that's why he didn't like them.

What's more, he was mistrustful of anything that wasn't instilled with qualities of good and evil. He delighted in proclaiming a machine 'poorly designed' (i.e. he just broke it), because that meant it was bad. But most things just are. They may be predestined for obsolescence, but not heaven or hell. It was no accident that my father became a judge, for when denied the power to praise or upbraid he felt helplessly irrelevant. Finding a whole three-dimensional universe outside his jurisdiction must have been horrifying.

My mother, by contrast, had an uncanny mechanical knack, and in the absence of my brothers would cajole my father away from his jammed typewriter, to fiddle with frequent success. She understandably identified with the inert, manipulated by its master, whose only capacity to resist resided in its passive inability to comprehend what was required of it.

Though dubbed The Bulldozer by my parents at an early age, Mordecai more than any of us had an instinctive grasp of lawnmowers that must have come from thinking from the inside, where my father would simply attack from without in blind, bigoted ignorance. Had Mordecai brought to his three marriages the same gentleness and intuition with which I had seen him tinker lovingly with his table saw, no woman no matter how crazy would have ever walked out. If relations to objects are at all evocative of relations to people, then Mordecai was naturally compassionate where my father was a brute.

I skipped Krispey Kreme and turned down Franklin Street, where the bumpers of Mordecai's army truck delineated the stumpy contour I associated with my brother. Everything he owned was thick and blunt; his suitcases were heavy-gauge aluminium with rounded corners, his three-mil leather boots had dull reinforced toes, so that bluntness is a physical shape I associate with stubbornness, resistance and relentless, ploughing aggression. One of his inventions was 'wooden pillows', two of which he'd given my parents for watching TV: great slabs of laminated oak with routered edges. Only Mordecai the Obdurate would think to make pillows out of wood.

As I skirted the truck down the drive, my pulse girlishly quickened, and I reminded myself I need no longer be so bowled over by my older brother's job as a small businessman. The shine might have gone off his colourful rebellions against my parents as well – mutiny against tee-totallers had been too easy and had gone too far. In his rejection of formal education, he was left defending a Swiss-cheese version of the world with the same preachiness of the father he overthrew. And while twenty years ago they'd seemed worldly with their Spartan mumbles, *Yeah, Mort, sure, Mort, cool Mort*, the truth was a lot of his friends were morons.

None of this prophylactic deflation went anywhere. I was visiting my big brother. My brother, the genius.

The door was open; I wandered in. My eyes took a moment to adjust. The sun was glaring outside, but no ray no matter how determined ever infiltrated this space. There were only two windows near the ceiling, their black curtains sealed with duct tape.

The Basement's sleeping quarters were relegated to a cramped corner of the floorplan. I ducked under its maroon drape to check if he was still in bed. It was, after all, only five in the afternoon.

'Mordecai?'

Quietly, I switched on the lava lamp, churning the matted shag with lurid red eddies. There were no windows in here at all, so the same air had recycled for two decades, thick with what seemed to be the pungency of dirty sheets. I knew better – Mordecai didn't own sheets. This outer room housed his office; the lamp illuminated rows of audio catalogues. Decibelle's crimson logo gleamed on his invoices: a sketch of Neil Armstrong's first step on the moon captioned, 'Nothing's impossible, just expensive.' An Iron Butterfly poster drooped off its Blu-tack, but as for ornament that was it; Mordecai's idea of decor was embodied in the ocean of off-white plastic beneath Inna-Godda-Da-Vida that constituted his exorbitant Compaq computer drafting package. The beaded curtain to his bedroom had abandoned all pretence of privacy, missing more strings than it retained, but Mordecai was not a prudish man. More than once I had heard grunting, glimpsed swatches of dark hair, as I suspect I was intended to.

'MK! Slide me over some one-by-fours, will ya?'

From behind the drape I heard metal echo, a saw shriek – he was up.

As a teenager, I used to tempt my brother's hirelings sidling in in tight cut-offs. They all had ponytails and low-riding jeans slung on lean hips, a scraggle of belly hair exposed through missing buttons. They wore wire-rims and amulets and puzzle rings; they ate carob bars and yoghurt raisins, or tahini-tofu pitta pockets with sprouts. Perspiration infused the thongs at their necks until the leather was slick and dense with a funk that still permeated my brother's Basement. The astringency of those men – a few years older than I, men who fasted, threw the I-Ching, and popped mescaline as casually as I might chew the bit of paper that wouldn't peel off my Tootsie Roll – the boggy pong of their brackish Birkinstocks and sharp weedy breath had steeped this whole warren. Their residue mingled with the mildew from Mordecai's bare mattress and mould spores rising from discarded coffee cups, with the singe of grinding metal, the char of drill-bits blackening good wood, the sting of hot oil.

I loved this cavern in summer, with the sealed cool air of a wine cellar, cement cold on my bare feet as Mordecai ritually rebuked me that the floor was rife with nails. Now in December the heat exhaled from an open duct overhead, breathing down my neck as I crossed the workspace. Sawdust caught in my nose hairs, and I couldn't quite sneeze.

'Core!'

Three seedy employees looked up. The heavy one winked. I may not have quite the figure I once did, but my brother is still proud when I stop by. Around Mordecai I am impressionable, acquiescent, soft. Around Truman I am caustic, canny, imperious. They have completely different sisters.

'Mort, you want this threaded?'

'Yeah, but for 1.2 cm and no more. If you can't get it exact, call me over; that rod's $3.80 a foot. Dix! Get my sister a drink, will ya? – For Chrissake, Wilcox, never operate that saw without the guard down!'

I enjoyed being ignored. I savoured my brother's self-importance.

'How ya' doin', girl?' Dix slapped me on the shoulder.

Of Mordecai's wives, Dix Ridelle was my favourite. I hoped he kept her. She was a carpenter by trade; her overalls swung with ball-peens and screwdrivers. A chipped front tooth gave her a pawky, tomboy grin, and her sandy hair was cropped as if she hacked it off herself with a razor blade. When they first married, she was tall and lanky, with sinewy arms and shoulders hard as oranges. I supposed she was still tall. But after putting in four years of overtime with my brother, even overalls couldn't hide the extra weight. Dix was turning yellow.

'Hanging in there,' I said, and collapsed in what passed for their kitchen. No wiener-cooker or bagel-slicer here. The blender hadn't a top, and if you didn't remember to put a plate over the strawberry daiquiris the nook took a blood bath. Often they hadn't, on the third batch, and the wall was mapped in these oversights, Rorschached with splurts of coffee-ground tomato sauce left on high, and Jasper-Johnsed from mustard jars that just missed Mordecai's head. Uncrimped aluminium containers littered the counter from month-old Indian take-aways. Few of the dishes matched; all of them were filthy. I needn't open the fridge to confirm it contained three six-packs and half a bottle of hot lime pickle.

Truman hated The Basement. He'd only been here twice, while living a mile away. For one thing, Troom had a passion for stocked pantries – lone bottles of Cremora nestled in dead silverfish made him feel desolate. For another, he was fastidious, and Mordecai's table was sooty with roll-up ash; the Toast-R-Oven doubled as a roach motel. Both visits, Truman had washed his hands within five minutes. And Mordecai's environs dripped with the neglect that Truman detested. Mordecai lost the cap to his Worcestershire sauce, and never shut the top of his doughnut box. His cups seeped coffee from hairline cracks; his amplifier adjusted with vice-grips. Broken-down flop-house furniture lay strewn about the place at queasy angles in misadventurous groupings like the slaughtered anti-heroes of *Reservoir Dogs*.

But Mordecai's negligence was selective. Over in the workshop, motors were oiled, drill-bits of ascending size coddled in felt, hammers returned to their Magic-Markered shadows on the pegboard.

The message was explicit: a genius did not lower himself to buy broccoli. Even I had objected that his bog, with a door that didn't shut, its stacks of *Mechanics Weekly* by the head and hardened Hilton towels in the shower, never had loo roll. Money down, however, that Mordecai never ran out of electrician's tape or five-amp resistors. According to Truman, his brother's domestic disregard was a vanity.

For me it was a liberation. Granted this was not a household that arranged sliced tomatoes with fresh basil on handsome ceramic, whose host would throw a fit on discovering they were out of balsamic vinegar. No basil, no tomatoes, no platter, Dix howabout Karen's, you game? I loved it. Personally, I'm a natural homemaker – I'd have the bloody vinegar.

'How's it going at the haunted house?'

'Horror show. Low budget. Had much truck with *Averil*?' I had a way of pronouncing her name.

'Sweet. But mousy.'

'Ever lived with a mouse?'

Dix laughed. 'Scrabbling in the rafters.'

'And how. Oh, she never complains to me outright. Only through Truman. I get the diplomatic version.'

'What's the beef?'

'You name it. I add too much detergent to the laundry, too much salt to the pasta, and too much cayenne to the salad dressing – that is, any. After a shower, I walk around in a towel: I have no shame.' I raised my eyebrows. 'She's right. I don't.'

'Mean she's lucky for the towel?'

'It's no accident she's a school teacher.'

'Bet they figured once your mother cashed in her chips they'd have the place to themselves.'

'They should have figured they'd be out on their ear.' The heat in my voice surprised me. 'There's no reason Truman should assume he stays in a house willed to all three of us just because he never had the wherewithal to leave home. – Hi.' I looked up shyly. 'What's up?'

'Just won the contract with Meredith College to overhaul their theatre. New sound system, lights, the lot. A plumb. Dix, you're remiss. Any clean glasses?'

'You mean of all the ones you washed?'

Mordecai slid me an aquavit in a Burger King tumbler glazed

with Daffy Duck – it looked so harmless. If spirits this early in the day were against my policy, I maintained most policies to make exceptions to them. Truman replaced my parents' regulations with stricter of his own: no pie. Mordecai chucked them whole-sale. Me, I teetered. My whole life I had never decided whether to be a good or a bad girl.

'So how's tricks at the ranch, Core?' Mordecai dumped his boots on the table; dope seeds rolled to the floor.

I sighed. 'We've reclaimed the place, little by little. But it's slow, and pretty depressing.'

'That house is full of the most godawful crap.'

'It's funny, we can't bring ourselves to throw anything away. Everything's in boxes.'

'It's not all yours to chuck, is it?'

'You want the yellow squash casserole?' I offered.

He skinned up a Three Castles. 'You don't know what I want.'

'Listen,' I raised cautiously. 'I wouldn't have thought you had anything to do with this, except the Britannicas disappeared at the same time.'

I darted my eyes towards the entrance, where the twenty black encyclopedias had been dumped not a foot past the door. An uppermost volume was squarely under a leaky pipe; a drop splat-ted as I looked over. The book's black surface had already bub-bled and blanched, its cover warped.

'You didn't, uh, borrow any tools, did you?'

He licked the Bambu. 'A few. One of my hand drills was on the fritz. We had a deadline. What's the problem? You guys get a half million dollar house, and I grab a bag of two-penny wood screws.'

I rolled a dope seed between thumb and forefinger. 'See, the drill and … little circular saw,' which wasn't little and was frig-ging expensive and about which I had already heard altogether too much, 'they're Truman's. So you might, um, drop them by. And maybe next time … make sure first?'

'I gotta ask Mommy?'

'You can help yourself to all the yellow squash you like. But if you run off with anything of Troom's I get the aggro. From now on it's between you and Truman.'

There was nothing between my brothers but me. If the matter were left to direct communication, Truman wouldn't see his saw

95

for fifty years. Ask my parents what happened when Mordecai 'borrowed' things.

I looked up suddenly. 'You have a key!'

'Sure. I left with one at fourteen.'

'In case you came back?'

'Maybe I still will.'

Dix got up for a beer, and slammed the fridge. 'Mort!'

'Dix, roll a joint, will ya? Anyway, Core, I did come back. When no one was home. When I couldn't stomach another heat-lamp casualty burger from the Red Barn dumpster. I'd fix a cheese sandwich.'

'With lots of chilli sauce.'

'And sometimes pocket a twenty from Father's dresser.'

I slammed Daffy Duck. 'That was you! I got scuppered for that! Twice I was grounded for a week, no dessert! They still think I did it!'

Mordecai hee-hee-ed. 'Naturally they wouldn't suspect little True, would they?'

'Oh, no,' I said. 'He was always Mister Perfect.'

'I rehabbed your rep, then. Added a dash of the unpredictable.'

But what came back to me were even earlier scenes, when Mordecai still lived at home. A crime would have been committed, petty – Father's scissors swiped from his desk drawer. 'I din do it,' I'd say, wringing my skirt – even telling the truth I looked guilty as sin. Truman swooned up at them with those big hazel eyes, mute with terror. Mordecai folded his arms and scowled. My father would arraign us at the kitchen table for mock juvenile court. We were not allowed to leave until someone came clean.

The culprit was always the same. But we would sit for *hours* at that table, Mordecai implacable, staring at the ceiling. Once I'd shaken my head to satisfy Truman that he needn't take the rap on my account, the toddler would rifle cereal boxes for snap-together prizes and draw pictures in poured salt. But I couldn't stand it. I wanted to go play. I eyed Mordecai with defeated admiration. He'd have sat at that table into the night with no dinner rather than cave in to my father. Every time, I took the blame.

While I was spanked, Truman would throw his arms around my father's ankles, imploring, 'Hit me instead!' I'd figure I deserved the beating, as punishment for weak resolve. And I have since found taking the fall enlightening, of the Birmingham Six or the Guildford Four: it is less humiliating to confess to something you didn't do.

'What bamboozles me,' Dix was saying, 'is how you could only take twenty bucks.' She turned to me. 'Kid out on the street, fourteen, fifteen, and they didn't give him jack? And his daddy a hot-shot lawyer?'

'As I recall,' I said cautiously, 'he didn't want their money.'

'Besides, Dix, it would just have been subtracted from my inheritance.'

'Your parents were remembering sons of bitches.'

'I'm surprised I didn't get deductions for the diapers.'

'Speaking of which,' I mentioned. 'The ACLU wants their dosh. Of course they asked nicely. This chap thought Father was Gandhi or something.'

'I could tell him a thing or three,' Mordecai grumbled.

'So we had the house appraised, and it's worth more than Hugh thought: $410,000. That means you'd be due about $100,000 clear … There's no reason to take this to court, is there? Between the cash and a mortgage, Troom and I could buy out the ACLU and you as well …' The proposition had seemed so straightforward, yet I couldn't look Mordecai in the eye.

'Yeah, right.' He knocked back another aquavit.

'Why don't ya'll put that albatross up for sale?' Dix exclaimed. 'You know how many rich faggots would leap at that pile of kindling in Oakwood now? Are ya'll out of your tree?'

I hugged my elbows; Mordecai flipped a catalogue.

'Heck-Andrews is irreplaceable,' I said feebly.

'Who would *want* to replace it?' She was furious; I wasn't sure why. Though she reminded me of my mother in her resort to slamming dishes, instead of rattling silverware she threw it away.

'What's with that brother of yours, anyway?' asked Mordecai. 'What's his game?'

'I'm not sure Truman has a game.'

'Well, that's pathetic.' Mordecai eyed his wife puffing away on her reefer and not offering him any, and reached for the baggie to roll his own. 'What are you up to?'

'What do you mean?'

'Why would you keep your share in the house? You said yourself your sister-in-law is driving you bats. Why not take the money and run? Buy a *flat* in England or something? Or are you planning to stay?'

'I don't know what I'm going to do. I had a bit of a mishap in London. All my work was – ruined.'

'That sounds careless.'

'I was living with two chaps and, ah, fucking them both at the same time. They found out.'

Mordecai guffawed and said, 'Nice going!' I know how to impress my older brother.

'– So I'm back in Raleigh for now. Thought I'd stay in Heck-Andrews for a while, pick up some work after the new year. Besides, without my help Troom would have to get out. They barely have an income.'

Mordecai snorted. 'That's just what he needs, Corrie Lou. If you really cared about the guy, you'd pitch him in the drink. Sink or swim.'

'Uh-huh. What if it's sink?'

'And you know he'd have taken care of Mother until she was a hundred and five.'

'That's so bad?'

'Criminal.'

I took a breath and launched. 'He lives in a small world. OK, he goes to school, but to classes, full stop. He does his homework. He hasn't any friends. He has his – wife,' I said with effort, 'like some – little sister,' I said with more effort, 'who I'm sure tells him everything since there's nothing to tell. He volunteers for Preservation/NC twice a week, but that's all about the house. He wants most of all to get Heck-Andrews listed on the National Registry so no one can tear it down. That's his world, see: Truman lives in a house. You want responsibility for taking that away?'

'I'd leap at the chance.'

I laughed, and poured another aquavit.

'What's that kid gonna do with a degree in philosophy?'

'Prove to Father he's got moral gravity. Now Father's dead. Leaves Troom in a bit of a corner.'

'The guy's head is in a fucking bucket. And the wife – !'

'Don't get me started.'

'What a dishrag! How do you explain it?'

'Good lay?'

'Even your hand moves.'

'Any lay?'

'Now you're talking.'

'So you think that out of affection,' I proposed whimsically, 'you and I should buy Troom out instead.'

Mordecai looked around to find Dix out of earshot, and then leaned forward. 'That's right.'

I stopped laughing. 'Come on.'

'He'd be testy at first.' Mordecai leaned back coolly. 'Later, he'd never stop thanking you.'

I choked.

'What's funny?'

'I'm trying to imagine Truman, shaking my hand. "I just wanted to express my infinite gratitude for your robbing me of the most important thing in my life." '

'It's not his house.'

'He thinks it is. With a vengeance.'

'Let me ask you this. What effect do you think living in that museum has on your little brother? Honestly.'

'It stunts him,' I conceded. 'He talks about Mother all the time. He feels guilty there. He's always scrubbing and hoovering, like a murderer washing his hands.'

'Don't you think that some people have to be pushed from the nest because otherwise they'll peep away their whole lives too scared to jump?'

'That's Mommy Bird's job,' I said warily.

'Mother's dead.'

I drummed my fingers. 'Mordecai, what are you getting at?'

'I told you: why don't you and me buy out your brother?'

'You're serious!'

'Damn tootin'.'

In truth, I had never been so flattered. I stalled for time. 'Truman wouldn't agree to sell to us for all the tea in China.'

'He wouldn't have to. You said it yourself: without your share, he can't swing it, can he? Together, we own half the house already; we've got the cash coming in from the will, and *you and I* could take out a mortgage. Sink that equity into Decibelle, it'll multiply; sitting there on Blount Street, it rots.'

'Truman would die,' I mumbled.

'He wouldn't die. He could take the money and pick up a condo where Mother didn't boo! around every corner and maybe, perish the thought, get a job. He'd squeal, you betcha. But getting booted out of there would be the best damned thing ever happened to the guy.'

'I don't understand. What would you want with Heck-Andrews?'

'That place is massive and right now it's wasted on flower vases and empty beds. My office is cramped, and we just broke our last coffee cup. Plenty of work space – why not? And you and I get on all right – don't we?'

I wanted to say I wasn't so sure; that he paralysed me with a deference as if I were always making up for something, though I had never located for exactly what. But that very deference guaranteed I would answer, 'Sure.'

I could hear his wife in the background, shouting instructions to his workmen. Though she once hired out at union wages, she now worked for Mordecai as his Vice President. Mordecai didn't pay nearly so well.

'But how does Dix feel about this?' I whispered.

'I thought she made it pretty obvious how she feels. Decibelle's in the red – though only for now, we've got this new contract – and a quick hundred thou with no strings would come in handy. But she'll come round. I have a feeling once the pigeons were cleared from the rafters she might like it there. So whatta you say?'

I opened my mouth and this is what I expected to come out: however hobbled he might seem to you, Truman is my beloved younger brother who might recover from moving house but would never recover from a sister's perfidy. Thanks, but no thanks. If you force the house on the market, Truman and I will make our bid, because that's the way it's always been – Truman and I are a team.

'Maybe,' I heard instead, to my own stupefaction. 'It's an idea. Can I think about it?'

'Not for long. That's why I'm going ahead with the partition suit, Core. The court will give you a deadline, and you need one. You don't like to make choices, Corrie Lou, but you're making them all the time whether you admit it to yourself or not. It's down to the wire: your neurotic, retarded kid brother, or me.'

Dix returned to the kitchen for a refill of aquavit, and looked from her husband to me. 'You asked her.'

'Yeah,' said Mordecai, spewing smoke.

'And what'd she say?'

'Think we may have a deal here.'

That's not what I said, but Mordecai was not The Bulldozer for nothing.

One of their last plates hit the concrete floor. 'Ya'll are out to lunch! What's that dump gonna do for you two but suck $100 bills like a leaf machine? I don't know diddly about real estate, and even I can see the place is falling to bits! Maybe you save a snapshot to remind you of your Mom and Dad, but you don't save a $400,000 hole in your pocket!'

'That house may not be my kid brother's, but it ain't yours either so stuff the attitude and butt out.' Mordecai's boots hit the floor.

'When my Daddy died, all I wanted was my Daddy's desk, which you gave me shit over –'

'OK, driving the truck all the way to Chattanooga for one lousy desk was a pain in the ass –'

'I didn't ask you to cart back the whole fucking house, did I? To remind me of my goddamned wonderful childhood?'

Mordecai stood up and advanced with a clump. Dix took a step back. 'I don't seem to recall you had such a goddamned wonderful childhood.'

'That's what I mean, you bastard, have you forgotten? All you were to them was a drunken chain-smoking cunt-fingering degenerate, and you're getting maudlin? When we're up to our eyes in debt –'

'It's my inheritance, which I'll take in the form I please, and you can keep your fucking desk –'

'You smashed it, in case you've forgotten.'

I might have left before she started breaking his records and he threw bottles, albeit not the ones with beer – he wouldn't waste it. Instead I withdrew just out of range, a vantage point from which to ascertain that like most battles this one had rules. Dix's eye flicked to the title before she grabbed an album to crack over his head, and once she chose another. The kitchen was open season, but they ate out. Not once was the slightest feint made in the direction of the workshop, *the tools*, with which Mordecai's crew continued to grind and hammer, shouting directions a bit more loudly as if Dix and their employer going at it were a car alarm that wasn't theirs. If she really wanted to whack him, she'd have abandoned Daffy Duck – an early casualty – in favour of a solid chisel blow to his Rockwell table saw. This fracas, therefore, was performed within strict theatrical boundaries, so when I interrupted that I needed to be off they dropped their weapons as if the director had called a tea break.

'You won't say anything to Truman, will you?' I pleaded. 'About what you proposed?'

'Since when,' said Mordecai, 'did I ever say anything to your brother, period?'

Fair enough. 'And I wanted to know,' I said, 'if you'd come for Christmas.'

Mordecai shrugged. 'Sure. I'll come for Christmas.'

Wrapped up with a bow.

8

Chewing peppermint to obscure the incriminating caraway on my breath, I found Truman and Averil in the kitchen with rolled-up sleeves. We were not nearly through with sorting and reclaiming this house for ourselves, and the kitchen remained the most dauntingly inhabited diorama of my mother's Gestalt. Though overflowing with comestibles, this had always been one of those mysterious sculleries whose pantry dropped cans, whose fridge bulged baggies, and whose freezer required a chair against the door to keep it from popping open, where you couldn't find a thing to eat.

We'd attacked the refrigerator the day before, and once we cleared out the fungus-furred yellow squash, liquefied lettuce, separated mayonnaise and crystallized strawberry jam there was nothing salvageable remaining besides a single jar of dubious peanut butter. After we scoured the ice-box with cleanser and propped it open to air I had gazed into that expanse of pristine plastic, for the first time guiltlessly glad on some account that my mother was dead. My whole life that refrigerator had been crammed full of stale margarine crumbed with burnt toast, cling-filmed half-cups of overcooked rice, and imploding green peppers sagging into the lower drawers' ad hoc vegetable soup. I had never been at liberty to thunk anything into the bin without suffering, 'Why, that's my *good meatloaf*!' to send her scraping diffidently at a glaucous brown scab. There was always one half-inch chunk of a Macintosh that was 'perfectly good', leaving me to question my mother's compromised version of perfection, and if I ever drew her attention to the fact that though apples by the bushel had indeed been cheaper than by the bag but these were nine months old, we would suffer reproof by pie.

In fact, my mother had not been a bad cook, but she was so

consumed with employing ingredients that 'needed using' that she'd contaminate five dollars' worth of lasagne with a handful of ammoniated mushrooms that cost ten cents. When she cut fresh pineapple, it so grieved her to slice off any of the fruit with the rind that she left the spines in, and dessert was like chewing your way out of a prison camp. This curious inclination to sacrifice the whole for the part – to leave mould on one side of the cheddar, to gouge out only half the tomato rot, or bake an otherwise gorgeous gingerbread with fermented molasses – must have had larger implications for her life. Had she been a Civil War surgeon, she couldn't have brought herself to chop off any of the 'perfectly good' leg and what's wrong with leaving just a little infection and all her patients would have died from gangrene.

Having so recently exterminated the refrigerator, I'd given her culinary edicts some thought: those imperatives both to *save* and to *not-waste* – subtly different laws with subtly different pitfalls. Saving became hoarding for its own sake; misers died with mattressfuls of cash, or, in my mother's case, a full row of spiced peach halves, which she adored, in the back of the pantry. But the upside of saving is a sense of preciousness. It gave my mother more pleasure to retain those jars than to dispatch them. She savoured potential, just as Truman treasured a stocked larder. I liked that, the keeping; it was a belief in the future, if misguided, since the peach halves had survived her.

Not-wasting was all the more rooted in preciousness. How could I fault that? Only for being a trap. Not-wasting was a bondage. Say the zucchini is sufficiently geriatric that when you pick it up with one hand it falls in half. Yet if you chuck it you become a person who throws 'perfectly good' food away and that is not the way you want to think of yourself, so into the stir-fry it goes, even if you have to ladle in the zucchini with a spoon. My mother served dinner, literally. Food was a responsibility, a ward she was determined to do right by, and as long as her charges were helpless she was a good mother. I can't count the times at a restaurant that she'd been given an absurdly large portion, when she was already too heavy and would feel bloated later, and still she could not, could not bring herself to leave so much as a morsel on her plate. She'd force herself through to the last forkful even to the point of nausea, because she did not understand that it was there for her and not the other way round.

My father felt superior to the inanimate and my mother was its love-slave.

However, my mother's sense of the precious beat the buy-another-one world in which a fresh sponge meant nothing. I enjoyed swabbing coffee grounds with bright yellow virgin foam. I wouldn't want to start a new sponge every day.

My parents never resigned themselves to the fact that anything wore out or spoiled. All was forever: from stereo speakers whose shot woofers my father refused to hear buzz to '30% More' saltines that Mother would 'crisp up' (burn) once the crackers were soggy. The night before, Truman and I had finally put to pasture the pepper grinder we'd wrestled since I was five, which had strained the tendons in even his arms for a weary baptism of imperceptible ash. It would never have occurred to them in a million years to buy a new grinder. They had bought one, with the finality of marriage.

Possibly this belief in the immortality of the inanimate was a stand-in for belief in their own, the refusal to recognize degeneration of foodstuffs commensurate with my mother's conviction that she had been born beautiful and could not, therefore, be fat. Stubbornly, she would deny loss on even the smallest scale since if 'perfectly good' brinjal pickle could acquire a suspicious fizz behind your back you entered an untrustworthy universe where romances could sour and sons could go bad. She refused to live on so unreliable a planet, and I couldn't resist a sort of dumb admiration for someone able to fly so magnificently in the face of fact. The pickle was from their trip to India eight years earlier and it was 'special' and it was therefore fine. Reality had nothing to do with it.

Consequently, my mother was a compulsive economies-of-scale shopper, for because she did not acknowledge the concept of the perishable there was nothing that wouldn't keep. It always amazed me that when her gallon can of olive oil went rancid she couldn't taste it. She would stash the same can in the pantry for five years, rust crawling across the catty-cornered punctures, until her dressings made me gag. If she could taste rancid oil, some override function intervened: it was more important to my mother to maintain her belief in the permanence of all things than to toss edible salad. Hers was a religious problem, or strength – my mother's obliviousness to corruption, her stoic Protestant palate, was a tribute to her faith in life everlasting; our every meal was a sacrament. Jesus in our family did not, alas, turn water into wine, but resurrected our vegetable drawer.

It was before the cathedral of eternal life that Truman and Averil now stood, stepped fearfully back with its great door agape: the awesome stand-up freezer. Truman had unplugged it, like the villain in *Star Trek* who turns off life support for space travellers in suspended animation. The baggies were just beginning to glisten, frost yielding to that treacherous world of decay that my mother spent her life defying. On the floor yawned two heavy-duty garbage bags, which I expected to prove insufficiently capacious for the ransacking we had planned.

'What took you so long?' Truman fretted when I walked in. 'I don't see how you can bear that rat's nest. And I thought you always say he's so boring.'

'Mordecai is endlessly entertaining, if often at his own expense,' I said.

'Anyway, you're just in time for a walk down memory lane.'

'Memory lane –' I poked at a fibrillated rump steak on the counter that had freeze-dried to umber with a distinctive greenish cast '– in winter. Bloody hell, do we have to do this now?'

'That's what you've said all week.' Truman prised a tupperware container from the upper shelf with the crowbar he'd marshalled for the job. '"Feta walnut pâté",' he read out. 'Corlis – when did you make that?'

'Ten years ago.'

I was not hyperbolizing; I meant ten years ago. When he prised off the lid, the frost had grown high and interlaced, reminiscent of that remarkable green fungus which had thrived on the yellow squash. He plonked it in the bag.

'But that's my *good feta* and *walnut* dip!' I exclaimed, once more the imitation too true for comfort. 'You're *not* going to *throw* it *away*!'

'Gross,' said Averil, exploring another corpse in cling-film. 'Is this fish, or fibreglass?'

'Three important heels of bread from 1977,' Truman announced, *ker-chunk*.

'That would make *perfectly good* french toast!' I cried.

'I don't believe it,' Truman groaned, fingers grown ruddy. 'Rice and cheese balls!'

I had helped my mother with a party, when? I must have been at UNC at Chapel Hill, and we'd rashly multiplied a recipe so fecund that the rice balls seemed to reproduce of their own accord, as if by cell division. Poor Truman ate those gluey fried dumplings for weeks – but not, it seemed, all of them. The second shelf was devoted entirely to neat packages of icy brown orbs, nesting nefariously like an invasion of aliens waiting to hatch. Just then I had a brief nightmarish vision of what might happen to our house if we allowed the undead to enter the room-temperature dimension. I cautioned Truman he should cart these bags to the kerb before their contents began crawling up the stairs to our beds, tongues of unnaturally preserved lasagne noodles trailing crenulated worms along the carpet.

'A quarter cup of chilli con carne, 1974 ...' Truman rooted. 'One half hot cross bun –'

'The Easter rising,' I said. '1916.'

'One ball pie dough scraps, one dollop leftover carrot cake icing, and – what's this – *salmon surprise*.'

'You know what she did, don't you,' I explained to Averil. 'When some yummy titbit in the fridge was turning to science fair project? Normal people throw it out, Mother put it in the freezer.'

'She believed in cryogenics,' Truman posited. 'Maybe she was hoping that over the years they'd come up with a cure for cancerous casseroles.'

'In the later years it became obsessive,' I went on, taking over while Truman breathed on his stiff red hands. 'They lived to freeze. A prune cake would barely cool before Mother was wrapping it happily into little squares and nudging them maniacally by the egg whites. Egg whites ... Egg whites ... Egg whites ...' I threw four successive plastic containers into the first bag, now full.

'I'm going to toss this,' said Truman, tying it up. 'I swear this bag was starting to move.'

When he returned we were down to the serious archaeological back layers, which had melded into a solid wall of petrified leftovers, the kind of Arctic dig in which you discover missing evolutionary links. Troom hoisted the crowbar again. 'Corlis,' he enquired offhandedly, using a hammer on the crowbar to chink the gooseberry crumble my mother only made once – when I was in tenth grade. 'What happened, at Mortadello's?'

'Oh, a lot of bitching about the ACLU, of course. Funny, too – most Yippie sons would be carping that their fathers *didn't* leave bequests to bastions of social justice. You can't win.'

'Uh-huh. And that's what you told him?'

I shrugged and picked shrivelled peas from the floor. 'More or less.'

'What about the house?' asked Averil squarely. 'Will he let us buy him out, or not?'

'Ah –' I was getting very thorough about the peas. 'Not exactly.'

Truman hit the crowbar again with the hammer, hard, and a glacier of clam chowder gave way. 'What do you mean, "not exactly"?'

'I guess I mean –' I scooped some frost from the floorboards. 'No. He won't. He's going ahead with that partition suit.'

'What the heck!' A chunk of cooked frozen oatmeal skidded across the floor.

'Would you watch what you're doing with that crowbar? I think you need an acetylene torch.'

'But why?'

I muttered, 'Mordecai's more complicated than you think.'

I took over from Truman so he could thaw again. Spanish noodles, pork barbecue, lamb curry – all my old favourite dishes had paled to the same morbid mauve. This was Mother's idea of preservation?

'All he's ever cared about is money. What's complicated?'

I noted with some surprise myself, 'He's sentimental.'

'Mother and Father didn't like him, I don't like him, and you don't like him, do you? *Do* you?'

In the crook of the freezer door, I was physically in a corner. 'Not much.' I qualified tentatively, 'I guess.'

'So what's to be sentimental about?'

'I did what I could, OK? The fact is, if the house goes on the market there's a chance the price will go higher than the appraiser's valuation and Mordecai knows that. Yes, he wants his money, but he wants as much of it as possible. That's why he'll force us to advertise, and it's not my fault!' I had made all this up on the spot.

'OK, OK – then why are you so mad?'

I had started hacking at the ice mural of dinners we didn't finish and hadn't enjoyed much the first time, wondering if the impulse wasn't to save most what you never really had in the first place. The montage of my motley childhood was in this layer so welded and blurred and twisted with interweaving plastic wrap failing to protect tuna bakes from the ravages of salvation that none of the dishes was recognizable any longer, or distinguishable from one another – just one big gunky smorgasbord of keeping elbows off the table and wanting to go play. Oh, she'd saved all right, but saved what? A life of freezing. That was what my mother did. She froze.

If I was angry at being jammed once more between two brothers, at that very moment I was furious with the woman who lodged me there. Like the sponge, this freezer was a point of view. Beyond rice-and-cheese balls, my parents had stored their courtship by the ice cubes, wedged their lives together and their first kiss between the chopped spinach and desiccated chuck steak, so that at the end of this project I half expected to find the two of them embraced over stiff slices of pumpkin pie. For my parents had not been brave enough to live in a world of spoilage and catastrophe, decline and obsolescence. Their marriage was in the freezer. Their versions of their children – The Bulldozer, The Scatterbrain, The Tender Flower – were in the freezer. The world itself – where grown children now have sex and drink 'the hard stuff', but not in their house – was in the freezer. The fixed tenets of Heck-Andrews – that we Loved Each Other, that we had a Happy Family – were in the freezer. So I was angry over ten-year-old feta walnut pâté because I'd have preferred warm-blooded parents who had rows and fell out instead of a couple rigidly holding hands like the top of a wedding cake preserved for eternity by the family-pack pork.

'You know,' said Averil, retrieving a casualty and sniffing, 'this might still be all right –'

I grabbed the pinkish chunk and hurled it back in the sack. 'Don't even think about it.' Averil didn't have the constitution for this work.

Eugenia Hadley Hamill met Sturges Harcourt McCrea when she was twenty-one at a Young Democrats conference in Richmond, Virginia. He was President and she was Secretary – too perfect, for 1952. Loosely speaking, she remained his secretary for the duration, dutifully remembering appointments while the Great

Man championed racial justice. (How appropriate that my father never appeared for a plaintiff in a sex discrimination case.) That there was never any question of equality between my parents probably made the relationship possible.

Initially, her looks would have nearly evened the balance with her husband – my mother was stunning. My father received flattering lambastes in conservative papers, but my mother got salesmen falling all over themselves to be helpful when she bought a hat. She sported generous hips, but a tiny waist and neat, close breasts. Over the years her knees got a little bulgy, but otherwise her legs were solid, and she had trim, diminutive feet. Her skin was a warm olive that didn't sunburn, which I inherited, while Truman was stuck with my father's freckling hairless white-bread complexion that seared and peeled with a vengeance. Only Mordecai, however, got her hair – a thick and lustrous mahogany like the pricey woods he favoured, with a natural curl and tendency to form ringlets around the temples after a light sweat. Mordecai bound that hair tightly away, but Eugenia Hamill had made the most of being a brunette, sweeping shocks back from her forehead where they would tendril free from hairpins down her neck.

Most riveting of all, of course, was her face. Even in crinkled old photographs she radiated with a smile like an open window, and chocolate eyes that simmered in the light, twin pots of dark fudge glistening on a stove. Mordecai got those, too – her firstborn was treated to the whole package, so that when the second and third came along it was as if there was less left for us genetically. But in my older brother those eyes had a muddier, more conniving stir, less like fudge sauce than brownie batter. They were flatter and more suspicious, and when they went pellucid it was never with desire but always with self-pity. Even in my mother's eyes you found a popple of mischief before she married, which by the way completely disappeared. All that church-going and oatmeal-freezing is hard on mischief.

In that animal way some women have, at twenty-one Eugenia Hamill marked my father as a male destined for the head of the herd. You'd have needed an eye for it, since I couldn't see anything auspicious about him in their wedding pictures. My father at twenty-five was a geek. He may have been president of the Young Democrats, but he cut his hair barbarously short so his ears stuck out from his head. Acne. He looked gawky and awkward, no chest, and the features in his face had not yet settled; they didn't seem to know where to be, as if at a reception where they weren't sure how to mingle and kept wandering off for a glass of Hawaiian punch. Were you stuck at cocktail hour with Mr Sincerity here, first of all he wouldn't drink; and second, he wouldn't let go, but would corner you to dissect Adlai Stevenson's strategy for derailing McCarthy while everyone else was swooning about James Dean and tapping their toes to Chubby Checker. He wouldn't dance, or remember jokes. The fact is, if I met my own father at a party I'd have ditched him in a minute for the guy with a sense of humour and a martini on the other side of the room.

My father may have been a swat, but even then – this is what my mother spotted – he must have been driven by a ruthless personal ambition that he disguised decorously, and with timely creativity, as burning social conscience. Their first few dates were spent picketing lunch counters, or leafleting for integrated education and then fishing their discarded hand-outs from black cotton Virginian mud. To give Sturges credit, with a woman from the midwest for whom the segregated South was the evil empire, a diner with Whites Only restrooms was a much more inspired locale to get her to clutch his hand than in the back rows of *Frankenstein Meets the Wolfman*.

My father must have had some cachet, a stalwart lefty in the days when it cost you, who had taken two years off after a history degree at Davidson to volunteer for – ever the sacred cow – the ACLU. Meanwhile he threw himself into the election campaign that so broke his heart that Truman Adlai had it to thank for his middle name. Anti-McCarthy, anti-nuclear testing, later to troop after Martin Luther King and help found the Southern Christian Leadership Conference, Sturges McCrea was in on the ground floor of all the noble sentiments that are now derisively dismissed as 'politically correct'. My brothers may have resented their father's staking claim to the big liberal issues not just because these were used to bludgeon the boys into submission, but because so little largesse was left for them. Truman did not champion the black and the poor but porch mouldings; Mordecai had thrown in his lot with high fidelity of only the most technical variety. If Eugenia Hadley Hamill had met either of her own sons at a

Young Democrats conference, after politely permitting Truman to regale her about the distinguishing elements of Second Empire architecture, and Mordecai to extol the components of his last recording studio, she'd have politely excused herself for finger sandwiches, leaving them both to goon mournfully after her as had so many young men in her youth.

I do not question that falling in love with Sturges McCrea was the biggest event in my mother's life. Before Sturges, she had tolerated countless suitors, gracious and considerate of their feelings, though firmly offended when their hands crept over her knee. But I figure when Sturges so much as grazed her blouse she couldn't breathe. My mother must have had a libido the size of South Dakota; though virgins when they married, for years after they were so self-congratulatory over their restraint that there must have been a fair fire to contain. They were apart during much of their courtship, hailing from different states, and she lived for his letters – stiff, formal protestations of undying love with a lot of God thrown in that we were still unearthing around the house. That his prose was stilted my mother no doubt overlooked, sweeping to her bedroom and throwing herself on the bed to hoard his onionskin as she would later stockpile Vidalias until they were black. The door locked behind her, she would pen a reply in that liquid, Palmer-method script of hers that made even 'ketchup' and 'light bulbs' look exotic magneted to the refrigerator door when I was young.

I had bosomed my share of *billets doux* as well. Yet she never gave me credit for the full-blown passion that enveloped her on her Iowa bedspread, and it was her very insistence that rapture remain foreign to me, her possessiveness over love itself, that first suggested to me that she was nervous of keeping it on her own account.

She did fall in love with him. I believe that. Their romance was the real McCoy at the start. But I think being happy must be a thoroughly petrifying experience. The first thing that seems to occur to people high as kites is that any time now the wind might die and there they'll be, torn in a tree. Exhilaration seems to arrive in tandem with the threat of despair; passion arrives hand in hand with the prospect of indifference. Maybe when you feel anything strongly the sensation becomes definitive of the state in which you feel otherwise. This dark alternative must have smacked my mother up-side the head. She was in love with my father, and the idea that the honeymoon might one day come to an end was patently intolerable.

I never met the woman in those early snaps. In all the pictures of our family where I feature even as a baby, her smile is no longer an open window but a shut one with the air conditioner on. Through the years, too, you can see her eyes change; they contract into themselves, shielded, a little blank. I've experimented with putting my hand over the cheesecake lower half of her face, and isolated from all those teeth her eyes look pained. The burden of incessant acting when she really hadn't a knack for it must have gradually taken it out of her. For well before I was born she had abandoned the precariousness of really being in love with my father for the surety of pretending to be.

No, I am not one more whinging offspring, begotten of two people who reviled one another, and now irremediably scarred. On the contrary, we were instructed from first grade on that my parents had the most wonderful marriage in the whole world, and that 'we should be so lucky', my mother would caution, to barely approach in our own tawdry adulthoods the elation of their ethereal communion. We were informed repeatedly that whom you married was the biggest decision of your life and that in the history of the universe never had this choice been more inspired than in our own house. We were the privileged witnesses to Wedded Bliss, whose literal expression was described as so 'beautiful' and so involved with Jesus that I always pictured the two of them kneeling in prayer by the bedside before they Did It. At any rate, hats off to my father for being able to get it up in such a sanctuary of a bridal chamber that their windows were stained glass, while beatified in rhetoric that urges most people to burst into the doxology.

Consequently, whenever my mother heard about another of my relationships biting the dust (though I shielded her from most of them), her comfort ran that my 'problem' was having 'such a remarkable father' and being the issue of 'such a spectacular union' that no one I found could measure up. Somehow this explanation regularly failed to console.

My parents were condescending about Truman's marriage, as if it were his sweet little boy's attempt to imitate their Tristan and Isolde, as if upstairs he and Averil were playing Doctor. My father expressed his contempt by never mentioning Averil, as if to do so would be vulgar; my mother by being too encouraging. Truman maintained at the time that he and Averil opted for a brief civil ceremony with me as their only witness because they were practical, and didn't like fuss. I think my parents had made them feel ashamed.

In any family there may be one worm, a single wriggle of corruption from which every other foulness spreads, and in the McCrea case the source-lie was that my parents were happily married. The irony? They were happily married. They just didn't believe it. They were afraid that, like the brinjal pickle, it might not keep, and so they turned a perfectly serviceable relationship into a religion and thereby into a fraud. Imagine how disconcerting this was for small children. We were told their marriage was as good as they come; yet there was something horribly hollow about it and so marriages didn't come very good. What they offered as promising merely depressed us.

If the stagy fakery that invaded my mother's behaviour had been restricted to her 'telephone voice' – she never answered the phone with anything less than, 'Hello, Eugenia Hamill McCrea speaking' – and that fossilized smile for strangers, I could have forgiven her as a socially formal woman covering for the fact that she was shy. But it was in private she was at her most false. And mind, she was a woeful actress, so that when she squeezed us for a beat too long and recited, 'I luv you, kiddo' we would squirm and refuse to meet her eyes out of the same raging embarrassment of watching Vivien Leigh overdo Scarlett O'Hara. And this is the bugbear: she did love us. My mother loved us. But she never, never said so *when she was feeling it at the time*.

My mother imitated her own feelings, that is, feelings she did truly stash somewhere. The interesting question is why, if she loved her husband and her children, did she have to pretend to? Why, if she was genuinely attracted to the man, was she moved to contrive loud, giggling recitations of amour with the bedroom door carefully cracked open so we could hear?

This may be why I get nostalgic for the days Mordecai issued his declarations of independence in our foyer while I secured my balcony view. The word 'fuck' was a primitive trigger for my mother's visceral acrimony, and it was only when she was lashing I could trust her: this was at least Real Mother. Frightening as she may have been while screeching at her eldest below me that his girlfriend was a slut, I cannot exaggerate my relief at hearing her voice both lowered and hitting harmonic squeals like an actual person trying to express an emotion she was undergoing right then.

As I posited to Truman, Eugenia McCrea was not a contented woman and she never knew it. Father may have been happily married (though obliviously – like a verdict he was not planning to appeal, the merger was simply decided) and Mother told herself she was. She never got around to the genuine article in the exhaustion of manufacturing a plausible mock-up. She was like a woman who lets her yard roses wither because she's always indoors watering the plastic ones.

In some ways a wholesomeness entered Heck-Andrews when my father died, a death whose survival had been my mother's greatest fear: at long last she had permission to be miserable. If anything, the trouble became that she wasn't as ecstatically miserable as she'd have liked. North Carolinian weather remained mercifully clement and the Russell Stover's Dark Selection insidiously seductive, and how relaxing it must have been to stop hamming it up.

Again, I don't mean my mother didn't love my father, but she was afraid she didn't – afraid to brave that one terrible moment when she had to entertain the notion that she did not. Then she'd have had to be truly bored with him when he went on about a case she didn't care about, truly irritated when he glued the coffee cup handles with epoxy glopping down the sides – it's not all it's cracked up to be, having real emotions. I know that with the most dazzling men there have been times I've been terribly bored and I am sure they've been equally bored with me. Then much of life is indeed boring and that's nobody's fault. The most positive thing I ever heard Truman say about his own marriage is that up in the dovecot he and Averil didn't always have anything to say to each other, but he refused to fabricate Topics simply to convince himself they were so suited to one another that they never ran out of conversation. Myself, I'd been in the very arms of a beloved and felt absolutely nothing, when the only choice was whether to admit I felt nothing or to lie. The hardest thing about loving someone is those moments when you're not. And there are inevitably such moments; the amount of trust required to get past them is stupendous. My mother didn't have it. For all her dogged Presbyterianism, her confidence in the durability of produce, my mother was a woman of quite tenuous faith.

Take family vacations. We were obliged to Have Fun. So we'd be wheeling through the Blue Ridge Mountains and my father would veer into an overlook for more exciting slides of rust-coloured bumps. My mother would exclaim breathily, 'Sturges! It's so – *exquisite*!' and immediately indicate that the vista of turning leaves was completely lost on her and that she probably needed to pee. A little later, she would chirp, 'Aren't we having a wonderful time!' and that was the point we knew she was nervous we were having a rotten time, as – after enough cooing about what a wonderful time we were having – would certainly be the case. She would fill the remainder of our holiday remarking on how we would look back on this time as so 'special' when what she was condemning us to remember was her saying over and over how we'd look back on this time as so 'special'. A vacation's one shameful redemption was our mean imitations of Mother behind her back.

Part of this removal in my family was relentless interpretation – no fact got left alone just to be itself – so that my mother's death by heart attack is left to me to find potent. Surrounded by photographs of my father – she would have liked that, she might have designed it, perhaps she did. But she wouldn't like my reconstruction one bit.

I see her sifting though the snapshots, as she'd done many times before. She gazed at my father's lopsided mug for the camera, and she felt – stricken, her heart *attacked* by his absence? No. My version? She felt nothing. One of those times. Nicht, nada, zip. Her mind wandered to lunch – yellow squash – though it was only ten. Here she was, smoothing photographs of her dead husband and she was thinking about squash – it must have killed her. My theory? It did kill her. She made herself cry. I know the sound: sobs forced from her lungs as if trying to dislodge a piece of popcorn – bad acting. Though no one else was in the room, most of her performances were for her own benefit. And the harder she pushed those sobs, the more she knew that she was faking. Whether she died from the exertions of fraud or the acknowledgement of fraud I couldn't say, but my mother did not die in a state of grace. Maybe there is no more grotesque a betrayal of yourself

– or of your husband: to parody your own passion. Up to the end she preferred the safety of pure if concocted grief to real loss mixing sordidly with squash.

On my mother's wedding day, the one thing she wanted above all was to spend the rest of her life married to my father. Barring two years, that's what she got. And she muffed it. She was so scared to permit the possibility for an instant that the romance wouldn't last that she put it in the freezer, and I tried to tell her long ago that even the omnipotent freezer doesn't keep things forever but gradually turns its charges tasteless, dry, and grey until preservation itself becomes a drawn-out crucifixion instead. Yet between the fickle if blood-warm treacheries of the perishable and the deceitful sureties of Freon she chose to put her heart on ice. And I am truly sorry. I imagine those two might, had they trusted their own ardour, made a reasonable pair.

9

I sighed. 'So are we doing the whole turkey number?'

We were in the sitting room, where I was depilating my legs in front of the fire. I'd donned a skirt for the occasion, which I tucked between my thighs as I nibbled the Epilady over my raised knee. Its sleek body purred, while at its mouth a loop of gyrating spring munched hairs.

'We've got to have a turkey!' cried Averil, who was signing Christmas cards. Her handwriting was rounded and neat; her tastes in Hallmark ran to snowmen.

'If we roast a turkey,' I said grimly, 'we'll end up with thousands of fibrous packages in the freezer. That's hardly festive.'

'With mashed potatoes and peas,' Averil determined, and I found myself wondering if she dotted her *is* with hearts. 'Pearl onions, gravy and pumpkin pie.'

I switched off the epilator, incredulous. 'You are not seriously proposing we make *pies*?'

The fact was, we were in a bit of a pickle. We weren't Christians, pointedly not, but we didn't have the courage of our lack of conviction. We couldn't quite turn the twenty-fifth into Friday. The fraud of which I accused my mother seemed only to compound; it was our legacy. At least she believed in God.

'Just because we make one pie doesn't mean we're all out of control and everything,' Averil muttered.

'We could have rice and chicken thighs,' Truman threatened from his armchair. He'd been reading Hegel, but I noticed he kept having to turn back to the last page he'd read and scan it again. 'Like always.'

'OK, OK,' I backed down, turning the epilator back on. 'I'll make the pie.'

Truman resettled his wire-rims on his nose; they gave him a puritanical air. I extended my right leg so the shin muscles rippled. He rearranged himself in his chair, and I couldn't tell if he was trying to improve his view of my calves or block them from his vision altogether.

'What are we going to get Mortadello?' Averil supposed. As kids, we'd approximated Mordecai Delano to luncheon meat. Grey-pink slabs with squares of white fat had sufficiently evoked his pasty complexion and little rim of belly flab to make the moniker usefully offensive; ever since Averil had latched on to it, I'd abandoned the nickname myself.

'What we should get him,' Truman grumbled, 'is a set of free weights, a nicotine patch, and a prescription for ala-puke, or whatever it's called.'

'And what we will get him,' I said, 'is a fifth of aquavit and tin of Three Castles. Unless you know five girls we could hire to descend on him at once with no clothes on. As I recall, he's a fellatio fiend.'

'How do you know?' Truman took off his glasses.

'That's disgusting!'

I smiled. Averil must say *that's disgusting* about ten times a day. I bore down on some straggling ankle hairs, *ah-mm, ah-mm.* 'You know Mordecai likes to talk smut.'

'I certainly don't,' said Truman primly, caging himself in wire-rims again.

The pine popped; I switched to my left leg. The hum of the epilator set a tremble in the air; the firelight flickered.

Finally Truman looked over from his book, as if noticing my appliance for the first time. 'How does that thing work?'

'I'm not sure.' I held it up, enticing Truman from his chair.

'Does it hurt?' He approached closer, and touched my thigh, once.

As he stooped by the fire, his jeans rode above his dark socks. I snagged a few exposed hairs before he exclaimed, 'Hey!' and jumped back.

It was like coaxing a pet from under a bed. 'Try it.' I handed him the Epilady.

'I don't need bald –'

'Not on yourself, on me.'

He traced the coil over my right calf in a deft circle. 'That's amazing!' He tried another patch in the hollow between tendon and knee. I rested back on my elbows.

'Corrie Lou's getting cellulite,' said Averil quietly.

Truman glanced at his wife, and handed the appliance back with, I thought, a trace of regret.

I had lived in Heck-Andrews just shy of three weeks by then, and though Averil had been by and large decent to me I couldn't escape the feeling that she regarded me as a guest whose welcome was wearing thin. We were not overtly hostile, but our relationship suffered an absence; we were polite. Amid the formal kindness, there were lapses: Averil would bring out only two wine glasses, apologize, and fetch a third. In compiling my own absurdly short Christmas list, I regularly left Averil off of it, and when I forced myself to try and think of something to buy my sister-in-law I'd grow irritable and write down one more present for Truman instead. I wouldn't go so far as to say we didn't like each other; I don't know what you call it when you have nothing against someone precisely except you wish they weren't there.

I told myself that Averil was simply not quite my sort. It was only at her behest we bought mild salsa for our corn chips; she wore pastels with high necks; she listened to Suzanne Vega and Janis Ian and still kept a teddy bear on her dresser. When we scanned listings of the oldie cable network, she rooted for *Room 222*, *That Girl*, and *The Partridge Family*. I think she was affectionate with my brother, responsible in her job, and technically quite bright. Nevertheless, Averil had an compliant intelligence. She rarely ventured an opinion she hadn't read elsewhere, and when she did improvise was given to outbursts like why don't all the governments in the world get rid of their weapons at once so there could be peace on earth. Fair enough, but she lacked a certain edge.

We collided in the most puerile contexts, and keeping a mature head above it all didn't come naturally to either of us. She liked her coffee weak, and when I brewed it strong and boiled water on the side to dilute her cup, she remained discernibly sulky and once claimed the watered coffee wasn't the same. She was touchy about being the one to iron and fold Truman's two dozen identical forest green workshirts, and had a peremptory way about her in the grocery store, when I'd been versed in Truman's dietary dictums since before those two met. If I ventured a new item in the cart, she didn't put it back, but her countenance darkened. She drank skimmed milk, which I couldn't abide, and acted as if keeping a quart of 4% for me was the worst sort of pampering. Just within my earshot she had started imitating my English accent, 'We're out of tinned *tomahtoes*,' and I wished she'd do it to my face so I could tell her she wasn't very good at it.

'Might I drive?' I enquired, as we three zipped jackets by the Volvo.

Truman assumed the wheel. 'Stiff clutch.'

I remained standing. 'I could get used to it.'

He started the car. 'You've made such a point of being accustomed to the left side of the road, I wouldn't risk your careening into oncoming traffic whistling "God Save the Queen".'

I actually had to stop myself at the age of thirty-five from saying, 'Can I have the front seat?' That Averil always sat beside her husband shouldn't have grated as much as it did. I swallowed, ducked in the back, and reflected that my return home was thus far having an alarmingly regressive effect. I had recently been tortured by cravings for Hostess Sno-balls, and during TV adverts would bark around on all fours in the sitting room and chew my brother's trouser leg. No one in London would have believed it.

I've wondered if everyone's emotional make-up isn't an eight-year-old's, and growing up is merely learning to disguise 'Gimme back my ball!' as lawsuits over contractual ownership and 'You cheated, I saw!' as high-minded editorial comment in *Harper's* – the difference may be essentially linguistic. If so, of late my real primary school interior was laid bare; I couldn't let the car business go. 'Averil, don't you ever drive?'

'Sometimes,' she said coldly.

'Averil has trouble with the clutch, too.'

'I never said I had trouble with the clutch –'

'Can we *please* – ?'

Good lord, he sounded exactly like my father.

We were going to buy a Christmas tree. The ensuing *déjà vu* was vertiginous. Traditionally this had been another Frolicsome Family Outing, which had reliably degenerated into my needing to pee and Mordecai hum-a-zooing 'Yellow Submarine' until I whined, 'Fa-ather! Make him shut up!' and 'He's *pinching* me!'

Mordecai would look all innocence, while Truman sucked at the blanket Mother was trying to break him of because he was too old for it –

'Muu-dder! More-cai took my *bembet*!' and Troom would start to cry.

Father would lurch into a Minute Market car park and swing to the back seat. 'If you kids don't quiet down I'm turning around and we won't have a Christmas tree this year, understand me?' We were always 'you-kids'. I don't think my father liked having children.

'Now, Sturges,' Mother always purred, 'this is supposed to be a special time. Let's try to have fun.' I must have been in university before I developed a normal concept of fun. I thought it was something you tried to have. Mordecai belting out '100 Bottles of Beer on the Wall' to the very last verse while I gripped my crotch so tightly that my dress would be crumpled for school the next morning and Troom picked morosely at the bubble gum his brother had matted into his blanket – I thought this was 'fun'.

We'd believe that we were indeed in danger of having no Christmas tree, so I'd stop whimpering about a restroom, Troom would sniffle into his sticky 'bembet', and Mordecai would give us Indian rubs with impunity since we could not howl. By the time we got to the tree lot, I'd be so incapacitated by the demands of my bladder that I could barely walk pigeon-toed, while Mordecai dissociated himself a hundred yards away with an I've-never-met-these-people glower and probably snuck off for a smoke. Truman dribbled after my mother chattering in his windbreaker, red nose drizzling as she debated evergreens; Mother was oblivious to fiasco since I'm sure the evening was already lodged imperviously in her psychic freezer as a 'special time'. My father, impatient to get the errand over with, regularly refused to let us buy candied apples like the other kids, guaranteeing the three of us would pout all the way home.

The flashback was forbidding. My God, I thought. I was thirty-five, still stuck scrapping in this damned Volvo, shopping for a dead tree to commemorate the birth of a Messiah I didn't believe in: having *fun*. So this was inheritance. Thanks, Mom. Thanks, Dad. Wish you were here. In fact, I rather felt they were.

However, I couldn't imagine my parents had had a 'special time' except in the sense of especially tortuous: cramped with shrieking, brawling, piss-filled children, barely able to drive or hear themselves think and expending huge amounts of energy just trying to keep from hauling off and belting the little bastards until they couldn't breathe. I am sometimes disconcerted why anyone has children voluntarily when I consider what it must have been like to raise myself. If wilful pregnancy is not the result of a convenient poor memory, it must be to atone, to drive yourself to the same wit's end to which you once drove your own parents. It was an ugly cycle of penance.

On one point, however, I vowed to do better: if any little girl in my back seat was gripping between her legs and breaking into a cold sweat, I would pull over to a loo.

I suspected the same string of lights was swinging in Truman's head, so I leaned forward with my chin on his headrest and mused, 'Would Father ever pull into a Texaco for you?'

'Of course not. But I learned not to drink anything, not on car trips. No juice, no Coke. I'd get thirsty, but that was better than busting my gut.'

'What are you talking about?' asked Averil.

'Our father,' I explained. 'He wouldn't make rest stops unless he had to take a slash, and he could slurp down a thermos of coffee without a twinge. Whenever we'd ask it was, like, "Can't you wait? We'll be there in another two hours."'

'That's horrible!'

'Well, it wasn't like being pistol-whipped or thrown in a frying pan or anything,' I apologized; yet my efforts to keep our middle-class tribulations in perspective never made much headway, for childhood grudges are pernicious. 'But it was painful and embarrassing. We had a hard enough time admitting we had *needs* in the first place, so that by the time I got around to tapping my mother on the shoulder I'd be about to explode. She'd lean over and whisper to my father and then I'd get this another-two-hours shit. Sometimes I cried. I suppose weeping was one way of getting a little liquid out of my body.'

'He was Mister Rights for Everyone in Raleigh,' said Truman. 'But his kids didn't have any rights. He didn't give a damn if we had to piss. He didn't have to.'

By the trifling thou shalt know them. I saw my father's whole character laid bare in our Volvo, speeding blithely past Sinclair dinosaurs, Shell scallops and Esso ovals while their keys to ladies' rooms glistened in his dashboard. To date my memory of drives to my grandparents' house is not of Dairy Queen breaks or jovial family sing-alongs, but of squeezing against the car door, my eyes shooting wide every time we hit a bump. Mordecai would tickle me, and I would seep. In my mind, my father's refusal to stop at Texaco was part of his awesome power.

Yet with the common enemy of the deceased, and the giddy freedom of being able pull over to a petrol station whenever we pleased, the three of us were allied for once, so for five golden minutes as the sun set over Taco Bell on Western Boulevard we had – we had fun.

The tree lot was swimming with screaming kids, faces crimson with candied apple, and with such a mirror before us we were adult for once and picking the tree took five minutes. For the way home, Averil offered me the front seat.

'Have you ever considered what they believed?' I supposed as the car infused with cedar fumes. 'That Jesus was the "son of God" and "born of the Virgin Mary"? Troom, our parents were intelligent people.'

'*I believe in God the father almighty,*' he intoned, '*maker of heaven and earth* … Can you finish it?'

Truman and I tried to piece together the Apostles' Creed. Two things impressed me: first, that though we had been forced to repeat this short passage every Sunday from the age of four, we couldn't place where Pontius Pilate came in and the last line was a muddle. The credo had not got in. My second revelation, though, was that when we managed to patch together the first bit (*crucified, dead and buried, to be raised again on the third day and sit* …) the hairs rose on my arms. Some germ of mysticism had successfully slipped under our skins, which helped explain why we had this bloody Christmas tree in the back of what was now our own car.

'It's bizarre,' Truman concurred, 'how two people with college educations could take part in gruesome ceremonies where tasteless wafers are the body of Christ and grape juice is his blood without taking serious drugs. But do you think maybe we were better off? Having parents with a catechism, even if it was crackers?'

'Why? So we could ruin half of every precious weekend piping "Nearer My God to Thee" wearing patent leather shoes?'

'I mean it gave us something to not-believe.'

I grunted. True: our rejection of Presbyterianism was so richly indignant that apostasy became its own faith. But now the oppressors of our religious scepticism were dead. We could call Christianity 'crackers' and no one objected. It was a bitch to be a heretic without a foil.

Then, belief in Jesus wasn't that much of a stretch when the gods of our family were human enough. So in decorating our tree back home, we constructed a pagan memorial. Truman balanced my father's gavel on an inside branch; we pierced a paperclip through the foetid sponge from the upstairs bath and bound it on top as the star. I folded my mother's last grocery list, inscribed on the back with my family tree of allegiances, and balanced it on the evergreen like a greeting card. We dug up an opaque Ziploc from the kitchen that must have been washed twenty times, filled it with my father's favourite cool blue mints and twist-tied it on a branch; though the candies had gone white and soft after two years in his desk drawer, their waft was still the sweet clear breath of our father when he would kiss us goodnight only when he thought we were asleep. Truman retrieved the photos that had been spread at our mother's feet when she died, and these we attached with clothespins: her flashy smile basking up at my father's squinting weathered face, which was faintly reminiscent of John F. Kennedy; his mortarboard at a cocky tilt as he accepted the honorary degree from Shaw University that meant so much to him because Shaw was black. Beneath the tree, we collected the coffee mugs he had shattered and glued so appallingly together again, and arranged jars of spiced peach halves like an offering to who we knew, even as young children, was the real Santa.

The results were a bit motley – the branches sagged with mementoes not one of which was pure, each with a Janus-faced ambivalence down to my mother's unconvincing smile. If we had made a shrine to our parents' failings, it was also to our fondness for them, for it is people's faults you cherish. As for anything our parents did properly, we were not remotely interested.

Yet when we turned off all the lamps and plugged in the coloured lights, something rippled over me. Maybe my childhood was not such an unremitting disaster as that, for as the hair had risen on my arms when we successfully recited *crucified, dead, and buried*, the glow off that Christmas tree gladdened some part of me immune to our mockery of Presbyterianism. For the first time I was grateful we hadn't skipped the holiday altogether. The parlour poppled with those tiny rare moments when my mother was looping Palmer-method tags on last-minute packages, giving coy hints about their contents in the days that we cared what was inside, when my father would peer over his glasses with a brief in his lap and slyly suggest we have pumpkin *pah*, while Truman victoriously caught me in the act as I palmed one more five hundred from the Monopoly bank. Mordecai would be off in his own corner taping together his first Mobius strip, while I hoped that my gyroscope might be one gift among the socks that he'd hold dear. The light from our commemorative tree was just low enough that in its subdued blur I could recall brief beats of time – though no longer – in which I did not chafe at my parents' moralism, at Mordecai's precocious recitations of college-level physics, or at the unsheddable devotion of my younger brother, but felt safe, round, whole; when my mother restrained herself from picking the calluses off her feet, and my father for once ceased his interminable droning about justice and made a joke. I wondered if you put all those moments together – the moments in which we truly were a happy family – they would constitute more than five or ten minutes, but I also wondered if those few minutes might arguably be worth suffering the balance, thirty-five-and-some years of crap.

The following day Truman directed before he left for Preservation/NC that I was not to forget what I'd promised. He insisted the job be finished by evening in the same stern paternal tone in which I was once admonished to clean my room, except this time the room I was to clean was my mother's. I'd volunteered to go through her things, keep what I liked and give the rest to Goodwill, and I'd put off the task for a week. When he returned late afternoon and I'd still not started, Truman threatened to forestall dinner until I'd at least made some progress. All right. Of all our sortings through, this was the task I most dreaded.

Among the several sensations from which I shrank was my own cupidity. A mother's trinkets, no matter how cheap or garish to the world, hold a kleptomaniacal allure to daughters. How many times had I watched, chin in hand, as she dabbed from bright pots I was not to play in, rubbed smoky perfume behind her lobes that only on the rarest occasions would she touch to my own wrists, and clasp a doublet of magenta beads behind her neck that I was not to snitch from her dresser when she was out because they were 'special'. I recognized that my mother's possessions could not be that commercially valuable, yet I still wished to steer clear of them not because I didn't want them but because I wanted them too much.

I trooped to the second floor, but baulked at the transom of the master bedroom. When we were kids we were warned to knock before entering and if we were ever discovered here without permission we got into trouble. The room retained an off-limits quality, but I forced myself inside.

It was a big, attractive room, with an arched double window in the pavilion whose antique glass rippled the scalloped slate porch roof below. Late afternoon sun glinted in the dresser's jars and little boxes that had entranced me as a girl.

The bureau drew me, and at first I touched things – unscrewed the blush, patted foundation on my cheek to discover it matched. I sniffed the cold cream, shook talc in my hands and spanked it off. When I opened the frayed red jewellery box, it tinkled brightly with Brahms's lullaby; I silenced it hurriedly, as if I might be discovered.

Just as on the cat's-away nights I'd disobeyed and crept in here anyway, I played through beads, humming. I coiled her wedding pearls in my palm, worked the neat closure on the rhinestone choker, sorting necklaces not into troves to keep and give away but putting all the green ones in a pile.

After piddling fruitlessly with Mother's jewellery, I slumped back on the bed, surrounded by the nosegay of her jars. I didn't cry; I might have liked to.

I reached forward and pulled open a drawer, rifling scarves, until my fingers hit a bundle of rubber-banded correspondence. I unfolded a letter: 'Dearest Eugenia ...' It was from my father on a trip to Washington when they were parted. 'I met Archie Ellman at the SCLC yesterday, and he thinks Mark Coe is the best candidate for the fundraising position –'

I couldn't finish reading it. Because I was prying, because I was afraid of unearthing hurtful secrets better left interred? No, I was bored. The events he described were meetings, and I found no mention of me at all. Nothing would have delighted me more than to locate a smutty passage, or to wrestle a girlie magazine from under the mattress, but the most depressing of my parents' secrets was that they didn't have any. I sure hoped at my own death there would be something shocking in my chest of drawers.

I resolved to be disciplined. I marched to the closet and flung open the door.

The hangers were jammed. She had lots of clothes, being fond of bargains and mortified by throwing anything away. I reached to the far end to screech two hangers apart, revealing a floor-length white cotton with a Nehru collar.

You should keep that.

Ten years before when I'd been home from New York with nothing but bluejeans, my parents had been giving a dinner that night. Ordered to this closet to find something 'nice' to wear, I'd been confronted with this same array of big buttons and tie-bows. Looking for something simple, I'd tried on this white Nehru. As I examined the fit I saw my mother's expression battle behind me in the mirror: rancour flicked to admiration, back to rancour again. I was her daughter; she should want me to be pretty. But I looked better in the dress than she did.

'You should keep that,' she'd said harshly.

I hadn't. I'd hung it back here as a malicious reminder of what I looked like in it. I doubt she ever wore it again.

I unhooked the dress, pleated from hanging. Curious, I dragged off my jeans and tried it on.

The straight-cut snagged on my hips, which had settled a bit. Frankly, I looked dumpy. I wondered if my mother would be gratified. So this is inheritance. Mother, you no sooner pass on your looks than take them back.

Behind the Nehru was a smart brown check with pert white collar that I couldn't remember seeing her in since I was in third grade; no doubt she had years before ceased to fit into it. I remembered the dress because she had worn it one day when I'd forgotten my lunch (again). She poked her head into my spelling class, whispered a few apologetic words to my teacher as she delivered my Yogi Bear lunchbox, and waved to me. I know children are chronically embarrassed by parents, but that morning I basked. The girl in the next desk leaned over and exclaimed, 'Was *that* your *mother*?'

I nodded.

'She looks like a movie star!'

128

For the rest of the day I was myself a celebrity. They couldn't believe that I, a klutzy schoolgirl with thin hair, crooked teeth, and psoriasis on my ankles, was related to that.

Going back even further in time, at the very end of the rack was my mother's wedding dress, preserved in clear plastic. Though the satin had yellowed a bit, the gown held its form, the delicately puckered bodice cinching to a petite waist, gently flaring to accommodate the next slight, seductive curve. That by her wedding Eugenia Hadley Hamill had been one staggeringly attractive woman became a bone of contention when I was in university, when on the phone with a classmate I referred to my mother's good looks. Anna, who had met my mother, scoffed, 'Get off it! Your mother's fat!'

My ear had tingled at the receiver. 'She's put on a little weight. But she used to be a knock-out.'

As Anna abjured that I must let go of this sad mythology, my umbrage rose. Off the phone, I rummaged for my copy of my mother's wedding picture, with that inhalation of a smile and a figure to stop your heart. I cycled to Anna's flat, said nothing when she opened the door, and presented the photograph. Diffident, she glanced at the portrait casually and handed it back. 'Not bad,' she said with a shrug.

Not bad?

I might have felt chagrined that to friends I exalted my father's heroics for the underprivileged, but only flaunted my mother's waist. Yet she was valedictorian in both high school and college; she founded a local day care centre and was president of the NC Consumer's Council –

No use. The most important thing about my mother to me was that she was beautiful.

But look, I observed, shrieking hangers across the rail: the newer dresses had gathered elastic waistbands; sizes were no longer sixes and sevens. The eights and nines were knits, expanding to encompass a generous self-deceit. I didn't want these dresses. I was too terrified that, sooner or later, they would fit me.

For if my mother lived 'beside herself', there was no one where she actually was; an elusive sensation of emptiness at last manifested itself in her diet. Deep inside, my mother was hungry. Her amplitude cruelly coincided with the in-house competition getting stiff. As her fourteen-year-old in a first pair of high heels twirled in the mirror, my mother had snapped, 'I used to have legs like that!' and stalked off to cut shortening.

My triumphalism was brief. The flake-by-flake larding of her ambrosial pies soon weighed as heavily on me as on my mother. I'd declared more than once in public, 'My mother was much better looking than I ever was,' and I said that with pride. My waist had never been that tiny, my cheekbones weren't as high. My feet were a size larger; my toes splayed; though I had her olive skin I also freckled. I'd clung to these shortcomings; I craved handicaps. Of course I'd won the contest. At twenty-five years her junior, I was cheating.

Now she was dead I could defend her: fine, she got heavier, but it wasn't fair, Anna, to call her fat. She was forever slimming, and until the accident delivered her half-eaten pie wedges to my father's lap. Past forty she drew wolf whistles; at fifty she qualified as handsome. When my father died she had a choice: to pine away to nothing, or to balloon. If, no drinker, she hit the chocolates, who could blame her? Siren for forty years, she may have handed the baton of family fox to me with some relief – she was tired of salad. The weight hurried her heart attack, but she wanted to die. The real accident, I had heard her claim more than once, was that she wasn't in the car.

I nestled my face between Eugenia McCrea's scratchy overwashed synthetics and sagging expanded knitwear. Oh, Mother. My alarm at your spreading backside was too much on my own account. But any man's head I ever turned was turned for you. Any sway of my hip, every gleam of my good white teeth came from your fine saddle. At my most magnetic moments I have most resembled you. I might offer as consolation that lately my own elbows dimple, my neck is creased, my stomach has an ominous curve, except you were far too generous a woman despite single moments of understandable bitterness to take satisfaction from my weakness for linguini. No, I think you would only mourn for my thighs as I mourned for yours, only forgive my pasta as I failed to forgive your pies. It was a tawdry woman's prayer. And I repented that I had not put my striking inheritance to its most redemptive use, by ducking into the classrooms of nine-year-old girls over a lunchbox to make their day. But I would not apologize for carrying that icon of nacreous satin and lush brown eyes from house to house, pointing: *that was my mother. Doesn't she look like a movie star?*

Several garments rumpled to the floor. I sighed and picked up the dresses; all this emotionalism was no help. I had a chore to do, and was torn between binning everything and retaining the lot. Yet if there was anything to be gained from this larger exercise of death and transference, it was to acknowledge that no inheritance need be absolute – that each generation wields partial power over what to keep and what to discard. In the end I developed a system: I would rescue the exotic, the dream – her kaftan from Ghana, kimono from Tokyo, sari from Delhi. I would salvage my mother's alternative lives, what she might have looked like born elsewhere or at another time – as me, for example. The more matronly frocks, with their belts pulled first at the third, then fourth, fifth holes, notching the progress of her dejection, I folded for Goodwill, for it does a generation a disservice to save the tarnish on its glory.

I'm not sure what got into me, but when the closet was cleared, I retrieved a floral sleeveless from the Goodwill bag – an older, smaller dress she had worn at the opening of her day care centre. I put it on. I was daring myself. It fit. On the back of the shoe tree were white pumps just broken down enough for my feet to squeeze in. Inside a top shelf hatbox I knew I'd find a curly brunette wig, for when her permanent was waning. I shoved my browning blonde straggles under its net. Seated at the dresser, I unzipped the make-up kit, smearing my face with foundation, tightening my lips in an O to apply pink gloss, and dusting my cheekbones with mauve blush. Clip-on earrings pinched me to consider that maybe this prank was nasty. A string of aqua beads completed the effect, which was – as I stood before the full-length mirror and recited, 'I *thought* you *liked* my *pie*!' – gobsmacking.

I crept down to the kitchen, feet swelling over the shoes. The table was deserted. Rooting through three storeys to locate that overly private, inexplicably contrary youngest, I felt possessed. Back upstairs, I tapped on the dovecot entrance with the same tentative don't-mind-me and I'm-coming-up-anyway that had driven him to the tower deck in December hail.

'Twooo-maaannn!'

'Corlis?' came from above, with a touch of puzzlement. By the old rules at least, his sister could just walk up.

I perched the prim white toes on the tips of his refinished stairs, wondering if he'd pulled up the carpet so he could hear her coming. Pigeons warbled warning from the roof. I tucked at the wig for errant sandy hairs. My step was timid, hands clasped at my waist in the posture of a woman who does not want to be a bother but has had far too many cups of coffee on her own today.

Truman was in his living room on the Victorian couch, frowning over a philosophy text. I poked my head in the doorway, hands pawed on the frame.

When he looked up his face drained of colour, as if a dusty window shade were pulled from brow to beard.

I'd an opening line ready: 'I made you and Averil a rhubarb cream ... !' but uttered nothing. It seems not only had I made a thin joke, or one in poor taste – I hadn't made a joke at all. As my too-perfect performance of my mother's slamming kitchen cabinets suggested, maybe you can't disguise yourself as what you already are.

'That's amazing,' he said leadenly. 'Take it off.'

My face heated until I could feel the make-up melt. I tried to grin, but my mouth curled up falsely so much like the latter Eugenia McCrea that the smile made matters worse. I stuttered, 'Sorry,' and clattered downstairs, to rub off the Almay Natural Cover with Kleenex after Kleenex sopped with cold cream. Though traces of foundation streaked my cheeks all night, the vision from that doorway would linger longer. I expect Truman Adlai has never thought of his sister in quite the same way since.

10

We were notified the will was out of probate. Hugh had expedited the title search and asset liquidation, I hoped, out of consideration for the fact that Truman and I were skint, but I later suspected extra pressure was brought to bear from a third party known since a colicky infancy for getting his way and fast. The Fourth Child, however, was still not paid off, and Hugh had received another letter, pointedly less polite, demanding the legacy be resolved. Smug in its assurance of our father's favour, the ACLU was the spoiled and peevish sort of sibling all children detest.

The very next day the doorbell rang. It was 19 December.

A functionary pumped my hand. Bobbing in an ocean of navy polysester, he flapped his papers and grinned as if I had just won the Publisher's Clearing House Sweepstakes. That's North Carolina for you – even a Wake County Sheriff comes on like your long lost buddy.

'Troo-man!' I sang up the stairwell, capturing the infuriating gaity with which my mother had roused her sullen children for Sunday school. 'We have a visitor!'

Truman was not by nature well disposed towards strangers of any kind. I had suggested to him that everyone starts out a stranger; if you don't get past that hurdle you don't make friends ever, but then that was Truman, he didn't make friends, ever. He could be so warm and garrulous, I didn't understand how he'd gotten through all of high school, a ten-year job whose only conceivable redemption was chatting up clients, and five semesters of university without once bringing anyone home. I think he was scared other people wouldn't like him and so beat them to it by disliking them first. This particular yuletide pop-by was unlikely to break him of the habit.

'What's the problem?'

'This is Mr Benson, Troom. He's a – ?'

'Process-server. Just need you two to John Hancock these here papers, and then I'll run them back to the courthouse. Won't take but a jiff.'

'Would you like to come in?'

Truman gloomed.

I drew Benson into the parlour. 'Does this have to do with the probate?'

'No, ma'am. A Mr, ah –' he checked his folder – 'Mordecai D. McCrea is filing suit for partition. These forms here are just a formality. Say you've been served and know to appear at the hearing and all. Nothing to get het up about.'

'What if we don't sign?' Truman jutted his chin.

Benson looked embarrassed. 'That'd just put me to the trouble of writing out an affidavit swearing you've been served. Somebody must have connections, though. Court's backed up to kingdom come, but ya'll's hearing's next week. Twenty-fourth.'

'We have a hearing on *Christmas Eve*?' asked Truman.

'Just another day, where I work. Get Christmas off, New Year's, that's it.'

'Maybe you could show us where – ?' I asked.

The sheriff spread his documents on the coffee table.

'You don't have to be so damned cooperative,' Truman growled.

'Well it's not his fault, is it?' I whispered back.

'Say, ya'll aren't related to Sturges McCrea, are you?'

'A.k.a. Dad.' I smiled; Truman rolled his eyes.

'Heckuva guy. That explains how this moved up on the docket. Terrible shame about that accident. Can't say I agreed with him on that bussing folderol – caused more trouble than it was worth and now it's the *African Americans* putting up a stink about riding across town. But Sturges start in a direction, he keep going, yessir.'

'That's for sure,' I said, thinking Benson could as well be describing my older brother. I added to Truman, 'Wouldn't even stop at a Texaco.'

'Texaco invest in South Africa or something?' Benson gaped at the cornice and chandelier. 'Never would have pictured Sturges McCrea in a place like this.'

'Sturges McCrea didn't picture himself in a place like this

either. Mammy's out back making Scarlett a dress out of drapes, but we try to keep the tenant farmers' jump-down-turn-around-pick-a-bale-of-cotton sotto voce so the neighbours don't complain.'

'Old-fashioned and the dickens to heat, I bet. But this house is a prize, it is.'

That's exactly what Heck-Andrews was, a prize. But I had not yet discerned whether the reward was for the best behaviour or the worst, nor if it had any real value or was merely an oversized trophy.

'Sign here, and here, too … You sure don't have much of a tar-heel accent, do you, miss?'

Having established my paternity, I couldn't pull off English origins this time. 'I never did, much,' I said.

'Sure you didn't, Corlis,' said Truman. His signature was a jagged scribble; his capital C tore the page.

'You two have a merry Christmas now –'

'How likely is *that*?' said Mr Friendly.

Benson had decided to leave, and I think he made the right decision. The veins in Truman's temples were beginning to pulse. 'Take care now. Gotta scoot.'

'This is ridiculous!' Truman shouted when the man was gone. 'Why is this going to court?'

For once I didn't quiet him with collusive disparagement of Mordecai's character by concurring that our brother was a bully and simply wanted to watch us cower and scramble to keep our ancestral home. I had some dawning appreciation for why Mordecai would bring the ownership of this house to a head, for when I considered telling Truman right then, *Troom, I know you and I have talked about buying this house together, but I'm not sure that would be the best thing for you and* … (I'd have sounded so unpersuasive already, like such a shyster, and he would stop me and say what do you mean Corlis, and I would stutter …) *Truman, I've talked to Mordecai about maybe buying the house with him instead, and you and Averil could* – Gentle as he seemed, I had a feeling that Truman was wholly capable of socking me in the jaw.

So I let Truman fume and said nothing of the sort. And Mordecai was right, I'd have put off opening my mouth to this effect for months, for years, forever. Often as I might have railed that I was born in the middle and it wasn't fair, much as I might have resented both my brothers for forcing me before I was old enough to understand the choice to pick one of them over the other, the middle was where I was stuck, again. I could not have both pie and ice cream, but instinctively I would take my pie and sneak the ice cream. I had always been like that. I was still like that.

My inclination with law was to duck it, though this evasion did not consistently translate into a life of crime. I preferred bicycles and scooters over cars, since the cops overlooked lesser transport , whereas an auto, with its attendant registration, insurance and driver's licence, entangled its owner in jurisprudence. Yet once on a bicycle, I stopped for lights and gave way at zebra crossings. Being an ex-pat had appealed because, while technically subject to British laws, they were not my laws; especially with no National Insurance number I felt out of their reach, a sensation on which I placed high value even with no plans to break them. For several years I paid the IRS more than I needed, having instructed my accountant that at any cost he must fictionalize a filing that wouldn't be scrutinized. My sole ambition with law was to slip out from under it. Hence I would never, myself, have filed a partition suit, thereby flying into the very web I went out of my way to avoid.

However, on 24 December Mordecai's nonchalant slump in the courtroom displayed the plumped lying-in-wait, not of the fly, but of the spider. He had arrived before us with uncharacteristic punctuality. Lolling on his bench with arms extended on either side, ignoring the armed bailiff when the man tapped his head to warn my brother to remove his hard-hat, Mordecai clearly saw the law as a weapon to wield or to defy, either of which he would do with zeal and in plain view. Mordecai regarded a courtroom as part of his inheritance and therefore as one more thing he might help himself to, like a celadon vase. Or this is the only way I could explain how a hippie anachronism in pigtails who was probably packing at least an ounce of dope at the time could slouch amidst all those uniforms in so relaxed and proprietary a fashion.

When I trailed into the court after Truman and Averil, Mordecai waved me over to the seat beside him. Refusing to so much as nod, Truman selected a pew two rows behind Mordecai, so I assumed the empty one between them. That my inability to sit in public incontrovertibly by either left me sitting by myself I might have taken as cautionary.

The case was before a single judge. Our verdict's dependence on the caprices of one man was all too evocative of my family, and it discouraged me when the larger world was as arbitrary as the small – there was no resort. Judge Harville had an immobile, deadpan face with stiff grey hair that moved like a solid object when he looked down at his files. His languid, congenitally bored manner conveyed that after thousands of picayune disputes paraded before his bench nothing fazed him any more. He kept his voice a level plainsong, except at the end of sentences where they pitched, like Truman's, in a minor key. Yet while my brother's voice fell a half step, keening a tune of tragedy and defeat, Harville's rose a half, lifting with a satiric little jest. From a distance at least, I got the impression Harville saw his job preponderantly as farce.

'Docket number 92-P648,' announced the clerk. 'McCrea vs. McCrea.'

Truman and I made way in the aisle for the blue-maned, blue-faced biddy who had failed to prove her hairdresser's negligence in placing a standing ashtray in the path between the dryers and the ladies' loo; when Truman tripped on her outstretched crutch she was elaborately huffy. We sat up at the left side of the court, where we were joined by a striking young man whose dark, drastic features suggested Sephardic parentage, though his surname, murmured hurriedly as he sat beside us, was Anglo enough: Grover. Truman sniffed, and worked his chair another few inches from the larcenous do-gooder. When I whispered that David Grover was pretty sexy, Truman's face curdled as if I had just confessed to a crush on Radovan Karadzic.

Mordecai swung behind the table on the right. My older brother was in his usual caked black jeans and lace-up boots, with bits of plaster clotting his eyebrows. He was joined by a lawyer whose attire was proper only in the most technical sense. The attorney's tie was wrenched aside; his suit jacket arms were shoved up his wrists, while his white shirt showed a tad of tail. Since they couldn't make a rule against it, he seemed to have bad skin on purpose. The lawyer lounged in his chair, savvy and familiar. As he chuckled with Mordecai, I wondered if he'd taken the case on contingency or just for laughs.

It was Truman's idea that we needn't hire counsel, though we had rung Hugh, who said he was too closely connected to the case and begged off. Truman figured that since we were in the right we might as well speak for ourselves. I suspected our error, but kept my misgivings to myself. In retrospect, I'd advise prospective defendants that sanctimony makes for weak representation at best.

'Mr McCrea,' Judge Harville began, addressing Mordecai. 'Remove your hat, please.'

'Sure thing, *your honour*,' he underscored, with the same knife-twist he'd used when deploying the address with my father. Mordecai's release of the chinstrap was leisurely.

'And there is no smoking in this courtroom.'

'Righty ho,' said Mordecai, tucking his Bambus back in his leather vest pocket and adding convivially, 'hard times for us retrogrades.'

'This is a courtroom, not a pool hall. Mr Shipley?' Harville sounded so fatigued I thought he might collapse. 'Exit the chewing gum.'

Mordecai's lawyer snapped a tiny bubble before picking the wad from between his teeth and jamming it under the table.

'Mr McCrea, can you explain to me why you have brought this matter to our court? Could you not resolve what to do with 309 Blount Street between you and your siblings?'

Mordecai lunged to the podium in front of his table, flipping a pigtail as he rose. He gripped the lectern and weighed on his elbows, tipping the podium on to its forward edge. 'My brother refuses to put the house up for sale, which ties up over $100,000 of my money. I run my own company, and am currently under financial duress. Meanwhile he claims he lives there, and won't move out.'

'Can your brother not compensate you for your share in the equity, then?'

'He doesn't have the cash,' said Mordecai bluntly.

'We do *too*,' Truman whispered fiercely beside me.

'You are Mr Truman McCrea, sir?'

'Uh, yes, yes I am – your honour.'

'Step up to the podium please?'

Truman stumbled to the lectern. While on the opposite side Mordecai had assumed the planted, squinty-eyed try-and-make-me stance from which he had refused to turn down the volume of Three Dog Night, Truman shoved his hands in his suit pockets and drew his shoulders together just as he would have hunched in our kitchen doorway delaying the inevitable relinquishment of his duplicate key.

'Do you have the financial resources to retain this property by yourself?'

'No, but –' Truman looked back at me. 'With my sister –'

'Do the two of you have those resources?'

'No,' I intervened from the table. 'I'm afraid we don't.'

'This is cut and dried then –'

'Your honour!' Truman pleaded. 'We were going to take out a mortgage. Sir.'

'You have arranged a mortgage?'

'How could we? He filed this suit the day the will was out of probate! The fact is, we made him an offer, and he turned it down!'

'If it may please the court,' intruded Shipley wryly, though neither he nor his client had gone out of their way so far to please anyone, 'The offer so made was spurious, sir, the money was not at hand. For the record, the junior Mr McCrea is an undergraduate at Duke University, with no income aside from a recent inheritance too slight to purchase my client's share of the property. His wife is a part-time substitute teacher in the Raleigh public school system, with an income, if my research serves me, of $10,000 a year. I would submit that no banker in his right mind would give such an individual a mortgage of fifty cents.'

'They would, too, with a half-million dollar house as security – !' Truman's voice was cracking.

'Which raises another of our contentions,' Shipley proceeded. 'The property's assessor has shared with my client that he substantially undervalued the real estate, by perhaps as much as $100,000. We have that in writing, sir.' He passed a paper to the judge, who refused it with a laboured wave of the hand.

'This court cannot weigh the credit-worthiness of prospective mortgage applicants. We are not a savings and loan. To bar partition, I need written proof that the respondent can buy out the petitioner. Mr – Grover ...' Harville shuffled paper with weary confusion. 'You are representing – the American Civil Liberties Union? I fail to see whose first amendment rights have been trampled here.'

'*Mine,*' grumbled Truman.

'If I may explain, your honour,' said Grover easily. 'The property was willed in equal parts to the three heirs and the ACLU; my organization is tenant in common of 309 Blount Street.'

'Who would write a will like that?' Harville supposed.

'Justice Sturges McCrea, sir.'

'Typical,' grunted the judge, and added without looking up, 'Seems to me you nosy parkers stir up enough trouble without being encouraged.'

'I beg your honour's pardon, what was that?' enquired Grover. 'For the record?'

'Never you mind, Mr Grover.' Harville whinnied, resuming his dreary professionalism. 'And how is the ACLU disposed in this dispute?'

'It is naturally in our interests that the property be liquidated. The ACLU has no resistance to this suit; in fact, we are eager to disentangle a charitable bequest from domestic politics that are none of our affair.'

Looking stranded at the podium – no one had told him to sit down – Truman smote David Grover with an evil eye. 'Why don't you sit over there?' he muttered, nodding towards Mordecai. Grover had no choice but to sit on our side of the court, but having him in our dugout was like hunkering down with a teammate whose uniform was the wrong colour.

'Ms McCrea.' Harville turned to me. 'What are your wishes in this matter?'

My heartbeat doubled. 'I'm neutral, your honour.'

'Would you not prefer to reap the proceeds of a sale?'

'I guess I'd like to see the house stay in the family, sir.'

'So you're not neutral.'

'I guess not, sir.'

'But you do not have the funds to purchase the house, even with your brother?'

I was grateful he didn't say with which brother. 'Not quite, sir.'

Harville shook his head in disgust, obviously ready to knock off for Christmas Eve with his own dysfunctional family.

'309 Blount Street,' he intoned, 'is to be publicly advertised for auction, proceeds to be divided equally among the four parties. Bids to be due February 5, 1993 – that gives you six weeks. Should any one party or combination of parties raise the funds in that time, you are within your rights to participate in the auction yourselves. I might add, Mr Shipley, that a materially identical course of action was available without judicial assistance, and there was no excuse for wasting the state of North Carolina's time with this case.' The gavel fell. We were excused.

I mumbled to Mordecai as we left the building, 'I guess you're not still coming for Christmas Eve dinner, right?'

'Wouldn't miss it for the world!' He slammed me on the shoulder to lumber off with his sleazoid lawyer, leaving me slack-jawed.

I shouldn't have been incredulous. While I was an avid voyeur – having acquired a taste for watching spit fly by eavesdropping on argy bargy from our landing – I preferred an eye on the storm to the eye of it. Like it or not, I resembled my mother in more than countenance; unless pushed to the wall she, too, would smooth over family cracks with pastry. Outside discrete bouts of hysteria, my mother did not believe in conflict, that there was such a thing. All enmity was misunderstanding; improve communication and everyone eats pie. I did believe in conflict enough to avoid it. Mordecai, by contrast, adored nothing better than a pretext to hurl crockery. I've wondered if our difference wasn't so much appetite for battle, one of us peace-loving, the other a warrior, for I became paralytically bored when stuck among softies who all ploddingly got along. Perhaps what differentiated our eagerness to enter the ring was the degree to which we were convinced we could win. If Mordecai stirred things up because he was sure to do more damage than have damage done, I envied him.

So, doomed to Momism, Christmas Eve I found myself in the kitchen peeling spuds for potato salad, all of us about to kill each other while I debated mayonnaise versus sour cream.

Truman was slicing Smithfield ham into the translucent slices tradition demanded. His brow was boiling, his lips were compressed. His wide forearm was flecked with the same once-blonde curls of my own hair, glinting with bygone gold. Often I barely recognized this meaty grown man as the fragile four-year-old who had stacked wood-blocks in our carriage house only for me to knock them down. Other times I recognized him more profoundly than any other child in the family. Despite the long string of failed Christmas Eves in this house, he would sliver yet another mound of exactingly thin Virginia ham in the naïve expectation that this time would be different, just as he had erected yet another playroom folly convinced, like Charlie Brown with Lucy's football, that for once I would leave it standing.

With blocks or Lego, Truman hadn't constructed phallic towers, but wombish houses, like a girl. There was, if I looked closely, a touch of the feminine about him still, maybe what all that weightlifting in his eyrie was meant to disguise. Truman's improbable guilelessness, at thirty-one, tempted me to knock it down. Fleetingly, I relished telling him that the future of Heck-Andrews had a Plan B.

Averil was stuffing holly-cornered napkins into rings carved with Santa's elves. She was wearing red and green. The kitchen was a disaster, and for what? I wondered how we'd bought into this myth of occasion, my mother's 'special times'. All this hustle-bustle, only to wrap the leftovers in cling-film, waiting to spoil so we could put them in the freezer.

'I thought you hated potato salad,' I mentioned at the sink.

'Yep.'

'Then why are we having it?'

'Search me.'

'... Do you like Smithfield ham?'

He shrugged. 'It's all right.'

'Then why are we bothering?'

'Search me.' He'd decimated a third of the ham. He seemed to enjoy cutting too much.

'Don't you think that's enough?'

'Fine.' He glared with a tight grisly smile, the knife raised point up.

'I guess we should have arranged some financing before showing up at that hearing.' My eyes met only those of the potatoes; my peeling was meticulous.

'I *guess* we should have.'

'You're the one who didn't want to hire a lawyer. I assume that's the first thing he'd have advised us, OK?'

'Too late now,' Truman clipped. 'Hindsight's about as useful as looking up your ass.'

I eased the cork from a cabernet.

Truman looked askance. 'At six o'clock?'

'It's Christmas Eve!'

'There's always some excuse.'

'For a drink? In this house? You bet.'

'You're drinking more than you used to, Corlis.'

'We both are, we didn't used to drink.' Which staggered me. I'd no idea how I managed my whole childhood without a bracer. 'What's biting your bum?'

'Besides the fact that my brother just made me look like a complete twit in public? Maybe I'm reminiscing.' I was relieved, though we'd more than enough sliced, when he applied the knife back to the ham. 'About last year.'

'I'm sorry,' I said.

'Yeah. You said that at the time. You were *sorry*.'

By and large, I was prone to the indolent emotions. I'd drop by if I was in the neighbourhood; I'd buy friends a little something, but only if there was a shop on the way. I was comfortably regretful when it was too late to remedy an oversight. I did whatever I wanted on the assumption that I could patch things up after. I was cavalier; I was sorry.

'Troom, how was I to know Mother would have a heart attack? She wasn't very old. Right, people can always die on you but you can't twiddle your whole life in the sitting room waiting for some member of the family to expire.' Well, of course you could; one of us had.

'Uh-huh. But you're home for Christmas this year. Now that she's dead.'

He hadn't let go of the knife. I whittled too many potatoes, reflecting that my little brother had all the makings of a serial killer.

'Maybe better late than ...'

'No,' he insisted. 'Maybe not better late.'

'I couldn't afford –'

'Mother said that she offered to pay for your ticket. And you said no.'

'I finance my own –'

'You're not too proud to take it now, though. Inheritance may be "evil", but you'll accept her money when it doesn't mean you have to put up with her company for a day or two.'

'I visited when I could.'

'You'd be out every night of a five-day stay. You'd apologize, of course. Think she didn't *twig*, Corlis?'

'All right.' I tossed a potato in the sink. 'Did you enjoy earnest evenings with Mother? Be honest.'

'Of course not, and that's the point!' He threw down the knife at last. 'Do you realize what it was like here last year? Mother had volunteered to pay your fare, and you said you'd rather spend the holiday with your *flatmates*. Did Mordecai stop by? When he lived ten blocks away? Not one phone call! So Averil and I went out and spent three hundred dollars on a bunch of presents she didn't need because *no one else bought her anything*. You didn't, did you, not even a little package of shortbread or a souvenir from Buckingham Palace. She'd have been touched by trash, Corlis, some stupid trinket. You didn't even send a decent letter, did you? A postcard! Which arrived, as I recall, in the middle of January.'

'The end of January,' Averil contributed.

'So we spent last Christmas Eve looking at slides of their travels with Mother's voice quavering, getting so puddly she couldn't focus and the ten million shots of ANC worthies kept wobbling into blurs. We heard, again, about how they met in the Young Democrats and how respected Father was and how Jesse Jackson came to his funeral. We made her dinner and cleaned up and wouldn't let her help, though that was mostly to get away for at least a few minutes, which didn't work because while I was sudsing glasses she'd droop over my shoulders and thank me for being the one kid who seemed to care and she'd cry. I may have wanted to hit her, but I didn't hit her, did I? You hit her.' Truman was hyperventilating.

'I had friends and a career and I lived in another country! That's what parents bargain for. They do not expect you to stay home until you're fifty-five, making repairs to the stoop.'

'Then what are you doing now? Except I don't notice you making repairs to the stoop.'

'I'm taking a little time to work out what to do next. Considering you wasted ten years driving a bloody hardware truck in circles for your in-laws while you decided what to do with your life, I think I've earned a few weeks of slack. That is, if you *have* decided. If studying philosophy isn't more navel-gazing procrastination. Fucking hell, you're one to talk.'

That did him. I was regretful – I was sorry. He looked at his big hands with his shoulders slumped. I was glad I could still make him cry. 'I thought –' His chest lurched. 'Christmas was hard, Corlis. I was tired, she was driving me crazy. I thought you might come home for me. You didn't bother. All you cared about was your boyfriends.'

Despite the plural dig, I said, 'I *am* sorry, Truman,' and this time the apology felt different; I meant it. 'Now –' I poured him a medicinal glass of wine, '– Mordecai will arrive any minute. Get this down you, and then some. You'll need it.'

Truman had not swilled nearly enough antidote when the kitchen table trembled as a military motor gunned outside. Mordecai managed to drive a vehicle that actually sounded like a bulldozer.

When he clumped in the back door with three of his workmen in tow, I noticed that his manner had altered. Ordinarily he had acted detached here, the avuncular visitor, but now he waltzed in with a feudal swag just like my father after a long day, who would slide his briefcase on the table and make for the freezer, to shovel ice cream straight from the carton before dinner. Mordecai now walked in this house as if, well, as if he owned it.

'Yo, you guys got something to drink?'

I scanned all four of them, and felt a little economic sinking that not one of them had arrived with a bottle of anything. Mordecai beelined for the cabernet on the counter, grabbed a gas-war tumbler, and upended the bottle. His roll-up bobbed and shed ash as he talked. Meanwhile his minions ambled through the first floor, poking into closets and picking up knick-knacks, as if considering whether to tuck them in an inside pocket. 'Hey, Mort, some crib,' the one with the dingy blonde ponytail murmured. 'Not bad.' I felt the impulse to count our silver, like some hapless Civil War widow when a Northern general occupied her vanquished house for bivouac. I expect Sherman didn't arrive with any wine either.

'Where's Dix?' I asked as Mordecai helped himself to ham.

'Spending the holidays with her snit,' he said with his mouth full. 'They were getting on so good, it seemed a shame to part them.'

'What's she upset about?'

Mordecai flicked his head in Truman's direction. 'Later.'

God forbid with the three of us together that anyone would confide anything to anyone. It may have been a luxury of a sort to be the centre of information, for each brother told me his side of things so long as the other was out of range, but as a consequence they left me full of secrets and turned me into a liar with both. Maybe that was the idea.

Mordecai having left home so early, I'd had little experience with the two of them in the same room. Since I assumed a radically different persona with each brother, they cancelled me out. Not only did I not know what to say, but how to say it. With Truman, my speech was distinctly British – I said 'con*tro*versy' and used a 'spanner'; with Mordecai, I fell in with his yahoo singsong, and said 'fuck' a lot. In Truman's company, I was careful not to drink to excess, never admitted I sometimes smoked a cigarette, wouldn't be caught dead nibbling biscuits between meals, and curtailed stories of sexual antics in the interest of portraying myself as a passionate woman with high standards just looking for love. Slumming with Mordecai, I tried manfully to keep up my end of a bottle, name-dropped multiple boyfriends, and snickered knowingly at any reference to pharmaceuticals, never letting on that I'd only taken acid once. Therefore when Mordecai thumped his muddy boots on the table, rolled a joint and passed it to me I froze. With Truman, I claimed I didn't smoke dope; with Mordecai, I had never refused a few hits. I compromised with a single drag and handed it back. Truman raised his eyebrows. I fled for ham.

Mordecai and his three grungy employees reached across one another for slabs of Smithfield, ignoring the holly napkins to wipe mustard on their sleeves. Bandying brands of audio manufacturers, they glugged great tumblers of Rosemont cabernet until in short order they'd decimated a third of our case.

We were never formally introduced, but I sorted out the names of our gate-crashers. MK was the smarmy blonde, whose ponytail hung stiff with a lacquerous sheen. His weight was cadaverously low, his face dappled with the purple undertone of volcanic acne in his youth. MK's drawl overplayed the dumb hick: *gosh-dang ain't that sump'm*. I figured him for one of those lowlifes who was always trading on a southerner's reputed buffoonery – sweet corn to divert attention from the switch-blade taped to his ankle.

When he followed me once to the sink – to get a glass of water he failed to drink – he may have been locating our case of wine. He said, 'Is it true, Corrie Lou, that Mort took a test at NC State that proved he was a *genius*?'

'So I've been told,' I said coldly. I noted MK had mail-ordered my brother's exact same style of leather boots, as he also rolled his own cigarettes and extolled that sickening caraway schnapps. Imitation made me edgy; it was a kind of theft.

''Cause that guy sure do run rings around me,' MK twanged. 'Half the time, I can't tell what he's gassin' about from the man in the moon.' Somehow I didn't believe that MK felt all that stupid.

Wilcox was the tall lantern-jawed fellow who didn't say much, though that left his mouth the freer to suck down drink. His head swivelled, following the others' chatter as they segued from speaker components to the US Marines' recent invasion of Somalia, but his pupils were inert and opaque. Wilcox looked like one of those kids in the back of the class who maintained an attentive expression, but if you called on him he'd sputter about the Revolutionary War when the class had long ago moved on to algebra.

Big Dave was the cut-up of the bunch, an amiable porker with a shameless guffaw. Maybe it was the granny glasses, but he seemed quicker than the other two and, more appealing still, I thought Big Dave liked my brother. When he chortled he seemed to have got the joke, where the other two laughed late, waiting for their cue. Big Dave was physically familiar, gripping Mordecai's forearm, but even this boisterous prole knew his limits and when Mordecai looked down at the hand Big Dave lifted it with a simpering grin. The whole trio demurred to excess and their good-timeyness felt forced, making me wonder whether Mordecai could be forbidding outside his family as well as in. I overheard Wilcox mumble to MK to 'keep an eye on Mort' because 'you know that fucker's a mean drunk'.

Under-breath asides as MK and Wilcox left in tandem for the loo confirmed that what they said in and out of my brother's earshot was chalk and cheese – *hear any more about fucking Somalia I'm gonna ... fucking skinny niggers, who gives a ...* Mordecai reared back as if his workmen were hanging on his every word, but I thought that their real concentration was on the potato salad.

While they helped themselves to our dinner and uncorked new bottles without asking, not one of them bothered with niceties like making conversation with Truman and Averil. Typically, no one had mentioned the hearing that afternoon, least of all Truman, who pulled his chair two feet outside the circle and said absolutely nothing.

MK asked about the folks their boss 'got this place from' – these three seemed under the impression that Heck-Andrews was Mordecai's alone. Though my brother described his father as an overbearing knee-jerk liberal, he went on to detail several landmark cases his father had tried, until it hit me like an anvil flattening Elmer Fudd: Mordecai was boasting! About his father! Then, MK couldn't have cared less, his eyes only following his employer's spliff as it stabbed the air for emphasis and failed to circulate around the table.

'You know, if either of you guys needs some extra dough,' Mordecai finally addressed his siblings, 'this contract's got us pressed. You're pretty handy with a hammer, ain'tcha kid?'

Truman shrugged.

'I pay fifteen bucks an hour. Think about it. And Core, I could use a hand in the office. Invoices, typing up bids?'

I looked at him in stupefaction. 'You want me to be your secretary?'

'Of course not, Core! You'd be my *executive assistant*.'

Having ravaged most of the food, Mordecai screeched his chair out and clomped off to the parlour, bottles in the crook of each arm luring his threesome along with him. Behind him, the table was strewn with potato dribs and half-gnawed carrot sticks, the floor tacky with flattened ham fat. Truman stayed behind to clean up.

That set the rest of the night: each brother in a different room. I kept excusing myself to the kitchen to fetch another cabernet where I would dawdle and dry glasses, drifting back to the parlour where Mordecai had put on Pearl Jam at a volume that would have broken another window in the door if our father were still alive. In neither room was I relaxed. After ten minutes I was acutely conscious of having left one brother for too long and began to fidget. Finally I gave up on trying to please both and no doubt pleasing neither, curling anti-socially in a far corner of the parlour. The music was too loud to talk anyway, so I amused myself by flipping a photo album that lay flat on a shelf in the absence of Britannicas.

I've wondered if personal memory hasn't been fundamentally subverted by photography. These crinkled snapshots objectified a past that would otherwise have remained a revisable blur. For example, when I remembered those years, I didn't envisage being a child. I may have recalled the sensation of not being wholly in control of my destiny, but I couldn't picture myself two feet high. Yet look: I was tiny, smothered in lacy frills that would repel me now, my arms spread with their Vienna sausage fingers groping at the air to embrace a world of which I have grown so much warier since. Photos were a corruption, however. That I did not remember feeling physically small had a truth to it. I'd noticed as well the seductive tendency to replace the quiver of real recollection with the steadied camera. I conjured my mother flat and artificially touched up at her college graduation, an event that I couldn't remember because I wasn't born then: photographs.

They did, however, have their uses, and though I was well familiar with this album I turned its leaves this time round as if consulting an oracle. I may have been a little stoned, but my questions were two: why was Truman terrified of his brother, and why did Mordecai revile him?

In the first four leaves, there is no Truman: Mordecai in our Hi-Flier wagon, holding the handle with two-year-old Corrie Lou between his legs. Here he already wears that signature smirk; by five, he has learned the f-word. I, on the other hand, am unrecognizable: decked in flounces, bouncing with blonde ringlets, gawking up at big brother with ga-ga adoration. He is about to go plummeting recklessly down the hill, and I haven't a care. My eyes are glad and uncomplex, without duplicity. Corlis Louise, dumb but happy.

More of these: Mordecai galloping with his baby sister on his back, bundling her on his sled for the scant two-inch snowfall on Bloodworth Street, the runners bound to scrape tarmac the second time down – snow in Raleigh is exotic, precious. Mordecai my protector escorts me, without my mother, to my first day of school.

The next leaf: my mother with fuller breasts, posing in front of the rental Tudor that preceded Heck-Andrews, a formless bundle in her arms. Mordecai is clutching me to his thigh, and averting his head with his eyes closed as if to say: this couldn't be happening.

In the following two panels Mordecai grips his sister with resolute possessiveness, plying her with stuffed bunnies, crayon portraits, bugs under jars. The third of our number is no more included in the drama of the moment than shirt cardboard. In Pullen

Park, Truman fists his mother's skirt and ducks in its folds as Mordecai, confident, tall and commanding in comparison, pushes my swing.

I had puzzled over these early shots of Truman before. All small children appear bruisable and undefended, but in Truman these qualities are extreme: his eyes are watery blue, large for his face and too wide open; his lips are parted, his hands held from his sides, wafting as if he doesn't know what they are for. He looks lost, the other two children colluding behind him, and his innocence is the kind that draws torment as irresistibly as flowers draw bees. These were the days of my first clear memories, when Mordecai and I would follow the toddler about the house ridiculing his first attempts at speech, exaggerating his mistakes; small wonder the little boy went mute for days.

Still there must have been an afternoon that I refused to participate in the game, though I do not remember it. When, instead of mimicking, 'Doh-nnn! Weave me awone!' in unison with Mordecai, stooping to leer into Truman's face as he flapped his arms in the hand-me-down jacket that was still too big for him, I snapped, 'Quit it, Mordecai,' put a hand on Truman's waist-high shoulder, and lent him my model palomino. There must have been an afternoon when, after school, instead of ritually threading down to the basement to peer at Mordecai's latest stink bomb experiment I searched out the four-year-old back from nursery school, still struck dumb from having spent the entire morning at West Raleigh Presbyterian in a corner with his blanket. An afternoon when instead of hiding the 'bembet' one more time in the couch cushions I helped him look for it.

For with a single turn of a page the groupings of our threesome transform – and one construction we never find here is the three of us playing convivially in the sandbox together. No, suddenly I am filling Truman's pail, edging forward to balance his seesaw, ketchuping his hotdog. These photos already capture the inseparable quality for which among my cousins we were renowned. And this is the first point in the album I recognize my own face. Its lines have sharpened and thinned; my eyes glitter with the quicksilver of a sovereign sibling. I am no longer a gurgly little sister; I am myself a protector, though in the way of most protectors, also the one you need protection from. We do what I say; we do not do what I proscribe, and Truman accepts both punishment and reward with equal submission because he has never stopped being grateful.

Truman was still grateful for my defection. That very evening, when I would pop back to the kitchen he didn't look censorious but beholden. Likewise, I concluded as I looked up from the album at Mordecai puffing away on his rollie, eyes cutting in my direction to make sure I had not abandoned him for the galley, my elder brother had never stopped being aggrieved.

You could see it in the photos. Often, in the later shots, Mordecai is out of the picture altogether. When he appears at all, he is remote from the rest of the family, sucking on candy cigarettes, looking daggers at his sister and her new-found sidekick. (In a single intimate exception, Mordecai is holding his little brother's waist as the youngest dangles on a jungle gym, but there's more than a hint in both Mordecai's sly grin and Truman's expression of abject horror that Mordecai is considering letting go.) Far at the edge of the frames, his eyes are slit with calculating resentment, as if he is plotting revenge, biding his time while he contrives the ultimate stratagem to win his sister back. When I glanced over at him in my father's old chair, boots on my mother's flimsy coffee table, knocking back our cabernet and casting about the parlour with an air of fresh reclamation, I realized that Mordecai was still scheming; he had not given up.

It had never occurred to me that my desertion might have hurt Mordecai's feelings. There was humility in my blindness – I never imagined I was that important to him – and admiration as well; he was my big brother, absorbed in pulley systems ingeniously driven by Erector Set motors, or nose down in his dinosaur book. Why would he covet the plaguesome curiosity of a little girl? For in my memory, Mordecai was sufficiently invincible that he didn't *have* feelings.

The other puzzle I hadn't fitted together was not only why I was forced to choose one brother over the other, but why I had selected the younger one. Was I naturally maternal? Did Truman's unguarded blue pupils cry out for my safekeeping? Or had I merely revealed a preference for the role of capricious leader over cowed fan? Did I only opt for Truman so I could boss him around? Or did I perhaps – like him better?

Whatever the answers, the consequences of our childhood alliances and betrayals were still playing themselves out in this household, so that one more time I would have to decide with which brother to throw in my lot. I slammed the book shut, having at least satisfied this much: Mordecai reviled his brother because the little twerp had swiped his sister, and Truman trembled because anything capable of being stolen can be taken back.

11

I fell asleep in that chair, and dreamt about my sculptures, tumbling down a muddy red hillside just out of my reach and cracking off their hands. These dreams were recurrent, and always the sculptures were wards in my keeping that I had forsaken or neglected and which suffered unduly on my account. Visions of clay figurines spliced with snapshots of my mother. To say I missed my art more than my parents would go too far, though my mourning for the objects was simpler. More accurately, the loss of what I had made and what I was made from had indistinguishably fused.

I woke to find Mordecai passed out on the floor, a wine stain spread at his elbow, a cold roach between his fingers having burned a black dot in the carpet. The flunkeys weren't in evidence and hadn't taken any care to cart my brother to bed and I hoped they'd gone. Groggy, I roused to switch off the stereo, still auto-reversing Smashing Pumpkins. I collected a few glasses and went to the kitchen; Truman had turned in, and I felt bereft. I wanted to explain to him that I had some new angles on our childhood and now I couldn't wake him up the way I used to and whisper secrets at his bedside because he was married.

I bundled to my own bed and didn't get up again until noon on Christmas Day. I found Truman downstairs, bent over the stove. It seems that Mordecai and his friends had made a late night raid on the fridge, decimating a whole pan of unbaked stuffing, one of my pumpkin pies, and most of the cranberry sauce. Truman had already stuffed the turkey, and was basting over the breast as if to soothe himself.

'I guess after I went to bed you guys had a high old time,' Truman clipped.

'Hardly. I conked out in the parlour and had nightmares.'

'Are those waste products gone?' Among their other unsavoury attributes, Mordecai's employees were *strangers*.

'I don't know. Want some help?'

Averil came in the back door having binned the rubbish, and the three of us put a shoulder to dinner, lopping radishes, splitting celery, peeling potatoes. Mordecai must have hauled himself to bed in the wee-smalls, so we salted the rug, though the burn mark was there to stay.

By three Mordecai shambled into the kitchen yellower than ever, the weave of his three pigtails afray. He made straight for one of Truman's cold beers, and within the hour it became apparent we had three charity cases for Christmas. They'd sacked out in the second-floor bedrooms, and by four-thirty had polished off two six-packs. I was reminded of a future whereby our father had let out spare rooms to the homeless after all.

When the seven of us milled around our Christmas tree it was nearing dark, though its carnival glow was unable to bathe our gathering in a persuasively festive light. I had fresh appreciation for how difficult it must have been for my parents to pull off this holiday with adolescent or grown children. Once we exceeded twelve or so and no longer wheedled outside their bedroom door to hurry up, pleading to open our presents while they exasperated us with breakfast, Christmas had acquired this same half-hearted, arbitrary quality. We had all become too patient and civilized and could buy ourselves what we liked; if we had postponed opening our presents another day or another year no one would have died. I'd always thought this failure of atmosphere was all my parents' fault, and now look, we couldn't do any better. One of the great privations in the demise of a generation over you is having no one to blame.

Averil put on 'A Music Box Christmas', but Mordecai said, 'Fuck this' not halfway through 'O Little Town of Bethlehem' and replaced it with Nirvana.

I apologized to our interlopers that we'd have wrapped them up a little something if we'd known they were coming, though what I really meant was this is our first Christmas without both our parents, it's hard enough and it was tactless of you three to butt in.

MK remarked, 'You're the one who's lived in London, ain'tcha, you sher have lost your accent.'

'I dare say I never had much of a drawl to lose,' I assured him, draping languidly on the mantle and wishing I had a fag to garnish the pose. 'Our mother was from Iowa and made such merciless fun of our father's Virginian accent that I pretty much grew up speaking like her.' I didn't mean to imply that as a child I had sounded like Walter Cronkite, but I guess it came out that way.

At which point, with a twinkle in her eye, Averil initiated our exchange of presents by handing me a wrapped packet. Her cornering was impeccable, the bow pert, the paper covered in reindeer, whereas I was given to swaddling presents in newspaper. The enclosed cassette was unmarked.

Averil took the tape from my hands, ejected Nirvana, and explained, 'We found it in your Dad's filing cabinet.' She hit PLAY:

– *Happay barthdie tew yew! Happay barthdie dayer fodder! Ha-apay barthdie tew* … (High nasal giggles and spastic laughter.) *Hey thar, fodder! Ah wonted ta ply yew ma reco-erder* – ?'

'Holy Christ,' said MK. 'Is that Corrie Lou?'

'None other,' said Averil. 'Sh-sh!'

'Averil, take that off!' I implored.

Averil placed herself bodily in front of the deck, treating us to a reedy rendition of 'Streets of Laredo', pierced not only with wrong notes and shrill squeaks but with plenty of interruptions from Truman:

– *Shud-up, Core-loo, ya don hayuv ta ply oll fave varses, ya dooface* – !

– *Trew-mayun! Ah ain't finished! Leggo* – !

Mordecai hee-hee-ed; his merry men snickered. Averil lost her guard over the tape because she was doubled over laughing. I reached to shut it off, my face hot. I was trying to smile, but I'm afraid I only managed the brave, nauseated simper of accident victims carted off on a stretcher when they don't want you to worry. That was the last time I ever apprised anyone that even as a kid I never had a Southern accent.

For Averil I'd got a blouse. It was pink, with a high neck and tie bow, a panel of lace down the front – much like my dresses when I was three. She was nicer about it than she should have been.

I had purchased Mordecai the obligatory litre of aquavit, tin of Three Castles, and cyberpunk novels, though there was something too generic about the gifts, like always getting my father aftershave. I had my theories from afar, but I didn't know Mordecai very well in an ordinary way. After ten minutes of chatting with him like anyone else, I'd have discovered what movies he liked to and whether he still read science fiction. When other people talked to members of my family, I'd often been amazed by how much they found out that I didn't know.

In exchange, Mordecai delivered me a small unwrapped vial, with speaker wire for a ribbon.

'The texture –' he leered '– is just like spit.'

It was sexual lubricant. Truman examined my present with a scowl; later he would remark that it was typical of Mordecai to give me something 'literally slimy.'

'This is a Gift of the Magi, Mordecai,' I said. 'I don't have a boyfriend.'

'We'll see what we can do about that,' said Mordecai. I scanned the trio on offer and wondered if they were part of my Christmas present.

I was looking forward to Truman unwrapping his hefty pile, all taped up in the *News and Observer*. I'd considered getting him some books on architecture, but that idea seemed staid. Things had been so ponderous around our house that I thought we needed to lighten up. By the time he opened the first package I realized the gifts would not be received in the spirit I'd intended.

'Well, well,' he said, his voice grey. 'Pick-up Stix.'

I had gone to Toys-R-Us and discovered that, amid the computer games and battery-operated doohickeys that did all your playing for you, many of the classic amusements we'd grown up with were still for sale. I got so caught up in my own reminiscence that I went a little over the top: Matchbox cars, Lego, Tiddly-Winks. I'd had a wonderful time and frankly spent a fortune. Yet as Truman dutifully shredded off the newspaper, revealed a box of coloured plasticine, and went, 'Huh,' I wished he'd hurry up and get this over with.

All right, so he took the presents as an insult, as if I still thought of him as a little boy, an impression the more distressing with Mordecai looking on. But the toys may have rung off-key on a deeper level. Having meant to trigger his nostalgia, I may have roused his memory instead, which is not the same thing by a yard.

For inevitably the Risk set would have recalled that it was a game Truman never won; the imperialists of his family had amassed great armies on his borders, which were inevitably overrun. Clue would have revived his rage at my record-keeping 'system' – after I'd guessed Professor Plum in the library with the candlestick, Truman would ball my scorecard of hieroglyphic triangles into the fire. Monopoly would merely remind him of my helpful advice that every property he landed on was too dear for the rent, leaving me owning the entire board and Truman with Go money. Perhaps he imagined the Lego blocks would be the usual motley mismatch of the corner pieces left over from my own three-storey hulk that had consumed all the windows. That Matchbox sedan would be his first, at thirty-one, in good nick – for when we'd built elaborate cities in the backyard I would get the convertible whose top went up and down, and Truman would drive the convertible only when the top had jammed or the door had been pulled off. As for that adorable stuffed gorilla, I wonder if Truman still expected me to mash its mouth and bulge out its eyes until the creature looked so deranged that he'd be afraid to take it to bed.

'Oh, yeah,' said Truman, his voice in a dying fall. 'The same fire truck.'

'It came to the rescue when we played Volcano, remember?'

Truman's head bobbled, like a plastic dog's in a car's rear window.

'We'd build a mountain in the sandbox,' I explained to Averil, speaking quickly and smiling too much, 'with houses and trolls and trucks. But the mound was constructed around the garden hose, and when the city was completed we turned on the water. It took a little while, but eventually whole sides cracked off and there went the neighbourhood. We got much more fun out of tearing things apart than putting them together.'

Truman sounded fatigued. 'All children are like that, Corlis.'

Mordecai, who I'd have expected to find my presents either dopey or equally evocative of an unsavoury past (we'd never played board games with him, since if he didn't win he'd fling the Chance cards all over the room and we'd be weeks finding them), crawled on to the floor and built a double helix with Tinker Toys. I wondered if he'd have preferred the tiddly-winks to cyberpunk, as he and Big Dave then scrambled on all fours popping bright plastic discs exuberantly among the needle droppings. To watch his mesmerized ching-chinging of the Slinky, you'd think Mordecai had never played with toys before.

In a way, he hadn't. His only resort when I deserted his wagon had been to withdraw to his famous precocity. He disdained our muddy fire engine rescues for his crackling Jacob's ladder in the basement – Mordecai had been in one basement or another for most of his life. Maybe he thought that this Christmas, as he and MK fashioned lewd plasticine figurines with outsized phalluses, we were at last including him in the games he once pooh-poohed but must also have envied.

Truman thanked me with a peck on the cheek, and tramped off to baste the turkey. Like the racoons he trapped, the roast was a helpless little animal and he felt sorry for it.

When Truman returned Mordecai said he'd brought a bottle of champagne for Christmas, and Truman said, 'A whole bottle?' deadpan. Absorbed in his rapid progress with the Rubik's cube, Mordecai gave Truman instructions where to find the champagne in the back of his army truck so we could start it chilling.

Before he trudged out the door Truman asked, 'You want to *time* me?'

Mordecai didn't seem to get the reference, but I did. When Troom was small we were always making him go fetch – crackers, Coke, especially anything to which we weren't supposed to help ourselves so if caught the youngest would get in trouble. 'I'm not your swave!' he might protest, at which point Mordecai would offer craftily, 'We'll *time* you.' Truman would race off for ginger snaps and tear back again; Mordecai would declare, 'Forty-three seconds!' Later, if we wanted a sandwich: 'We'll *time* you.' It worked without fail.

When Truman bustled back into the house his face had paled a shade, and he whispered to his wife furiously; something was up.

Truman composed himself and announced in that woeful tone of his that my own present was out back and I would have to put on a blindfold – no peeking. I taped a holly napkin around my eyes. He took my hand and guided me through the back door and across the porch, until I recognized the hollower resonance of the carriage house platform. I stumbled up its rear stairs to the door on its second floor, which Truman had stolidly refused to unlock for three weeks. Then I heard a click, and 'We Wish You a Merry Christmas!' boomed in his own hearty baritone from speakers in front of me.

'You can take it off now.'

The light was bright, since someone had finally replaced the shorted overhead socket. As my eyes adjusted, I noticed the big room was cleared of broken rockers and withered forsythia, and repainted white including the floor. The tacked-tin sink was no longer clogged with leaves and dead crickets. Along two sides were newly installed counters sealed in thick enamel. At one of these stood a high stool, before an armature board.

'Truman,' I gasped. 'What is this?'

'Your new studio,' said Truman. 'You said you wanted to move to bronze casting, so your sculptures couldn't get smashed by jealous boyfriends any more. So I bought you some wax. Did a little reading up on what you might need.'

He'd done his homework. There were three blocks of microcrystalline by a two-burner hotplate, along with a battered pot, a bag of resin chunks, some pallet knives and a coil of aluminium wire.

I walked around the studio, tracing the neatly rounded counter edges with my fingertips. I was abashed. It suddenly occurred to me how I might have felt if, instead of getting up early to paint and pound nails, Truman had bought me dollies that wet and an oven that baked add-water cakes with a light bulb. As if he knew what I was thinking, Truman quipped behind me, 'I figure you can work on sculpture while I play Volcano with my fire truck.'

I tried to say thanks, but the words stuck. What jammed in my throat was not only this studio, but the brownie batches he'd cooked for my girl scout troop when I was behind in my homework, the cage he'd laboured over when I decided to raise gerbils, the bookshelves he'd built for my Chapel Hill flat. I could go on. All my life Truman had patched my punctures and carried my suitcases, and though I may have become jaded I couldn't resist the notion that some of these gestures were not because he was 'grateful' or obsequious or frightened, but because he loved me.

'You don't like it,' he said morosely.

'No –' I coughed. 'I do. It's – swell.' Lame, but since awkwardness and inadequacy are the flag of sincerity in our family, he must have known I was impressed.

'Listen –' Truman hustled me to the stairway landing. 'Is there something you need to tell me?'

'Thank you,' I remembered.

'No, is there something I don't know?'

'Sorry – ?'

His whisper was harsh as we huddled down to the back porch.

'When I went for that champagne. Mordecai's truck – it's all loaded up, Corlis.'

'So? Maybe he's got a job –'

'No, there are bags of dirty clothes, filing cabinets, a photocopier, that computer drafting rig – to the gills, Corlis, like, everything he owns is in there!'

'Troom, I haven't a clue –'

When we reached the parlour again, Mordecai was reclining in my father's chair, hands clasped over his middle, with a feline smile of having just eaten the canary. For the first time all day, he spoke directly to his brother.

'Bet you thought I forgot you, bro,' said Mordecai. 'That I didn't get you anything.'

'It wouldn't be the first time,' said Truman warily.

'Au contraire, kid. I saved the biggest box for you.' Mordecai spread his arms in benediction. 'Voilà. Erry-may Istmas-cray, O-bray. You did *finally* figure out pig Latin, didn't you?'

'I fail to get the joke,' said Truman coldly.

'That's 'cause it ain't a joke, True. I am your Christmas present.'

Bloody hell. Mordecai was moving in. That's what the peons were for, and to earn their turkey dinner the three hirelings reluctantly smashed their fags, crumpled their beer cans and ambled to the army truck in the drive. As cartons of hand tools were hefted past me and Mordecai's voice sharpened to a foreman's once more, ordering the tools to Truman's workshop, I got snippets of the story. Dix had staged a bit better than a 'snit', and though he didn't say so outright I suspect their loggerheads were over whether Mordecai would try to buy this house. She'd kicked him out of the Basement, and in the meantime he needed a place to live. He was under contract to Meredith College, so Decibelle had to relocate somewhere, right? Wasn't this a third his house, as much his as mine or Truman's, and weren't we two availing ourselves already? You couldn't argue with the legality of the situation, though more to the point you couldn't argue with Mordecai full stop. Neither Truman nor I could keep Mordecai from shifting wholesale into Heck-Andrews because he was our older brother, The Bulldozer. That was a kind of law, more binding than statute.

Poor Truman was drafted into the work crew, and his hangdog expression as he shouldered the computer down the truck's ramp was of a prisoner building his own gallows. It took three of them and a hand truck to move the hulking Rockwell tablesaw into Truman's workshop. Once the workshop was chock-full, Mordecai instructed that the lathe and standing drill be carted to my new studio. MK dragged the machine tools across the floor, scraping Truman's fresh paint job. As for the aluminium suitcases of dirty black jeans, Mordecai gave Wilcox directions, not to his adolescent hovel, but to the master bedroom. It had never occurred to Truman or I to sleep there. It had never occurred to Mordecai to sleep anywhere else.

Concerned that Truman might regard me as complicitous, I didn't lend a hand myself. I watched in the parlour as Big Dave shoved the encyclopedias back in their shelves. The spines had frayed, the pages splayed, the covers mottled. After two weeks in Mordecai's possession the Britannicas had aged fifty years. He had a similar effect on wives.

Mordecai managed to distribute at least one carton in nearly every room of the first two floors. That he steered clear of the dovecot was wise, but I suspect he was less canny than disinclined to tromp up an extra set of stairs.

Between trips to the inexhaustible troop transporter, Truman returned to the kitchen to baste. The turkey long done, he'd turned the oven down low and tented the bird with tin foil. Truman had coped through his whole childhood this way, by coddling creatures even more powerless than himself – fallen baby bluejays, fireflies in jars. As he knelt at the oven and swabbed, I wanted to advise him that what you were meant to do was find something weaker than you were and beat the shit out of it.

'I'm not hungry,' he grunted to Averil.

'You can't let him get away with this!' she whispered.

'What am I supposed to do? Huh? Just what?' He was shouting.

Mordecai sauntered in for his champagne. 'Krug,' he purred, untwisting the wire. 'Seventy-five bucks.'

Mordecai popped the cork deliberately at the ceiling and promptly put out the kitchen overhead light. He laughed, and left us in the dark.

Truman groped to his overrun workshop and fetched a torch; I held the light on the fixture as Truman climbed on the table and incrementally unscrewed the smashed bulb with needlenose pliers. 'Isn't that typical?' Truman mumbled, dodging falling glass. 'We buy all the groceries, get presents, put up a tree; he and his freeloading buddies drink up all the wine and beer in the house and what do we get? One bottle of overpriced champagne. I guess we're supposed to fall all over ourselves.'

It was eleven o'clock, so Christmas was almost over, which couldn't be soon enough for me. Truman hauled out the turkey, withered and cowering, slopped out the reheated mashed potatoes, and ripped the cling-film off the relish tray. The peas had pocked, but according to Averil they were obligatory, and I have to express some incredulity that while our house was being occupied by foreign troops she could still panic that we were short on cranberry sauce.

Mordecai hove into the dining room and hacked off a drumstick whole, dousing it with Open Pit barbecue sauce and setting to with both hands – if Truman would have made a credible antebellum gentleman, Mordecai belonged in the Middle Ages. Meanwhile, his henchmen didn't avail themselves of plates, but wrestled scraps off wings and fingered the stuffing, picking out all the chestnuts.

Alcohol was in tight supply – the beer was finished, and to my amazement our entire case of cabernet had evaporated the night before. I got one dribble of champagne, but otherwise had to rely on Mordecai's aquavit, which he doled out in parsimonious trickles while he himself slugged straight from the bottle, never releasing hold of its neck. The ABC stores were shut, and a dry dinner with dry turkey made everyone petulant.

Yet despite my irksome sobriety, I remember that night physically teetering. Once more I swayed between spheres of influence, helping Truman and Averil slice pie in the kitchen while Truman muttered that it 'didn't make any sense', if Mordecai was trying to sell this house out from under us, for the son of a bitch to move in; then gravitating to the dining room, where I tried to tease out titbits about Mordecai's altercation with his wife, and enquired tentatively – wasn't it a terrible lot of trouble moving *everything* over here if they got back together and he moved back?

'Of course not,' Mordecai scoffed. 'When you and I buy this place, I'll have to shift my crap here anyway. What's the diff?'

All right, I can be slow, but I got it. Mordecai and Dix may very well have had a fight, but I was not convinced it need have result-ed in Mordecai's every hand-drill and paperclip shipping into this house. I may not have known Mordecai so well, but he had a fair measure of me. Anyone who didn't like to make choices often made them by default. If I was already living with Truman, I could choose my prince by doing nothing. If I was living with both brothers, I would have in any case to *do* something, force one of them out. In a stroke, Mordecai had evened the score. Moreover, if Mordecai acted as if we had reached an accord when we had done no such thing, I would have to ram that absence of consensus forcibly down his throat, and Truman was not the only sibling in this house afraid of an older brother.

12

Walking in the back door two days later, I recalled the flamboyant baking projects Truman and I undertook as kids. Flour fogged in the air, chairs lay overturned, silverware spilled from the drainer. A copper bowl rocked on the floor with a new indentation the shape of Mordecai's crown. Himself was at the sink, running water over a chicken breast, then testing if it was thawed enough to slab over his eye. His hair, full of flour, had gone prematurely grey.

'You missed the show,' said Truman, emerging from the pantry with a broom.

'Who starred?' At first I assumed that with me out of the house for only an hour the two of them had gone at it tooth and nail.

'Dix Ridelle, who else?' said Truman, with the smugness of I-was-here-and-you-weren't. 'The harridan.' He began sweeping up the shards of his panda mug from the National Zoo.

'Mordecai, are you all right?'

Mordecai flinched from my hand, shielding his face with an elbow. A cut above one eyebrow was bleeding.

'Why don't you let me –'

'Leave it!' he said sharply, wadding paper towel over the eye. He shook water off the chicken breast, still stiff, and stalked out.

I said, '*What* on *earth*?' before I could stop myself. That was my mother's expression, which had been insinuating itself into my moments of alarm with ominous frequency.

'There's more,' said Truman. 'A straight-back in smithereens on the landing. That woman's got some arms.'

'What were the ructions over?'

'Money. Mordecai didn't leave her any.'

'I thought she was Decibelle's vice president – ?'

'VPs are a dime a dozen,' said Truman with authority, and I

wondered, with incredulity and even a trace of vexation, if he had talked with his own brother. '*MK* is a vice president. Dix can't sign cheques.'

I began sponging cabinets, which were glopped with crusting raw egg. 'I must say, had Mother and Father fought like this from time to time it would have done them a world of good.'

'You're not honestly saying you wish Father heaved ten pounds of flour around the kitchen on a routine basis.'

'Once in a while, yes.'

He stopped, standing the broom on its handle end. 'You admire this mess?'

'In a way,' I conceded. 'Our parents acted as if they agreed on everything. But how is that possible? Father kept her under his thumb for nearly forty years, and she never tried to wriggle out from under. She'd take it out on me, when I got big for my britches and didn't expect to become some man's secretary –'

'Except Mordecai's –'

'I wish Mother had thrown something – once.'

'Averil and I don't fling dishes. Is there something wrong with our marriage, then?'

'No, but –'

'In a good relationship you have brawls and smash furniture, according to you? That's real communication? That's love?'

'There must be nights that Averil complains one more time about raisins in the chutney, and you'd like to punch her in the gob.'

'First you're commending gross physical destruction, now wife beating. Mordecai's only been here two days, the house is already a trash heap, and he's clearly had a glorious effect on your version of the good life.'

'Never mind.' Convincing Truman that disarray had any merits whatsoever was a lost cause.

'If and when our parents did have a difference of opinion,' he said, sweeping again, 'they kept it civil and between themselves. If you imagine that makes us anything but lucky, you're pig-ignorant.'

I kept my clean-up cursory, and marched from the kitchen. I would not have my sheltered, shut-in little brother lecturing me on the harsh realities of the big bad world.

*

Within a week the discipline that gripped our household when Truman ruled Heck-Andrews fell to ruin. Sometimes I missed it: the cereal-sandwich-chicken-thighs battery, two measures of wine, a rigorous walk around the same cemetery circuit; a niggardly finger of Wild Turkey, after which we would brush our teeth and go to bed with the regimentation of children with school in the morning. Other times I recognized that life for what it was: compulsion fuelled by terror, as if with a single step off his treadmill Truman would freefall hedonistically off the deep end. He was afraid of fat, indolence, drugs, drunkenness and constipation. The strictness of his habits gave him away. He legislated against sloth and intoxication because he was so powerfully drawn to them. More than biscuits or a second bourbon, Truman was afraid of himself.

Mordecai and I discussed it more than once – how Truman was squandering his life as a milquetoast, how more than any of us three he was haunted by the stern apparition of his moralistic parents, how staying in this house dwarfed him while for Mordecai rolling joints on his mother's bureau was a victorious coming of age. Mordecai's adolescent rebellion may have seemed tawdry once we were grown – he'd stood his ground on his right to fuck, his right to get hammered – but surely the battle was the point, its pretext spurious. Maybe every generation was revolutionary or should be; maybe you were obliged by the very process of replacing it to overthrow the existing order, or surrender and so prove unworthy of its mantle. By that definition, Mordecai was my parents' only progeny who did his job, who most deserved the house and its intangible accoutrements; Mordecai was the good son, where Truman, in his very acquiescence to his elders, had remained too much of a son and therefore a rather bad one.

Mordecai took his castle by force as he'd once wrested power from our parents. He appropriated Truman's workshop, where their tools miscegenated on the same pegboard. The Hewlett-Packard laser printer and Design Jet plotter, IBM photocopier and Compaq Prolinea 4/66 high-capacity computer were installed in our sitting room, where the television whittered all night, competing with Urge Overkill pounding from the parlour. The C. S. Lewis Narnia series that Mother had read to us as children was thrown in the corner, their shelf space devoted to electronics catalogues.

Upstairs in my father's office, Mordecai squared his Toshiba laptop and Bubblejet on the big black desk and tossed the *Law Weeklies* on the floor. A length of casebooks gave way to *Doonesbury* anthologies and old *National Lampoons*. He unhooked the framed diplomas from Davidson and Harvard, masking the resultant white patches with his poster of Iron Butterfly. Burying flyspecked Supreme Court stationery, Decibelle invoice blanks gloated: 'Nothing's impossible, just expensive.'

In a matter of days, the master bedroom stiffened with crusty denim and unmatched socks; the dresser was scattered with alligator clips and grew hairy with threads of Three Castles. The room reeked of aquavit like mouldy rye. Mordecai kept the drapes pulled all day, just as he had at thirteen in the room across the hall, until leaching from under the door came the unmistakable whiff of Basement.

This sounds more unpleasant than it was, or at least to me. I liked that smell. It may have been stagnant and a little stale, but the odour was full and human and inhabited the whole second floor. The house needed inhabiting. Mordecai may have spread himself in Heck-Andrews the way he sprawled on court benches, but this was a cavernous barn of a place; Truman, Averil, and I had not been able to make enough sound here. Our steps were too timorous and made a hollow tiddle down the hall, where Mordecai's boots boomed to resonate all three storeys. The yammer of WRAL, the pulse of Nirvana, the scream of his circular saw filled a void. Mordecai wasn't shy, whereas Truman and I had lived here with post-funereal deference, as if asking permission. Mordecai had never asked permission for anything in his life, and he took Heck-Andrews like a rake who knows you never get anywhere with women by asking for a kiss.

Moreover, his three confederates never quite left. Oh, they didn't spend every night here, but no one in Mordecai's crew spent a 'night' precisely; they slept during the day. Big Dave assumed the bedroom next to mine, and I'd hear the mattress wheeze and springs squeal about the time I was getting up. Wilcox drifted sullenly in and out of Truman's old room, and kept the door shut possessively even when he was out. Since that room faced the entrance to the dovecot, I would sometimes see Truman and Wilcox emerge at the same time, to confront each other with the flat anonymity of hotel guests. MK made for

Mordecai's former nest, ploughing down the hall with a familiar side-to-side lunge. Not quite ballsy enough to plait his hair in three pigtails, he had opted for five instead. MK's aping of my brother unsettled me, for I was convinced that he didn't want to emulate Mordecai so much as to replace him.

However, if I relished the sweet funk infusing the second floor, it made Truman gag. He did have a legitimate gripe that the rooms were not self-cleaning. Wet towels left splotches on oak floorboards. Throw rugs grew lumpy with smudged Y-fronts toed out of view; the furniture fluttered with stray Bambus and cast-off foils of paracetamol, their quick-fix hangover cure of choice. Gradually we'd find ourselves short on cups and glasses, and retrieved them from the guest bedrooms, curded with soured milk and grey coffee, or sticky with J. D.

As for how the habits of our latest 'tenant in common' clashed with Truman's it is hard to know where to begin. Certainly their schedules collided, for after New Year's – an evening of merry-making that so resembled all the others that I have no distinct recollection of it – Averil went back to substitute teaching and had to get up at seven, right about the time Decibelle called it a day. And Decibelle was aptly named. With Mordecai shouting brand-name electronics, the table saw shrieking at four in the morning, all-night gospel shows chorusing from the sitting room, and Bash and Pop interminably auto-reversing in the parlour, few sugarplums danced in anyone's head. After a week of sleep deprivation, Averil acquired a vagueness whose consequent suggestion of apathy could be misconstrued. The panda rings around Truman's eyes deepened and darkened, and provided him the look of a Boris Karloff zombie who might prove murderous later in the movie.

Yet the mounting issue of groceries – not to mention drink – was at least as volatile as that of sleep. The amount of time and money we were spending to keep our new housemates fed and soused was building into a sizeable grudge, apparent by the rarity with which this resentment was voiced. Then, that is the nature of resentment, as distinct from anger – it is an emotion you can only feel if you are not doing anything about it. While Truman and I appeared pagan in comparison with our devout Protestant parents, a constraining propriety and embarrassment about money betrayed that our souls were Presbyterian.

Before Mordecai moved in, I had calculated my share of the

bills to two decimal points; my payments were prompt but bashful, since heaven forbid anyone should *ask* for my cheque. I knew that Truman had an exacting sense of justice, if not arithmetic. Well, Mordecai's sense of justice was rough at best, if not opportunistic. He did splurge – on another bottle of Krug, a side of the best smoked salmon, Haagen-Daaz liqueur that I'm afraid Truman detests, or a tiny jar of Beluga caviar whose price tag of $79.00 Mordecai left ostentatiously stuck on the box. Nevertheless, it would have meant more to us had Mordecai humbled himself to rattle a cart down the aisles of Harris Teeter and remember we were out of ketchup.

I'll grant there are oblivious people. They do not question full pantries, and if the cupboard is bare they don't question that either and somehow they don't starve. Mordecai's head was not in the clouds, however. In his work he was consumed with the cost of materials, and could quote the per-foot price of oak two-by-fours to the penny. He was not the kind of Einstein unable to deduce from the sticker that a can of tomatoes cost 89¢. He would have been aware then, perhaps with no small amount of satisfaction, that someone else had bought the loo roll every time he wiped his bum. The hint of literal brown-nosing would have pleased him.

Truman would not go back to school until 21 January, so when he was not out shopping, now a daily preoccupation, he was home during the day, studying, or pretending to study, for his upcoming courses. Naturally, he ate the same lunch every day – a ham sandwich with a third slice of Branola for extra carbs, lots of mustard and pickled banana peppers. Like all his exercises of Zen-like repetition, the sandwich both entranced and saddened me. However, keeping all these ingredients on hand in the downstairs kitchen, subject to regular 3 a.m. plundering, was nearly impossible within any 24-hour period. Truman would launch downstairs at one to find his Branola gaping open, its heels stale, the mayonnaise hours out of the fridge and toxic, and pepper juice spattering the floor.

Troom's first gambit was to stock his lunch provisions in the dovecot kitchen, but this only guaranteed that, finding the downstairs fridge absent of sandwich makings, the entire crew would tromp up his stairs, and Truman would wake to jar lid clattering and the intricate details of Meredith College's lightboards in the

169

middle of the night. They'd figured him out fast: Truman ate the same lunch every day and would therefore always have ham. By the time Truman remembered that he'd installed the means of locking them out ten years earlier, Mordecai or one of his lackeys had drawn my mother's spare from the dovecot lock and pocketed the key.

Therefore Truman's very last resort was to address the issue of sandwich makings to his brother directly.

'Mordecai,' Truman raised early that evening (breakfast), backed up against a counter and trying furiously to sound by-the-by. 'Do you, um, include lunch as part of your pay?'

Mordecai had fumbled to the freezer and poured himself a wake-me-up of aquavit. 'It's not in their contracts, if that's what you mean. But those boys work fucking hard and I figure they deserve a fucking sandwich. Gotta problem?' Mordecai was not paying much attention.

Truman retreated out of his brother's path as Mordecai nosed into the breadbox and scouted the last of another loaf of Branola. 'It's just, the ingredients, you know,' said Truman faintly, 'are adding up.'

Mordecai looked up with an expression of unutterable disdain. He hauled out his fat wallet, bulging with receipts and high denominations, and frisbeed his brother a hundred dollar bill. 'Happy?'

It fell to the floor at about the place where Truman's spare key would have dropped at my mother's feet, only this time it was Truman who stooped and mumbled thanks, his face burning.

I shook my head, marvelling. Though a hundred bucks might seem excessive for a little ham and mustard, after two solid weeks of pillage a C-note was a drop in the bucket. Still, Mordecai's contempt, coupled with the appearance of overpayment, ensured that Truman would never again ask Mordecai for lunch money as long as he lived. Was this calculated? I was beginning to concur with NC State: my older brother was a genius.

One of the horrid things about families is that they are largely about the past, but one of the pleasant things about the past is that it reprieves you from the future. Or seems to, though attended to or not the future does come romping along of its own accord. I could spend my time grieving for my sculptures or grieving for my parents, but grief as an activity doesn't fill the day. We'd finished shoving trinkets into boxes. With little to do with myself I had, for the maw between Christmas and New Year's, conceded to type up invoices for Mordecai, run his post and print out his orders. I was only allowed to work on the laptop and Bubblejet upstairs; he would not let me near his Compaq Prolinea and Design Jet plotter in the sitting room. That these hallowed toys, along with the state-of-the-art Autocad software, were worth $30,000 I probably heard at least once a day.

Even those five days in his employ had been illuminating. He'd left me far too much to my own devices; mitching would have been a doddle. I'm pretty dogged in the docking hours department, but his other henchmen, for all their 'fucking hard work', were doubtless taking advantage of similar independence. My younger brother was not the only patsy. When Mordecai explained his Lotus software, he went through the keystrokes much too fast and assumed I knew more than I did; while I was flattered he gave me so much credit, I was also relieved to find a manual among the catalogues when he was gone or I'd have been lost.

I thought I'd managed pretty well, considering Mordecai's explanations were worse than none, but then I made a mistake. I wiped out a file. He yelled at me – he'd been drinking, if that bears mention that any more – and called me a 'ditzy broad', and a 'brain-dead bimbo'. I said, well you're the one who didn't keep a bloody hard copy back-up and screw this, I quit. Typical fucking girl, said Mordecai, can't take a little flak, one sharp word and it's I quit – what a fucking baby. All of Mordecai's wives had been employed by Decibelle at one time or another, and fired at one time or another, or that's what Mordecai said but no doubt they walked out, as they also walked out of his life. On his payroll I was in perilously familiar territory, his and mine.

Licking Mordecai's envelopes I'd felt so like my meek mother and her lowly tending to the great man's needs, that a few days into January I got a job at a framing shop in Crabtree Valley. It was shit work that paid less per hour than Mordecai did, and pretty depressing. I was pained to see people spend all that money to gilt-edge wide-eyed kittycats, under-exposed sunsets, and weeping Christs on velvet, but at least Frames got me out of the house.

Alas, nine-to-five was the least strenuous segment of the day – when Decibelle slept, Truman burrowed in philosophy texts, and

Averil was at work. It wasn't as if I, like Truman, couldn't bear it when Mordecai awoke, rankled by his presence in our house. No, I liked having my older brother home at last, and I was happy to make him syrupy black coffee and perch on the outside rail of the carriage house as sawdust billowed out the door and swirled in the floodlights. Mordecai would chat to me about 'strange attractors', monologues that didn't require much more than *uh-huh* and my mind could graze.

What I could *not* bear was being stretched on a rack between the first and third floors. The longer I spent on the porch, the more vigorously I would later have to thaw Truman's icy demeanour in the dovecot afterwards. The longer I spent in the dovecot, the more snippy remarks I would be obliged to make about Truman the next time I perched on Mordecai's rail. The whole cycle of conspiracy, abandonment and placation made me feel despicable. I was beginning to wonder if rather than be the lucky one in the triangle, the privileged middle member whose attentions were so coveted, I was instead the victim and pawn. Worse still, they both liked to ruminate about what life would be like 'after partition', when each assumed he would be snugly ensconced with his sister for life.

Therefore, having squandered the peaceable hours of our household's day conferring with old ladies about which frame best picked up the lovely fleck of green in their pooches' eyes, at the beginning of my second week of work I returned home at six for the agonizing half-hour when both brothers were in the same kitchen. I burst in acting falsely effervescent – just like my mother – telling stories to neither in particular while they kept their backs to each other. Truman was silently preparing chicken thighs while Mordecai groped half-blind and just out of bed to the freezer for aquavit. Fortified, Mordecai mounded so much coffee into a filter that there was no room in the cone for hot water. I assumed Truman was making that horrible splatting sound by hurling skin in the sink because he'd bought that pound of French Roast two days ago and it was already shot.

Then I found the *Raleigh Times* on the table, open to the real estate section with an advert circled in red marker:

SALE AT AUCTION – Judicial partition. Grand Reconstruction mansion at 309 Blount Street, Oakwood, Raleigh. Three

storeys; seven bedrooms, plus separate apartment. Assessed
valuation $410,000; minimum bid $250,000. Bids taken
February 5, 1993, 9 a.m., Jaycees Center, Room 112. To view,
contact owners at (919) 828-5292.

'Wonderful,' I muttered.

'We got a couple of calls today,' said Truman, 'from our new little friends.'

His tone was smouldering. He was yanking skin off the chicken
thighs like Crazy Horse scalping Custer's soldiers.

'What did you tell them?' I asked.

'To go stuff themselves,' said Truman.

'You didn't,' I said.

'All right, I didn't. But I didn't suck up to them and act all
grateful that somebody was willing to buy my own house from
under my feet. I told them the place was a wreck –' He cut his
eyes towards Mordecai, whose few tablespoons of hot water had
indeed failed to trickle through the filter. Mordecai poured in
more water anyway; the cone tipped off the thermos and spewed
its moist grounds like diarrhoea all over the floor.

'– Which it *is*,' Truman finished.

Mordecai glanced at his brother and the coffee sludge with
equal boredom, settled for one more shot of aquavit, and walked
out.

'One of the callers,' Truman grumbled, his eyes narrowing after
his brother, 'was *Japanese*.'

'So?' I asked from the floor. The coffee muck rapidly demoted
our new sponge from *special* to *perfectly good*.

'First they're buying Rockefeller Center, now my house. Fiftieth
anniversary of Pearl Harbor's barely over, and for all their gosh-
we're-sorry they've figured out a much sneakier way of taking
over this country. Sell us Nissans and use the profits to buy this
place up. You see them in Oakwood in droves, you know. Taking
those Capital City Trail tours of all the old houses, clicking away?
They love this neighbourhood. Sushi's old hat. They want buffalo
wings and hush puppies. They wear Caterpillar Tractor caps and
say "ya'll" and titter behind their hands. I've heard them. They
collect out on Blount Street and ogle our house and sometimes
they knock and want to look around, as if we're some sort of state
museum, and now, I suppose, I've got to let them inside.'

'In that the Japanese are also known as inveterate racists,' I said sharply, squeezing out the sponge, 'I guess they'd fit into this neighbourhood just fine.'

My father would turn in his grave. If his public exhortations to tolerance held little sway with his children, his private intolerance of any infringement on his convenience had passed to the next generation perfectly intact.

I had dinner with Truman and Averil, though we couldn't hear one another over the din from the back porch, which Mordecai was using for an impromptu sawhorse. We'd only discovered that his rotary saw had completely severed two floorboards the week before when Truman's foot crashed through to the ground. Mordecai had been in residence not three weeks, and he'd already clawed a four-foot scrape down the mahogany panelling of the foyer while hand trucking the Compaq Prolinea to the sitting room, put out one of the carriage house windows when angling a two-by-six on to his table saw, and shattered a balustrade in a fall when staggering up to bed. It was hard to resist the notion that Mordecai wanted possession of his inheritance largely to be able to destroy it.

While Averil cleaned the kitchen, I joined Truman for tea (there was no more coffee) in the dovecot, where they barricaded themselves against Mordecai most evenings as they once had against my mother. I'd have expected the usual impotent rage in response to the advert. Instead I found Truman sobered, philosophical.

'Something isn't adding up, Corlis,' he said, staring into his tea as if trying to read the leaves. 'Mordecai wants his money, right? But we made him an offer and he turned it down. He didn't try to get us to go higher, he took us right to court. I understand he likes to throw his weight around, but that suit was a lot of bother. Then he moves in here. With the house going on the market. He lugged in all that heavy equipment which next month he'll have to drag out again. And with the minimum bid set at two-fifty, he runs the risk of the house going for less than the appraisal; if those Japanese are tightwads, you and I may be able to scarf up our own house at a bargain. Nothing he's done seems logical to me. He's supposed to be so smart. What's going on? Or has he really taken too many drugs?'

I knew I should play dumb, but couldn't stop myself. 'Have

you ever thought that Mordecai might feel shut out of our family? A little cheated? He left here at fourteen – he seemed so towering to us then, but he was just a kid. And on the rare times he visited, he had to play the big man. Mordecai barely had a childhood, barely had a family. So he concocts an excuse to come back home.'

'What, he's trying at long last to get close to his brother? He would say more to a dog.'

I thought I would burst. I was dying to tell Truman that Mordecai wanted the house for himself, if only so we could brood over why. 'He wants something. I doubt he's quite sure what it is or how to get it. Maybe that's why his moving in seems so irrational.'

'It's not so confusing, what he wants,' Truman countered. 'He wants you.'

I pretended to take a sip from my tea, but it was gone. 'Come on.'

'Think I haven't noticed, how he asks you out to dinner and gets you to fix him a sandwich and print his invoices? He wants you to hang out by the carriage house, *my* workshop, and treats you to his perpetual yammer about chaos theory –'

'He's separated from his wife, don't you think he gets lonely?'

'CORRIE LOU!' bellowed up the stairs.

I stood up.

'You always scurry when he calls.'

'Don't I scurry when you call?'

'I don't call.'

Funnily enough, Truman was right. He never summoned me, as he hadn't begged for my companionship when he was four. He presented himself, to be played with, or not. His only solicitation had been to look forlorn.

'I'll go see what he wants,' I said.

'I've made an appointment with a banker,' Truman said behind me, 'to finance a mortgage. Next Tuesday, the nineteenth, at three. Make arrangements to take time off work, Corlis. The auction's just over three weeks away. Be there.'

For once: a summons.

13

My presence had been commanded because one of Mordecai's braids had come unclipped, and waist-long hair was flying free – a hazard around machinery. Mordecai asked while I was at it would I reweave all three pigtails; this used to be Dix's job, and he didn't know how to do that nifty plaiting across the scalp. I sat him down in the kitchen and untwisted his hair, combing it out until the crimps lifted into a thick messianic ripple. I'd rarely seen Mordecai with his hair down, and I took longer than I needed teasing out snarls. The cascade was so wild and lustrous unbound, suggesting there was something in Mordecai himself that was too tightly wrapped and yearned for open air.

If Mordecai had been courting my company of late, he didn't know what to do with it when he got it. He was more in his element holding forth to groups. Maybe he fought with his wives because screaming and smashing furniture was the only mode he had mastered one-to-one. As I combed down his back, he reached for the *News and Observer*, and lit on Bush's declaration that American forces would definitely be out of Somalia by March. 'Man, this reads like a Christmas wish list! Somebody should tell Georgie it's January ...'

Mordecai's theatrical ridicule would have passed for conversation with a larger audience, but came off as nervous prattle with his sister. The majority of his discourse consisted of either harangues, or set-pieces that might have been lifted wholesale from a Britannica entry; Mordecai talked a lot and communicated almost nothing. He must have felt desolate, trapped in an echo chamber where he could only hear his own voice, a chorus that surely rang hollow to Mordecai himself. You'd think it inevitable such a man would begin to conclude that talking didn't work.

He never mentioned his marriage. He didn't discuss how he

felt about his parents' deaths. Though I'd heard from Big Dave that Decibelle's balance sheet was increasingly bloody, Mordecai never said thing-one about his finances either. As he'd tell my parents about his imminent successes and never allude to a single failure, he allowed himself two emotions in public view: pride and disdain.

Gathering the first three strands of the left braid, I was staggered at how hard it was to ask a simple personal question. 'Mordecai – do you miss your wife?'

'Of course I do,' he said gruffly. 'What do you think I am?'

Ah. So we were to dismiss his finer feelings as self-evident, in the interests of discussing the less obvious foibles of American foreign policy.

'And what about Mother and Father?' I experimented. 'Do you miss them as well? Or not?'

That got him. This answer, for Mordecai, was not beyond dispute. As I finished weaving the scalp and proceeded to the main braid. He said nothing.

'If I died,' he asked at last, 'do you think they would have missed me?'

Typically, he would boomerang the question to himself. 'For twenty-five years, you made yourself so scarce that you may as well have been dead. In a way, they wouldn't have been able to tell the difference.'

'You mean no.'

'I don't,' I insisted. 'I think they'd have both been awfully upset. But I also think,' I added, since there was no use in glossing over, 'that, well, especially Father would have been surprised at that. At his sense of loss. Shocked, even.' I fixed the end with an alligator clip. 'But you didn't answer my question. Do you miss them?'

He said with a sigh, 'Shit, I did all my missing while they were alive.' He turned his head, seeking my eyes, and I lost the threads of his right braid and would have to start again. 'It wasn't easy, fending for myself at fourteen, you know that? And they disowned me.'

'Oh, they did not –'

They disowned me.

In the wake of his vehemence, I physically stepped back.

'They were ashamed of me,' he went on bitterly. 'I didn't have a law degree from Harvard. I'm the grubbing capitalist, right? Well, Father passing judgements from on high was the one with his head in the ozone. Money makes this country tick. Without people like me the great state of North Carolina wouldn't have had the tax base to pay him to flaunt his ideals in his big black robe –'

I was losing him. I tugged sharply on a strand to reign him in.

'Say you miss them,' I whispered in his ear. 'Say you remember Father going bananas when his typewriter ribbon jammed, banging around his study shouting "I'll be swiggered!" and that makes you smile. And Mother could sing, couldn't she? She had a gorgeous voice –'

He laughed a little, and for once it was not a snicker. 'She had a gorgeous body, fuck the voice.'

'Yes. She was beautiful. She sang you to sleep – "Day is Done" or "Grandfather's Clock" and though you were nodding off you would beg her, beg her for another. And she made wonderful pie.'

'All right, all right!' He raised his hands in surrender. 'I do, I –'

When Truman and Averil walked in at that moment I could have kicked them.

Then, it was eleven o'clock, and time for grapefruit, one of the key elements in Truman's anti-constipation programme. Mordecai shied at my hand, complaining the right braid was too tight, would I do it again. Before I resumed, he launched to the pantry and returned to the table with a bottle of Lindemann's shiraz. Truman's eyes followed the wine while he stooped at the open refrigerator, whose light glinted in his pupils with a cold blue tint.

'Like I said, Core,' Mordecai boistered, cutting the lead foil with his Swiss Army knife. 'There's no fucking way the US gets out of that mudhole in *six weeks*. It's a cinch to step in dogshit, a lot harder to get it off your shoe.'

Frankly, I was a little mystified how Mordecai was aware we'd invaded Somalia. I had never seen him actually read a newspaper, merely declaim over it. He tuned the TV to Oprah rather than to MacNeil-Lehrer. The only texts I'd seen him devour since he moved in were a Zap comic and the 1993 Blaupunkt catalogue. For all his references to Kafka and Nietzsche, I'd never seen him open a book, and I suspected his familiarity with these writers was derived from Junior High, when he would carry *Thus Spake*

Zarathustra through the halls of Leroy Martin to impress his teachers. Yet since his information did not entirely date back to the Johnson administration, he must have read something some time – he was like one of those obese people you never see eat. I pictured him holed up in a closet with a torch over *The Economist*, because if Mordecai imbibed information he didn't want to be caught at it, much as my mother claimed he would never allow himself to be seen sleeping in his crib, but would pull himself up on the rails wide-eyed and weaving as soon as the nursery door cracked open.

Popping the cork for emphasis, Mordecai was paralleling Somalia with Vietnam. If the comparison was none too novel, it did provide another pretext for reminding Truman that he was from a less tested, if not trivial generation. My mother had been determined to blame her first-born's 'disturbance' on the Vietnam War, but I was never persuaded. True, Mordecai's draft number was in the early twenties, but by the time he turned eighteen it was mid-'72 and the war was winding down. That he was never forced to flee romantically to Canada seemed the source of both his relief and his regret. In my view, the stress in Mordecai's adolescence wasn't the turmoil of the Sixties so much as the anxiety of nearly missing out on them. Mordecai had played the geeky egghead mascot for the hip Chapel Hill crowd, popping tabs of acid in the back of vans and extemporizing on the theory of relativity in garrulous detail that before you're old enough to drive is rather sweet. If this is not too great a leap, I believe his wait-for-me experience at fifteen explained why I was still braiding his waist-long hair. There's nothing like lingering on the fringe of a movement to make an enthusiast for life. It's the last-minute add-on at the end of a guest list who is sure to show up at a party first and leave last, as if he senses how close he came to not being invited at all. Most of the slightly older ex-hippies I knew had flat-tops and horn-rims and MBAs. They voted Republican, parroted Milton Friedman, and sat transfixed by CNN all through the Gulf War, cheering and raising beers when Patriots intercepted Scuds as if they were watching the Brooklyn Bridge Fourth of July fireworks.

'Mark my words,' Mordecai proclaimed, gulping half a glass of shiraz in a swallow. 'Those marines will end up whacking twelve-year-olds in technicals and look like child-killers.'

He drained his glass. That was our last bottle.

'The United States had no choice,' said Truman, clawing at his grapefruit peel while eyeing the demise of our wine. 'Popular support for intervention –'

'Was trumped up by a load of damp-eyed journalists hungry for another we-gotta-do-something poor-dumb-nigger story.'

Another glass; that bottle cost nine dollars.

'But those poor people were starving!' peeped Averil.

Mordecai didn't turn his head.

Truman's hands were dripping with grapefruit juice. 'The operation has succeeded in getting food to –'

'Pull out and the bastards will be right back at it,' Mordecai overrode. 'Didn't those bloodthirsty funks bring the famine on themselves? There wasn't a drought or a plague of locusts, was there? They were just so busy mowing each other down with AKs that nobody bothered to plant crops. Why garden when you can act in your very own spaghetti western?'

'The people who were starving,' Truman submitted doggedly, 'weren't necessarily the people who deserved –'

'Somalis,' Mordecai cut him off, 'are assholes. They all – deserve – to die!'

The Sweeney Todd refrain was off-key, but I laughed. Truman shot me a look as if I were an effigy of Guy Fawkes he personally planned to torch. Nodding at the depleted shiraz, he muttered, 'You'd think that Mordecai of all people would support the doctrine of overwhelming force.'

Now that Truman had finished peeling his grapefruit and removed every trace of membrane, Mordecai polished off several segments. The muscles in Truman's jaw began to pop.

'It's a question of national sovereignty,' said Truman, leaning back from his plate as if no longer interested in his citrus once Mordecai had touched it. 'Do you let societies do whatever they like to their own people as long as it's within national boundaries? Or when human rights are being sufficiently violated do you have a moral imperative to intrude? In some ways it's analogous to cases of domestic violence.'

With Truman doing isometrics with his grapefruit peel until my eyes were stinging from its spray, mention of domestic violence made me edgy. But Mordecai was oblivious to the set of Truman's jaw, and slurped down his second glass of vino.

'Intervention has diddly to do with national sovereignty, True, it has to do with money like everything has to do with money. Cold War's over, kid, and the United States can't afford to be every barefoot country's mom. At the very least you've gotta do the job right, so if we go into Somalia we're obliged to take over the whole shebang and cobble together a new government. That takes years and moolah and who wants that shit-hole for the fifty-first state? Fine, human rights, all very worthy, but justice is expensive, and we've got our own problems. Fucking downtown Raleigh is a shambles, Belks closing, jigaboos shooting scag on every corner? I say, let Somalia rot in its own stinking pit. Let them shoot each other until there's not a Somali left standing and then the problem takes care of itself and we can fund urban transit and health care in the U. S. of fucking A.'

Yet another champion of the downtrodden for whom my father could take credit.

'What do *you* think of intervention in Somalia?' Truman charged me as I combed out Mordecai's unwoven middle hair.

Truman didn't give a toss what I thought about Somalia. He wanted to know whose side I was on and why I was braiding that wanker's hair. I walked a diplomatic middle line: 'Bush's last bid for nobility as a lame duck. Or maybe he's hoping to hand Clinton a headache, a little welcome-to-the-White-House present, like a whoopie cushion.'

Truman wouldn't let me get away with it. 'That was a political analysis. What about a moral one? Would you go in to stop the famine, Corlis? Or not?'

'Me, personally? Of course not. We've had this discussion, Truman – I'm not benevolent.'

'*Father* would have approved of intervention,' said Truman slyly.

'Maybe after a lot of backwards-and-forwardsing, but he wouldn't have been gormless about it. He wasn't simple.'

'Like me?'

I merely sighed. Before I began the last braid, Mordecai ranged to the fridge and browsed the groceries Truman had installed yet again that afternoon.

'Food aid is disastrous anyway,' Mordecai declared into the ice box. 'Creates a dependency economy; local markets dry up. Ethiopia's turned permanent panhandler, eighty per cent fed by the WFP.' Having picked through the upper shelves, he returned with an unopened camembert, neatly crated like a Red Cross air-drop.

Truman stared at the box. A vein on each temple had risen and was pulsing a vivid blue. He didn't eat a lot of cheese (it was greasy and constipating) but did allow himself a morsel before dinner with his wine, and I dare say that one wheel would have lasted him a week – under ordinary circumstances.

No such luck. Mordecai unwrapped the velvety white puck on to the table and stabbed the rind with a table knife. When the ripe inside spilled on to the wood, he smeared it up with a moistened finger, then sucked the cheese from under his yellowed nail. In about sixty more seconds he had dispatched a third of the wheel.

'That's my cheese.'

I looked around to see who had said that. I didn't recognize the voice, which was deep and low and horribly controlled.

'What did you say?' Mordecai's knife froze over his next wedge.

Truman cleared his throat. 'I said, that's my cheese.'

'Oh, right,' said Mordecai. He glanced at his brother as if Truman were crazy. But also as if he were dangerous.

Maybe it seems bonkers, Troom popping up with 'that's my cheese' all of a sudden, but I had some insight at the time. If I may avoid clichés about straws and camels, we had read a book as children called *The Boy Who Swallowed the Sea*, about a kid who could suck the ocean into his mouth, leaving fish flopping on the sea floor so that his friend could run about collecting the catch into a sack. The boy warned his friend that he could only hold in the ocean for so long. His friend paid no heed, and kept stuffing his sack until finally the boy could no longer contain the water inside his cheeks. I don't remember the ending too well besides that the friend was drowned, but I picture at first a little dribble down the boy's chin, just like 'That's my cheese' burbled out of Truman, before the sea of his indignation spewed over Heck-Andrews and consumed his brother.

Truman himself may have had no idea why the camembert in particular oozed from the ocean of impositions he had swallowed – all the pilfered cases of wine and sandwiches and leftover chicken. The trouble was, conventions between people are established overnight. Maybe if we'd told Mordecai the very first time he reached into our refrigerator that he wasn't to filch food he didn't buy, he'd have made the odd trip to Harris Teeter himself, though I find that hard to imagine, both Mordecai in Harris Teeter at all and Truman or I saying any such thing without being pushed to the absolute limit. Yet furtive presumption becomes unabashed presumption in no time; privileges advance to rights.

Though side-eyeing Truman as if the boy had lost his marbles, Mordecai also took the mauled cheese and *wrapped it up* in clingfilm and *put it away* in the refrigerator, which was collectively on a par with Helen Keller folding her napkin. Truman took a sip of Mordecai's third glass of wine. Mordecai didn't reach for it again; Truman moved the glass to his place. In fact, Mordecai absented himself after I hurriedly finished plaiting his third braid. It hung crooked for the rest of the night, like a question mark – quizzical, perplexed.

The following Saturday our first prospective buyers came to view the house. At first I worried for George and Magnolia Johnson, since all week Truman had been practising his rudeness for their tour. At least we needn't strew towels through the house and leave food on the floor, as we had for Tom Wheeler – we had Mordecai.

I don't know if Truman would have been able to pull off a frosty demeanour; he was naturally too decent. In any case, when we opened the door a cold shoulder was abruptly out of the question. The Johnsons were black.

When we were young, a good proportion of the discrimination cases our father handled involved housing – black families trying to purchase property in solid white neighbourhoods would find their bids turned down and the houses hurriedly sold to white couples. It didn't take much digging to discover that in many instances the new owners had underbid the black buyers and still got the house. These flagrant civil rights violations in Raleigh were largely a thing of the past, but subtler practices like accepting a higher bid without giving the black buyer a chance to return a better offer or realtors simply not showing certain properties to black buyers were still not unheard of. Truman might rail against the slopes or Mordecai write off bongos in Africa, but our father had made marginal headway with his children, and with blacks at the door we were all smiles.

Magnolia Johnson was a tall, elegant woman with spindly legs and a remote, collected manner; when Truman shook her narrow hand he crushed it. Her husband George was round-faced and robust; yet his two-jaw smile gleamed with a funny conditionality, as if his glad-handing could turn on a dime. They were both better dressed, I think, than even most well-off whites would have been for a Saturday afternoon real estate foray – Magnolia was wearing a green raw silk suit, tasteful accents of gold jewellery and a sable coat. George's three-piece was tailored to smooth his paunch, and when we shook I noticed his chunky watch was spinning with extra dials. That his tie was of Ghanaian kente cloth had a bit of an in-your-face quality, though George had hardly arrived in a dashiki.

They were polite but never gushy – they weren't Toms. This part of the country may have come a long way since 1964, but when we opened that door the Johnsons knew very well we were thinking, *Oh, fuck, they're black,* and we knew they were thinking, *That's right, what of it – welcome to the New South, too bad, and watch yourselves, we know the law.* Their having rocked up at the McCreas, this subtext was more convoluted still, since Truman and I felt compelled to insinuate *you don't understand! We're on your side! Our father was a renowned civil rights advocate!* Though somehow from the straight-backed bearing of this couple I suspected we would simply inspire, *so what, do you want us to kiss your feet or something*? and we would only dig ourselves in a hole.

Therefore, when George mentioned in his introductions that he was a lawyer, Truman commented, 'Is that right? You must have known our father, then.'

'Who might that be?'

'McCrea, of course. Sturges McCrea.' Truman looked expectant.

George's face remained blank. 'I'm sorry, I –'

'Sturges Harcourt McCrea,' Truman insisted.

'Nope,' said George firmly. 'Can't say I had the pleasure. He was – ?'

'Another lawyer,' said Truman, deflating. 'Never mind.'

The only thing that got up Truman's nose more than all the people he met who remembered his father was meeting someone who didn't.

'You and your wife the owners?' asked George as Truman led them to the parlour.

'Sister. With one other brother,' said Truman, 'and the ACLU.'

The Johnsons didn't pick up on this. So much for making points as heart-in-the-right-place white folk.

Where before we'd been grateful for scattered drinks glasses, smelly socks and stale, overflowing ashtrays, now the shambles embarrassed us. 'Sorry about the mess,' said Truman. 'My brother's a slob.'

They were duly admiring of the architecture, and Truman warmed. 'This house has a long history of lawyers,' he narrated. 'It was designed in 1872 by G. S. H. Appleget – I've got a picture of him framed upstairs. Carpetbagger, probably got the land for a song, but he was at least good at his job. Designed four other houses in the neighbourhood, but this one's the most magnificent. It was built for Colonel Jonathan Heck, who was a lawyer and an officer, I'm afraid, on the wrong side of the war – what can you do, this is North Carolina. The Heck family sold to A. B. Andrews, another Raleigh lawyer, in 1916, and that's where the house gets its name.'

Truman had a future on the Capital City Trail. When we reached the kitchen, Magnolia exclaimed, 'Oh, dear, we'd have to do *this* over, wouldn't we?'

With a shudder, I had a vision of this room lost to the Johnsons at auction, our criss-crossed wood and tacked-tin counters slapped over with spotless white Formica, the loyal yellowed porcelain sink lost to stainless steel with a disposal; the funky ash cabinets scrapped for walnut veneer with spring closures, the oak floor glued over with E-Z-Kleen lino. A lot of cold classy equipment, sleek low-slung kettles from Conran's and avant-garde tableware whose spoons you couldn't tell from the forks. The Johnsons wouldn't be nostalgic about Reconstruction.

When they ducked into the carriage house, Magnolia supposed she'd return the outbuilding to servants' quarters. I sensed a taste for turned tables; I bet Magnolia's maid would be white.

Truman led them upstairs, and apologized that people were sleeping in four of the bedrooms (it was only 3 p.m.), but we might peek inside. When she ducked her head into the master bedroom, Magnolia cried, 'Pee-yew!' and held her nose.

Gracious as he'd become, Truman must have got nervous about doing too fine a sell, since on the way to the dovecot he tried to put them off with Gladys Perry.

'When my parents bought this house it was pretty run down, and I don't think it's ever quite recovered. Gladys Perry was the last owner, some really ancient creature who wore scads of talcum powder; neighbourhood kids thought she was a ghost. She lived by herself and was obsessed with saving money. She became a virtual homeless person in her own house – collecting huge black garbage bags full of you-didn't-want-to-know. The family across North Street say they'd see her shifting these bags back and forth all day; they worried she didn't feed herself, and sometimes left her covered dishes on the porch.

'Anyway,' he went on, I think to distract them from his beloved dovecot, by which they seemed altogether too charmed, 'one day no one had seen her for a while, and a neighbour called the cops. The police had to break in, and they could hardly move, the place was so cram-full of bags. When they cleared a tunnel to the second floor they found Gladys in bed with frostbite. She'd been too stingy to turn on the heat –'

'Mother didn't keep the thermostat much higher,' I intruded. I'd always had Gladys Perry in the back of my mind as an image of my mother ageing without Truman to take care of her, getting scattier and cheaper and storing international bric-a-brac in big black bags.

'The state stuck Gladys in a nursing home, and finally she agreed to sell to my father. I was only two at the time, but he says clearing out those bags was a horror show. The whole place was knee-deep in talcum powder. He never forgave this house for that operation. The smell took *ages* to dissipate,' he stressed, maybe suggesting that the master bedroom would reek of aquavit and Three Castles for a long time to come.

'We'd have to cut some skylights,' Magnolia reflected.

'Oh, no,' said Truman. 'You wouldn't want to do that. The architecture –'

'At least four, I think. The way you've done this up is quaint, isn't it? But I think we'd knock out these two walls. And the paper is terribly old-fashioned.'

Truman looked mournfully at the hunting scene whose panels he had painstakingly lined up so the hounds had tails.

Back downstairs, Magnolia conferred with her husband, but didn't seem to mind if we could hear. 'It would have to be gutted and revamped from the ground up. But the shell has possibilities, George. Nairobi would just adore that little tower deck.'

Truman watched them climb into their Mercedes and whispered, 'House hunters from hell.'

None of the other parties were black, so we didn't have to be nice to them. The novelty of these tourists wore off, and Truman developed a cursory patter, with no more discursions about Colonel Heck and the Carpetbagger. Instead he hurried them through our lives so they had to jog to keep up, barking, 'Parlour, right? Dining room, right? Kitchen, right?' until by the end they were panting.

Yet the Johnsons would not display the only gross insensitivity to our thirty years with this structure, about which we might be expected to harbour some sentiment. House-hunting is an imaginative exercise, and solely about the future; other viewers as well seemed to take a sadistic pleasure in their potential to plaster over our past. Chrome-and-glass furniture imposed alternative groupings in their eyes; I could see my parents' Indonesian batiks vanish from the walls, slap-dash abstracts popping up over the fireplace. I'd never before considered the fickle nature of property. Heck-Andrews had seemed to cling to us, but no, she would desert for a price and remember us little beyond however much we scarred her. Maybe Mordecai had the ticket after all – by gouging his hand truck down her mahogany panelling, he'd made a more permanent impression than all of Truman's TLC. If the metaphor were extended to people, the precedent was gruesome.

That night, I convened with Truman and Averil in the dovecot, and the atmosphere was like a wake. Truman rose to readjust the frames of Appleget, Heck and Andrews as if to reassert himself, treasuring the fact that Magnolia could not yet rip down his hunting scenes and knock out the back wall.

'Too bad Father didn't live to see this,' said Truman. 'Real Negroes wanting to buy his house! He'd have paid *them*.'

'Don't worry – one way or another,' I promised, 'we'll keep Heck-Andrews in this family.'

'A public auction is unnecessary and all Mordecai's fault.'

'At least the auction,' said Averil, 'sets a date by which Mordecai has to move out.'

'Maybe we're going about this all wrong,' I suggested.

'Together you, me and Mordecai own three-quarters of this house; why not share it between us? We're all living here now, aren't we?'

'You have got to be joking,' said Truman. 'This Three Bears routine is impossible.'

'It's obviously possible, Truman – we grew up together, in case you've forgotten. And history is full of awkward divisions of territory that last uncannily. Look at Ireland: a "temporary" partition put together in 1921 until they sorted out something more intelligent. No one ever got around to it. They got used to the arrangement instead. I know we've looked at these three weeks as temporary, but all over the world, the temporary becomes the permanent.'

Averil gripped the couch, her knuckles white. 'Permanent!'

'Yeah, well in Ireland they're still fighting about it,' Truman snarled.

'I never said they didn't fight about it. That's one of the things you get used to.'

'Do you *like* having all of us here?'

'Yes,' I admitted. 'But what if splitting the house three ways were the only way for you to keep it at all?'

'How could that be? You and I will take out a mortgage and buy –'

'No, what if I refuse to buy the house with you unless Mordecai is in on the deal? What if I said I won't kick my older brother out of his own house?'

It was to Truman's advantage that my kicking brothers out of houses did not come easily.

'I'd say you were out of your tree. Besides, Mordecai said he wanted his money. Are you telling me that now he wants to *stay*?'

'I'm not sure,' I hedged, 'but he seems to like it here. Don't you ever stop to think that our handing him a cheque and buying him out of the only family he has left might injure him? Just a little?'

Truman looked at me as if I had just objected that before scouring the sink with Ajax we should stop to consider the feelings of a stain. 'This is just a game to him, how much bother he can subject us to, and how completely he can take over. So far? The sitting room, Father's office, my workshop, the spare bedrooms, half your studio – he thinks he's playing Monopoly. Any day now I expect him to scrap Heck-Andrews and put up a hotel.'

'Mordecai was a pretty sore loser at board games.'

'He can't throw the pieces all over the room if he isn't in the room. We'll bid as high as we have to, and have him evicted. Bring in the cops, if need be.'

'On your own brother?'

'That's what cops are for, your own brother. As for the happy threesome idea, Corlis, no deal.'

'You're not in a position to deliver me ultimatums, Truman. Controlling interest you don't have.'

'Neither do you.'

Controlling interest was exactly what I had.

When I tripped downstairs, any giddy burn I might have felt from flexing my muscles in the dovecot was short-lived. The last thing I ever felt around Mordecai was powerful.

'Yo, Core,' he ordered. 'Fix me some java, will ya? Make it strong this time. That last pot was like camomile tea. Oh, and I almost forgot – we've got an appointment with some mortgage banker. Monday afternoon, at three. You'll have to wake me up. Bring a hammer. '

'Mordecai, I've been thinking, we've got to have a talk about all this –'

'Save it. Monday, we'll do dinner – Karen's, on me. Now, hurry up with that coffee, girl. Get a move on.'

My margin had narrowed from thin to microscopic. Rather than panic at the prospect of taking out mortgages with two different brothers on the same house, I was actually grateful that the bank appointments were on successive days and not on the same afternoon.

14

I had always got a child-like buzz out of riding in Mordecai's army truck, so high above the cars, intimidating traffic with that military roar. Commonly surly in what was to him early morning, Mordecai was forcing himself to be matey on my account. Monday was Be Nice to Corlis Day, as Tuesday would be for Truman, yet Mordecai's warmth had a cheap feel to it. I had fleeting sympathy for the rich or influential, having to suffer the synthetic, ulterior kindness of people who want something from you. On the other hand, it works. No matter how often I reminded myself that Mordecai merely needed me for the sake of this mortgage, when he effused that in portfolio photos my sculpture looked 'dynamite' I peered regally out the window and twirled my hair into an impromptu bouffant. If Mordecai ever regarded me as having a life outside full-time sisterhood I was overcome.

Though Mordecai had worn his slightly less filthy black jeans for the occasion, he'd donned the hard-hat as well, as if in all encounters with authority he expected the powers-that-be to bash him on the head. Peacenik that he had once been, Mordecai approached the least rendezvous as battle.

He pulled into the Wachovia on Hillsborough, a tiny red-brick Tudor branch that had a doll's house aspect even when we were children. The green-tinted drive-in window had been replaced with an automated teller, but otherwise this was the same bank where all three of us had started our first savings accounts with the vast five dollars we were each given on our tenth birthdays; the gifts were earmarked for Wachovia and not to be squandered on Raisinettes. The ploy succeeded with Truman and me – I have a packrat side; Truman did what he was told. However, the idea of getting Mordecai to start a savings account made me choke. The first thing he did with his passbook was pull the five dollars out.

Mordecai lifted me from my seat by the waist and swirled me to the pavement with a flourish of chivalry; maybe having sway in important matters was not overrated. He clumped ahead and held the door. I'd worn a skirt, a rather short one; as I passed, Mordecai whistled softly and said I had mighty fine legs. Ordinarily I found anything related to finance an ordeal, but I was starting to enjoy this.

A gangly man who introduced himself as Claude Richards shook hands and led us back to his office. He was one of those scrawny men who'd had a few too many chicken-fried steak specials, but the weight he'd put on had consolidated in a discrete bump above his belt and hadn't spread an ounce to his thin, indefinite face and underdeveloped limbs. He looked like a boy acting an older part in a school play with the aid of a throw pillow. I noticed a wedding band. Envisioning the woman who had singled out this nondescript from all other men and their ensuing ardour stretched my imagination beyond its capacity.

'Have a seat. You probably don't remember me, Mordecai, but we were in the same class at Leroy Martin.'

'Sure I do!' Mordecai geezed. 'Clyde Richards, what do you know. Trig, right?'

'No. Social Studies, with Mrs –'

'Townsend!'

'No, that was the fast-track class,' he said, with a trace of acid. 'Seventh grade, before they put the whiz-kids in one group. Mrs Gordon. She hated you.'

'That's because she couldn't make head or tail of my papers,' said my brother, putting his feet up on Claude's desk. 'She circled all the ten-dollar words and wrote I was using vocabulary "beyond my years" that I didn't understand. So I looked them all up in Webster's and wrote out the definitions. Took the essay to Mr Hawkins, and he made her change the grade from a C to an A. That put a chip on her shoulder the size of a pine tree.'

'Can you blame her? I remember that story – you told everyone, and made her look like a dolt to all her students.'

Mordecai was unmoved. 'She was a dolt. A dolt adult – hah-hah.'

I was rolling my interior eyes. If Mordecai wanted to ruin his chances of getting a mortgage by boasting over seventh-grade conquests, fair enough, that would simplify my life enormously.

'I don't remember seeing you at Broughton, though,' Claude noted. 'Did you go to Sanderson?'

Mordecai grinned. 'I took early retirement from the public school system. Wasn't sixteen yet, so had some shrink verify that I was nuts. Sent that poor meathead to the dictionary a few times, too. Personally helped him fill out the diagnosis: delusions of grandeur, narcissistic personality disorder, with a little paranoia thrown in for salt. It was a scream. Sort of sad when our sessions ended – I was working up my psycho deferment for the draft.'

I kissed our mortgage goodbye.

But Claude seemed intrigued to have snagged this specimen from the past in the middle of another drab banking day; he handled Mordecai with care, like an antique. 'You were the one printed that underground newspaper, weren't you? *The Butt End*. Signed, The 'Shroom.'

Mordecai raised his hands. 'You found me out, bro. So did Jesse Helms.'

An overweight, tiny-eyed J. Edgar, Helms had gone straight to the Senate from being the regular Channel 5 commentator for WRAL. Though we McCreas had our differences, Jesse Helms had long been the family scourge, on whom even Truman's antipathy would converge. Mordecai had savalged a mimeo machine from Leroy Martin's dumpster, tinkered it into working order in his basement, and used the school's own purple drum to roll out *The Butt End*: a hodgepodge of teacher-baiting, editorials on dress codes, erotic cartoons and the usual anti-war, workers-unite rant that Helms singled out in one of his TV editorials as pinko propaganda. How a grown-up television commentator came into possession of Mordecai's stapled lavender handouts, or how the man could spend five minutes of the public's time on a junior high school newspaper and still go on to assume the chairmanship of the Senate foreign relations committee, I'll never know; all I do know is that that broadcast was the highlight of Mordecai's life.

'He accused me of "fostering the festering red corpuscles of communism in the blood of the Southern young". From the nattering-nabobs-of-negativism school, but I never thought Helms had Agnew's flair. Never could figure how a clown with a room-temperature IQ got elected to the Senate even in North Carolina.'

'I voted for him,' said Claude.

Mordecai shrugged. 'Guess that's the way it happened then. Son of a bitch must be desolate without the Cold War. Thank God for school prayer.'

'Well, all those beads and bangles seem a long time ago now,' Claude submitted equably.

'No,' said Mordecai. 'They don't.'

Mordecai was right. It didn't seem long ago at all. If we had grown up in a country that was divided, it was still divided. However shifting or elusive the line between two tribes in this culture, Mordecai and Claude lived on either side of it. I hadn't a clue how we were going to get money out of the geek at this rate.

'Maybe it seems like yesterday to you –' Claude eyed Mordecai's pigtails. 'But you have to admit that at a distance all that peace and love, drugs and group sex seem pretty silly.'

Mordecai tilted his head at Claude's fuzzy short red hair and tortoiseshell spectacles. 'You don't look like you got in on much of that group sex.'

Claude laughed, and for the first time I liked him. 'Even if I did, you'd better not tell my wife. Now, let's get down to business.'

As he loaded our file on-screen, Claude was easy to picture as a teenager. In film and fiction, his era was portrayed as wall-to-wall radicals, but in truth Nixon's 'silent majority' had persisted in force – most of the girls wore saddle shoes and shaved their underarms and dabbed nail polish remover on nylon ladders; most boys never came to school without a belt and wore noxious deodorant. North Carolina's hell-no-we-won't-go brigade formed a tiny, persecuted, if sanctimonious corner in otherwise straight-laced, docile student bodies, of which Claude would have been an inconspicuous member. He made B-minuses. He believed smoking marijuana led to heroine addiction; at pep rallies, he knew all the words to the school song and nudged recalcitrants next to him who refused to stand for the national anthem. No one sent him valentines. Reminiscence about the Sixties with Claude was almost wicked; retrospective versions of his generation left him out altogether, and he was left out enough at the time.

'There's one thing that bothers me here, Mordecai,' said Claude. 'Your books and your tax filings don't square.'

'Of course they don't,' said Mordecai. 'I'm an American.' My brother had come to patriotism late in life.

'Which am I to believe?'

'I'm a businessman. You figure it out.'

'That does leave us with a rather unorthodox –'

'You're going to tell me,' said Mordecai, lighting a roll-up under the no-smoking sign, 'this is the first time you've come across discrepancies of this kind?'

Claude smiled. 'Hardly. If these books are correct, you've got quite a net turnover. Pretty impressive.'

'Damn straight,' Mordecai puffed. 'Fuck the peace armband shit, Clyde, I'm a company man now. A productive member of society. Which is more than I can say,' he added, 'for my brother.'

'Who is also a co-owner of this house, I see?'

'For now,' said Mordecai coolly. 'He plans to move out.'

'Mordecai, I –'

'He just doesn't know it yet,' Mordecai cut me off.

'So the house is up for auction in –'

'Just over two weeks. Chance we can get it for less than the appraisal, if the public competition's not too stiff.' Mordecai cocked his hard-hat, no longer The 'Shroom, but a hard-nosed good-old-boy capitalist – which is, underneath those pigtails, what he was.

'And your inventory is worth –'

'Two hundred grand. At least. But I'd like to expand. Use Blount Street for my offices, and you've a picture of the house there, it's presentable. Good location, right downtown. Plenty of those Reconstruction shells converted to commercial premises already; zoning's no problem. There's some machinery I'd like to invest in, which is why I'm asking for such a sizeable mortgage.'

'How sizeable?' I asked.

Claude turned to me. 'I thought you were a co-signer of this application.'

'Sure, she just forgot. Two-fifty, remember, Core? There's a lot of audio work in the Triangle, and I need the wherewithal to cash in. Hire a bigger crew, take on more than one contract at a time. That dough will come back in spades.'

My mouth was hanging open. 'But Mordecai,' I whispered, 'doesn't that mean I'd be responsible for – ?'

'It's a dead cert, Claude. And you know Oakwood; even if my expansion didn't pay out, that property's going to keep appreciating. Any trouble, sell the place off in a couple of years and make a wad.'

'But the whole point,' I objected, 'is to keep the house in the family –'

At last Claude paid me attention. 'Now, Ms McCrea, your source of income is – ?'

'She works for me,' Mordecai intervened.

All right, so it wouldn't help our case for me to be making $4.75 an hour at Crabtree Valley. I shut up.

'You'll also note –' Mordecai leaned forward and mashed his roll-up on his boot sole. 'My sister and I have $140,000 each, clear, inheritance from my parents. Of course we don't want to tie it all up in real estate, but the money would cover mortgage payments for the next several years. Pretty safe bet, Clyde. Offered to me, I'd take it.'

Claude rubbed his chin. 'You're pushing your luck, Mordecai,' he said appreciatively, tapping at his terminal. 'That's a fair proportion of the value of the property, but ... let's see what we could do with a 25-year term.'

As Claude entered figures into his computer, I began to panic.

'Listen, I – Mr Richards, I don't have to sign anything yet, do I?'

He shrugged. 'Of course, nothing's binding until you acquire the property. But in a public auction, you've got to have financing right up front – that is why you are here.' He looked at me as if I were *a dolt adult*.

'You'll be in touch, then, on February 5?' Claude shook hands with my brother. 'Have to say, never would have thought my bank would be lending The 'Shroom two bits. Life sure is funny.'

Mordecai gave me a friendly pat on the rump as I hauled myself into the truck. 'Quarter of a mil. Not bad for an afternoon's work.'

My mind was churning. The entire transaction had been conducted over my head. Large amounts of money intimidated me, and I tried to keep out of the clutches of financial institutions just as I avoided the long arm of the law. Now I was potentially snared into owing that little Tudor gingerbread $250,000.

I tried to take it slowly. 'Say the house goes for the appraisal. We own half of it –'

'So we pay off the do-gooder and the do-nothing with $205,000,' Mordecai finished for me. 'Leaving you with your $140,000 untouched, with which you can contribute half of the mortgage payment every month, and buy yourself a few chocolate-covered cherries to boot.'

'But if Wachovia gives us two-fifty, there's $45,000 left over. What happens to that?'

'I pay off the lease on my Prolinea 4/66, for a start.'

'It all gets sunk into Decibelle? Wouldn't half of it be mine?'

'Technically,' said Mordecai, clicking his eye teeth together with an edge of irritation. 'You could become one of my investors.'

'What would I get out of investing in your company?'

'Or you could take your damned money, but I'd say that was pretty ungrateful.'

'For what should I be so grateful?'

'You can't imagine that our friend Clyde would give you a mortgage for two-fifty on the basis of that job framing kitty cats in Crabtree Valley. Without me and Decibelle, the best you could hope for would be to get on his Christmas card list. So, yeah, I think you should be grateful. Still want your money?'

I folded my arms. 'I'll sleep on it. I have to remind you, this whole proposition is hypothetical. I haven't decided to buy the house with you. I haven't decided what I'll do.'

Mordecai gunned the motor in exasperation. 'Well, you've got eighteen fucking days to make up your mind, baby. For Christ's sake, Corrie Lou, how can you live in that mealy head of yours? I'd shoot myself.'

I pouted, silent and purple like my mother, staring pointedly out the window and tugging my skirt as close as it would come to my knees.

'Hey, loosen up,' Mordecai cajoled. 'Sure it must be pretty tricky, you being True's big buddy and all. I'll put in a little work, you get freshened up, I'll take you out to dinner and we'll talk all this through. Wear something slinky, huh? We're gonna show this punk town a pair of legs.'

'Why are you getting so gussied up?'

'Karen's is chi-chi. For *Raleigh*, anyway.' I fastened my mother's pearls. The way Truman was glaring you'd think I had a date with Jesse Helms.

Yet by the time I had finished dabbing a bit of perfume behind each ear, repairing my eyeliner and working the grey heel smudge on my white hose into my satin pumps, Truman's antagonism had given way to disconsolation. His face slackened much as it had when I hobbled down the front walk to my first prom. My mother reported that as I swept my Lurex gold formal into the waiting Mustang, Truman had collapsed on the stoop and announced with chin in hand, 'I've lost my sister.' Melodramatic, but he was right: once I hit sixteen, I bounced from boyfriend to boyfriend, and didn't give my little brother the time of day. If this evening he was only losing me to his older brother, the dynamic of desertion was if anything compounded.

I kissed Truman on the forehead and promised I wouldn't be late. Mordecai was waiting – in a clean white shirt, turquoise bolo tie and freshly shined boots.

'Happy chicken thighs!' I shouted out the door, relieved to escape the monotony of perfect nutrition for one night. As I clambered into the adjutant's seat, trying to protect my pantyhose, the incongruity of my slit-skirted hot-pink silk in Mordecai's army truck was lost on neither of us, but then Mordecai looked on all ceremony as satire.

At Karen's, the sign about jacket and tie did not, apparently, apply to my brother; I knew of no rule to which Mordecai did not regard himself as an exception. The maitre d' looked happy to see him, though only when the bill arrived would I realize why. Mordecai didn't wait to be escorted, but lumbered to his 'regular' table in the corner, where a chilled double of aquavit had arrived before he sat down.

'We'll keep you taken care of, Mort,' the waiter whispered, and my brother beamed at the schnapps. I was not sure I wanted Mordecai taken care of all that well.

I stuck with wine, and pulled at the silk under my thighs so it wouldn't wrinkle from nervous sweat. I liked wearing dresses sometimes, but they could have a dismal effect on my personality. Mordecai already made me timid, and the dress clinched it. In a skirt I grew demure; I scissored my legs where I was more given in jeans to prop an ankle on the other knee, like my father. Though I usually bantered with waiters, 'gussied up' I seemed to think 'that sounds terribly tasty' in response to the specials was enough – I traded in my wit for looking pretty.

I nodded. 'No hard-hat. This must be a *special time*.'

I twirled my wine stem, and surveyed the restaurant. Karen's had low-lit billiard-green and white-linen decor, its hushed tuxe-doed waiters gliding between tables as if on casters. Its curiously conspiratorial atmosphere was enhanced by a mural covering the far wall, in which outsized diners lifted champagne flutes to mythical triumph. The women in the painting bulged from skimpy black dresses; meant to appear voluptuous, they looked puffy. Their bow ties choking too high on the neck, the men seemed desperate to get home to flannel plaid. Rosy brush strokes in cheekbones, intending the high colour of good cheer, instead evoked over-indulgence. Smiles were stiff, eyes vacant, and even in the mural waiters leaned towards one another, collusive. Surely the commission was designed to present clientele with a picture of themselves as chic, glossy, urbane, but the artist had depicted the reverse: a crowd of trussed up tar-heels dining in a dreary shopping centre of the American hinterlands; they would just as soon be tucking into a Roy Rogers quarter-pounder as veal piccante. It was a painting about fraud.

'So, how'd you like Clyde?' Mordecai polished off his double; a replacement appeared silently within five seconds.

'I always wondered what happened to people like that, after school,' I said. 'The low-profile, undistinguished sorts. I guess they really do become accountants and bankers.'

'Among other things, they marry your own brother.'

'Was Dix a nerd?' I asked innocently.

'I wasn't talking about Dix, and you know it,' he said sharply. 'For that matter, True himself was a nerd, wasn't he? His reports were on time, with nifty binders. You said yourself he had no friends. His room was neat.' For Mordecai, the only habit more damning than a well-kept room was legible handwriting.

I had come out this evening having made a promise to myself, and I would soon find how difficult – how astonishingly difficult – it would be to keep. This constant sniping at one brother to pla-cate the other was topping me up with unspeakable self-loathing. I would not, I swore, be enticed into whittling down my unde-fended little brother from salad to mints. So I curved the conver-sation, stalling while I came up with something brutally nice to say about Truman McCrea.

'I'm always gobsmacked,' I said, 'by proles who doggedly exe-cute those dumpy jobs. Grocery management, soap distribution, even work that pays – law, stock trading. They're welcome to the money. I need shop-keepers and soap-sellers; they allow me my fringy, irresponsible life, and without them I guess I'd have to take that sodding job at Wachovia myself.'

The latter section of my speech I hurried. Whenever I talked to Mordecai I heard a clock ticking; if I tried to tell him a whole story, I pared the details until it was boring – just what I was afraid of becoming. One of the most gracious privileges you can extend to others is permission to be dull; surely it is only when provided this relaxing latitude that most people will successfully amuse.

Indeed, Mordecai had ignored my recitation in favour of the menu, and proceeded to order an excess of its most expensive dishes. Besides, he would not be wrested from his pet subject of the night, which if allowed he would worry like a vicious cat with a mouse that was already dead.

'Maybe it's about time you explain to me how your brother and I could be biologically related,' he began, popping olives. 'Do you realize that every time I lay eyes on that henpecked asshole he's vacuuming the stairs?'

'He likes order,' I submitted. 'And every time I lay eyes on you, you're spilling ashes on the stairs.'

'Who gives a fuck, Core?' The second aquavit was beginning to take hold; his voice was louder, his accent more Southern.

'Truman does. It's daunting, growing up as the youngest. Here's a little chaos theory for you: when everyone around you is more competent, more powerful, your universe is anarchic. Everything takes place out of your hands and over your head. So you have a neat room. It's a way of taking control.'

'It's a way of wasting your fucking life dusting your fucking bureau.'

My arbitration wasn't making a lot of headway.

'You didn't grow up in anyone's shadow,' I persevered. 'You were free to invent yourself. By the time Truman was in first grade, you were already established as the family bright spark, and I'd cornered the market on creativity. What was left for Troom?'

'Only the rest of the whole goddamned planet.'

'That's not the way it seems, in a family. You didn't come of age thinking of yourself in terms of other people. Truman couldn't help but compare himself to us, because everyone else did. He went to Martin, too, and had your teachers – they remembered you. Boy, did they ever remember you. Mrs Gordon failed Truman for the first half of a term before she figured out he was –'

'A rabbit.'

I took a breath, and stirred my arugula. 'I've always thought of you as courageous. Well, Truman is afraid. You remember how long it took him to give up that decrepit blanket, how long he sucked his thumb? How for hours at a time he'd go mum? Maybe you can call that a failing. Fine, it's a failing –'

'I can see quailing from spiders, but that's not what we're talking about. Ever hear of *pantophobia*? That's the kid's problem. Fear of everything.'

'But he was born that way, Mordecai; you can tell from his photographs. I'm not a hopeless determinist, but some traits of character are not our fault. I'm a little devious, and I was probably born that way, too; you were born stubborn. You were, according to Mother, an obstinate baby. Still, of the failings, isn't trepidation defensible, even rational, given what you know about the world? It's a ghastly place.'

'It's a fucking riot, if you don't let it get on top of you. There's nothing about "the world" that makes everyone cower in the attic of their parents' house until they're twenty-whatever. Besides, what's the guy got to be afraid of?'

'Walking into his own parlour and finding his mother dead, for starters.'

'Cookies crumbling. Any day of the week you can walk into a room and find yourself dead.'

Mordecai was subdued for a moment by the arrival of his carpaccio. He prided himself on his taste for raw meat.

'I know you especially fault Truman for not leaving home,' I continued carefully, 'when you couldn't wait to get out, even if that meant flipping hamburgers at the Red Barn. But when you're the youngest you look at a family from the other end. You and I regarded our parents and Heck-Andrews as this big heavy immutable thing we had to get away from. But Truman watched us go, our parents get older. The youngest is clued up, actually. He knows that a family isn't some permanent burden but a tremulous and temporary coalescence, because the youngest is around to watch it fall apart. That makes you conservative. That makes you stay home, because you're afraid that if you turn your back for a minute there won't be a home. And you're right. There won't be.'

Visibly unmoved, Mordecai washed a clump of French bread down with schnapps. 'OK, so he's stayed in that house because if he stepped outside the bogeyman would get him, or the fucking thing would disappear. But sheer timorousness or "conservatism", as you call it, didn't necessitate that into old age he buy Mommy's groceries and mow the lawn. I can't believe that every youngest kid is such a snivelling, ass-licking toady.'

'So you never tried to earn your parents' approval?'

'That's right.'

'Get off it! Didn't you run home with that IQ test result that proved you're a genius? Didn't you leave your 100% Algebra II tests on the kitchen table? Even as an adult, weren't the only times you stopped by when you had a big contract coming in and you wanted to trot out those big figures, and didn't the fact that Father was never impressed by money drive you to distraction? For that matter, didn't you bring your girlfriends to your bedroom instead of taking them to a Motel 6 in order to make Mother jealous?'

'There's a big difference –' He took a deep drag on his Three Castles, '– between expecting recognition for achievement, and wanting a pat on the head for obsequiousness.'

'Truman wasn't obsequious, he was *nice*!'

Our waiter cleared the starters and smoothed in the main course: for me, fish; for Mordecai, a thick black-and-blue fillet steak. I found the waiter's air of indifference feigned. I was sure they routinely eavesdropped on Mordecai's tirades, looked forward to the show even, while Mordecai was careful to give them one. I'd gone through twice as much wine as I would normally in less than an hour, and I, too, was getting rather loud.

'Now that's a loser attribute if I ever heard one,' said Mordecai, sawing into the meat savagely and exposing flesh so red it was probably cold. 'Every screw-up ever lived was *nice*. That's just another way of saying your brother's a rabbit! Sure you're *nice* when you're afraid, otherwise somebody's gonna bite your head off.'

'Aren't you glad he took care of Mother? Wasn't that better than her being all by herself, aren't you thankful –'

'I thank my lucky stars it wasn't me, that's for sure.'

'And Truman's been nice to me. Nicer than you by a mile. And kindness isn't a "loser attribute"; most losers are sour prats. The number of things Truman's done for me –'

'When was the last time you *asked* me to do something for you, Core? When you were six years old.'

I picked the bones from my haddock. 'My first day of school,' I said. 'You held my hand. I asked you.'

Mordecai swabbed his meat juice with a fistful of bread, intently. 'You spent so much time with that kid, and I have tried to understand why, tried to figure what you saw in him I didn't, but I'm just flummoxed, Corrie Lou – I mean, where's that kid's spunk? Did he *ever* say no I will not go to church this Sunday, I don't believe in God? Did he ever shoplift a roll of lifesavers, has he ever been *bad*? Has he ever said fuck-you to anybody, Core? In his life?'

'He's said fuck-you to you a few times.'

'Not to my face he hasn't. And I would shake the guy's hand, I would! I would pay the little bastard money just to hear it!'

I drummed my fingers. 'I doubt that. I doubt that extremely. And Truman did rebel, in his own quiet way, if that's what you're after. Father pooh-poohed Troom's interest in architecture to his dying day, but that never stopped Truman from campaigning against the beltway –'

'What a cause, boy. A highway. Really something to get distraught over.'

'See, you're just like Father. And Truman persisted despite that derision, which shows backbone. Besides which, to imitate you I'm afraid, he held off on going to university for years, under considerable duress.'

'And what's he doing now?'

'Paying his dues, I'll grant, trying to please Father when it's too late. But you don't realize – both Troom and I were told over and over how you'd made Mother's and Father's lives hell. From the time I was ten, we were drilled with how mortified they'd be if our teenage years proved just as horrific. Yes, our parents exaggerated their suffering out of self-pity, just like –' I was about to say, just like *you* do. 'But we were under a lot of pressure to be decent kids because you used up all the patience and forgiveness our entire generation had coming.'

'They never forgave me an ever-loving thing.'

That stopped me. No. They hadn't.

'But what's with this house thing?' Mordecai mumbled through his steak. 'True talks about that house as if it's his fucking mother.'

'Maybe to Truman,' I said, 'it is his mother. Or all he has left of her. You can't imagine it's just a building.'

'It is to me.'

'Oh, horseshit. You're going to tell me that the only reason out of all the houses in this town you've decided to try and buy Heck-Andrews is because it's a bargain or you need that many bedrooms? If so, you have the self-awareness of a flea.'

'I'm not "trying", I *am* buying that house because I already own part of it and you own the other part and I happen to think you and me'd make a team.'

'What if Truman didn't want it?'

'What say?'

'You heard me. What if Truman didn't want the house? What if it was an albatross to him, and he'd be thrilled for you to take it off his hands? Would you still want it then?'

Mordecai smeared his mouth with a napkin and said, 'Sure,' indistinctly.

I snorted. 'And Mother thought you were so smart.'

The waiter cleared our entrées, mine barely touched. Here was dinner almost over and we'd only danced around our official agenda – typical McCrea evening. Mordecai must have assumed that if I stuck up for his brother I was preparing the way for no thank you, I'd prefer to live with Troom. In truth, far from it – I'd so rarely had a real conversation with Mordecai rather than serve as his cooperative, conveniently taciturn audience that this was the first time I thought, you know, I *could* live with my older brother.

'Core,' Mordecai slurred, a fresh aquavit at elbow. 'I wish you'd just tell me yes or no, hey?'

He was courageous. I played with my spoon. 'I told you, I thought we should talk about it.'

'Fine,' he said. 'Talk.'

My mind went blank, save for one simple question. 'If I say yes,' I said softly, 'could I have the dovecot?'

15

I did not get home early. Mordecai kept us on through three more rounds. Though my older brother has the chemical resilience of a walking medical experiment, there is no constitution on earth that could metabolize that much alcohol and not show it.

'I'll never forget,' he croaked, bolo tie askew and beef juices down his white shirt. 'In eighth grade, we got back a chemistry test. The whole class flunked. The whole class, except me. I got a D. I came home to Mother, really pleased with myself, you know? Told her out of thirty-five kids I was the only one to pass. She scowled.' Mordecai did a plausible imitation, crinkling his lips into a butthole. 'She shook her finger. *You mustn't compare yourself with the bottom,*' she said. Jesus H. Christ!' With a sweep of his arm, he shattered his coffee cup, water glass and empty schnapps tumbler on to the floor. '*You mustn't compare yourself to the bottom.* They were never fucking satisfied ...' His chin dropped to his clavicle.

'Mordecai, I really think we should go.'

The waiters were putting chairs on top of tables; we' d been the only remaining customers for over an hour.

'One for the road!' my brother roared.

I shook my head at our waiter, and scribbled the air for our bill.

'Come on,' Mordecai wheedled. 'One more. You've hardly drunk anything.'

'On the contrary, I'm plastered,' I said. 'That's enough.'

'You're just like *Mother,*' he groused.

'I don't recall Mother ever telling you to lay off after a full litre of hundred proof,' I said crisply.

It took him minutes to dig out his credit card; watching him page through every receipt and video membership in his wallet was excruciating. When the imprint arrived Mordecai's pen hovered over the gratuity, looping confused squiggles in the air. I reached for the bill and filled in the 15 per cent myself, pausing to scan the itemized printout. Each double aquavit was ten bucks, inflating the total to $280. I felt less guilty about the tableware we'd broken; fob off that much booze on a single customer, and a few smashed glasses were figured into costs. After Mordecai trailed the pen aimlessly across the carbon, the waiter had to bring it back because he'd signed on the wrong line.

On the way out the door, Mordecai slumped on to my shoulder; I staggered, glaring at the maitre d' – this was my brother, *taken care of*. Mordecai lunged at the mints by the register, upsetting the bowl and clattering pink buttons across the counter.

We had a tussle over the keys in the car park, where I discovered Mordecai was stronger than he looked. When I finally prised them from him I threw the chain into the azalea bushes, and threatened if he didn't let me drive I would walk. By the time I recovered the ring from the mulch, Mordecai had begun to snore in the passenger seat, leaving me to figure out how to operate an army troop transporter all by myself. I supposed if I lived with my older brother I'd get pretty good at it.

I woke the next morning thrashing from pillow to pillow as I racked my brains to remember what I had promised Mordecai about the house. As far as I could piece together, my older brother had spent $300 on another glorified maybe, and the only thing that had changed as of this hangover was that I no longer had eighteen days to make up my mind, but one less.

I tugged the duvet to my eyes, then pushed it back to my chin because my breath stank. I squinted at the seedy wash of winter light. In July the sun threw a vivid harlequin patchwork on my quilt, but in January the pale rays filtering through the panes of stained glass cast weak, uncommitted colours on my bed, like the blah pastels of Averil's blouses. Core-less! I chided myself. You cannot sign for two different mortgages on the same house. You cannot divide your future into parallel universes where you live with Truman in one, walking the straight and narrow of chicken thighs and brisk cemetery constitutionals, and with Mordecai in the other, dragging him to bed at cock-crow and hauling off his boots.

All month I'd been tormented with dreams of raising my left

hand in the Jaycee Center, then outbidding myself with my right, eventually raising the price of the house into the several millions. Once I roused, 5 February would keep a drowsy fog about it, as if the date would never arrive after all. Maybe I was too accustomed to double-dealing and getting away with it.

I collapsed over on my side, cool air spraying from the pillowcase on to my cheek. There was more to it than that. While still backed by middle-class parents, all my decisions had exuded a probationary aura – as if my hand hadn't left my checker, and I could always slide to my last square. In this respect Heck-Andrews diminished me as much as it did Truman. Though my parents were dead, their house propped me up with paternal solace, its moist motherly air nursed me with there-there-dear. I still felt taken care of. Perhaps this was one reason we were all three holed up here: our trio had regrouped to its lone bunker, sandbagged against an army of alien surnames. We were cleaving to the last vestige of a generation that had buffered us from the rest of the world, where we were nobody in particular and were expected to fend for ourselves or take the consequences. It may indeed have been 'only a building', but Heck-Andrews was the only refuge we had left.

Consider your options, girl. I flapped the duvet off my shoulder to slap the skin with a shock of cold draft. Yet no usefully contrasting fantasies came to me: the snug groove I might wear with Truman versus the wild, unhinged carouse of life with Mordecai. Instead I weighed competing dreads, estimating which sibling might be visited with more devastation by my betrayal. My solicitous, timid younger brother? Or the older, whom I had already betrayed once, if all those afternoons of abandoning him to his basement didn't count as thousands of individual treacheries? Could I bear to add one more?

Then, most decisions consumed no more than a nano-second, and this ritual agonizing was cheap theatre. Trying to make up my mind might be transparent flight from the fact that I had made it up to begin with. My stomach yowled. *Maybe I knew all along which brother I would choose.*

So in preference to dwelling on my dilemma, I lacerated myself for being duplicitous: you waffler, you snake, you slag. Self-disgust was an indulgence.

I got up, since I had another mortgage appointment today! Nuts.

Dressed, I groped down the banisters, giving the gargoyle at the bottom a pat – this morning it looked like a self-portrait. As my hand felt the kitchen doorknob tremble with Truman's murmur to Averil on the other side, I paused. A memory descended to me unbidden, like the Good Witch Glinda when all seemed lost. Disheartening at the time, now the flashback was a burst of light: I was not the only member of this family whose loyalties were provisional.

About three years before I had been visiting from London. I often slept in, and they can't have expected me to be up. I'd trundled downstairs and around into the hall between the foyer and the kitchen; this door was not quite shut. Voices emerged.

'– I just think she should get realistic!' When Truman was strident, he said *just* a lot. 'She's thirty-two, and what's she going to do, drive a moped around London delivering other people's memos all her life?'

'Well.' I knew that *well*: throaty, seemingly apologetic – it meant, I-don't-like-to-criticize-you-kids-to-each-other-but-just-this-teency-weency-once-I'll-make-an-exception; I'd heard plenty of *wells*, plenty of exceptions. 'I've tried to be encouraging about Corrie Lou's artwork, but I am beginning to worry that she's a bit of a dreamer. Of course, the pictures I've seen of her sculptures are very *attractive* –' Mother emphasized the moderation of the word.

'Oh, they're OK, I guess, but how many other people can make passable figurines, Mother? She's living in a fantasy world! Do you realize how competitive art galleries are? I don't keep up with that stuff, and even I know that field is a crapshoot. I just think she should consider another career, maybe one in which she could be useful, help other people –'

Like *nursing*, I thought sourly.

'– Like working with handicapped children.'

Even better.

'I'm more worried about whether she'll ever be taking care of her own children,' said my mother.

'Don't hold your breath,' said Truman. 'Corrie Lou just seems to go from man to man –'

'I am *simply* in *despair* about that girl!' Mother cried, italicizing with lots of air. 'I cannot understand how, after witnessing her parents' deeply loving marriage, she could *cheapen* herself like that – !'

'It is, it's cheapening,' Truman chimed in. 'She sells herself short. I guess when you've been with enough guys it doesn't mean much. And the riff-raff! I have no idea where she digs these people up.'

'I think it's been hard for her to find any man who measures up to her father. But that's no excuse for jumping into bed with the first fellow who comes along. I've been *so* relieved that you and Averil have a committed, faithful relationship. You two had the restraint and respect to wait and explore the delights of each other's bodies until your wedding night.'

'I think it made a big difference, actually,' said Truman. 'Holding out, and being first for each other.'

That lying sack of shit! In whatever cursory a fashion, Truman was no virgin when he met Averil; he'd cut the teeth of his zipper on one of my best friends. As for having 'waited' for his wedding, what about tucking Averil naked up to the tower deck?

'But your sister!' Mother gasped. 'Why, she must have given herself to at least three or four –'

Truman guffawed. 'Three or four! Mother, you're joking.'

'What's that supposed to mean?'

'Well.' My brother's *well*. 'She told me that this last month –' I could see him through the crack, leaning forward with an elbow on each knee, chin thrust, eyebrows arched, as he lowered his voice and disciplined himself not to smile. 'Last month, she was with three different guys. That was just one month, Mother.'

I'd had enough. That morning, I went back to bed. In the end I may have been less offended that he grassed about my sleeping around than that behind my back he called me 'Corrie Lou'.

I realize that eavesdroppers are supposed to 'get what they deserve', but I find the snooped-on will leap at the violation of their privacy to divert you from what you overheard. It was not from shame at having pressed my ear to the kitchen door that I never discussed this cosy dialogue with Truman.

I guess I never brought it up from a depressing shrewdness; if he was a quisling, so were we all. Given half a chance, I had sold him downriver as well, though always to my father – *Can you*

208

imagine why Truman doesn't have more friends? How do you think he came to be so unadventurous with parents who love to travel? Hasn't he had a desperate time finding his professional niche … ! Alone with either parent, all three of us disguised our reflections on our siblings as concern when in truth we were ripping each other to shreds. The subtext was obvious: how much more wonderful we were than their other worthless children. I didn't know what else to do but find it funny. With one another we would collude in beastly imitations of our mother's 'telephone voice', but throw a parent into the ring and it was a free-for-all fight-to-the-finish for the trophy of parental adoration. Maybe the sibling relationship was intrinsically penultimate; maybe all our alliances with each other were brief marriages of convenience, and we tread a thin crust over a boiling magma of rivalry, which could readily spit to the surface as outright hatred. Maybe the real marvel was that we ever got along at all.

'Looks like you had one swell time last night,' Truman snarled at my rat's nest hair and baggy eyes when I bumbled into the kitchen.

I rang Frames and informed them that I was still unwell which, considering the state of my head, was accurate enough. I brewed my coffee extra strong, and choked down a rare breakfast. Today, I'd need it.

I showed up in the kitchen that afternoon in jeans, the novelty of bankers having already worn off, but Truman squawked and said, yesterday you took off work to give *Mordecai* a hand and wore a skirt to go to Ferguson's Hardware, you could at least – I said OK, OK, so changed into the outfit I'd worn on Monday; it was still on my chair. Truman was trussed in suit and tie; there was no danger that in any encounter with authorities Troom would show up in a hard-hat.

I know it was only a second time, but for me the drive threatened to become one of those hellish Nietzschean re-enactments – this woman who had zero interest in finance of any description would be spending the rest of eternity going from one mortgage appointment to another. The sensation of being trapped in an infinite loop intensified when Truman replicated the route Mordecai had described in the army truck the day before, though it was only when Troom turned into the little Wachovia Tudor branch on Hillsborough that I realized we were applying for a loan at the very same fucking bank.

Which may seem a Dickensian coincidence, but wasn't. Both my brothers have a provincial side. They had started their first accounts at this branch when they turned ten, and neither had ever moved their accounts elsewhere.

'Ms McCrea?'

The fog surrounding 5 February was apparently only possible if my double-bind were kept shrouded in the clouded privacy of my head; when I shook hands once more with Claude Richards, it was like reaching out and touching my predicament, hot, solid and clenching. The expression on Claude's face was of rapacious narrative hunger.

'How nice to see you,' I said, lying.

'This way,' he said familiarly, and tucked me in front of him to lead off to his office. I glanced behind me, imploring; I prayed that the confidentiality accorded clients of lawyers and doctors applied to bank patrons as well.

I assumed my usual chair in the corner, as the onlooker of my own life. Truman took the hot seat in front of the desk. He clasped one set of fingers around the other as if holding a hat in his lap, cleared his throat, and straightened his back. His bearing of formal appeal reminded me of nineteenth-century suitors asking for a daughter's hand – the steadfast, stolid petitioner who plans to stay and work the farm and meanwhile the dashing ne'er-do-well officer has eloped with the girl.

Claude shifted papers and kept us waiting. Seen through Truman's eyes, Richards no longer appeared a nebbish, an overgrown boy fevering at his report on Abraham Lincoln, but an imposing and unruffled bureaucrat on whose caprice our fate depended. The throw pillow over the man's belt inflated to a complacent paunch. His hair, yesterday a silly orange, now looked fiery. I noticed touches like the white-on-white monogram at his collar and tasteful pewter studs at his cuffs, where the day before his costume had seemed drearily generic, though I was sure he was wearing the same suit. His tortoiseshell spectacles, with Mordecai trite and dorky, now refracted the sun from the window, their gleam stylish and power-lunch.

'You can see we've applied for a mortgage of up to $100,000,' Truman intruded into the silence. 'I know that seems a lot, so maybe

210

I should explain. My sister and I have $140,000 each in liquid assets from my parents. We're willing to contribute most of that to buy the other half of our house, but would like to have a little left over, if that's all right ... To keep from being flat broke, you know, and be able to make the first payments and everything ...'

'Yes?' said Claude, with a maddening absence of response.

'If we get the house for the appraisal, of course, technically we only need $25,000, but there's a chance other parties –' Truman darted his eyes to my corner, 'like those *Japanese* people, will be bidding against us, and we'd like your permission to go higher ...'

'You may well have competition for 309 Blount Street,' said Claude, looking at me.

'I'm sure $50,000 would be more than enough!' Truman burst out.

Claude held the paper before him by the very edge, as if it were smeared with something sticky. 'I see here that aside from your inheritance you have little – or no income?'

'I'm a student at Duke, with another year and a half before I get my BA. I know I'm kind of old for college, but I went through a long period of trying –'

'To *find yourself*,' Claude provided helpfully.

Truman slumped. 'You could call it that. Anyway, after I get my degree, I should be applying for academic jobs ...'

'And you're studying – ?'

'Philosophy,' said Truman morosely.

'I see.'

'My wife works. She's a school teacher.'

'And earns – ?'

'Subbing's not full time, so about $10,000; good years more like twelve ...'

'I see. And Ms McCrea?'

'She's got a job in a framing shop in Crabtree Valley, but that's temporary,' said Truman hurriedly.

'But I thought – ?' The banker raised his eyebrows, and stopped. 'No matter.'

'She's sure to get something more remunerative soon,' Truman went on. 'Besides, she's an artist. Her stuff is really good, you should see it, and some day she's certain to be making scads –'

'Once she's *discovered*,' said Claude drolely.

'I realize it doesn't seem like we have much money coming in,

211

and I guess we don't,' said Truman. 'But that will turn around, we're sinking a lot of our own money into the house and not asking for all that much – are we?'

Claude's face remained stony, so Truman kept talking.

'Heck-Andrews itself is an astonishing Reconstruction estate, a supreme example of Second Empire architecture.'

'It is a remarkable house.' I thought I should be supportive. 'You should stop by some time.'

'Yes,' said Claude. 'I'm beginning to think that could be quite an experience.'

'One of the first things I'd do once we got the title,' Truman enthused, 'would be to get the house listed as historic on the National Register.'

'You're aware that such listing actually lowers the value of a property?' Claude leaned back, tapping his pencil eraser on our forms. 'By legally restricting what can be done to the structure, you make the real estate unattractive to developers.'

'Of course. That's the idea.'

'I'm telling you that your intentions make 309 Blount Street less attractive, thereby, to Wachovia as well.'

Truman craned forward. 'You wouldn't want the house to get torn down, would you?'

'My feelings on the matter are neither here nor there.'

'People used to think these old houses were white elephants, but not any more! This state's beginning to wake up to the value of its heritage. You know, strangers *stare* at our house? Knock on the door and want to walk around?'

Back hiking Capital City Trail.

'You're aware we're in a recession?' asked Claude.

'I read the papers.'

'The market in North Carolina is depressed. Should you default on your payments –'

'Then you own a half-million dollar house after having paid, what, fifty thousand for it. A steal.'

'Such a holding is only of value to a bank if it is sold. As an historic property in a sluggish market, it could be difficult to unload.'

'"Unload"! A house like that – ?'

'The point is, mortgages are only arranged when the bank does not anticipate foreclosure. We accept land holdings as loan security, but do not actually wish to enter the realty business. I can only approve this application if given sufficient evidence that you and your sister can make the payments according to schedule.'

'We wouldn't even need you if it weren't for my father!' Truman exploded. 'Without his greasing the stupid ACLU we'd have plenty of cash and we wouldn't be here!'

Claude turned pages and indulged himself. 'I see. Your brother … is co-owner of the property?'

'A profiteer,' Truman growled. 'He just wants his money,'

'Oh, does he?'

'Mr Richards,' I intervened. 'I don't mean to press you, but I suspect you've already made up your mind about this mortgage. Maybe you should cut to the chase.'

'You're quite right, Ms McCrea, I'm afraid my feelings are rather conclusive. Without a little more earning power demonstrated here, a loan of $100,000 is really out of the question.'

'Say $50,000, then!' cried Truman. 'Or thirty! We might only need twenty-five!'

'Mr McCrea, no bank parts with so much as a half-dollar that it doesn't expect to get back.'

'Twenty-five grand for a $410,000 house? And you won't take it? Are you crazy?'

Claude stood up, ending our meeting. 'I'm sorry, but I must decline this application. I would advise you to take your custom elsewhere; another bank might feel differently, since the equity you're offering as security is considerable. Do not give up.' He directed the advice to me.

I shook his hand. As Truman shuffled despondently ahead, I hung back and whispered, 'Truman's application isn't that absurd, is it?'

Claude shrugged. 'Judgement call. Try Hanover Trust, just down the street. They might not regard your affairs as quite so – complicated.'

When he saw me off at the waist-high gate by the tellers, Claude couldn't control himself, and lowered to my ear. 'What are you *doing*?'

I muttered, 'I wish I knew.'

Truman rested his forehead on the steering wheel and didn't start the car. 'That was humiliating. I felt like I was asking for a raise on my allowance and got turned down.'

'Maybe that was the problem,' I said. 'That you acted as if you were asking for a raise on your allowance.'

'What was I supposed to do, swagger in there and puff out my chest and say I'm the big man and I'm going to make lots of money, gimme yours?'

'Well,' I said. 'Yes.'

'It would never work. You've gotta prove stuff. Have things on paper, tax records … I don't have the income and he has evidence of that.'

'You can always lie.'

'Not with a bank, not without the goods –'

'I don't know a lot about high finance, Truman, but I sense it's like every other profession – personal. You have to snow them, put one over. Why, maybe asking for only a hundred grand was a mistake. Maybe you'd have had better luck insisting on two – or two-fifty.'

'When he wouldn't come across with twenty-five?'

'He'd least of all come across with twenty-five. It's like a lot of things in life – have the gonads to shoot for the moon, and the green cheese lands on your lawn. Ask for dirt, people think that's what you're worth; and you don't get the dirt, either.'

Plausible sidewalk philosophy, but I took Claude's wink and nod, that a small mortgage on a valuable house was not unheard-of even with meagre income stats. I rang Hanover Trust that Wednesday from Frames, taxied by for the forms on my lunch hour, and filled them out that evening, in my room with the door shut. I did the photocopying and made yet one more appointment – if my life was degenerating into a series of mortgage negotiations, I might as well take charge. This time I wore my primmest blouse and a skirt of conservative length; since I was assuming the driver's seat in every other respect I demanded the keys to the car. On the way to the bank, I tutored Truman that he was not to mention his philistine brother, not to rant about the ACLU, and not to apologize for being in college at thirty-one. He was not, in fact, to apologize for a bloody thing, and he would let me do the talking.

At Hanover, I took the chair closest to the banker, crossing my legs the way Mother had taught me and not like my father. I dealt with the transaction as if it were a simple, straightforward formality, and that is the way the banker dealt with it in return. In fifteen minutes we had the go-ahead to bid for Heck-Andrews up to $490,000.

All of this felt right. I was the Big Sister. Truman did what I said.

But why did I go to such trouble? Why didn't I leap at the chance for circumstances to make an odious decision for me – tough nuggies, Truman, the bank won't lend us money but will to Mordecai, so to keep the house in the family I'll purchase the place with him? Wasn't I letting a golden opportunity to weasel out from under slip by?

There was a purity to my Hobson's Choice that I wanted restored. If both brothers secured financial backing, I had evened the odds. It seemed more fair, or more perfectly unfair, for whomever I bid with on 5 February to depend wholly on the whim of my devotion. So I reinstated the allegorical starkness to my dilemma that with no little perversity I enjoyed. I would retrace the points of my triangulated childhood like a victim leading policemen step by step through her trauma at the scene of the crime.

16

Truman returned from Hanover Trust ebullient, a welcome relief from the twelve days previous, during which he had been unremittingly frantic, especially when we had three more prospective buyers tour the house. His idea of celebration was to cut his required pre-dinner reading of Heidegger from fifty to thirty-five pages, open our bottle of wine in fifteen-minute violation of the Eight O'Clock Rule, and merrily rip the skin off chicken thighs.

'You wouldn't consider,' I proposed, 'going out?'

Truman dismissed, 'Restaurants are a scam.'

I was familiar with this reasoning. It was the same irrefutable practicality that had ostensibly kept Truman living with his parents: it didn't 'make sense' to rent a separate flat when he had a 'perfectly good' apartment upstairs. Truman never went out to dinner, for commercial establishments cooked with too much grease, and it was just as easy to cook up a more nutritious meal at home. Granted, for pouring calories down the gullet restaurants were a gyp, but surely my brother was missing something. Restaurants were decorative, having your own flat was decorative, but Truman, so much of life is frou-frou.

Yet I had learned, within the rigidity of his routine, to multiply modest diversions from it into the extravagant. When Truman offered to buy me a beer at Player's Retreat after dinner, willing to spring for a $3 draft when we could as well have uncapped a Molson in the dovecot for 60¢, I knew this to be roughly the equivalent of Mordecai's $300 tab at Karen's two weeks before. It was merely a matter of moving the decimal point.

Truman made a more considerable gesture still when we drew on our coats and he mentioned Averil was staying behind. I hadn't been on a single social venture with Truman without his wife along since the stroll we took through Oakwood in December; subsequent ambles were taken as a threesome. I wasn't sure what I'd done in the past to require a chaperone, nor how I had reformed to earn a single evening of Averil's trust, but my gratitude was reminiscent of birthdays, when I'd get a *whole hour* alone with my father.

We strode down North Street across Wilmington to the Mall, where the great white hulks of floodlit governmental granite had more the look of sheer Dover cliffs than urban build-up. The air was sharp, the stars refreshingly oblivious – all that tension over who got the house when what I wanted more than anything was to get out of it.

My sudden sense of freedom was spurred by the absence of Averil, with whom I tended to be ickily well-behaved. Out of consideration, I avoided clubby references to our childhood; hence we three would prefer flat, neutral subjects like the merits of homosexuals teaching primary school. When we traded impressions of others, I made sure to say something kind even about people I despised, since I feared that in Averil's more extreme moments she regarded me as a scathing, bossy, impossible-to-please elitist. She thought I was snooty about having lived abroad, and that I wanted both to help myself to my younger brother, imperiously, when he was in my reach, and to disavow him, along with the rest of the McCreas and North Carolina into the bargain, when it suited my convenience: I wanted to have my cake and lose it too. She considered her sister-in-law arrogant, glib, domineering – everything Averil perceived had a truth to it except, I wanted to object, you could describe anyone, accurately, and make them seem odious. That she was driven to reduce me in order to enlarge her husband was, I begrudged, to her credit.

While Averil might have kept absolute condemnation in abeyance, she was ever vigilant for my slips of unwitting candour that might confirm her most damning intuitions – for example, that I didn't like her. In fact I neither liked nor disliked her. She didn't pertain to me, and maybe that was the insult she was waiting for. Personally, I would rather be loathed than overlooked. Then, when you are always watching what you say for some incriminating remark, every time you open your mouth the sensation is of digging your own grave. My conversation around her was so circumspect that it became suspect for sounding sanitized.

217

Overly edited discourse draws attention to what's been left out.

My staunch refusal to give her a reason to hate me was exhausting. Should I buy the house with Mordecai, one of the dividends would be to throw this fight. Averil would never forgive me, and simple enmity would be so much more relaxing than tiptoeing down the Mall on eggshells night after night.

Truman sighed. 'Averil's going insane.'

'Why more so than the rest of us?'

'She's furious with me. Or rather, "disappointed in me", as Mother would say. I'm sleeping on the couch.'

I confess this information cheered me, though I didn't know why. 'Whatever for?'

'She thinks I'm a wuss. She thinks Mordecai's moving in is all my fault. That if I were a real man I'd have kicked him out.'

'Doesn't she understand, legally –'

'No, she doesn't understand anything except that our home has turned into a frat house and we can't sleep and we can't keep cheese and she's sick of hearing Nirvana until six a.m.' He balanced along the rim of the Legislature fountain, which splatted like far-off applause. 'I wish he would just go away.'

'Your own family,' I said, 'is the very definition of what doesn't just go away.'

'Mother and Father did.'

'No they haven't. That's our problem, isn't it? They peer through every board of your bedroom. No wonder you're sleeping on the couch.'

He lunged down the wide white steps two at a time, and meandered down the pedestrian mall, hands in pockets. 'I just wanted to thank you for helping to arrange that mortgage. The last few days, Averil's barely spoken to me, Corlis. When we thought we might lose Heck-Andrews ... Because Averil likes that house. Really likes it. This last week she hinted that if she couldn't live there she wouldn't want to live with me at all.'

'That's daft, Truman. Venal.'

'It isn't,' he insisted. 'Places – they're part of life. And when you marry someone you marry lots of things about them outside their personality and stuff. A three-storey Reconstruction mansion is part of what I have to offer her, Corlis. It's part of who I am.'

'You give a few scraps of pine and mortar an awful lot of weight, Truman.'

'That's all our house means to you?'

'No, but I'm not going to let it ruin my life. Have you ever considered,' I suggested, 'rather than buying, moving out instead?'

'Not for a split second!'

'But this operation is turning into such a pain in the arse, Troom – mortgages, auctions. You and I don't have much money, and there will be upkeep, property taxes …'

'Are you backing out now? When the auction's in four days?'

Tentatively, I tested Mordecai's theory: 'Maybe it would be good for you to leave. To make a fresh start.'

'There's no such thing as a fresh start! Part of what you are is what you have been. That's what's wrong with this country: start over, bulldoze the last generation, and put up identical lobotomized squares with no memory like individual amnesia units, as if to deliberately make yourself stupid – look around you!' He gestured to the Legislature behind us, sleek but too slick, at the thick, chunky new History Museum, with no suggestion in its dumb polished beige slabs that it knew what it was for. 'No wisdom, no style – nothing aggregates, it just gets uglier.'

'But our own past wasn't that great, Truman, if you'd be honest –'

'So what?'

'To keep something simply because it's old is just as witless as promoting any innovation because it's new. You have to pick your spots, Truman. What's worth saving about our parents isn't what they dragged with them by accident – like Mother's sexual hysteria, which she caught from her own mother like a disease. Father did make some progress on how you should treat blacks when Grandfather was a card-carrying Kluxer. Keep that. Forget the *house*. It's not that important.'

'That's where you're wrong. You've got to hold on to something. In a way it doesn't matter what you stick by, only that you stick by it. If you let certain things go, you let everything go. Heck-Andrews is mine. It's me.'

'It's only you,' I said huskily, 'if you let it be. And that's a mistake.'

When we arrived at Player's Retreat, a dark divey place off Hillsborough with fish tanks and mint machines for the blind, we hunkered into a booth and Truman, too, seemed to find his wife's absence liberating. On his second beer he confided that she had done nothing lately but complain. If he went out of his way to buy her Doritos, he'd inevitably bring home Ranch Style when she was craving Nacho Cheese.

'You know,' I sidled, 'the last few weeks, she has put on a few pounds.'

'Yeah,' he grumbled. 'You may think this sounds petty, but that's the one thing I don't think I could take. That could break up my marriage, if she got *fat*.' He had a way of saying that word, the *a* bloated, the *t* rebukingly sharp.

'And she's so afraid of Mordecai,' he continued, 'that she only carps to me, so it's as if *I'm* playing screamy music, wolfing down all the groceries, and drinking us out of house and home. She claims I never stand up to him.'

'You don't,' I said.

'Not you, too!'

'Hey.' I patted Truman's hand. 'I don't stand up to him, either.'

Truman toyed with his glass, and edged the beer away. 'Isn't it time we face the fact that Mordecai is an alcoholic?'

'Oh, I don't know about that,' I *pshawed*. 'Believe what you read these days, you and I are alcoholics.'

'Maybe we are.'

'Go on!'

'Except next to Mordecai, we pale. I'm not talking about nou-veaux-dipsos, who rush off to AA after a single spritzer because it's become fashionable to diagnose your "addictive personality", and have a problem to recover from. I mean the old kind. I mean alcoholic.'

'Mordecai would never go to AA. He's not a joiner.'

'He's a drunk!'

I'd have been more open to Truman's suggestion if I thought it pained him more. 'I wouldn't use that word.'

'What word would you use? Corlis, he gets up and goes straight to the freezer!'

'At seven p.m.'

'It's breakfast to him. You remember that Wild Turkey I bought, for our thimble-sized nightcaps before bed? A fifth *used* to last a month. I hid the bottle, under my sandbags. That stash worked with Mother, inveterate snoop. Then, she wasn't nosing around to whet her own whistle. My first day of classes? *He found it*. Sniffed it out like a dog. Admit it – when you went to Karen's, how much booze did he swill?'

I shrugged. 'A few shots.'

'Like fun,' Truman scoffed. 'Or last Sunday – when for once we hadn't been to the liquor store for a day or two? The house was dry, the ABCs were closed. You know I came down the next morning and the *cooking sherry* was upended in the trash can? There are whole hospital wards for people like that. Why can't you call him what he is? Why's it any skin off your nose?'

'So he has a dependency.' Defiantly, I drained my beer.

'*Why* are you always defending him?'

'Somebody has to. You sure won't.'

'The man's entire character is a write-off!'

I would not, would not bandwagon to please him. 'Mordecai drinks because he's troubled.'

'What has he got to feel so all-fired sorry for himself about?'

I gripped the edge of the pine table, carved with 'Go Wolfpack!', as if to keep myself physically from backing down. 'You know he was an unwanted baby, don't you? That when Mother found out she was pregnant with Mordecai she was livid?'

Truman shrugged. 'I was unwanted, too. They never made any bones about that.'

True enough, that I issued from their only planned pregnancy was one of the family's Known Facts; presumably I was to take this as flattering without the other two receiving a slight. In her lilting *Winnie the Pooh* voice Mother had informed us all that when the doctor told her she was carrying her first child she flew into a 'conniption fit'.

'You were different, just timing,' I reminded Truman. 'They'd wanted three children, already had two. Mordecai invited himself on their honeymoon.'

'How do you think that happened?' Truman reflected. 'They had birth control back then, didn't they? Just bad luck?'

'I've worked it out. Mother was using a diaphragm –'

'How do you know?'

'She told me plenty of details about their sex life – to rub salt in the wound that she slept with Father and I didn't.'

'Is the diaphragm that unreliable?'

'When you don't put it in.'

'She told you that?'

'No, but I know Fifties double-think. She was a virgin at the wedding – you heard *that* a thousand times – and proud of it. Positive urine tests were in her mind reserved as punishment for sluts. She was married. That meant sex with impunity. And diaphragms are embarrassing at first – you have to excuse yourself to the loo, suspend operations. They were inexperienced, Father was jumpy; she wouldn't have wanted to risk losing his hard-on while she struggled with her little rubber hat. Never mind that they had no desire to have a kid right away. She thought if you were married you were covered morally and that's all that mattered. I'd lay money on it: Mother got pregnant out of sheer self-righteousness.'

'All the same, Mother said she gave Mordecai more attention than the two of us combined.'

'Over-compensation. I bet a kid can tell. He can certainly tell when he's apprised point blank that his arrival was one of the worst things that ever happened to his mother.'

'Why do you think she told him that?'

'Maybe she figured if she was no-nonsense about it he wouldn't take it personally.'

Truman jeered. 'With Mordecai? Mr Self-Pity, Mr Leap at an Excuse to Cry in Beer? Fat chance.'

'Or maybe –' I tapped my forefinger. 'She wanted him to feel literally guilty for living. If so, it worked.'

'Mordecai is a horror show all because he was an "unwanted child"? That's pretty trite, Corlis.'

'I never said Mordecai was a "horror show". And I'm not saying it explains everything, but Father never stopped resenting his first kid. After waiting for a year to get his hands on this 100-pound hot number, the first month she starts to balloon. So, all told, Mordecai's led a stressful life, Truman. With no formal education –'

'Which is his fault, since he thinks he knows everything already –'

'You've got it the wrong way round. He acts as if he knows everything because he's afraid he doesn't. You're in college now –'

'Which only gets held against me, as if going to Duke is a weakness, a confession of ignorance. Just like my making good grades: by some twisted logic, a 3.8 GPA makes me pathetic. I'm one of those little rote people. Well, you went to U.N.C, didn't you – ?'

'Yes I did, shut up, that's the point. We've both walked those supposedly hallowed halls. Don't you remember, before you enrolled, how you privately worried that there were all these secrets in a university education, that it was an initiation you'd been left out of –'

'Which is a load of hooey. It's not that different from high school. Books and lectures and bullshit.'

'Precisely. University's not a masonic society whose handshakes you can't research in any library. I know that, you know that. Mordecai doesn't know that, he's never been. I've met other auto-didacts, Troom, and they're all the same: brassy, seemingly conceited, always spouting off what they've read. Because they don't buy their own schtick. We know the emperor has no clothes. Mordecai doesn't.'

'So he's insecure. That doesn't explain how you can sit on the back porch hour after hour submitting to that stultifying gibberish about the Mandelbrot Set –'

'It's not all boring, Troom. Have you ever listened? I didn't have any idea why drains clear in opposite directions north and south of the equator.'

'Uh-huh. Why is that?'

I cracked a splinter from the table. 'I don't remember.'

'See? You don't listen, either.'

I took a breath and regrouped. 'Can't you cut him a little slack? He started his own business at nineteen, with no capital –'

'Since when was gross profit something you were taught to admire?'

'It wasn't what we were taught to admire. Just as we weren't raised with an appreciation for *architecture*, right?'

But Truman was in no mood to suffer the same compliment I had paid his brother. 'All your anti-US guff, and you're as American as they come. What do your respect? Making money.'

'What I respect, which you should as well, is how hard it was to rebel against someone like Sturges McCrea –'

'Rebel! Give me a break. Pigtails and yin-yang rings? Mordecai's a throw-back, a cultural Cro-Magnon. For all his talk of revolution, Mordecai's never managed to overthrow himself.' Rather pleased with this formulation, Truman tossed back the last of his beer, licking off the moustache with a smack.

'You don't think it took guts to go it alone at fourteen?'

'Plenty of kids run away, Corlis. They don't get medals. So he flipped hamburgers instead of peddling his ass on the street, but it amounts to the same prostitution in the end.'

'But he left home before –'

'Unlike sappy little Truman,' he ploughed on ferociously, 'strangled in his mother's apron strings, just gullible enough to care about his own parents and how they felt –'

'I was *going to say*,' I overrode, 'that Mordecai is "troubled" because he left home before he knew he was loved.'

'Maybe he wasn't.'

'That's a hideous thing to say about your own brother.'

'So? He cut out when I was seven years old. He'd come home a couple of times a year and ask what *grade* I was in. I got more probing enquiry about my life from Father's partners. Just because he's family doesn't mean I care for him, does it? Doesn't mean I *love* him? It's not enough, being born a brother. You have to act like one, too.'

I leaned back appreciatively. If what Truman felt about Mordecai could not be called love, from the quaver in his voice along with its sheer volume – causing men in Cat hats at the pool table to look over – I was satisfied that Mordecai stirred passion of some kind. That was a start, and if anything what blood relations were good for. However we might enrage one another, we would never, as Averil to me, not pertain.

'Meanwhile,' Truman continued, 'he was held up to me as this freakish cross of paragon and anti-Christ, the genius of whom I was meant to be in awe but whom I must never, never emulate. What am I, a retard? Nobody ever called me "too intelligent for my own good".'

'That reputation boomeranged. It isn't an advantage in adulthood to have been a precocious kid. When you grow up, suddenly speaking in complete sentences isn't amazing. Everyone else knows those big words, too. You pontificate and no one falls off his chair. Mordecai's still trying to impress the way he did at twelve, and it doesn't work any more.'

'I'm not impressed, that's for sure. The best thing about this last month has been to get a good look at Mr Larger-Than-Life up close, who cast his fat black-sheep shadow over my whole childhood. He reads comic books! He watches TV for hours, and any old game show will do. He's stoned half the day. As for glorious

Decibelle Inc., with which he bootstrapped himself into the fast-lane world of commerce, I've seen what he does – he's a construction foreman!'

I was wincing. 'He may not be as towering as you were led to believe, but that doesn't make him a dwarf.'

'No, according to you Mordecai is this remarkable renegade self-made man, whose drinking you excuse as drowning his abandonment at fourteen. But first, he abandoned us, not the other way around, and second, that was ages ago, Corlis – !'

'Not to him.'

'Are you ashamed of me, then? Because I haven't left three wives and taken drugs and grown my hair to my waist? What do I have to do?'

I was afraid he was going to cry. Even as an adult, Truman wept often and freely. For men of our generation that was meant to be an achievement, yet I found I was from the old school – the shine in his eyes, before the voyeurs at the pool table, embarrassed me.

'Why,' I said, keeping my voice low, 'do you insist on regarding any credit I give Mordecai as criticism of you?'

The question was rhetorical. Though sympathetic with my own frustration, I was hitting my head against the brick wall of the way things were. However irrational the perception, sibling assets would always appear zero-sum; among brothers and sisters, any comment on one implicitly passed comment on the others. If Mordecai was bright, we were dumb; if I was imaginative, my brothers were prosaic; if Truman was loyal, Mordecai and I were traitorous.

'I'm not ashamed of you,' I mumbled as Truman paid our tab. 'You're considerate, responsible, industrious.' These adjectives had a kewpie-doll quality, second-prize. I added as forcefully as I could, 'I always hoped you'd to come to London so I could show you off.'

Hiking back towards the capitol, Truman hunched. 'I realize you know him better than I do. On the face of it, though, I can't point to what's so overwhelming about the guy. Even if he's not a villain, it turns out he's pretty ordinary. Which only makes me more miserable. He's ordinary and still makes me feel like a zero. What does that make me?'

'Different. You wouldn't want to be like Mordecai, and this family couldn't take two.'

'Maybe I'm too hard on him. I'm sorry if I was mean.'

I took a deep breath, and felt I'd achieved something.

'At the least,' he added, 'admit that he always pushed us around.'

'He had two little kids at his mercy; we must have been tempting. I suppose we've all got it in us to be fascists, given the chance.'

'Me, too?' Truman sounded hopeful.

I nodded towards Oakwood. 'Remember those twins we pestered, on Bloodworth?'

Of course he did. We hadn't been cruel children, relatively speaking. We went on sprees of stomping the crickets that periodically infested our carriage house, but never picked their legs off one by one. Neither Truman nor I were prestigious enough in school to torture the lower echelon; we were the lower echelon. Meanwhile, we were subject to the despotism of Mordecai's dread babysitting: gagged by deliberately lumpy powdered milk, pounced on until we couldn't breathe, red from his 'Indian rubs', sore from his prodding for 'pressure points', if relieved we weren't paralysed from the neck down.

So we two perpetual victims discovered a pair of twins who lived a few blocks from our house. They were perhaps three years younger than Troom, and played in their front yard wearing twee lacy dresses, daintily snagging at bits of grass but never mucking into puddles for fear of getting their pink skirts dirty. I'm not sure what got into us, but one day we sauntered past them and began to call them names. 'Barf-brains!' They whimpered. 'Spaz butts!' They balled their fists in their eyes. This inspired us. We rushed at them. When they wrung their skirts in anguish, we sniggered that we could see their underpants and we'd tell their mother.

'We'll tell!' they sobbed.

We guffawed, with a hard yucky laugh that was itself a discovery. We threw rocks. Little rocks; pebbles, really – we were new at this game. In the end they wailed so loudly for their mommy that we thought it judicious to skedaddle.

Troom and I went back several times. Taunting the twins became our private filthy pastime, and I will never forget that sensation which, incredibly, I have never quite experienced since: our small, pure sadism. I don't think we ever hurt them, physically, but it was obvious when we appeared that the twins lived in mortal fear of our arrival and had discussed our terrorism between times. This enthralled me. Our new-found taste for their mewling also made me nervous, the way every squeal baited us to cruder threats, dirtier epithets, larger rocks. Relish mingling with revulsion left behind a flavour like the ambivalent corrupted sweetness of high cheeses. After a handful of sessions Truman and I never went back, in tacit agreement that the experiment was over. We were both ashamed, and gratified, that we, too, could be bullies.

'I felt like a creep for that,' said Truman. 'But I'm glad I know what it's like, being a Big Kid: fun. And bad.'

'And fun,' I reiterated. 'So can you blame him?'

'Of course I can. We stopped teasing those girls, after a while. In the end, we didn't really enjoy abuse of power. Mordecai did. He still does.'

Back home, I turned in early, and lay on my back in bed, staring at my ceiling as if I could drill a hole to Truman's dovecot. So he was *sleeping on the couch*. I was happy as Larry.

Still, I had at least stuck up for each brother to the other, if my testimonials seemed to fall on deaf ears. At best when you're telling someone something they don't want to hear you'll get through on delay, and I liked to think that later they'd each remembered what I said. Probably the entire exercise in fealty was for my own sake; it made me feel a tad less of a rank shite.

17

That night I dreamt about the auction. Not the house but I was on the block, up on a dais with my hands tied behind my back. The auctioneer observed that I had good teeth, and demanded I grin for the buyers and then he said, look, she has her mother's smile! He used his pointer to lift up my skirt and leered at the audience. Someone shouted, 'Two bits!' and cackled. The auctioneer said there, there, we can do better than that for this fine filly!

'Four dollars and ten cents,' came from the back.

The gavel fell, like Judge Harville's at our hearing. 'Sold!'

A muscular black man roughed me off the stage for my new life. I woke rerunning the end of the dream, trying to recapture the face of my next master in case it might be a sign. No use – I could only dredge up a hand in the crowd. Wanting to burrow, I had tunnelled under too many duvets for this southern winter; I woke clammy and parched, and rubbed my wrists.

I had three days.

That morning at work a young woman came in with a print of David Inshaw's 'The Badminton Game', asking for my advice on a frame. I made a few inattentive suggestions, transfixed by the painting itself. Two long-skirted girls with flowing hair extended their rackets towards a mid-air birdie, on either side of a jauntily sagging badminton net. Unlike the dim chill overcast outside this unsightly mall, the light within Inshaw's margins was lush, its shadows lean and summery. Behind the girls, bulwarked, blunted evergreens cut phallic silhouettes against an untroubled cerulean sky. Beside these trees rose a solid three-storey house, covered with ivy and crowned with a tower deck. The toasty brick mansion looked immovable and safe, where inside I envisaged steaming, milky tea and cleverly iced petits fours waiting on a doilied tray, for the girls when they had tired of their game. I was sure the young women were sisters, and that they got along famously. It was a painting about balance and joy and affection and suspended time, though I could not identify with either sibling – only with the shuttlecock.

That afternoon I framed the print, envious of its contentment and even more of its infinite arrest, the birdie floating over the net; ever incomplete, this match would never see one sister triumph over the other. I'm afraid my mind was skipping tracks like a scratched record, my blade unsteady at the matt. When the woman came to collect the job before we closed, she was irate that I'd used the wrong frame. I volunteered to do it over, but wouldn't get the chance.

'Look at those corners,' my employer chided when the woman had harrumphed from the shop. He pointed to where the exacto had overshot its pencil mark and crossed into the card. 'Slipshod, and costly. That Inshaw frame will get deducted from your pay cheque. Your *last* pay cheque.'

'Sorry?' I must have looked bewildered.

'Three sick days in three weeks, sloppily noted orders, and the matt you just mangled is $5.50 a sheet. Your mind is not on your work, Ms McCrea. Art History degree or no, our arrangement is at a close.'

I told myself it was a rubbish job anyway and good riddance, but my cheeks stung and I hung up my smock with no comment. I didn't have my older brother's imperiousness – he'd shrug off dismissal with a sneer – and had more than a petal of Truman's tender-flower frailty. I didn't cry in public, though, and kept my dignity out the door.

When I returned home, I didn't tell either brother I'd been made redundant (a grim UK expression, so much more discouraging than being 'fired' – as if there were two of you, and the clone functioned as well or better). Nosing about the kitchen for a snack between their two turned backs, I was disinclined to confide in either if with each I had to leave something out. That wasn't real intimacy, was it: I'll-tell-you-anything-except? As well, I wasn't convinced that either brother would give a toss about my petty misfortune – or, for that matter, about any misfortune that befell me. Despite being fought over, I felt isolated and lonely and increasingly unpersuaded that either brother cared for me in the slightest. As with so many prizes when the contest is all, not only was Heck-Andrews itself irrelevant to the partition suit, but perhaps I, too, was irrelevant to my brothers' dispute over me. That was the first time I considered that maybe Truman and Mordecai had a relationship after all.

'You're pretty aloof.' At least Truman noticed.

'That's right. I'm aloof.'

'Did I do something wrong?'

Where to start? We had all done something wrong. Three days to zero-hour, when I would have to make an absolute choice between two men who were equally my brothers, however much Truman might assert that Mordecai had acted less than his part. If I didn't know what to do or which to choose, I was at least firm in my view that this shouldn't be happening.

'After supper,' said Truman, 'I want to call a meeting.'

'You mean with me?'

'With Mordecai, too.' This was a first. 'Would you ask him? To the kitchen table, about ten?'

'Why don't you ask him?' I said crossly.

'He'll be too busy, if I ask him. You do it. It's important. I have something to discuss with the *family*.' It was impossible to use that word now without being sardonic.

My stomach went gluey. Since when, so formal? Had he overheard something? Would Mordecai and I be carpeted for our alternative mortgage? Had I left a letter out, post from Wachovia that Truman would assume was for us? This was bad life, I thought. I used to enjoy chicanery, but that was when I was hiding my diaphragm from my mother, smug that I knew how to use it; I didn't like concealing anything from Truman. If I had tipped my hand, left an inculpatory scrap on the counter, I decided I must have done so on purpose.

When I informed Mordecai in the carriage house of his appointment at ten, he asked, 'What's this about?'

'Haven't the foggiest.'

'Since when does little True not tell you everything?'

'Since,' I said, 'I stopped telling *him* everything.'

When I was heading for the door, Mordecai put his arm across the exit. 'Made up your mind yet?'

'About what?'

'You know damned well about what.'

'Oh, that,' I faltered. 'I could use a little more time.'

'You don't have more time.'

'Tomorrow?' I pleaded meekly.

'Do me a favour. At least tell me yea or nay the day *before* the auction? I don't want to have to get up at the uncivilized hour of eight in the morning only to be told I can go back to bed.'

'Sure. In two days, then. I promise.'

The hour after dinner and before our 'meeting' was absurd.

From the carriage house: 'CORRIE LOU!' What-you-were-known-as-before-that-dipshit-existed. Summons of the first-born, yank of the past.

From the dovecot: 'Cor-lis!' I'll-call-you-what-you-like; I-know-you've-always-hated-*Corrie Lou*.

Carriage house: 'Core! Come here a sec. will ya? CORE!' In shorthand, familiarity; in naming, possession.

Dovecot: 'Gir-el!' A monicker from when Truman was twelve or so – pre-Averil, when I was all-women. Apt, of late; tugged between them, I was 'girl,' me-Jane.

I would be paged on the thinnest of pretexts: could you find Big Dave a – ? Did you get Mordecai to agree to – ? Wanna hold this while I – ? Would you like the last cup of – ? In the fetching was the game: how eagerly would I shout, 'Coming!', how quickly would I vault the stairs, how long would I linger in the enemy's lair.

By ten, I was tired.

Truman, Averil and I assembled in the kitchen in silence. Truman assumed the head of the table, once my father's place; now, of course, Mordecai's chair. Troom looked downcast, deflated, even morbid. I thought, he's found out. The solemnity of the occasion recalled our convocation for my parents' Living Will, and just like that evening Mordecai was predictably late. I was sent to retrieve him, and he was occupied; on arrival, impatient, clumping his boots on the table with a black glance at Truman, who had appropriated the seat of the eldest male. In our rustles and subdued coughing I heard the restless shuffling of a congregation before church.

Truman put his hands flat on the table. 'We thought you all should be the first to know,' he croaked, his throat dry. 'There are going to be some changes around here.'

231

I said nervously, 'Naturally, after the auction –'

'This isn't about the auction,' Truman interrupted.

I was faint with relief.

'Go on,' coaxed my sister-in-law. She was sitting on the other side of Truman, picking at grains of rice hardened on the walnut. She seemed unable to look her husband in the eye.

'Averil and I have been talking about this on and off for a while. We've put it off for ages because we wanted to be sure about the decision, not do anything rash we might regret. It's easy to just go through a phase or something, but the proposition kept coming back up, and by now I don't think we're in a phase.' The going-through-a-phase fear was a gift of self-doubt from my father. 'So we made up our minds, and we're sure it's the right thing ...' He sounded, as so often, exhausted, his chords minor, the end of sentences dropping that half-step of resignation.

My God. Sending hot ripples from my hairline down my neck, the nature of his announcement washed over me. Hurriedly I rearranged all he had told me the night before to assemble a situation of considerably more gravity. *Sleeping on the couch ... does nothing but complain ... the one thing that could end our marriage is if she got fat.* Not just talk, whingeing behind-back. The estrangement upstairs had widened more irreconcilably than I'd imagined. They were getting a divorce.

My reaction to Truman's news was complex. I felt sorry for Averil, as she peeled flakes of flagging pink polish from her nails. This was cheap pity, however; how effortless to have sympathy for an adversary when she is vanquished. With compulsive calculation, my mind flew forward three days and tried to decipher, with no success, just what effect this new turn of events would have on Truman's desire to buy the house. Yet trickling underneath all my astonishment, poor-Ave and poor-True, was an insidious, horrible little delight.

Which I instantly had to cover. I reached over and grazed Truman's little finger, not presuming to stroke his hand and rub his wife's nose in her lame-duck status.

'Maybe it was inevitable,' I comforted him. 'But you'll be all right.'

'Of course I'll be all right,' said Truman tersely, pulling his hand out of my reach. 'And, yeah, it was inevitable. You know what I'm like.'

'Sure I do.' I tried to keep my voice level, a little sad, but it came out unctuous instead. 'Remember, you've most of your life ahead. It's going to take a different course than you thought. But the future may surprise you. Though it probably doesn't seem that way now, this may be, in the end, a good thing.'

He looked at me askance. 'Of course it's a good thing. I just meant, you know, I like to take care of people.'

'I realize that.' I nodded vigorously. 'Your sense of responsibility is what makes this so hard.'

'It's not really that hard!' His callousness quite shocked me. 'We've been married ten years. We think it's about time.'

'Would someone clue me in here on what the fuck you're talking about?' Mordecai growled.

Truman shifted his gaze to his brother and said, 'We found out this afternoon. Averil's pregnant.'

I had been about to touch Truman's shoulder, ever so gently, but recovered my hand mid-air to fasten another button on my shirt, securing the demure neckline more in keeping with an aunt.

'If it's a girl,' said Averil softly, 'we could call her Corlis.'

'Anything,' I muttered, 'but *Corrie Lou*.'

'Congrats, kid,' said Mordecai gruffly. 'And when's the little bundle of joy due?'

'August ninth,' said Truman, for the first time in this funereal proceeding puffing with a bit of pride. 'Mother and Father's anniversary.'

'Well, isn't that touching,' said Mordecai, without quite as much sarcasm as I suspect he would have liked. 'Break a leg,' he said, 'or whatever. I gotta get back to work.'

Averil confessed to having already started sewing booties or something in the dovecot and excused herself, but not before Truman put a hand on each of her cheeks and kissed her forehead. *How sweet*, I thought before I could stop myself. He patted her bum as she left the kitchen, a gesture I recognized as my father's playfully condescending cheerio to my mother.

I carted coffee cups to the sink, grateful for stray dishes, and rummaged for our new bottle of Wild Turkey. It was slipped under the turned-over lip of the bin liner in the rubbish pail – Mordecai hadn't found it yet, since he never took out the trash. I poured a hefty double.

233

'You don't seem too thrilled,' Truman said as I rinsed cups, 'about our announcement.'

'I'm happy for you!' I chirped, not turning around. 'Could you hand me that sponge? You know, it really does improve quality of life when they don't stink.' I had swallowed a belt of bourbon too quickly, and my voice rasped.

'Did you suspect? Before?'

'Oh, sure.' Having run out of dishes I started gouging a knife into the cracks around the rim of the sink, scraping up grey gunk. 'A woman knows these things.' (I actually said that.) 'As I told you, I'd noticed she'd put on weight,' I pattered on, with the Pollyanna lilt I'd learned from my mother, 'but since you'd never let her eat too much, oh no, I put two and two together before you did.'

'Averil is pretty disciplined, about cookies.'

I was amassing a mound of dead paste on the edge of the counter, carving into every crevice I could find. 'Then, only one thing didn't match up. I thought you were sleeping on the couch.'

'I didn't say –' He took a swig of my bourbon. 'All the time.'

'Apparently not.'

'Well, don't act as if my sleeping with my own wife is some kind of crime.'

'Don't be silly.' I poked at my puddle of scum with a bare finger. It was sticky, sucking; it clung to me, and emitted a putrid road-kill smell like mice caught long ago in traps you forgot you set. *Grey matter*: what it looked like inside my head. 'And where do you plan to put this baby?'

'Corlis, we've got a huge house. We can finally put one of those spare bedrooms to better use than for Mordecai's filthy hirelings.'

'Don't you think the pregnancy is a bit premature?'

'Averil's twenty-eight!'

'There's a trend lately, women having them late.'

'Corlis, this is nuts. Averil's six weeks pregnant. That's not up for debate.'

'I meant premature in relation to the house. Remember the beloved house? That's your very self, as I remember?'

Truman pulled a selection of fag butts and paperclips from his pockets and collected them on the counter by my goo; he was scrupulous about sparing the hoover scraps that might clog the hose. 'All right, so that equation was a little extreme. But for once something has happened in this excruciatingly long month that doesn't have anything to do with the damn house!'

'It does; all roads lead to Heck-Andrews now. You don't know who's going to own this place, and you're already prepared to introduce a new resident.'

'There is no confusion over whose house this will be. It will be ours. Ours, right?'

My fingers were now covered in unspeakable ooze up to the second knuckle. Sliming the sink-rim paste between the pads of my fingertips was like wallowing in a distillation of all that was vile in me, yet also intrinsic to who I was, as Heck-Andrews was to Truman. 'It's a clever gambit, I'll grant that,' I said, allowing myself. If I had to live with this filth every day I might as well spread it around, the way Mordecai as an infant had decorated his crib with his poo. 'It's even sly. But you know, any of us could have kids.'

'Well, you haven't –'

'There's nothing in Mother and Father's will about grandchildren! There's nothing in the will that gives you more rights to this house just because you have a child!'

'Nobody said anything about the will, blast it, and I thought you and I had an understanding. I never once suggested that when Averil has the baby we'll kick you out.'

'You can't. You can't kick me out, I live here and this is my house, too!'

'You're getting overwrought, Corrie – Corlis.'

'What am I supposed to think?' I blubbered. 'How do I know you and Mordecai aren't plotting behind my back to throw me out on my ear? Look what you're planning to do to him, send him packing as soon as you've got the title in your hot little fist! When you can't trust your own brother, who can you –'

Truman grabbed my wrist and wrested my hand from the gunk, wheeling me to face him. 'Listen. I'm going to be a father. Even Mordecai congratulated me. Why can't you?'

I touched him on the shoulder, as I would have before it turned out he didn't need my consolation but good wishes; I had always been a dab hand at consolation. 'Congratulations, Truman,' I recited, getting glop on his forest green workshirt the way Mother had smeared it with weepy mucus.

'Thanks a lot.' He released my wrist, and sponged at his sleeve with disgust. 'Surprised it didn't take a gun to your head.'

He marched out and up the stairs to his darling wife, leaving me behind to feel ashamed of myself. I refused.

Of course, I recognized that the previous half-hour had featured the least gracious moments of my domestic career. But I had always been suspicious of being 'happy for' other people; I wasn't sure there was any substitute for being happy on your own account.

I did find the prospect of being 'happy for' others is charming; I would have liked it to be possible. So more particularly, neither of my brothers had ever been 'happy for' me and I had never been 'happy for' them. Truman may have been dead comforting when my sculptures were destroyed, but I doubted he'd have marshalled convincing exuberance had I instead flung open the door with the announcement that I had just made thousands of pounds and I was suddenly a famous artist in London. Deep, deep inside I was afraid that we wished each other, if not ill, at least *less*, and I prayed that this was what all siblings were like and not solely what McCreas were like. Oh, we could commend one another on trifles. I'd been elaborately encouraging when Truman got into Duke at the ripe age of twenty-eight, but maybe what I was really 'happy for' was the modest scale of his achievement. And yes, we presented brilliant shoulders to cry on when the chips were down; for secretly, we rather liked it when the competition was gaming with fewer chips.

Averil, pregnant? There was nothing in it for me. It was not my baby, and more, a foetus was tangible evidence of an intimacy Truman and I were forbidden, proof of the final severance of our childhood bond, the reward of his desertion to another woman. I was jealous. We'd have all lived in a finer universe by far if, when I heard Truman was going to be a father, I felt festive, glowing, genuinely buoyed and inclined to hum 'Day is Done' as I rinsed at the sink. But I couldn't, and I didn't, and in a funny way I'm glad I didn't. I may have been a bitter, spiteful shrew of a sister, but I was not a fake.

The following morning, in an irrational frenzy I set about pounding tacks into the perimeter of a square plywood frame. Then I snipped loops of knackered knee-highs I found in my upstairs dresser, and used them to weave potholder after potholder on the makeshift loom. This was a tried-and-true rainy-day childhood pastime, and potholders from old socks were a favourite Christmas present for my mother, since they didn't cost anything to make.

However, it was after Christmas, we didn't need potholders, and the busy warp and woof of argyles failed to spare me the gloom from their interstice: I had promised to give Mordecai a thumbs up or down in just twenty-four hours.

He roused earlier than usual, evidenced no interest in or surprise at my ridiculous crafts project, and ploughed off in his truck. Neither brother had noticed that I hadn't gone to work.

That evening I couldn't eat much dinner, for my sickness of heart had sunk to my stomach. Truman and I kept up a pass-the-Worcestershire dialogue that substituted for not speaking.

When Mordecai returned around nine, he was loaded down with plastic bags, and made more than one trip to lug them all inside. He literally threw the bags at Truman, but they bounced off harmlessly enough.

'What's all this?' said Truman, and peeked in one.

'Go ahead,' urged Mordecai. 'They're your Hide-the-Salami presents.'

Truman made a face at the phrase, and began pulling out stuffed animals – bunnies, opossums, elephants; Mordecai must have bought out the store. The overkill was typical. No doubt Truman would have been more chuffed had Mordecai lingered thoughtfully over a vast selection until he found a single doggie with an appealing expression, rather than snatching every fur-ball within reach. But that was Mordecai; never anything by halves. It struck me that all he and I had bought Truman in the last six weeks was toys.

The menagerie was a sop: Mordecai was filling his brother's arms with stuffed bears just like at the NC State Fair, where the giant panda was meant to distract you from the fact that it had cost you fifty dollars in pitched quarters. Mordecai planned to leave Truman with the bunnies and swipe the house. Look, the gifts said to me, don't feel guilty! We'll fob off a lot of little furry friends on your brother, slip him a cheque, and he'll just be too bowled over with gratitude to squeal. Wouldn't it be bad form for him to keep so many monkeys and lambikins and insist on a mansion as well?

Furthermore, Mordecai announced that in celebration of Truman's glad tidings he would take the night off and spend it with 'the family'.

We settled in the sitting room. Mordecai chain-smoked doobies until a cloud hovered at the ceiling like a gathering storm. Since I had failed to slip the bourbon back between the bin-liner and the pail, our Wild Turkey was soon shot, after which Mordecai moved to red wine, and only once our rioja was dispatched did he retrieve his own aquavit from the freezer. Averil, newly responsible mommy, wouldn't touch a drop. Truman wasn't party-hearty, either. He was mobilizing to demand that after the auction will his brother please remove himself lock, stock and barrel from the premises, and was not in the mood to be cajoled with bunnies or booze.

Yet if I could not have called it nostalgic, there was something familiar about us three, scrapping in front of the TV amid a herd of stuffed animals and an assortment of hand tools Mordecai had dribbled through every room of the house even as a boy. Just like old times – when I would lobby for *My Favourite Martian*, Truman would whimper for *Mr Ed*, Mordecai would insist on *The Dirty Dozen* and guess what we watched.

'*Bleh-eh-eh!*' bleated the pink lamb, as Mordecai turned it over one more time. The mechanism in its belly made a gagging sound like spew. '*Bleh-eh-eh!*'

The Caine Mutiny was on, which Truman had seen once and Averil never; they were both keen. Mordecai, however, had commandeered the remote control, and continually channel-surfed. We only got Bogart in snippets, after which Mordecai would flick to a fundamentalist Jesus programme he found campily entertaining. He made the opossum go down on the beaver and made off-colour slurping noises.

'Can we *please* stay on *The Caine Mutiny*?' Truman requested.

'*Bleh-eh-eh!*' The sheep looked half-slaughtered, having suffered a bloody baptism of spilled rioja. For his lamb-puke retort, however, Mordecai had let go of the remote control. Truman snatched it from beside Mordecai's boot and wouldn't give it back.

Unfortunately, the film was on one of those channels that has adverts for Pocket Fisherman every seven minutes. We might reasonably have switched to another show during the breaks, but

Truman was intent on not missing any of José Ferrer's monologue at the end.

Mordecai was getting surly. We were used to his varying degrees of inebriation, and it was often hard to tell if he was drunk. This evening, however, he was shitfaced. Poor Mort, spending all that money on presents for a sibling he didn't even like. One more slugfest with Dix in the Basement the day before had doubtless left Mordecai in no mood to hear that his brother was starting another happy family. Moreover, his wishy-washy sister was making him wait until the very last minute to know if he was about to be master of a demesne or was, within days, on the street.

Luckie Buddie was not warming the atmosphere. On every commercial break the advert for Luckie Buddie's Used Cars came on at twice the volume of the film, an announcer screeching, 'I'm crrr-AZY for deals!' while being hooked off camera in a straight-jacket: the sort of advert that works because you'll go out and buy a car that very instant if that would get Luckie Buddie to shut up. As if the line weren't repeated enough times, Mordecai had start-ed mimicking it when *The Caine Mutiny* came back on, and there was a creeping tone of menace in Mordecai's *crrr-AZY*!

'Man,' he drawled, 'Ain't no movie worth this shit.'

'Well, that ad's no worse than your lamb bleating every five seconds,' Truman sniped.

'Hey!' Mordecai jabbed at Truman's leg with the sheep's wine-stained muzzle. 'It's your lamb! I go out and buy presents for your kid and look at the thanks I get: Luckie Buddie.'

The film came back on, and Truman turned stoically to the screen, trying to rise above.

'If that ad comes on one more time,' Mordecai snarled, 'I'm putting a brick through the set.'

I glanced quickly around the sitting room to make sure there was no brick in sight.

We made it through one more set of handy kitchen gadgets safely to the next seven minutes of Bogie without Luckie Buddie, though Mordecai seemed only to smoulder at the lot owner's absence. We were into the penultimate scene, just a stone's throw from the credits, when –

'I'm crrr-AZY for – !'

The smash of broken glass was followed by the dry pop of an

imploding vacuum. As the tube tinkled to the carpet, a serpentine hiss sighed from what had been, not so very long before, our television set. Smoke threaded above the wreckage no thicker than the coil from Mordecai's roll-up.

Mordecai had not, after all, been pernickety about his choice of projectile. Truman rose stonily, unplugged the set, and dredged from its innards the electric drill that Mordecai had 'borrowed' or 'inherited' from Truman's workshop and never returned. The bit was bent.

None of us said anything. Averil inhaled, with a detectable sough. I attempted a chortle of sorts, but it sounded more like the gasp it was. Truman held the drill like a loaded Mac-10, pointing the barrel at his brother, but the bit drooped ludicrously towards the floor. Head tilted back on the sofa, Mordecai was beginning to snore.

18

'You call wrecking my electric drill and a $300 television having "style"?'

'Admit it,' I coaxed. 'Life around here has gotten a lot less boring since he moved in.'

'Maybe I want to be bored.'

I stopped smiling. 'Maybe you do.'

We were in the kitchen, of course – where my mother had conducted most of her life, and where I seemed destined to waste mine. Averil was at work, and I envied her. It was D-Day. My mind was conspicuously blank.

'So did Mr Dramatic Gesture manage to crawl upstairs?'

'When I peeked in this morning, he was still in the sitting room. I draped him with a blanket.'

'I think it's wakey-wakey time.'

'Truman, it's not dark yet!'

'Well, I'm going to find out just how grisly Dracula looks in the light of day.'

In six weeks, neither of us had ever roused Mordecai from his sleep. It wasn't done.

I followed Truman to the sitting room. The air was stinging with Three Castles, the carpet splattered with red wine. For once Truman hadn't cleared the bottles and butts; shattered glass was sprinkled before the gaping TV, whose open black maw still seemed to be sucking slightly. Stuffed animals were face-down or belly-up on the floor, stuporous. Mordecai, stiff in the same lolled position we had left him, might have been a wax Duane Hanson that museum visitors step around. His complexion was so bloodless, like dryer lint, that I was relieved to see him move when Truman kicked him.

'Get up!'

Mordecai groaned. Truman whipped my shroud from around his brother's shoulders and flung it to me. When the blunt toe of Truman's gumsoles thunked his ribs once more, Mordecai curled to the side and threw up.

I handed Truman the blanket back to clean his shoes.

'That's style for you,' said Troom, swabbing reddish chunks of his own tandoori chicken and dropping the blanket on the stain.

I suddenly recollected how Truman had finally been cured of his 'bembet'. Mordecai had nicked it, and used the tattered flannel to blow his nose until the little rag was crusted with boogers. Then he gave it back. Truman had been so repelled that even after Mother had washed the talisman he wouldn't come near it.

'Fuck off,' Mordecai grunted, cuddling into vomit and clutching the blanket desperately, as Truman had at four.

Truman wrapped the three foot-long braids around his hand, and heaved his brother in one motion to a stand. Behind Truman's open collar, bands of muscle stretched taut from skull to shoulder like two tethers.

I trailed behind as he half-lifted our brother down the hall and deposited his charge at the proverbial kitchen table, where we'd so often faced the music as kids.

Squinting, Mordecai patted his pockets. In his book report on *Lord of the Flies* in eighth grade, Mordecai had waxed eloquent not on Ralph or Jack, but on Piggy – the poor pudgy, misunderstood intellectual, blinded without his spectacles. So I went back to the sitting room to locate Mordecai's glasses, though I could hear, 'WHO DO YOU THINK YOU ARE?' boom from behind.

I returned with the thick yellow-tinted lenses, their frames bent and glass streaked with spew, and washed them at the sink. I had to remind myself that I was not being a voyeur, that this was my family and I had every right to listen in.

'What'd I do?' Mordecai whined, rubbing his eyes.

'You don't remember pitching my drill through the TV tube?' Truman stood bracing his hands on the back of my father's chair, as if threatening to brandish it.

Mordecai shot me his twelve-year-old grin. 'I did that?'

'Yes, Mordecai, you did that,' I recited at the sink, polishing his glasses with a dish towel.

'What'd it sound like?'

'*Poochhhh!*' I laughed. '*Hsssss … !*'

'You're going to pay for it,' said Truman.

'Sure,' said Mordecai as I brought him his glasses, but I recognized in the easy acquiescence that he probably wouldn't.

Mordecai raised himself in his seat, gathering his unbuttoned shirt to protect his pasty hairless chest, of late a bit breasty. He dabbed at his sleeve with a napkin, and mewled for coffee. Two alligator clips had come off his braids, which were unravelling in withered kinks.

'You come into my house –' Truman began.

'Troom, let him clean up first.'

'I'll let him clean up, all right. The sitting room, for a start.'

'Your house, kid? It's a third –'

'You never earned .01 per cent of this place. Who's repaired it for fifteen years? Who's painted it, refloored it, rewired it, roofed it, landscaped it and renovated the attic into a separate apartment?'

'No one asked you to –' Mordecai began.

'No one had to! And who has single-handedly sawed a hole in the back porch, gouged the hallway with his hand truck, and broken two windows, and whose wife has scrawled YOU BASTUD in red lipstick all over the master bedroom wallpaper like a serial killer?'

Mordecai was blasé. 'Division of labour.'

'But let's talk morally, *bro*. Did you ever come see Mother when she was grieving for Father, even once? Did you ever come visit either of them when you didn't want money? And do you think they didn't notice? Think Mother didn't remark on how happy you were when they signed that Living Will, and observe that it was "chilling"? How dumb do you think they were? They may have left a quarter of their assets to you, but that's only because they were hung up on this simplistic sense of fairness. And they thought about doing otherwise, they thought about it a lot. You weren't here, but they even asked me: should they maybe just leave the house, for example, to me and Corlis. I said no, because I didn't want to be greedy. In my shoes, would you have asked them to cut me out? At the drop of a hat.'

'You're shitting me, True.' Even magnified by lenses, Mordecai's eyes looked small. 'They'd never have disinherited me.'

'You treated them like chewing gum on your shoe, why not?'

'I didn't treat them in any way whatsoever,' Mordecai said wearily. 'I got on with my own goddamned life. That's what kids are supposed to do, shit-for-brains.'

'They're supposed to be grateful. And you're right, Mother and Father never seriously considered removing you from the will, but if they were just slightly different people you wouldn't have seen a red cent. A little more Old Testament, a little less New.'

'Read your Bible,' spat Mordecai. 'They'd have killed the fatted calf for me and you know it.'

'Fatted calf, is it? To listen to Father talk, he'd have more likely Isaaced you on some mountain top –'

I had a passing presentiment of what Truman was about to say and I didn't know how to make him stop. Outside rare blow-outs, our family was congenitally civil. That doesn't sound like such a curse until you consider that as a consequence we didn't know how to fight; that is, fight within limits. Families accustomed to airing grievances understand that even when things heat up the rules may change, that does not mean there are no rules; another set slides in, with wider margins but margins all the same. But we were conflict amateurs – we couldn't even tell my mother to her face that her rice was mushy – so that when we finally said what we were thinking all hell broke loose. It was a big Protestant problem and I'd seen it in other homes as well: once we allowed ourselves to say something, we allowed ourselves to say anything.

'– You know you were unwanted, don't you? That when Mother found out she was pregnant with you she was furious?'

'So she took pains to inform me,' said Mordecai dryly.

'Well, it's one thing to regret a kid before he's born,' said Truman. 'An embryo, a blank slate. It's another to regret him when you know what he's like.'

'What are you driving at?' Mordecai's impatience was nervous. 'Father.'

'Truman,' I interceded, 'I really don't think –'

'Four years ago. Right here at this table –'

'Troom, that's enough.'

'I'm the one who's had enough. You remember, don't you, Corlis? As I recall, you were on one of your charitable visits home.'

I nodded unwillingly. *Unconditional love.*

My father had been objecting there was no such thing.

Philosophically, I'd seen his point: that between any two people lurks the unforgivable. I could fling Truman's textbooks from his tower deck and though he'd be angry we'd be reconciled. If instead I threw Averil off the tower deck and she miscarried his first child, no handshake would smooth the way to nightcaps and chicken thighs. Some are more fragile than others, but all relationships are breakable if you kick them hard enough. Yet reasonable as it sounded, I remember resisting the proposition from my father, getting uneasy.

'Know what he said?' Truman leaned forward. 'Direct quotes. *If I'd known at the time what he'd put me and your mother through, I'd never have had my first-born son.*'

Mordecai snorted. 'Big deal. Parents toss that shit off all the time.'

'You think so?'

I didn't think so. The most harried parents I knew didn't rue their children as persons, but lamented the generic state of being unable to go to the cinema. The night my father issued his belated call-back of Mordecai was the only time in my life I have ever heard a parent – let's not beat around the bush here – wish his own child dead.

'So he was pissed off,' Mordecai dismissed.

'No,' Truman levelled. 'He wasn't.'

Mordecai looked to me with an expression I could only describe as pleading.

I turned away. 'Truman's right,' I said huskily. 'Father was pretty matter-of-fact.'

Composure had made his assertion so grim. He wasn't raving; no one was upset. My father made that unsolicited, unequivocal statement, having obviously given it some thought. The funny thing was, though aimed at Mordecai, the remark had tightened my own stomach. If perfectly durable devotion is a fiction, it is a myth any child of sound mind would preserve. For under my father's wishful retraction loomed the warning: *be a good girl, or we'll regret you, too*. With the divine power of parenthood to bring you into the world in the first place, it is hard to resist the fanciful notion that they could send you back.

And it was all very well to observe that if we turned into homicidal maniacs we could expect rebuff. But what had Mordecai done? He wasn't a thief or a junkie; he didn't even lie. He drank and philandered; he used bad language, but so does the London *Independent*. Mordecai was not malevolent but merely difficult, and that was enough. If this was conditional love, the conditions were stringent indeed.

'So the guy was an asshole,' said Mordecai, hardening. 'I can't say that comes as a surprise.'

I was impressed; I'd have cried.

'Then this won't come as any surprise, either. We're buying this house tomorrow morning, and you're out on your ear. No more free lunch; no more free maid service; no more free flophouse. We're kicking you out.'

'*We*, is it? Who's *we*?'

'Me and Corrie Lou,' said Truman proudly.

Mordecai turned to me and asked, 'Is that so?'

I panicked. I wasn't ready. I hadn't 'decided'. My gaze shuttled frantically from brother to brother.

If a stranger had walked into our kitchen right then he would have found: a pushing-forty Sixties throw-back with a violent hangover, streaked in vomit, moist in wrinkled slept-in clothes – a small-time businessman sunk in debt and not even bothering to battle the bottle. Not very tall, gently overweight, with a third broken marriage; a junior high school drop-out with a taste for cartoons.

Facing? A beamy-shouldered stalwart, handsome and showered, well-nourished and rested. Married, issue on the way, ensconced in a lordly manor he considered his own. If unadventurous, safely bulwarked in a small world whose perimeters he had no intention of pressing; if kind, fully capable of deploying unconscionable weapons at his disposal; if younger, grown.

But what did I see? In Mordecai, an edifice – the girds in our Hi-flier, my shelter on the first day of school. The foreshortening, pleasantly patronizing paragon actually allowed behind the grill at the Red Barn, who lured two hour-glass older women to the same Hillsborough mattress. King of the Basement, Godfather of the underworld below the post office. And the only man I had ever met who could stand up to my father.

Opposite? A delicate and ingenuous Tender Flower, with too-wide eyes and a kick-me smile, bedevilled by a wayward gold cowlick, and so shaken by nursery school that for hours after he would only speak in signs.

'Mordecai.' I looked at the floor. 'You don't need me.'

In my defence, I believed that.

'Yeah, right.'

Mordecai drew himself up with obvious reluctance, the Big Brother, the Genius. Though we serfs would have traded places in a minute, the imperial mantle of the first-born must have weighed heavy at times, and as Mordecai squared himself in the back doorway he didn't manage to right the slump of having been woken in what was to him the middle of the night.

'You,' he told Truman, 'are the one who's had a free ride, but if our parents never jump-started you into adulthood I will. You've always borne me a grudge, because I got out from under. You think being good wins the day, don't you? Oh, you've been perfect, all right. The perfect baby. Mother might reward that, but I won't.

'I've got the financing to outbid the both of you tomorrow, and I'll put in an offer you two couldn't touch with a barge pole.'

Before about-facing to the porch, Mordecai shot me one look and I met his eyes because I thought I deserved at least a glare. I was prepared for scathing, if not exposure. With some wonderment I found my older brother's brown eyes behind the yellow lenses for once unhooded, softened. I was braced for a parting shot to Truman and would submit to the consequences: *You realize that for two months your beloved big sister has seriously considered buying this house with me, don't you? We had a mortgage lined up. Put that in your pipe and smoke it.* That's what Mordecai might have said, or ought to have said, at which point Truman would never trust me again.

But Mordecai's lips remained closed and for once they didn't purse but smiled slightly; cleansed of sarcasm, the smile was relaxed, symmetrical, gentle. *I still don't understand what you see in that kid,* his shrug as much as said. *But if he's that goddamned important to you, keep at least one brother if only to remind you of me.* Then Mordecai's face resumed its military implacability, and he marched out the door to his truck.

A soldierly performance, but his flash of superior finance had been less than blinding; his swagger of seniority echoed hollow from the damaged boards of the back porch. I had long envied Mordecai's reputation for intellect, though his reputed brilliance served my parents' vanity as much as his. I realized that we exalted one another to exalt ourselves, and bestowed qualities to personalize the incomprehensible, but in the end we did each other a disservice. When your brother is the Genius, he is also the enemy. If the upside of families was that we meant something to one another, the downside was that we meant too much. We were never allowed to be regular people, just as Heck-Andrews was not allowed to be a plain old house. We turned each other into abstractions. So there was little mystery in why I had, at eight as at thirty-five, chosen Truman over Mordecai. The Tender Flower had laid exclusive claim to fragility, as The Bulldozer had title to brutality; that Truman could be cruel or that Mordecai could be injured was lost on their sister. I had been hoodwinked by my mother's nicknames, and seeking purpose more than power I would leap to the side of the helpless, who required my protection. In this preference I betrayed that I was, profoundly, a girl.

19

After Mordecai left, our capacious kitchen closed in, the long counters fencing us, a smell cloying the air like kippers, as if the altercation had left a residue. Though this room had commonly appealed to me for feeling untampered, that morning it felt excessively so – tired, worn, over. I scanned the crannies by the stove that my parents had cluttered with broccoli rubber bands, washed Ziploc bags, lidless jars and coffee-ringed coupons. Though we'd swept away the detritus in December, I saw these orphaned objects had gradually been replaced with our own: folded tin foil we'd ridiculed my parents for obsessively recycling but re-used three times ourselves, dried-up ballpoints, grocery lists we never remembered to take with us to Harris Teeter, and the same 'perfectly good' rubber bands. That we'd proved genetically incapable of tidy counter tops oppressed me.

Truman and I said nothing. Our imbroglio ended, for a few minutes it appeared that with the rules of normal discourse restored we had lost the knack of communicating within its strict and rather dull conventions.

At last he scowled at me as if I were the single lemon in a row of slot machine cherries. 'Why aren't you at work?'

'I was fired.'

Truman grunted and didn't pretend he cared why.

'I've gotta do something,' he muttered, and lunged from his chair.

I could hear him trudge up the first flight of stairs, then creak overhead towards the front – to Mordecai's room, or MK's. I didn't dwell on what he was up to, I had plenty else to dwell on, but Truman must have been gone for twenty minutes. When he came back, he didn't explain. He paced, jerkily, in various directions, and kept smoothing his palms down his jeans as if to rub something off.

'I don't have any classes. But much as I like this house, I'd really like to get out of here today,' said Truman, jittery. 'How about it? A walk, a museum, I don't care. You game?'

The claustrophobia wasn't like him, but I shared it. 'By all means,' I assented. 'I feel like all three storeys are resting on my shoulders.'

At first we walked our regular circuit, which seemed longer than usual; like the kitchen behind us, Wilmington, the Mall and Peace College felt overly known, washed out and washed up. For once I didn't stride with my head bent towards Truman's in conference, but maintained a wary space between us that would fit a whole person, as if a whole person were missing. I stepped toe-first on the pavement the way children balance along a wall, and superstitiously avoided cracks, though my mother was dead. After a while I said, 'I've never seen you like that.'

'Maybe I've never been like that. You're the one who said I should stand up to him.'

'I never said any such thing, that was Averil. And if I had, I'd have said *stand up to him* and not *stomp on his face*.'

Truman flapped his hands. 'Classic! My brother craps all over me for weeks – not to mention years – swiping my tools, defacing my house, eating and drinking everything in sight he didn't pay for and inviting half the town to do likewise, and *finally* I say something, *finally* I dish out what he has coming, and *who* gets the dressing down? Mordecai's the maverick, which I suppose elevates him above common decency whereas the obligations of politeness still apply to me.'

'I know Mordecai's been inconsiderate, but he hasn't tried to hurt your feelings.'

'What do you mean, he called me a "perfect baby"!'

I said, true.

At Krispey Kreme, neither of us had an appetite for bavarian creams, and we settled for tepid coffee. I couldn't be bothered to sharpen my English accent for the waitress, who commented when we ordered that I had 'started sounding like a local in no time'.

What all did we do that afternoon? We took a guided tour of the Legislature, which I hadn't done since a sixth-grade field trip. We roamed around the art museum; we canvassed the capitol and read Civil War inscriptions. We ended up in front of Green Street about six, too early for a beer really, but Truman seemed keen to make another exception to the Eight O'Clock Rule. I was weary of exceptions, and craved one day when, according to our old form, we sipped only two glasses of wine, after eight. It was odd, me wanting order and Truman acting devil-may-care.

I was tired of meandering, especially considering how little Truman and I seemed to have to say to each other. I'd have liked to catch MacNeil-Lehrer. 'Come on,' I urged. 'Let's skip Green Street, go home, and put our feet up.'

After glancing at his watch, Truman was adamant. He'd not go back to Blount Street; I supposed he dreaded running into Mordecai. So we pushed in the double-doors of the micro-brewery, all done up in snooker-green and brass like a British pub.

I collapsed in a booth, leaning into the corner. Truman fiddled with the hot mustard, stirring the pot with the tiny spoon and gazing dolefully at the Colman's. I realized I was waiting. All afternoon Troom had blown off blasts of hot air about his brother, but in the last hour he'd run out of steam. I knew Truman. He may have unearthed a buried penchant for sporadic biliousness, but it wasn't in him to keep it up. Once we had ordered bangers and mash to pick at, he mumbled, 'Maybe I shouldn't have said that, about Father.'

'Mmm-hmm,' I hummed. 'Maybe not.'

'I never thought I could say anything to Mordecai that would affect him in the slightest.'

I knew that. A man who regards himself as impotent is surprisingly lethal. He doesn't take care. No one tries to control power he doesn't recognize he has. And with a chronic victim, the idea that he might himself victimize other people never enters his head.

'You had an effect, all right.'

'You think I should apologize.'

'Yes.' I took a deep breath. 'And I may owe an apology to you.'

'What for?'

Mordecai had made me a gift of Truman's trust when he left that morning, but I didn't want it. So I told Truman everything. Mordecai's proposal, my openness to the coalition, even why Wachovia really cold-shouldered Truman's application. He didn't go ballistic, but kept his hands in his lap and took it all in like a good student.

When I was finished, I qualified. 'Don't get me wrong. I'm not apologizing for considering a different arrangement. I'm only sorry I wasn't dead straight. I still think Mordecai may have been right. That staying in that house isn't good for you, Truman.'

Though he might have chosen to lose his rag, or slump stiffly away from his scurrilous, two-timing sister, Truman instead looked four years old again, open, hopeful, obedient. I think it hit him, just like that first afternoon after school when I played Tinker-Toy with Troom instead of scampering down to watch Mordecai preserve mice in formaldehyde, that once more, astonishingly, the weaker had won. He seemed less interested in my duplicity than in nailing down the future.

'Do you really think Mordecai will make a bid for the house tomorrow?' Truman leaned over our sausages. 'And will he be able to go higher than $490,000?'

The house, the house, the house! I was bloody sick of it. I hated the *word* 'house'. So I peeked under our booth and once more discovered Dorothy's shoes. There was little use being in a position of influence if you weren't willing to exploit it.

'Now, listen, Truman,' I began. 'Yes, I'm uncomfortable with inheritance in general, something for nothing. But this situation has degenerated into a horlicks Mother and Father never intended and would have deplored. In leaving us with a piece of property and a nest egg, they were trying to do us a favour, not set us at each others' throats! OK, so I said I'd go in with you, but how does that make Mordecai feel? How does that make me feel? Like one of those medieval torture victims ripped limb from limb by Clydesdales. Well, I bow out. No, I won't buy the house with Mordecai, but I won't buy it with you either. I suggest tomorrow morning we all sleep late.'

'You don't mean that.' His voice was faint.

'Try me. Now can we please go home? Or do you want to check your watch again?'

He did. He checked his watch.

As we walked back to Blount Street, Truman tucked in his shoulders and hung his head, using short, shuffling steps and turning in his toes. His speech had gone tiny and simpering. The whole beleaguered, woeful schtick was getting powerfully on my nerves.

252

We trudged up the back porch stairs at about eight o'clock. Averil's PTA meeting mustn't have been over yet; the drive was empty of both army truck and Volvo. Truman took out his key, sorrowing up at the structure as if to goad me that if I had my evil way he would open this back door at best a handful more times in his life. The key would only turn a few degrees; the door was unlocked.

The first glaring absence was the kitchen table. The chairs had vanished, too.

'Truman,' I said slowly. 'What is wrong with this picture?'

'The kitchen does seem –' he cleared his throat, 'more spacious than usual.'

I wandered to the foyer. The stand by the door was missing, though its mat was rumpled in the corner under a scattering of stamps and menus for take-away Chinese. The oriental carpet, however, had disappeared.

'*What* on *earth*?' I was doomed to become my mother in a crisis.

With a methodicalness just this side of insanity, I walked calmly to the parlour, noting with the excessive moderation that is a substitute for screaming, uh-huh, so the couch is gone, so the stereo is gone; armchairs, check them off; coffee table, check … Though *Slavery and Social Death* and *Blacks in American Society* and their like were still shelved in the otherwise starkly naked room, the Britannicas were missing.

I pointed out the gap to Truman, where our family photo albums flapped open in the Britannicas' place. 'A signature, wouldn't you say?'

Across in the sitting room, the photocopier, plotter and Compaq computer were cleared off, too. Alone on the carpet with its smattering of shattered glass, the gaping television and stuffed animals had been graciously left behind, mementoes of our last lovely night together as a family.

As we ascended to the second floor, I noticed the carpet was torn on the stair lips; it was easy to imagine the legs of hastily hefted bureaux bump-bump-bumping to the front door. I called out, 'Mordecai? Big Dave? MK?' but heard nothing but an unusually resonant echo.

In the adjutants' rooms, we found the usual paracetamol foil, Bambus and dirty highball glasses, along with some balled-up sheets and a few soiled clothes, but with no beds to strew them on all these remnants were on the floor.

Like Hansel's bread crumbs, paperclips, pencils, address labels and my father's soggy blue mints were dribbled down the hall from the study, spilled from the drawers of the unemptied desk. Inside the room, the only component remaining of Mordecai's Toshiba and Bubblejet was his power strip. The study in particular had been ransacked. The floor was ankle-deep in tossed Supreme Court stationery; books my father had authored were splayed with their spines cracked underfoot. All that was left of Mordecai's dominion here were a few crumpled *National Lampoons*.

With foreboding, I ventured into my own room, where one of my stained glass panes was put out, perhaps from dismantling the bed frame. I would miss that bed, and not. Its mattress had hosted sweet dreams in my youth, but recent visions had been anguished, and that wadding had absorbed a lot of sour sweat I would happily donate to someone else's hell. A brief inventory found my clothes still about, the dresser having been disgorged, though a more thorough inspection would turn up that I'd been relieved of three pairs of lacy knickers. In a corner, I located the severed hand I'd brought back from South Ealing, now in pieces. Though I'd rescued the fragment in November as a relic of my sculptures, in the last two months the keepsake had transformed into a souvenir of deceit, and I was glad enough to throw the shards away.

Meanwhile, Truman had vaulted to the dovecot. Protected by that extra, troublesome flight of stairs, it was unmolested. The boot sale Victorian couch nestled in its throw-rug depressions; the portraits of Heck, Andrews and Appleget peered tranquilly from their frames.

Truman slumped in his baroque armchair. For a man who had so recently discovered his nascent powers of indignation, his reticence struck me as queer.

'I may have said you don't call the cops on your own brother,' I said, too restless to sit myself. 'But I'm coming round to your view. You don't remember his licence plate number?'

'No.'

'There can't be that many privately owned troop transporters on the road in North Carolina. We could still have him stopped.' I paused, puzzled. 'How do you figure he got all our furniture into that truck? It's big, but not that big.'

'Search me,' said Truman lamely.

We heard a car pull in the drive, and Truman bolted upright. 'I'd better catch her –' He scrambled out the door. 'Shock – the baby ...'

I followed him downstairs, at which point Averil was already wandering the foyer, looking dazed. She insisted on touring the denuded mansion as well, since some things you have to see for yourself.

We reconvened in the dovecot, the only area remaining with chairs. 'If he took two loads,' I supposed, 'then the stuff can't have been carted very far, right? The Basement!'

Truman groped for the phone. His colouring was a touch orange, as if he'd swallowed something that disagreed with him.

'Howdy!' Dix's voice carried beyond the earpiece.

'Dix, this is Truman McCrea.'

'If you're wanting to talk to Mort –'

'No!'

'Well, that's good, 'cause he ain't here, and if he do poke his head in my door he ain't gonna have one more than thirty seconds longer.'

'Listen, nobody's brought any – furniture over there, have they? Office equipment? A four-poster bed ... ?'

'Honey, nobody's brought so much as a six-pack by here in weeks, much less a four-poster. You offering? Though between the two, I'd go for the Miller, personally.'

Truman said, 'Never mind,' and clunked the receiver from an inch above its cradle, that's-that.

Experimentally, I ambled downstairs to take in the atmosphere. Switching on overhead lights as I went, I kept waiting to feel incensed. Yet my step was deft, my fingers extended from my hips like Ginger Rogers about to tap dance. My eyebrows arched, and as I threaded through the desolated bedrooms the corners of my mouth kept tugging upwards. When I tripped down to the parlour, so vast and austere unfettered, I could only feel refreshed. Their drapes away, the bays had widened, as if the house had opened its eyes after a heavy sleep. The room seemed to breathe more deeply, and to stare out at the lights of the capital city rather than squint in dark self-absorption. I'd never thought this so bluntly before, but this room's jarring mix of Danish Modern and newlywed bargains had always rankled. I hadn't really liked, I submitted briskly to myself, nearly everything my parents owned.

I trod pensively back up the stairs. If by clearing out this house Mordecai had evened our score, I was thankful; I wanted the score even. More, if in some unknown hovel on the other side of town my brother was unloading his booty – couches stained with chewy ten-year-old cacciatore from the freezer, end-tables adrip with my father's ghastly epoxy repairs – he was welcome to it. For this cleanly wiped slate was a dream come true. Though I wouldn't have wished to assume the onus of discarding the accumulated chattel of their lives, my parents' belongings had not been a record of my own sprees or my own penny-pinching. Now that my brother had obliged, I was free to inhale the bright release of oak fumes from the slightly lighter patches of uncloaked flooring, to saunter uncluttered rooms which, for the first time since my mother's death, seemed to have a future. He could assume the burden of all that imperfection and making do, for almost every object my parents had ever bought was their second choice because it was cheaper. In fact, this looted mansion had the appeal of a recycled canvas, fresh gesso whited over a failed painting. I had transient second thoughts about boycotting the auction fourteen hours hence. For perhaps the first time in thirty-five years, I liked it here.

Back in the dovecot, Truman was brooding. We started at the distinctive churn of another motor from below.

'Bloody hell,' I wondered. 'Why would he come back?'

We tumbled downstairs again, though Truman lagged behind. Alone of us, perhaps preferring the dramatic entrance, Mordecai often came in through the front door. When we reached the landing, there he was, slumping on the knob in the foyer, still wearing the same stained clothes from that morning. His left hand noosed a paper bag, and he was waving it aimlessly, unable to locate a table to set it down.

'You're going to explain –'

'Where did you take –'

Averil and I spoke at once. We shut up at once. Mordecai peered blearily up at our trio, his thick eyebrows tangled. He glanced beside the door, and toed the stamps and Chinese menus on the floor. When his eyes grazed the blonde square where the oriental carpet had lain, the sunny rim around his pupils sulphured to a more troubled hue.

'What now?' Mordecai scanned our formation. 'Mother didn't want me, Father didn't want me, you don't want me, I already know my wife doesn't want me, who's left?'

I stepped down the last few stairs. 'I can see how you'd be angry, and I'm sympathetic, to a point,' I began evenly. 'It's the presumption that gets up my nose, and the spite. The sheer spite! You know if you wanted a table or a mattress we'd have given it to you gladly.'

'Say what?' said Mordecai.

I held out my palm. 'I'm afraid you've used the key to this house for the last time and once too many.'

Mordecai stared at my hand, as if struck by the sheer emptiness of it, how little I had ever offered.

'If that's the way you feel about it, sis. Blood is sicker than water.' He tossed his whole keyring at my feet.

As Truman grabbed my arm to keep me from picking it up, I was visited with the unsettling recollection that Mordecai didn't shop for broccoli. Though he may have 'borrowed' Truman's electric drill, he'd never abscond with our food processor.

Mordecai trooped to the kitchen; I followed. He walked through where the table had been without flinching, but when he returned from the cabinet with a glass he started to put it down on a surface that was no longer there. 'What the fuck.'

'You mean, you didn't – ?'

He wouldn't answer, but left his bottle on the stairs and crossed to the parlour, where even an indifferent bohemian would notice something had changed. At which point he rushed to the sitting room, to be confronted with the lone bashed-in TV and hungover stuffed animals. 'Where's my IBM? Where's my Design Jet? *Where's my Compaq Prolinea*?'

Double-time, boots pounding, Mordecai clumped out the back to what was once Truman's workshop: the tablesaw was gone. The hand tools were gone. The lathe, the welding torch …

Rapidly losing energy, Mordecai dragged himself up to Father's office and shuffled through the spilled stationery. I think by this time he hardly expected his fax, laptop and printer to be plugged in and purring; his kicking at scattered *Law Weeklies* was perfunctory.

Mordecai trudged down the first flight again and sank on a bottom stair. 'Dix.'

'Your own *wife*?'

'My floppies are lifted. Software, including the back-ups – Lotus, Autocad, AC; all my designs, client records. Know any common thieves who'd steal a Blaupunkt catalogue?'

'Or the Britannicas,' I remembered. 'But why?'

'She badgered me just this last week that I never bought her so much as a Coca-Cola and then I'd go and invest in this Blount Street clunker that ought, she claimed, to be filled with nothing but foul memories. You gotta admit, she had a point.'

'But Dix couldn't have dragged all this crap out by herself.'

'She got help, sweetheart. I was at Meredith this afternoon. We were supposed to start installing the new sound system today. My whole crew went awol.'

'Your own employees would rip off your furniture?'

He rose up, splashing shnapps. 'Furniture? *Furniture*? That Compaq package cost thirty thousand bucks! I've got net assets of over two hundred grand. Don't you understand what's happened here, you nitwit? You're in a lather about throw pillows, and I've lost Decibelle!'

I had never heard him nearly as distraught when a marriage collapsed. Both my brothers were given to ulterior affections, as if they'd been rewired and all the current that might logically have been channeled to Mother or Wife got rerouted to House or Company instead.

'But why would they –'

The one outburst was all Mordecai could manage. He sat back down, his face gone slack, and it seemed to take effort to reach for his bottle. 'My payroll was a little behind.' He smiled, an ugly smile, and slugged his aquavit.

'How behind?'

'It doesn't matter.'

I bet it did to them.

'Shouldn't we call the police?' said Averil.

'And tell them what?' said Mordecai flippantly. 'To look for which truck? I bet they've crossed the state line by now. Dix is smart.'

'But Dix is at the Basement,' I objected.

'You're insured, aren't you?' Truman intervened.

'Couldn't afford the payments,' Mordecai reported almost cheerfully, draining the tumbler. 'Decided to risk it for a few months, save some dough. Dix knew we weren't insured, of course; the whole crew did. That standing drill is heavy. Wouldn't want to go to all that trouble to reward me with a cheque.'

'Dix is home!' I insisted. 'We called her, and she didn't seem to know anything about it –' No one was listening to me, but I wanted my sassy sister-in-law, whom I quite liked, exonerated.

'But the house is insured,' said Truman.

'Won't cover commercial property,' said Mordecai with a trace of his old authority. 'Most valuables worth over a couple hundred bucks have to be listed on the policy, and I bet the last time you checked Mother didn't remember to itemize her Rockwell table saw.'

'What are you going to do?' asked Averil.

'No tools, no crew, no work.' His tone had that soprano whimsicality of total apathy.

'Mordecai, I'm sorry,' said Truman.

There are two kinds of 'sorry': isn't-that-a-shame and it's-all-my-fault. Truman's sounded curiously like the second sort.

I ignored him; this was no time for Truman to indulge another bout of his compulsive flagellation – if-only-we'd-stayed-home-today or whatever. 'Mordecai, when the house is sold tomorrow, you'll have at least $100,000 disposable. Surely that much cash could get Decibelle on its feet?'

'Truman and I could help you out,' Averil volunteered, to my surprise.

'Huh.' Mordecai's laugh was halfway between a hiccough and a gag. 'I'm in debt, children.'

'But a hundred –'

'Drop in the bucket. You poor bastards all still think owing money means you have to give Daddy back the twenty he lent you for a secondhand bike. No, we're talking bankruptcy, the Big B. Sell the house tomorrow, some companies in this town gonna be very, very happy. As I recall –' He looked at his wrist. 'They let you keep your watch.'

'Mordecai, I'm *really* sorry.'

This time even Mordecai seemed to notice Truman's peculiarly culpable tone.

'It was your workmen, Mordecai, but Corlis is right, I doubt Dix had anything to do with it. I did, though.'

'How's that?'

We all three swivelled our attentions to Truman. This was the notoriety that he'd long envied Mordecai, and now, I sensed, could have lived without.

'This morning,' Troom went on heavily, 'I gave MK enough cash to rent a truck, and a fee for his trouble. I even suggested he get Big Dave and Wilcox to help. I guaranteed that no one would be home until at least eight –'

I interrupted, 'You hired that sleaze-bucket to gut your own house?'

But Truman disciplined his gaze at Mordecai. 'He was supposed to cart your what-all – tools, files, clothes – back to the Basement where it came from. I had it planned from way back. I thought Corlis and I would buy the house tomorrow, and I wanted you out. I was afraid if we didn't remove you by force you'd never go.'

Mordecai nodded appreciatively. 'Touché. You're on the money there, kid.'

A propos nothing, I asked, 'Why would those pinheads take the Britannicas?'

'I might have mentioned they were worth a lot of money,' said Truman, eyes stumbling to his feet. 'Anyway. He was only supposed to lug Mordecai's junk home. He wasn't supposed to take everything. And he wasn't supposed to keep anything that – didn't belong to him.'

'Perish the thought,' I quipped.

'Just because you're so cynical about people!' Averil snapped at me. 'It's not Truman's fault if he doesn't assume everyone's a jerk!'

'Congrats, kid,' Mordecai commended his brother. 'Direct hit. You delivered my business to a douche-bag, who will fence my entire inventory in Florida for about fifteen per cent of net worth. I couldn't have customized payback better myself. Too bad I can't remember what I did to deserve it.'

I suppose we might have invited Mordecai to the dovecot, with a table for his glass and cushion for his head, but we had never

asked him up there before and it seemed late in the day to con-
struct a happy threesome we hadn't even managed as children.
Just because he was hurting and intimacy would be handy, we
couldn't pull it out of a hat. If he felt alone, he was.

Then, what did we expect Mordecai to do, curl up on the bare
floorboards of his parents' bedroom? So he hauled himself up by
the banister and steadied before grunting, 'I need some air.' He
scooped up his keyring from under the lip of the last stair.

Truman, Averil and I measured his bottle in unison. It was two-
thirds empty.

These were sensitive times about Driving Under the Influence,
but in our family the issue was more than usually charged. On the
subject of booze my mother had always been reproachful, summarily corking our unfinished wine to the back of the fridge, but
for her final two years she'd been fanatic, smelling our breaths
before we drove. Truman submitted to the humiliating sniff-test
without complaint, because she had her reasons. In the winter of
1990 my father had attended a meeting in Durham about integrated public housing that ran late. It lasted, in fact, for ever.

His was a common enough death; too common, we all agreed,
for a man who adulated Medgar Evers and Martin Luther King.
My father was killed by a drunk driver – by a man who was just
about as poleaxed as his first-born son was now.

Truman and I locked eyes for one long beat, until I broke it by
raising my palms in a gesture of helplessness for which I could
feel no admiration. Yes, he was our big brother, and we had never
told him what to do, but if there was any point at which we
should have tried to it was at that moment. I think we were
exhausted. We both wanted Mordecai to go away. Not out of dislike, or from any of the old resentment that he was a despot or
that he got to be the genius while we cretins did our spelling
homework. But because if his intelligence had always seemed
more towering than ours, so had his troubles as well. Now those
troubles were more monumental than ever, and we simply
couldn't afford him any more that night. As soon as he heaved
into his truck we could tell ourselves he was no longer our problem.

Mordecai took the bottle with him, and his boots clunking
down the bare oak for ten paces put me in mind of game shows
where the clock is ticking and you have ten seconds to punch

your bell and stop the host and say *I've got it!*, but when we let him cross the transom the buzzer sounded: as if from a sudden blankness or failure of nerve we had just lost the jackpot.

'But what should we do tomorrow,' Truman called after him. 'About the house?'

Mordecai paused in the porch light, glancing backwards with distaste. 'Torch it.' He slammed the door.

While the truck revved and lurched out of earshot Truman and I couldn't look each other in the eye.

Then we lied. 'We shouldn't have let him drive,' said Truman.

'I guess you're right,' I agreed, colluding in the conceit that gosh, that just occurred to me too, and now, darn it, it's too late to stop the guy.

When we lumbered up to the dovecot, conversation was halting. I remarked, 'That was pretty gormless, Truman,' and 'MK was a dirt bird, the smallest little child could see that,' but otherwise let Truman off the hook. As the minutes ticked arduously on, I found myself straining for the grind of an engine, but caught only the odd whoosh from Wilmington Street, and once in a while the *wow-wow* of a police siren which I could not peremptorily dismiss as a stranger's disaster.

We agreed to call it a night, set an alarm, and deal with the issue of the auction at breakfast. Truman made up the sofa for my bed.

But there was no way, lying on the couch, that I was going to sleep. I kept rehearsing a story that Truman had told me only once. While small, short, and even ordinary in its way, the tale of ninety minutes in this dovecot two years earlier had printed itself with cinematic clarity on my brain, perhaps because it was the real-life version of every child's nightmare.

My father was due back from Durham. Another meeting, nothing special. My mother had tapped on Truman's door around midnight, the timid tiddle-tiddle of her nails setting his teeth on edge. She poked in and said Sturges was awfully late and she was concerned. Truman was impatient. He said, 'You know Father, he stays and talks to people forever, and it's a good half hour from Durham.'

She'd padded back to her bedroom in slippers, though Truman realized she wanted to come upstairs. Later he must have hated himself for not keeping her company, though there'd been so many other evenings when he'd been just as terse and closed and stony that if Truman were to hate himself for every one of them he'd hate himself pretty much all the time. Come to think of it – maybe he did.

An hour later, Mother hadn't stopped to knock as she'd been trained to, but shuffled straight into Truman's bedroom, though her son was a married man now, with a naked wife on his arm. She shook his shoulder. 'Truman?'

This time it was I who trundled into his bedroom to rouse my brother and whisper, *I can't sleep, I'm worried*, adding, *he's not back yet and he's nowhere else to go*. Truman mumbled much what he'd told our mother two years before: *if there's anything wrong, we're sure to hear. Go back to bed.*

But my mother had remained hovering at his bedside, while Truman's standard irritation battled a five-year-old's butterflies. As a boy, the nights Mordecai babysat, Truman had stayed awake for hours listening for our parents' car. He was always afraid something dreadful had happened to them, and the perfumed peck on his forehead and brusque *Eu-GEENya! Let's get a move on!* would constitute his final memory of our mother and father. Older, you get casual, credulous, but the child's mistrust is actually more intelligent.

At last the phone arrested Mother's fussy folding down of Truman's bedspread. It was 1.20 a.m., too late for Common Cause fundraising or gossip from my aunt. The dovecot had a separate phone line, so they could only hear it purring from downstairs. Troom said, 'I bet that's him now.' But he thought: I should really get up and answer that for her. He didn't. She bustled to catch it, though I figure if she had that flight to run over again she'd have taken her time, savouring the last few seconds of her life in one piece. The ring cut off. Truman held his breath. A minute passed. And then a cry rose from the master bedroom like a wild animal's, and it didn't stop and he knew what it meant and that once again Truman would be called upon to be the one good son.

I, too, paused in the darkness of Truman's bedroom, but no phone purred from below, no ululation curdled up the stairwell. *Hooo-IH-hooo … hooo … hooo …* Morning doves soothed from the yard. After a while I shambled back to my sofa. There I remained rigid, face up. What kept running through my head was the kind of sophisticated ethics my father had drilled into his children, easy axioms of don't-fib and thou-shalt-not-kill qualified with more demanding reminders that there are lies of omission and crimes of simply doing nothing, and by Sturges Harcourt McCrea's exacting standards we were murderers.

All repetition arrives with variation. In fact, the phone downstairs didn't ring until three.

20

At Rex Hospital, Truman and I filled in Mordecai's admission papers; our brother was in no condition to sign his name. I clued up pretty quickly as to the primary purpose of these forms; the section about drug allergies was a mere while-you're-at-it.

'Mr McCrea was carrying a Blue Cross-Blue Shield card, ma'am,' clipped the reception nurse. 'It was expired.' She made a face, as if Mordecai had been wearing dirty Y-fronts.

Truman whispered, 'If Mordecai wasn't even covering Decibelle, what are the chances he had any health insurance for himself?'

'Zero,' I said, and turned to the nurse. 'What does that mean?'

'We'll need some guarantee of payment, ma'am. A credit card imprint would do. We accept ...'

'Put it on mine,' said Truman, taking out his wallet.

I stayed his hand. 'Our brother's broke,' I said to the receptionist. 'What if we weren't here?'

'We do accept indigents, but for emergency care only,' she said, nose in the air.

'Corlis!' said Truman, straining to offer his card. 'We have to –'

'On the phone we were told he might need surgery,' I pursued, still holding Truman's wrist. 'Are you telling me that if my brother couldn't pay for it, you *wouldn't do it*?'

'That's correct, ma'am.'

I took Truman's credit card and tossed it through the window, the way Mordecai had frisbeed Truman a C-note. 'Not that long ago you people wouldn't accept blacks. Current policies don't strike me as all that improved.'

'This is not a charity ward, Mizz McCrea.' She slapped the machine over Truman's card with a flourish.

'All I can say is, thank fucking hell I voted for Bill Clinton.'

'There's no need to curse, ma'am.' Truman was now physically dragging me across the lino. 'And North Carolina voted overwhelmingly for George Bush,' said Miss Priss behind me.

'God!' I exclaimed. 'Take me back to London!'

'Corlis, this is no time to get into politics.'

'It's just the time! This is real politics, Troom. Not a load of waffle and bunting.'

Of course, alienating the admission nurse was a mistake; our frequent inquiries about the state of our brother were met with a cool lack of urgency.

After an hour, a doctor emerged with an update. Mordecai would need an operation on his back; a length of spine was crushed. An anesthetist had advised delay until morning; the alcohol levels in the patient's bloodstream were so extreme that putting him under could be dodgy.

'I should warn you –' The doctor touched an elbow of my tightly crossed arms. 'According to the X-rays, three vertebrae are compacted; extensive nerve damage is inevitable. There's a high likelihood that your brother will have lost the use of his legs.'

'Permanently?'

The physician took a breath; no doubt he had to decide all the time how much hope to offer relatives, and as to whether too much or too little did the most harm he seemed of two minds. 'There are therapies,' he said reluctantly. 'Let's skip the second-guessing until we have a clearer picture, shall we?' He squeezed my shoulder.

Truman went to ring Averil, whom we had left behind on the premise that she'd 'lost enough sleep over Mordecai already'. I'd already rung Dix from the house, and when she said, 'Keep me posted' rather than 'See y'all at Rex,' I knew Mordecai's marriage was scotched for good.

Truman returned to slump in the seat at my side and announced soddenly, 'It's all my fault.'

He sounded like Mordecai. Truman blamed himself for everything and Mordecai blamed other people for everything, but the absolutes were two sides of the same asinine coin. In truth, it's-all-my-fault was a plea for me to absolve him every bit as utterly as Truman damned himself, but I wouldn't cooperate.

'We might have tried to stop him from driving, but I doubt we'd have succeeded. What *is* your fault is that Decibelle's assets have been sent to the Twilight Zone. Limited liability, OK?'

'I could have scooped up his keys before he did –'

'Leave it!'

I guess Mordecai had been ploughing aimlessly around Raleigh in the truck. His wife wanted him decapitated, and his house had been co-opted by a fair-weather sister and a gullible brother who'd fashioned far grander revenge than the kid ever intended – where could Mordecai rest his head? I do not imagine, however, that his veering off the Cary Road and flipping the truck a full roll in a ditch was intentional. Mordecai may have not been a seatbelt sort of guy, but he was not self-destructive. He was destructive of everyone and everything around him instead. At least this time he'd not dragged an innocent down with him, so there was balance, if not justice, in the crumpling of a drunken driver two years after his father's death at such similar hands. (As so often in such incidents, the tippler who ran my father into an interstate rail tumbled about his two-door like a baby and got off with a broken ankle.)

'The auction's in four hours,' said Truman. He sounded embarrassed at bringing it up. 'I guess you want to let it go, huh?'

I used my thumbnail to press cuticles down one by one, as if counting up pros and cons. I'd enjoyed my brief burst of chuck-the-past, let's-get-on-with-our-lives, hasn't-that-house-become-merely-divisive, but down to the wire I was abruptly disinclined to throw myself, among other people, out on the street in four hours. If Truman and I thought we were exhausted at eleven, we were now catatonic, and I wanted a home to collapse in. The decision may have come down to this primitive and trivial a matter: I was in no mood, with my older brother crippled on the other side of that wall, to move house.

'Oh, I don't know,' I said at last. 'I'm not all that keen to have some little twerp scotch-taping lollipop trees to *my* bedroom wall. And the idea of a spanking new mod-con kitchen in 309 makes me want to hurl.'

Truman looked up at me and smiled. 'You're in, then? You and me against the Japanese?'

'No, Truman,' I said firmly. 'Not you and me. You heard Mordecai. If we buy him out, the money will go to his creditors.'

'You swallow that business about bankruptcy?'

'Why not?'

'What has Mordecai ever neglected to exaggerate by a factor of ten?' Truman said this with surprising affection.

'Since when has he exaggerated failure, Truman? Big contracts, big expertise, yes. But whether or not Father was bowled over, Decibelle is Mordecai's greatest achievement. If he's sufficiently against the wall to admit, to us of all people, that his darling company is in a state of collapse, I'm inclined to believe him. Besides which, Mordecai's a train wreck in there. You want him to have no one to take care of him, nowhere to convalesce?'

'Oh, I guess not.' Truman scuffed at the lino with his gumsoles. 'So what do you suggest?'

'Show up at the Jaycee Center, and buy it off the ACLU for the three of us. We already own three-quarters, right? No problem financing that last 25 per cent. Screw the Japs, we can go as high as we have to.'

'All three of us?' Truman squeezed his fingers between his knees; his neck extended parallel to the floor like a turtle's. 'You mean, like, Mordecai staying in the house – *staying*?'

'Yeah.'

I think the sheer hideousness of the vision recommended it as proper penance for donating Decibelle's assets to Florida. Truman put his face in his hands and mumbled through his palms, 'Oh, all right. Averil's going to die.'

'But Mordecai isn't,' I reminded him. 'There's at least that. And you're glad. Right?'

'Yeah,' said Truman with a sigh. At which point I regarded our family as having made some tangible progress.

I stood up and stretched. 'We can't do any good here. Let's go home, get showered, have breakfast, and go buy our own fucking house.'

The Jaycee Center was a prosaic brick one-storey sprawl, and Room 112 was a far cry from the dark, sconced hall full of stoogie-puffing toffs where I imagined auctions were properly conducted. The Formica desk and rows of blue plastic chairs replicated a primary school classroom. Though Truman and I were more than on time, the Japanese couple had preceded us, having demurely assumed a back row; we shot them refrigerated smiles and took our rightful places at the front.

Within a few minutes, we were joined by the Johnsons; three

other couples that I recognized from cursory tours of Heck-Andrews; David Grover, who must have come in an observer capacity and once more struck me as terribly handsome; and two suited men, whom I did not recall having met. I whispered to Truman that I'd never seen them before, and he grimaced. '*Developers*', he determined, as if the devil himself had sent his fiends to leer at these proceedings disguised in ties, and only Truman could spot the hellspawn for what they were.

Presumably developers wouldn't bother to poke their heads inside Heck-Andrews, since all they could see when they looked at our house was a high-rise car park.

The court commissioner, our auctioneer, pulled out his chair at the front desk and opened his briefcase with a nod to the boys and girls. The feeling in the room was halfway between an arithmetic test and a relay race, and I expected the commissioner either to announce we had fifteen minutes and we should put our pencils down when we were finished and no talking, or to unholster a gun, shout ready-set-go, and shoot out one of the ceiling tiles.

There was no question about anyone talking. Each party was surrounded by empty seats, the way we had to sit in third grade so that nobody cheated. We shot one another compressed little smiles when caught sizing up the competition, but no one seemed under the illusion that the people in this room were anything short of outright antagonists.

The commissioner began with information we all knew; he was soft-spoken, and the buyers strained forward to hear. When he started the bidding at the ridiculously low figure of $250,000, I missed the blended monotone I associated with an auctioneer, *I've-got-two-seventy-five-two-seventy-five-do-I-hear-three-hundred-going-once-going-twice-THREE!-three-hundred-do-I-hear* ... , that mesmerizingly unintelligible keen like a Catholic mass in the days it was still in Latin. No, this man had no romance whatsoever, and the primary school aura of the event only intensified when we all raised our hands at once to meet the early figures, as if we each knew the square root of sixteen.

The price rose in jumps of twenty thousand rapidly to $350,000, and each time George Johnson or an agent of Mephisto flicked his fingers Truman stabbed his hand in the air. Ever the good student, Truman was easy to picture in grade school, never wisecracking or folding cootie detectors at his desk, but vigilantly following the lesson while his classmates were reading Spiderman, sopping spitballs, and jeering at the goody-two-shoes in the front row.

I noticed the Japanese were keeping their hands folded, and wondered if they'd simply come along to witness this quaint American custom until the price hit $370,000; two couples and one developer dropped out, having hoped, no doubt, that a court-ordered auction would be serendipitously ill-attended and they could walk off with prime property for a song. In their stead, our eastern friends began to bid, the man never raising his single fore-finger above shoulder-high. Each buyer had a distinctive style of indication, the remaining developer's flip of the hand almost side-ways, sneering, while Truman jabbed his arm perfectly vertical, like a *Sieg heil!* salute.

The auctioneer began to jack up the price $10,000 a go; at $410,000 we lost the Johnsons, at which point I let the nightmare vision of our kitchen hanging with matching Conran's pots merci-fully vanish from my future. One more couple quit at $420,000, but the second developer persisted to $440,000. When he appeared to have given up hopes for expanded downtown park-ing, Truman's eyes lit with evangelistic triumph, and he turned to me with an Onward-Christian-Soldiers gloat at good smiting evil.

At $450,000, it was down to the McCrea kids and the Japs. Though, true to their race's reputation, the faces of our remaining rivals remained largely impassive, I did detect a shadow of confu-sion ripple over the little man's brow as we met $470,000 and $480,000 without hesitation. In fact, the last few minutes of this exercise achieved the surreal quality of my dreams, the price ris-ing and rising with no end in sight. Despite their renown as cold customers, the Japanese at our auction, in their willingness to so exceed the official value of Heck-Andrews, must have been bid-ding with a degree of infatuation. $500,000, $510,000, $520,000 ... something about our Reconstruction mansion had captured their imagination, the way so many profoundly American emblems – Big Macs, Big Head Todd and big tits – had caught on in Tokyo. When Truman once again stuck his hand up at $560,000, the cou-ple in the back looked to their laps, and bowed slightly. Sold, to the gentleman in the front.

It had been giddy, being able to bid as high as we liked, since every raise of $10,000 only cost us $2,500. David Grover was beaming, since the real winner was the ACLU, which would now get several thousand more than if the organization had settled for a quarter of the appraisal. Then, such inflated beneficence would only have delighted my father. And I enjoyed our determined fidelity to what was no longer a mere house even to me, but a threesome united for the first time in our lives. $560,000 for that house may have been absurd, but there seemed worse foolishness than overvaluing your own family.

* * *

It has been three-quarters of a year since Mordecai arrived home, his month in Rex Hospital having given Truman time to fashion ramps for the front and back stoop, and to install a wheelchair lift on the main stair and handrails in the bath.

We also managed to pick up the odd bit of furniture from local auctions – Troom and I acquired a taste for them, and grew accomplished at appearing blasé about the loveseat we were, in truth, desperate to snap up. The kitchen table and chairs were first, without which the social fabric of our little crew would have disintegrated completely. Yet for the rest we've been picky, having learned that possessions are not to be assumed lightly – Truman's kid might be saddled with unsightly investments for the duration. Little by little the household has taken shape, and the new version is spare, funky and belligerently American.

That first March afternoon when Truman lifted his brother from the Volvo and wheeled Mordecai up the back porch ramp making *vroom-vroom* noises I realized that something more profound than Mordecai's mobility had changed. Even more than I, Truman had regarded his brother as someone who didn't need his help, and Truman cannot relate to autonomous wise-guys who scorn his samaritanism. Confined to a wheelchair, abandoned by his cronies, no longer flapping a six-figure chequebook, Mordecai has ceased to intimidate. Moreover, I doubt Truman gives his brother a hand in the loo or hauls Mordecai into bed out of guilt or duty; as he relishes hefting my luggage, he likes putting brawn to practical use.

My older brother had never let anyone take care of him before, not even my mother, much less his wives, which may have helped explain why three marriages in a row imploded. Finally something has turned in him, and I like to think it is not that he's given up.

Perhaps because the succour comes from so unlikely a source, Mordecai now basks in being tended, and has proved less than eager to learn to dress himself and prepare his own breakfast.

Likewise Mordecai went through bankruptcy proceedings in the spring with festive relaxation, making obnoxious jokes in court about whether they'd let him keep his wheelchair; then, in failure is reprieve. For years Decibelle had been over-extended, taking on bigger jobs than his small workforce and limited equipment could quite manage, and Mordecai took to his retirement from deadlines and payrolls like a hard-earned holiday.

To protect his interest in Heck-Andrews from creditors, Mordecai sold his share of the house to Truman and me for 'one dollar and other valuable consideration', the latter of which would later come down to frequent free babysitting. We drew up a contract giving Mordecai the right to buy back should his ship come in. It was small sacrifice to allow him the hope that through some unlikely entrepreneurial sleight of hand he might once again be flush, throwing around Beluga and salmon and Krug like the old days. That before he buys back his share of Heck-Andrews Mordecai owes Truman and me almost $100,000 for covering his medical bills – for which we did indeed hit up Claude for a mortgage – tends to slip Mordecai's mind.

Paraplegia suits my older brother. For years he'd felt sorry for himself, but had I asked Mordecai before the accident what exactly was so terrible about the way life had treated him, I doubt he'd have been able to say. Now he could point to his legs – despite frequent water immersion therapy, dead weight. Routinely awash in self-pity, he might have wallowed to the neck in that wheelchair. Instead, Mordecai has a sense of humour about his disability – rueful, like his father – and never once have I heard him blame anyone for the accident but himself.

Mordecai is not above exploiting his condition, however; he wheedles all of us into running his errands or fetching things he might retrieve himself ('I'll time you,' he promises), and has developed a plaintive, peevish tone I suspect he cadged from Truman. But when he's alone in a room, I doubt he blubbers, but remembers he's in the middle of *A Brief History of Time* and gets down to it. Mordecai was never an anyone-for-tennis type anyway, and claims to find the excuse to read for hours on end luxurious.

However, a glimpse in the door of the carriage house this

summer sobered me. Mordecai was feeding a sheet of plywood through the Rockwell table saw, which Truman had replaced. Before his accident, I had often seen Mordecai slide boards gracefully under the blade, walking them out the other side. This time, from his wheelchair, Mordecai couldn't reach over and around; the plywood stalled and began to smoke. He tried again. The wood burned, the saw jammed, and the safety mechanism shut off the motor. As I walked away, leaving him to it, he was still rushing his chair around the machine, and I will never forget his expression, which was of pure, furious concentration; he pursed his lips so that they wouldn't wobble. Briefly, I appreciated how much he spared us, and how to keep up a really good game-face you have to maintain it for yourself.

His greatest indulgence is to watch videos about disabled war vets – *Coming Home*, *Cutter's Way*, *The Saint of Fort Washington*, *Article 99* – after which he is noticeably more irascible, playing the angry young man betrayed by his country. I think he indulges himself the fancy for a few hours that he did not live through the Vietnam War unscathed only to be felled by a bottle of his own aquavit. When we take Mordecai with us to Harris Teeter, shoppers steal glances at the longhair in the chair with elaborate sympathy. They've seen those videos, too, and Mordecai is careful not to disabuse his onlookers of their misapprehension. Later we ride him for these pretensions, but still keep an eye out in video stores for new feisty-vet-cripple releases.

Truman took a leave of absence from Duke to make Heck-Andrews wheelchair-friendly, but I doubt he'll ever go back. There seems little point in attending classes to examine why bad things happen to only half-bad people when the conundrum lives with you downstairs. And Truman has never cared for abstractions; like the Moser house, he likes causes you can touch. So together my brothers have launched a new business from Heck-Andrews: renovating old properties in the neighbourhood. They've quite a trade going; many of the outlying houses bought by well-heeled professionals are in poor repair. There's now a sign on our porch, 'The Mortis and Truman Joint', and those two have more business than they can handle.

Truman does the heavy work; Mordecai can operate their new lathe and hand tools from his wheelchair, and scrolls beautiful porch ornamentation or hand-routers finely detailed baseboards.

He can volute the fiddly sawnwork and does the fine sanding, though lately his most vital contribution to the business is to watch over Delano while Truman lugs banisters in their new army surplus troop transporter.

Delano Adlai McCrea was indeed born on my parents' anniversary, and though babies generally don't send me, this one has character. A bit too much, for Averil and Truman, for he was a collicky child like Mordecai, and though he seems to have stopped shrieking on the hour Delano is already attempting to stand in his crib whenever the nursery door cracks open. I'd never have pegged Mordecai for an infant lover either, but since Truman is not the only one in this family who's been a 'perfect baby' into his thirties, I guess it's not so surprising that Delano and Mordecai get along like a house on fire – not Truman's favourite expression.

I've tried to be of use, but Truman is possessive about taking care of Mordecai, and in no time I began to feel superfluous. Truman even controls the cooking, having put Mordecai on a strict diet. It's worked – at least, Mortis (as Truman now calls him) has lost weight, and looks in better trim in his wheelchair than he ever did standing up straight. As for booze, Troom hasn't disallowed it altogether, but Mordecai is allotted no more than the two glasses of wine and slight finger of Wild Turkey per night that the rest of the household is rationed. Aquavit has been banned outright. Mordecai manages to break the rules from time to time – Truman kept the bourbon out of reach, so Mordecai spent days designing an ingenious grasping gizmo with which he could wrestle bottles from high shelves. But Truman caught him after a week, and simply removed contraband to the dovecot, whose stairs his brother can't climb. Frankly, the difference between babysitting Mordecai and Delano is marginal.

Through months of living and working with one another, my brothers' natures have orbited closer together, like two planets pulled by each others' gravitational fields. Truman has grown more aggressive, sure and socially adventurous, some nights inviting his hired crew (though Truman refuses to employ 'waste-products') to dinner. He's got funnier, easier, less judgemental – the puffs of reefer he will now indulge make him giggly. Mordecai, on the other hand, is more responsible, and even Averil trusts him with Delano's care. And I'd say that Mordecai is kinder; for kindling empathy, a little disadvantage goes a long way. My brothers have confirmed my impression that, born or raised as polar opposites, only fused would those two make one whole, decent, daring person.

Meanwhile, I figured I was getting a bit old for one more minimum wage job, so on a whim I rang up David Grover. He seemed happy enough to hear from me, and ever since then I've been working for the NC chapter of the ACLU, mostly doing legal research. Truman was disgusted with my new employment at first – he called it 'brown-nosing the paternal grave' – though he concedes that pay cheque by pay cheque is one way of earning our inheritance back. I like the work, and several lawyers around the office knew my father. I don't find that eclipsing; it gratifies me, and eventually Father's old colleagues will retire and the younger attorneys will remember me instead.

Last spring I started going out with David Grover, and the first time he kissed me I swooned, if only from the shock that so recently I'd been willing to trade that infinite tunnelling for the shoulder-clapping of brothers. Sure, there was an element of courtship and even of flirtation in our threesome's Virginia Reel around Heck-Andrews. Yet no brotherly love could compensate for that kiss. Siblings aren't enough. They live beside you; I am glad for them; they are better than nothing. If I had often found myself torn between two men, when you can't make up your mind between alternatives the odds are they're both wrong.

So when Delano was born, David and I started living together in his house near my old junior high school. I'll never forget the contempt with which Truman first pronounced *David Grover!*, whose name is still associated in Truman's mind with nearly losing his house; though a sneer in Truman's enunciation persists, gradually they're getting on. Of course, Mordecai thinks David's a 'spoon-fed candy-ass'.

I've kept my equity in Heck-Andrews, as the one contribution I can make towards alleviating Mordecai's misfortunes. Besides, having gone on record as condemning inheritance as 'evil', I can't righteously demand $187,000 for signing my name.

However, as for accepting what I don't deserve I've learned to become less exacting. My whole life is something-for-nothing. I owe my mother for almond eyes and olive skin, my father for a better than scathing attitude towards black people. After my afternoon drives to buy *The Raleigh Times* for the crossword, I'm in debt to strangers for internal combustion, the ballpoint, a three-letter word for 'lament'. Most of what I use or regard as technically mine is rightfully claimed by centuries of industrious predecessors; purchase is more like renting or theft. I would never have invented plastic – much less electric kettles, or the concept of 'reckless endangerment'. There seems little point to feeling sheepish about what amounts to massive inherited wealth, so I'll take it all with a handshake and try to make my own contribution on however meagre a scale.

Therefore I've moved my studio to David's, and still do sculpture avocationally on weekends. The waxwork is sweeter without the pressure to please galleries, and I've used the little of my cash inheritance remaining to cast a series of six-inch figures in bronze. I'd completed enough of these light, lissome pieces by this Christmas to give Mordecai, Averil, and Truman each a gift of one, and now instead of international gewgaws my tiny bronzes will decorate the still spare furnishings of that house.

In fact, yesterday's Christmas Eve of 1993 went far more warmly than '92's. When David and I arrived for dinner, Mordecai had already sliced the ham, Truman had whipped up a potato salad he could stand, Averil's holly napkins blossomed around the table; there was nothing left for me to do. Truman had granted an extra wine allowance for the holiday, and the three of them were polishing off a cabernet. Though Averil is often touchy about Mordecai's assessment of her intelligence, last evening she was braving a few good-natured potshots of her own. In fact, the banter in that kitchen flew so fast and loose that I couldn't get a quip in edgewise, and so I lingered on the sidelines with David while Truman explained to me why drains clear in opposite directions on either side of the equator.

David and I were spending Christmas proper with his family, so at Heck-Andrews we exchanged gifts last night. This time Mordecai had fashioned a present for everyone, each hand-crafted. Not once did he goad Truman for being 'good' or too obliging; he could hardly ridicule his brother for a tenderness that for Mordecai himself has proved a windfall. I gave Truman grown-up presents and he seemed thankful, but it was all very civilized between us. Yet with Mordecai, Truman would wisecrack, and they'd cackle. Those two have developed a whole vocabulary grown from renovation fiascos and eccentric clients; last night I felt like Truman listening to his siblings speak pig-Latin before he broke the code. The exclusion was fair, but smarted. All my life I'd been fought over; I'd never felt left out.

Before we left, I broke the news that David and I had decided to move to London, where we'll both work for Amnesty International at its world headquarters – David as director of legal affairs, I as regional information officer for North America. I may no longer consider Raleigh nowheresville, but I'm restless, and inevitably in a hometown one feels stuck. I'm rapidly losing every trace of my English accent, which I miss, and the other day caught myself saying *ya'll*. That was the limit. Truman seemed a bit sad, but I wouldn't call him broken-hearted. He wished us the best of luck in Britain, and then he wheeled Mordecai to the middle of the kitchen, slipped out his comb, and unclasped the alligator clips. As Averil, Truman and Mordecai sang 'Day is Done' in three-part harmony, my little brother began reweaving Mordecai's hair.

EXCLUSIVE EXTRAS

❖ ❖ ❖

Meet Lionel Shriver

Return to Raleigh: Writing *A Perfectly Good Family*

Read an excerpt from *The Post-Birthday World*

Author's Picks

Have You Read?

MEET LIONEL SHRIVER

AH WAN OW! It took a while for my mother to decode the first words from my crib as "I want out." Since, *Ah wan ow* has become something of a running theme.

I wanted out of North Carolina, where I was born. I wanted out of my given name ("Margaret Ann"—the whole double-barrel; can you blame me?), and at fifteen chose another one. I wanted out of New York, where I went to university at Columbia. I wanted out of the United States.

In 1985, I cycled around Europe for six months; one hundred miles a day in wretched weather fortified a lifetime appetite for unnecessary suffering. The next year, I spent six months in Israel, including three on a kibbutz in the Galilee helping to manufacture waterproof plastic boots. Thereafter, I shifted "temporarily" to Belfast, where I remained based for twelve years. Within that time, I also spent a year in Nairobi, and several months in Bangkok. Yet only my partner's getting a job in London in 1999 tore me decisively from Belfast, a town that addictively commands equal parts love and loathing. As *We Need to Talk About Kevin* attests, I'm a sucker for ambivalence.

Though returning regularly to New York, I've lived in London ever since. I'm not sure if I've chosen this city so much as run out of wanderlust here. London is conventional for me, and I'm a bit disappointed in myself. But I've less appetite for travel than I once did. I'm not sure if this is from some larger grasp that people are the same everywhere and so why not save the plane fare, or from having just gotten lazy. My bets are on the latter.

At least the novels are still thematically peripatetic. Their disparate subject matter lines up like the fruit on slot machines when you do not win the jackpot: anthropology and a May-December love affair (*The Female of the Species*), rock-and-roll drumming and jealousy (*Checker and the Derailleurs*), the Northern Irish troubles and my once dreadful taste in men (*Ordinary Decent Criminals*), demography and AIDS in Africa (*Game Control*), inheritance (*A Perfectly Good Family*), professional tennis and career competition in marriage (*Double Fault*), terrorism and cults of personality (*The New Republic*, my *real* seventh novel, which has never seen the light of day), and high school massacres and motherhood (*We Need to Talk About Kevin*). My latest, *The Post-Birthday World*, is a romance—about the trade-offs of one man versus another and *snooker*, believe it or not—whose nature seems in context almost alarmingly innocent.

For the nosey: I am married, to an accomplished jazz drummer from New York. Perhaps mercifully for any prospective progeny, I have no children. I am confessedly and unashamedly fifty years old, and never lie about my age because I want credit for every damned year.

Lesser known facts:

I have sometimes been labeled a "feminist"—a term that never sits well with me, if only because connotatively you have no sense of humor. Nevertheless, I am an excellent cook, if one inclined to lace every dish with such a malice of fresh chilis that nobody but I can eat it. Indeed, I have been told more than once that I am "extreme." As I run through my preferences—for *dark* roast coffee, *dark* sesame oil, *dark* chocolate, *dark* meat chicken, even *dark* chili beans—a pattern emerges that, while it may not put me on the outer edges of human experience, does exude a faint whiff of the unsavory.

Illustrating the old saw that whatever doesn't kill you makes you stronger, I cycle everywhere, though I expect that eventually this perverse Luddite habit will kill me, period. I am a deplorable tennis player, which doesn't stop me from inflicting my crap net-game and cowardly refusal to play formal matches on anyone I can corner on a court.

I am a pedant. I insist that people pronounce "flaccid" *flak-sid*, which is dictionary-correct but defies onomatopoeic instinct; when I force them to look it up, they grow enraged and vow to keep saying *flassid* anyway. I never let anyone get away with using "enervated" to mean "energized," when the word means without energy, thank you very much. Not only am I, apparently, the last remaining American citizen who knows the difference between "like" and "as," but I freely alienate everyone in my surround by interrupting, "You mean, *as* I said." Or, "You mean, you gave it to *whom*," or "You mean, that's just between you and *me*." I am a lone champion of the accusative case, and so—obviously—have no friends.

I read every article I can find that commends the nutritional benefits of red wine; if they're right, I will live to 110. Though raised by Adlai Stevenson Democrats, I have a violent, retrograde right-wing streak that alarms and horrifies my acquaintances in London and New York.

Those twelve years in Northern Ireland have left a peculiar residual warp in my accent—house = hyse, shower = shar; now = nye. Since an Ulster accent bears little relation to the more familiar mincing of a Dublin brogue, these aberrations are often misinterpreted as holdovers from my North Carolinian childhood. Because this handful of mangled vowels is one of the only souvenirs I took from Belfast, my wonky pronunciation is a point of pride (or, if you will, vanity), and when my "Hye nye bryne cye" (= how now brown cow) is mistaken for a bog-standard southern American drawl I get mad.

RETURN TO RALEIGH
Writing *A Perfectly Good Family*

A PERFECTLY GOOD FAMILY is about inheritance—in the general sense of what our parents bequeath to us genetically, psychologically, and morally. How much do we have a choice in what we would keep, what we would discard? Yet the novel is also about a literal, nitty-gritty inheritance, the disposition of goods—likewise, what we would keep, what we would discard. Most of all, this is a book about a house.

A house, and who gets it. In my experience, a house is never a mere building. According to standard Jungian interpretation, in dreams a house is a stand-in for the self. The house where you grew up must have more power to evoke that house=self formula than any other. An inheritance dispute between siblings over the family home often grows so nasty because you are inevitably fighting not just over title to a property, but title to parental preference, or title to the past itself.

A Perfectly Good Family—which my mother prefers tellingly to misremember as *The Perfect Family*—is the only novel I've ever written set in North Carolina, where I was raised. When I was a kid, it wasn't yet fashionable to hail from the American South, and once I came of age I fled my Tarheel heritage—as well as my accent—for New York. I never looked back until I wrote this book. When I returned to Raleigh to do the research (and how odd, to discover that you still need to do "research" on a town where you lived for ten years), I was surprised to find Raleigh a much more fascinating, particular place than I remembered, with a rich Civil War history; why, it was a lovely city in which to live, and I was lucky to have grown up there. In fact, I located an entire neighborhood called Oakwood, in the very center of downtown, of which

I'd been utterly unaware as a teenager—full of fabulous Reconstruction mansions that were being restored to their original splendor by the wealthy gays who had recently colonized the area.

I fell in love. Specifically, I developed a crush on a massive three-story manor on Blount Street replete with widow's walk, wrap-around porch, and carriage house. Yes, Heck-Andrews is a real historical home, and in the novel I kept its name. But when I came upon it, the place was a shambles. The windows were boarded up; the roof was dropping slates. It hadn't been painted in decades. Digging through local records, I learned that the old girl had been inhabited for years by another old girl—an agoraphobic who was bats. Charitable neighbors used to leave casseroles on her steps. When she'd ceased to retrieve these offerings for weeks, the police finally broke in to find not only the owner's corpse, but bin liners bulging full of newspapers and bric-a-brac that so filled the first floor and on up the stairway that the cops could barely push in the door. You know the type: she never threw anything away.

With no living relatives, this old woman had willed Heck-Andrews to the State, but North Carolina couldn't afford to do the place up, so the poor house was falling to bits. Well, this once-grand manor captured my imagination, which for me is the same thing as capturing my heart. With the help of photos of the house from better days, I duplicated the same endeavor of those wealthy gays, albeit the low-budget version: I renovated the house on paper.

Of course, this novel isn't only about a house; it's also about a love triangle. The fact that the triangle is between siblings makes it no less charged than the romantic sort.

Like Corlis, I grew up sandwiched between two brothers. Only in retrospect have I appreciated the political complexity of growing up between two boys. During most of my childhood, I was pressured—sometimes subtly, sometimes blatantly—to ally myself with one brother against the other. Thus our household was forever teeming with subterfuge, capricious betrayals, and ongoing seductions to switch camps, of which my parents were blissfully unaware. When there had been only two kids in the family, life was simple: my older brother and I were a team. But once my younger brother entered the picture, ultimately I switched sides. For years, my older brother was scheming to win me back. Perhaps he still is.

While the structure of the McCrea family mirrors my own, I would hope that these characters live and breathe independent of my real relations, to whom they bear only modest resemblance. The story is fictional. At this writing, my parents are—touch wood—still alive and well. Thus I have never wrangled with my brothers over real estate, and we weren't raised in a house anything like Heck-Andrews—more's the pity. Nevertheless, underpinning this sometimes sour, sometimes comical story is gratitude for much of what I have inherited from my own parents, like an aptitude for language and an awareness of the world outside the United States. As the dedication notes, ultimately I came into "more strengths than foibles, which is the most parents could hope for any child."

While I do believe that the profound affection that underlies these retouched portraits is obvious in the text, when this novel was first published some members of my family took offense. So just in case one of them trips across this edition, I would append a truism that should be self-evident to anyone who's ever been a member of a family: We are not always loved for the reasons for which we want to be loved. That is, we are often loved not so much *for* who we are as *in spite of* who we are, making the experience of being "loved" at points rather unpleasant. Rest assured that my family loves me in spite of myself as well. But hey, when it comes to love, I take what I can get.

Oh, and I am pleased to report that when I returned to Raleigh a few years after this novel was first published, North Carolina had mobilized funds and was then putting the finishing touches on a complete restoration of the Heck-Andrews house. I was ambivalent; I had enjoyed having sole proprietorship of that house at my keyboard. But Truman would be delighted.

READ AN EXCERPT FROM
THE POST-BIRTHDAY WORLD
(2007, HarperCollins)

Can the course of life hinge on a single kiss? That is the question that Lionel Shriver's Post-Birthday World *seeks to answer with all the subtlety, perceptiveness, and drama that made her last novel,* We Need to Talk About Kevin, *an international bestseller and winner of the 2005 Orange Prize. Whether the American expatriate Irina McGovern does or doesn't lean into a certain pair of lips in London will determine whether she stays with her smart, disciplined, intellectual American partner, Lawrence, or runs off with Ramsey—a wild, exuberant British snooker star the couple has known for years. Employing a parallel-universe structure, Shriver follows Irina's life as it unfolds under the influence of two drastically different men. In a tour de force that, remarkably, has no villains, Shriver explores the implications, both large and small, of our choice of mate—a subject of timeless, universal fascination for both sexes.*

Chapter One

What began as coincidence had crystallized into tradition: on the sixth of July, they would have dinner with Ramsey Acton on his birthday.

Five years earlier, Irina had been collaborating with Ramsey's then-wife Jude Hartford on a children's book. Jude had made social overtures. Abjuring the airy we-really-must-get-together-sometime feints common to London, which can carry on indefinitely without threatening to clutter your diary with a real time and place, Jude had seemed driven to nail down a foursome so that her illustrator could meet her husband Ramsey. Or, no—she'd said, "My husband, Ramsey Acton." The locution had stood out. Irina assumed that Jude was prideful in that wearing feminist way about the fact that she'd not taken her husband's surname.

But then, it is always difficult to impress the ignorant. When negotiating with Lawrence over the prospective dinner back in 1992, Irina didn't know enough to mention, "Believe it or not, Jude's married to *Ramsey Acton*." For once Lawrence might have bolted for his *Economist* day-planner, instead of grumbling that if she had to schmooze for professional reasons, could she at least schedule an early dinner so that he could get back in time for *NYPD Blue*. Not realizing that she had been bequeathed two magic words that would vanquish Lawrence's broad hostility to social engagements, Irina had said instead, "Jude wants me to meet her husband, Raymond or something."

Yet when the date she proposed turned out to be *Raymond or something*'s birthday, Jude insisted that more would be merrier. Once returned to bachelorhood, Ramsey let slip enough details about his marriage for Irina to reconstruct: After a couple of years, they could not carry a conversation for longer than five minutes. Jude had leapt at the chance to avoid a sullen, silent dinner just the two of them.

Which Irina found baffling. Ramsey always seemed pleasant enough company, and the strange unease he always engendered in Irina herself would surely abate if you were married to the man. Maybe Jude had loved dragging Ramsey out to impress colleagues, but was not sufficiently impressed on her own behalf. One-on-one he had bored her silly.

Besides, Jude's exhausting gaiety had a funny edge of hysteria about it, and simply wouldn't fly—would slide inevitably to the despair that lay beneath it—without that quorum of four. When you cocked only half an ear to her uproarious discourse, it was hard to tell if she was laughing or crying. Though she did laugh a great deal, including through most of her sentences, her voice rising in pitch as she drove herself into ever accelerating hilarity when nothing she had said was funny. It was a compulsive, deflective laughter, born of nerves more than humor, a masking device and therefore a little dishonest. Yet her impulse to put a brave, bearable face on what must have been a profound unhappiness was sympathetic. Her breathless mirth pushed

Irina in the opposite direction—to speak soberly, to keep her voice deep and quiet, if only to demonstrate that it was acceptable to be serious. Thus if Irina was sometimes put off by Jude's manner, in the woman's presence she at least liked herself.

Irina hadn't been familiar with the name of Jude's husband, consciously. Nevertheless, that first birthday, when Jude had bounced into the Savoy Grill with Ramsey gliding beside her—it was already late enough in a marriage that was really just a big, well-meaning mistake that her clasp of his hand could only have been for show—Irina met the tall man's grey-blue eyes with a jolt, a tiny touching of live wires that she subsequently interpreted as visual recognition, and later— much later—as recognition of another kind. . . .

AUTHOR'S PICKS

THE AGE OF INNOCENCE, by Edith Wharton

I love virtually all of Edith Wharton, but this one's my favorite.
Why Wharton, in general? I admire her prose style, which is lucid,
intelligent, and artful rather than arty; she is eloquent but never
fussy, and always clear. She never seems to be writing well to show
off. As for *The Age of Innocence*, it's a poignant story that, typically
for Wharton, illustrates the bind women found themselves in
when trapped hazily between a demeaning if relaxing servitude and
dignified if frightening independence, and that both sexes find
themselves in when trapped between the demands of morality
and the demands of the heart. The novel is romantic but not
sentimental, and I'm a sucker for unhappy endings.

FLAG FOR SUNRISE, by Robert Stone

I'm a big fan of most of Stone's work. This one's the best, though—
grim and brutal. Stone has a feel for politics in the gritty, ugly way
they play out on the ground. His cynicism about what makes people
tick, and his portrayal of how badly they behave when either
desperate or given free rein to do what they like, jibes—alas—with
my own experience of the species.

AS MEAT LOVES SALT, by Maria McCann

I include this more recent title if only because, especially in the
U.S., it didn't get the attention it deserved. A historical novel—

which I don't usually read—set in Cromwellian England, it's about a homosexual affair in the days when same-sex marriage was hardly in the headlines; rather, man-meets-man was a hanging offense. I relished the radical sexual tension McCann created, without ever becoming sordid or even very blow-by-blow (so to speak), and the story is sexy even for hetero readers like me. In fact, this riveting story works partly because it's told by a straight woman, and so isn't tainted by the faint self-justification of many gay authors' work.

PARIS TROUT, by Pete Dexter

I'd recommend all of Dexter's books, but he may never have topped this one. He writes about race and bigotry without the moral obviousness that this subject matter often elicits. His prose is terse and muscular, but not posy and tough-guy.

ATONEMENT, by Ian McEwan

A terrific examination of guilt and exculpation—or, as for the latter, lack thereof. He writes about childhood in a way that isn't white-washingly sweet, and he doesn't endorse cheap forgiveness, of yourself or anyone else. There's a powerful sense in this book that sometimes seemingly small sins have enormous and permanently dire consequences, with which you're condemned to live for the rest of your life. I read this while writing *Kevin*, and I think some of McEwan's and my themes must intersect.

ENGLISH PASSENGERS, by Matthew Kneale

Once again, I include this novel for its relative commercial obscurity in the U.S.—though it did, justly, win the Whitbread in the UK (and should have won the Booker). Seven years in the writing, *English Passengers* follows the hapless journey of a ship bound for Tasmania in the mid-nineteenth century to find the original Garden of Eden. The novel demonstrates the value of good research, which is seamlessly integrated into the text, and it's hilarious.

HAVE THE MEN HAD ENOUGH?, by Margaret Forster

Forster is underappreciated even in the UK, and shamefully neglected in the U.S. This book takes on subject matter from which most novelists have shied: the increasing decrepitude and dementia of an aging relative. Given the demographic future, this is material that most of us will soon have to contend with, like it or not.

REVOLUTIONARY ROAD, by Richard Yates

Yates was able to look at the disturbing underside of so-called ordinary life, and even more successfully than John Cheever exposed the angst and dissatisfaction that teem beneath the placid suburbs. I don't think anyone's life is simple or easy, even with enough food on the table, and Yates was depressive enough as a person to appreciate this fact.

THE IDIOT, by Fyodor Dostoevsky

Of Dostoevsky's novels, most writers would cite *The Brothers Karamazov*. Which I also adored in latter adolescence, but found I could not bear when I tried to read it again in my thirties. I hadn't the patience. By contrast, re-reading *The Idiot* as an adult rewarded the return. At that time, I was writing my second novel, *Checker and the Derailleurs*, and also grappling with how difficult it is to write about goodness. Virtue in literature, as it is often in real people, can be downright off-putting. The secret, I discovered, was to put virtue at risk—thus guaranteeing that our hero is misunderstood and persecuted. I preferred to confirm this with Dostoevsky, though if I hadn't acquired an allergy to all things religious during my Presbyterian childhood, I might also have located the same ingenious fictional strategy in the New Testament.

ALL THE KING'S MEN, by Robert Penn Warren

As I scan these (hopelessly arbitrary) selections, I note that a number of novels that have made a big impression on me have somehow managed to incorporate a political element—without being tiresome or polemical. In my own work, I've often tried to do the same. Penn Warren's loose fictionalized biography of Huey Long has stayed with me for so intertwining the personal and the political as to expose the distinction as artificial. Unfortunately, when I tracked down his other books—and there are not many—they were all disappointing in comparison. Read *All the King's Men* and forget the rest. Years hence folks may be dismissing most of my own novels in just this manner, but if they're still touting one title, and it's as good as this one, then I'll still be very lucky.

HAVE YOU READ?

WE NEED TO TALK ABOUT KEVIN (winner of the 2005 Orange Prize for fiction)

In this gripping novel of motherhood gone awry, Lionel Shriver approaches the tragedy of a high-school massacre from the point of view of the killer's mother. In letters written to the boy's father, Eva probes the upbringing of this more-than-difficult child and reveals herself to have been the reluctant mother of an unsavory son. As the schisms in her family unfold, we draw closer to an unexpected climax that holds breathtaking surprises and its own hard-won redemption. In Eva, Shriver has created a narrator who is touching, sad, funny, and reflective. A spellbinding read, *We Need to Talk About Kevin* is as original as it is timely.

"Impossible to put down."

—*Boston Globe*

"In crisply crafted sentences that cut to the bone of her feelings about motherhood, career, family, and what it is about American culture that produces child killers, Shriver yanks the reader back and forth between blame and empathy, retribution and forgiveness."

—*Booklist* (starred review)

GAME CONTROL

Do-gooding American family-planning worker Eleanor Merritt
was drawn to Kenya to improve the lot of the poor. To her dismay,
she falls in love with Calvin Piper, a beguiling misanthropic
demographer with chilling theories about population control. Surely,
Calvin whispers in Eleanor's ear, if the poor are a responsibility, they
are also an imposition.

Set against the vivid backdrop of shambolic modern-day Africa,
Lionel Shriver's *Game Control* is a wry, grimly comic tale of bad
ideas and good intentions. With a deft, droll touch, Shriver
highlights the hypocrisy of lofty intellectuals who would "save"
humanity but who don't like people.

"[O]ne of the best works of fiction about Africa."

—*The New Statesman*